In the wee small hours

Gil McNeil

In the wee small hours

BLOOMSBURY

First published 2005
Copyright © 2005 by Gil McNeil

The moral right of the author
has been asserted

Bloomsbury Publishing Plc, 38 Soho Square,
London W1D 3HB

A CIP catalogue record for this book
is available from the British Library

ISBN 07475 7902 4

ISBN-13 9780747579 021

10 9 8 7 6 5 4 3 2 1

All papers used by Bloomsbury Publishing are
natural, recyclable products made from wood grown in
well-managed forests. The manufacturing processes
conform to the environmental regulations of the country
of origin.

Typeset by Palimpsest Book Production Ltd, Polmont, Stirlingshire

Printed by Clays Ltd, St Ives plc

www.bloomsbury.com/gilmcneil

ACKNOWLEDGEMENTS

With special thanks to everyone at Bloomsbury,
and PiggyBankKids, and extra special thanks to
Ann Scott, Arzu Tahsin, Dad, Katie Bond,
Mary Tomlinson, Minna Fry, Mum, Rose Davidson,
Ruth Logan, Sarah Brown and Sheila Crowley.

For Joe

I

Sunday Bloody Sunday

IT'S SUNDAY MORNING, AND I'm wondering why I'm up to my armpits in fairy-cake mixture with a child who's threatening to throw up all over the living-room carpet instead of having a proper Sunday morning like people do in magazines, lounging about in crushed velvet and cashmere socks reading the papers. And it's Valentine's Day, not that you'd know it from the complete lack of cards landing on the mat yesterday. Our postman, Dave, looked especially apologetic as he handed me the gas bill, and one of those letters inviting you to take out a new amusingly shaped credit card and spend thousands of pounds that you haven't got so they can take your house off you six months later. Valentine's Day is so much more humiliating when you know your postman, and round here they pretty much insist on the personal touch. The milkman, Ted, also likes a nice cheery chat in the mornings and is always blocking the lane with his milk float to tell Charlie how many flaming badgers he's seen so far this week, when it's perfectly obvious to anyone with even half a brain that we're already late for school.

Sometimes I really miss the anonymity of living in London, though not when I'm expecting a parcel, obviously: Dave tends to put them in the garage if you're out, and write you a little note. And he's an excellent source of gossip. There's absolutely no chance of lying on your kitchen floor for six weeks before someone alerts the emergency services round here; but that doesn't stop it being embarrassing when you open your front door at the crack of dawn only to be told that Mrs Nesbitt has a dressing gown just like yours, only she's still got the belt.

'I feel sick.'

'I told you not to eat so much cake mixture, Charlie.'

'Yes, but I feel really sick. I think I've got semolina.'

'What?'

'Semolina. Nana says you've got to be very careful with eggs or you get semolina. And that's awful. Were you careful, Mummy? Because I think I've got it.'

'It's salmonella, Charlie, and you haven't got it.'

'Stop being horrible. I feel all fuffled up now.'

'Not half as fuffled up as I do.'

'I hate you, Mummy.'

'Go and lie on the sofa. You'll be fine.'

'I will not. I'll be sick. All over the carpet probly. And it will be your fault.'

'Well, that'll make a nice change then, won't it?'

'Horrible Mummy.'

I don't know why I'm even bothering with sarcasm, since I already know it's a total waste of time with six-year-olds, especially ones like Charlie.

'I FEEL SICK.'

He's yelling now, and stamping round in his slippers, clutching his stomach to highlight his tragic plight. I

2

wonder if I should give him some bicarbonate of soda or something. I think I've got some baking powder, which I'm pretty sure is the same thing, although it might just make him foam at the mouth, which on balance I could probably do without.

The phone rings. It's Kate, who's also been volunteered for baking duties. I did try telling Mrs Harrison-Black that home baking wasn't exactly my forte. Although to be honest I'm not really sure what is, unless getting into a complete panic and swearing a lot counts. But she wasn't having any of it, and stuck me and Kate down for cakes on her clipboard, and that was that. Once you're on one of her PTA Lists there's no escape. Kate's doing gingerbread people, because she says they make her less tense than cakes.

'I've just finished icing on faces but they all look rather sinister. Do you think anyone will notice?'

'Don't worry, they'll be too busy laughing at my fairy cakes. They always go like biscuits, it's really annoying. I bet Mrs Harrison-Black will make one of her Comments.'

'Well, we'll just have to call her Betty all night then.'

Mrs Harrison-Black hates being called Betty, and signs all her PTA letters Mrs Robert Harrison-Black. Maybe we should call her Bob.

'Did you get any Valentines?'

'No. But Phoebe got one. And it's driving her demented.'

Phoebe is Kate's nine-year-old daughter, nine going on nineteen. She's a vegetarian, keen on eco-warriors and desperate to get her tongue pierced, but she also wants to dye her hair blonde and have acrylic nails, a bit like Hippie Barbie, if they make one. Which, if they don't, they bloody well should because they'd make a fortune.

'Does she know who sent it?'

'No, but she's hoping it was David Pettifer.'

3

David Pettifer's sixteen. He's got a leather jacket and half the girls in the village in a complete state. And most of the parents too. He's thinking of getting a motorbike to go with his jacket, apparently.

'She's refusing to come out of her room. I think she's hoping she'll wake up and magically be sixteen and old enough to interest David. James is watching wrestling on the telly and beating up the sofa, and we've still got lunch with my mother to get through. And I can't decide what to wear to this PTA Barn Dance thing. We're bound to end up dancing with each other, you know, unless we want to upset all the women who've still got husbands. Whatever happened to Valentine's weekends in posh hotels and champagne breakfasts?'

'We had kids, that's what. And look on the bright side – we might finally get to see Betty and Ginny punching each other.'

Betty's run the PTA for years, and has two boys, Edward and Harry, three Labradors, and drives an enormous Volvo, in a typical Volvo-mother fashion: slap in the middle of the road with erratic signalling and absolutely appalling parking. Her coterie of supporters all wear padded waistcoats like she does, and sensible navy skirts or slacks, and are fond of saying things like 'Jolly good' and 'Oh well done'.

Ginny Richmond on the other hand drives a Mercedes sports car, wears an ankle chain, and always has perfect nails and full make-up, even at eight-thirty in the morning. And her daughter Olivia is unfeasibly petite and perfect, and a rising star at ballet. Ginny says 'Super' and 'Gorgeous' a lot, and recently got elected on to the PTA Committee, mainly because most of us voted for her just to annoy Betty. But instead of settling down and becoming one of Betty's helpers she's embarked on a series of outflanking manoeuvres. Tonight's Barn Dance was Ginny's idea, and Betty's doing a cake stall, so there's likely to be a fair bit of seething tension between the two rival camps.

'Well, if there's going to be punching it might be worth going, I suppose. I'd love to see Betty get a shiner. But I'm not dancing. I hate country dancing. I had enough of it at school.'

'Fair enough.'

Kate went to a very posh boarding school and knows how to waltz. In fact she's rather posh altogether: she's been known to go riding for fun, and could probably pluck a partridge in under five minutes. But despite her *Horse and Hound* tendencies she's great, and my best friend in the village, which is lucky really because Charlie and James are best friends, and virtually inseparable. Miss Pike has to make them sit on separate tables now because when they're together they tend to go off into a world of their own; and it's not a world that's very interested in maths or nice handwriting.

I've just managed to get the fairy cakes in the oven when the phone rings again. I hope it's not Barney ringing to talk about work; he's up in Northumberland, looking at locations for the job we're doing in a couple of weeks' time and he's bound to have a list of things he wants sorting.

It's Barney. Excellent.

'What's the weather like?'

'Fucking awful. It's freezing.'

'Oh.'

'Lawrence has gone into shock.'

'Shame.'

I hate Lawrence. And he hates me. He's our executive producer, whereas I'm the freelance dogsbody producer who Barney calls in on shoots because he hates having Lawrence: he's great at all the meetings with agencies and landing us work, but he's crap on shoots because he panics too much. I'm in the office once a week to catch up on paperwork and annoy Lawrence, but the rest of the time I'm based at home, which is perfect. And Barney's a brilliant director, even if he is completely round the bend.

'I've found us a beach – the ones the location guy came up with were pathetic – and the weather's spot on, gales and sleet, and the forecast's for more of the same. And the light's fantastic. But we're going to need a boat.'

'I beg your pardon?'

'You heard me. A boat. A fishing boat will be fine. Just sort it, all right. Lawrence has got some numbers for you.'

'Well, get him to email me then and I'll see what I can do, but I'm warning you, Barney, I'm not going on another boat with you. Especially not in gales and sleet.'

The last time we used a boat on a job Barney managed to get the fisherman into such a state he crashed it into the harbour wall.

'Sorry, I can't hear you. This line's fucking awful. You practically have to climb a tree to get a fucking signal round here. It's like the Dark Ages. Poor old Lawrence asked for decaff skinny latte at breakfast and they looked at him like he was mad. Mind you, I don't really blame them, he's wearing those leather trousers again. Anyway, just sort out a boat, all right, and I'll run through the rest with you later. OK?'

'Fine.'

'Oh and, Annie?'

'Yes?'

'You have still got your woolly hat, haven't you? Only I think you're going to be needing it.'

Oh brilliant. When you tell people you're a producer

they always seem to think you spend most of your time in Barbados, or lounging about in Soho, whereas the truth is almost the exact opposite really. I've never even been to Barbados, but I've certainly spent vast chunks of my working life hanging around various parts of Britain in wet-weather gear while Barney gets the light right. I knew this job was going to be annoying, and Lawrence is bound to have booked me into a really tragic hotel, because he always does; he books luxurious five-star places for him and Barney, with Michelin-starred restaurants, and plunge pools in every room, and sticks me in the kind of hotel where all the furniture's bolted to the floor.

This job's an ad for insurance, with a woman walking along a beach in a storm protected by a huge umbrella with the name of the insurance company on it. Although how we're actually going to get her to be able to walk along holding an umbrella and not get blown into the sea isn't exactly clear to me at this stage, but Barney's bound to have come up with loads of brilliant new ideas while he's been up there finding the perfect beach; shoot the whole thing dangling off a rope from the cliffs possibly, or hire a fleet of helicopters. It's going to be a total nightmare, but at least it'll keep the bank manager happy, and I'll be able to continue with my ongoing research into exactly how many layers of clothing you can fit under a cagoule.

Actually, I must remember to buy a new cagoule at some point tomorrow, because my old one's got a hole in the sleeve where I managed to shut it in the lift doors at the hotel after a particularly trying night shoot. Maybe I should get some of those plastic trousers that pull up to your neck as well. Actually, I'd better start a list. Cagoule, plastic trousers, woolly hat, find out about boats.

* * *

'Mummy. I'm hungry.'

'I thought you said you felt sick.'

'Well, I do, but a nice little snack might make me feel better.'

'Charlie, you've only just had breakfast.'

'Yes. But I'm starving. Edna makes me nice little snacks. She says I'm her best boy. And she lets me watch *999 Emergency Action*. I wish I lived with Edna.'

So do I, at this precise moment.

'Go and watch a video or something and let me finish these cakes, and then I'll make some lunch, all right?'

'All right. But not soup. Soup is disgusting.'

'OK. Not soup.'

I must remember to give the kitchen a quick clean before Edna arrives. She's looking after him tonight while I go to the PTA thing, and she'll spend half the night with Mr Muscle and a damp sponge if I don't have a tidy up. She's very keen on clean work surfaces. As well as television programmes about people who have hideous accidents with agricultural machinery, and then survive by dragging themselves across six fields after making a tourniquet out of their trousers. I know she lets Charlie watch them, and I don't, but she's so good with him I can't really say anything. And anyway, I suppose it's got to be handy having a childminder who's so up on first aid, especially the more unusual kind involving hang gliders and electricity pylons, just in case. And at least it means they're not watching *Buffy* and frightening themselves witless about vampires.

Mum rings while I'm grilling the sausages for lunch, to check that I'm still going over to see Uncle Monty this afternoon. Obviously being the person with cakes to make and a Barn Dance looming, and a big job on the horizon that I haven't even had a chance to start panicking about

8

yet, I'm the perfect choice for the woman with the least on her plate who should be visiting mad eighty-two-year-olds on a Sunday afternoon instead of having a nice little lie-down.

'And take him something for his tea. He doesn't eat properly, you know.'

'OK, Mum. I said I'd do it, didn't I? I've made him a shepherd's pie.'

'Well make sure you heat it up for him then. I don't think he knows how to use that oven. Mind you, I don't blame him, it could go on *The Antiques Roadshow*. I just don't know how your Aunty Florrie managed, I really don't.'

Aunty Florrie was Dad's aunty, so Uncle Monty isn't what Mum likes to call Proper Family, but since Florrie died last year she's been trying to keep an eye on him. Mainly by sending me round, because she doesn't really get on with him. He told her to bugger off a few years ago, when he'd had a bit too much to drink at Christmas, and she's never really forgiven him. So it's pretty vital I get her off the subject sharpish or she'll be on the phone for hours: How Florrie Ever Coped is one of her favourite subjects.

'Mum, I promise I'll heat it up, OK. It'll be fine. Have you spoken to Lizzie lately?'

'Yes, and she's writing a birth plan, for all the good it'll do her.'

She certainly likes to be organised, my little sister, although she's nearly six months pregnant now, and not quite so little any more. She's asked me to be with her and Matt at the birth, which I'm trying not to panic about, but I really can't wait to see the baby. And not just because newborns are so sweet, especially when they're not yours and you can hand them back when they start to get narky, but because it's going to be completely fascinating watching to see if Lizzie unravels like the rest of us do once we crash land on Planet Motherhood. And I'm particularly looking forward to seeing just what kind of impact the baby will to have on her and Matt's beautiful we're-both-architects-so-we-live-in-white-minimalist-heaven lifestyle. A pretty major one, I'm betting.

'She says she wants a water birth. In a great big paddling pool. She was telling me all about it, she's got books and everything. Someone called Boy something is all for it, apparently. Have you heard of them?'

'Leboyer. He's French.'

'Oh well, that explains it then.'

'He's big on keeping everything dark and quiet so it's not such a shock for the baby.'

'Oh I see. So being born head first into a paddling pool's not going to be a shock then? Poor little thing.'

'Mum, it is up to her, you know. Birth's a very personal thing.'

'Well, thank you for telling me that, Annie, I mean I've only had two of my own, I'd never have guessed. Honestly. What's wrong with popping on a nice clean nightie and getting into bed like everyone else, that's what I want to know. And what's she going to wear in the water, anyway? She'll catch her death, and that'll be a lovely start for the new baby, won't it, a mother with pleurisy.'

'I'm sure she'll be fine, Mum. You write all sorts of things in your birth plan, you know, and then when it comes to it you just go for the drugs like everyone else.'

'Well, I think it's ridiculous.'

'Right.'

'Tell her, will you. She listens to you.'

'OK.'

She bloody doesn't, but never mind. She stopped

listening to me years ago. Probably around the time I kidnapped her Cindy doll and cut all its hair off. But the only way I'm going to get Mum off the phone and get a few minutes' peace before we go to Monty's is if I agree with everything she says. Which means I'll have to ring Lizzie later on, and be supportive, because Mum's bound to call her straight after she puts the phone down on me and say that I think a water birth is a daft idea too. And the last thing you need when you're writing your birth plan is other people chipping in and telling you it'll all end in tears and sick. Which would make a pretty good birth plan, come to think of it, but I don't think I'll tell her that.

The smoke alarm suddenly announces the sausages are done. Quite well done, actually.

'I must go, Mum, I'm in the middle of cooking lunch.'

'Other people use a kitchen timer, you know, dear.'

'Thanks, Mum.'

'I don't like my sausages so crispy, you know, Mummy. Edna doesn't make them go black.'

'Yes, well, I'm sorry, Charlie, but Nana was on the phone.'

He gives me one of his special new looks that he's been perfecting over the last few months. A kind of cross between pity and disgust at finding himself with such a sub-standard mother. It's mesmerisingly annoying, but I've decided ignoring it is probably the best plan.

'Come on, Charlie, hurry up. We're going to see Uncle Monty after lunch.'

'Can I bring Buzz and Woody?'

'No.'

'They'd love it on a farm, they could play with the other rabbits.'

'Yes, but Uncle Monty shoots rabbits, remember. He told you last time.'

'Yes, but not in the daytime – they do it at night.'

Damn. I didn't think he'd remember that.

'No, but they might get lost. And anyway they don't like going in the car. Remember when we took them to the vet's?'

The car was rocking from side to side so much that at one point I thought we'd have to stop and sedate them. Although I'm still not really sure how you'd go about sedating a pair of over-anxious rabbits, but somehow I don't think Calpol would do the trick. And it would be bound to go everywhere, because I'm not sure rabbits are terribly clever at drinking sticky pink stuff from little plastic spoons.

'Can I bring my bow and arrow then?'

'OK, but you'll have to find it quickly.'

God knows what Monty's going to make of Charlie turning up with a bow and arrow, but as long as he doesn't shoot any of the sheep I'm hoping it'll be all right.

The farm is about twenty minutes from us, in a little valley that always seems to have completely different weather to everywhere else. It'll be pouring with rain on the way there, but as you drive down the hill the sun will come out. There's a stream running through the fields, and a pond at the front of the house, and the house itself is really pretty, apart from the old lean-to kitchen, which looks like it might give up on the leaning thing at any moment and just collapse.

Last week when we arrived Monty was shooting pigeons out of the living-room window, so I'm hoping for something slightly less dramatic this time. The dog rushes out to greet us, followed by Monty who looks like he hasn't the faintest idea who we are for a moment, but then suddenly remembers.

'Hello, Annie, what brings you out here? Get down, Tess. Daft dog. I don't know why I don't just get the vet round and be done with it, amount of use she is. Fine guard dog she makes, out here licking your hands and muddying your coats.'

Tess is Monty's sheepdog, and from a long line of prize-winners. She won all sorts of trials and things years ago, and he's got all the cups in the sideboard; I used to help Aunty Florrie polish them when I was little, and Tess is so well trained she can almost read his mind, a bit like Aunty Florrie could.

I know he's missing her terribly. It was awful watching him at the funeral last year, standing there looking bereft in his best suit, which he'd obviously tried to iron himself, and it had gone all shiny. And one of the cuffs of his shirt was all frayed, so he kept pulling his jacket sleeve down to cover it up, like he thought Florrie would mind that he'd put a shirt on with a fraying cuff. Which of course she would have done. And then he stood by the grave for ages, while we all walked back towards the cars and then milled about awkwardly. In the end Dad had to go over and put his arm round his shoulder and help him back to the car.

'Will you get down, you daft dog?'

Monty's smiling.

'She's like that with everybody. Greeted that flaming Meals on Wheels woman like a long-lost friend.'

Tess is jumping up at Charlie now and licking his hands, which he's loving. He's doing his special I'm-a-boy-who-desperately-wants-a-dog routine, which involves lots of stroking and kneeling down, with occasional filthy looks directed at me, just in case I've forgotten that it's All My

Fault that he has to make do with other people's dogs. Shame.

'I heard all about it from Mum, Monty, and you're lucky she didn't go to the police, you know. You can't go around threatening Meals on Wheels ladies with shotguns.'

Mum was absolutely furious, mainly because it had taken her ages to persuade them to put Monty on their list in the first place. Apparently there's quite a queue of people who need lukewarm food delivered daily, poor things.

'I didn't threaten her, stupid woman. I was going out for pigeons. Pick a whole field clean, they will, if you let them. Mind you, I'd have done a few people a favour if I had been after her, could have put that van out of action for a bit. Saved a lot of poor souls a lot of bother.'

'I would have thought a nice hot meal every day would have come in handy, Monty.'

'Well, yes, it might well have done. But not that muck she brought. Not fit for pigs.'

'Have you got pigs now, Uncle Monty?'

Charlie's hopping up and down now, desperate to get round and see all the animals.

'No. Used to have, though. Very intelligent animals, pigs are. Had one who could have given your Aunty Florrie a run for her money any day.'

He smiles, and offers us a cup of tea.

I'll have to be very careful how I bring up the subject of the shepherd's pie I've made. I don't want to be marched off the premises at the wrong end of a shotgun. Although no doubt Charlie would love it.

'We've made you a shepherd's pie for supper, Uncle Monty. Well, Mummy made it, but I helped. It's all right. Well, it's better than fish pie anyway, and at least it's not all black like my sausages. Do you like crispy sausages,

14

Uncle Monty? Only Mummy always makes mine too crispy.'

'Oh I don't know about that, Charlie boy. I'll tell you a strange thing, shall I? There'll come a day when you'll prefer things just like your mother used to make them, trust me. My mother was a terrible one for burning bacon, and your Aunty Florrie, well, she couldn't make a Yorkshire to save her life – flat as anything, they were. Like little rubber pancakes. But I prefer them like that now.'

Charlie considers this for a moment.

'Well, you can always give it to Tess if you don't like it.'

Monty smiles.

'Thanks, Charlie boy, but I'm sure it won't come to that.'

'Where's your gun, Uncle Monty?'

'Locked up in its case. You can't leave guns lying round the place – very dangerous.'

Monty winks at me.

'Can I see it, please, Uncle Monty, please?'

'Well – '

'Charlie, I told you last time, guns aren't toys. They're very dangerous, and not for children.'

'That's right, Charlie, listen to your mother.'

Charlie does one of his special pleading looks and Monty winks at him. Bugger. He really is barking mad, and always has been. His dad was too apparently, he was the local mole-catcher, and lived here all his life just like Monty, who carried on the family tradition, along with a spot of sheep farming and a mad passion for collecting bric-a-brac. Poor old Florrie fought a losing battle against a tide of old tat for years. But Monty says it'll all come in handy one day. Visiting him is a bit like stepping into the twilight zone; you're never sure when you're going to get back again, but you know you'll have an unusual item with you when you do. Last time it was a mangle, and the time before that a really horrible old hat rack.

We go into the house for tea and a glass of lemonade for Charlie, which turns out to be soda water but he pretends to drink it and then I pour it down the sink when Monty's upstairs finding me one of his latest treasures: a hideous old Bakelite radio with no plug.

'How lovely, Monty.'

'Yes. They don't make them like that any more, you know.'

I'm not bloody surprised. It's not exactly what you'd call portable. It must weigh at least a ton.

'You can have it, if you like.'

'Oh thanks, Monty, but we've already got a radio. Save it for someone who really needs one.'

And does weight training on a regular basis.

'Well, I'll keep it for you, just in case. The new ones are always packing up on you.'

'Great.'

'Fancy a walk, Charlie, see if we can't scare up a few pheasants?'

'Oh yes, please.'

Charlie's got a look of total devotion on his face, because he adores pheasants, and has done since he was tiny, and Monty knows a walk with pheasant-spotting opportunities is always pretty much top of his list. God knows why he's so keen on them, but it's bloody annoying given that we live in the country and the flaming things are always loitering around the hedgerows looking like they're about to hurl themselves into the road right in front of the car. Charlie insists on stopping every time he spots one, for a quick chat or another doomed attempt to catch one by charging across a muddy field. Sometimes I manage to distract him before he spots them, but I've lost count of how many times the five-minute journey to school ends up taking nearly half an hour due to unusual amounts of pheasant activity.

We start walking round the farm.

'It's beautiful here, Monty.'

'Yes, but farming's finished, what with the price of land, and those Mafia bastards. Stands to reason.'

The Mafia bastards are the officials from MAFF, who Monty's been having a series of battles with for as long as anyone can remember.

'The only way to make a living is to sell up and let them put up a load of houses, take yourself off to the knacker's yard, one of them old people's homes. Load of old codgers sitting about in chairs all day. Kill you off quicker than anything, that will.'

'What about the farmers' markets? They're doing very well, aren't they?'

'I wouldn't know about that.'

'Yes, but you get much better prices, don't you?'

'Oh I dare say. But if I wanted a job in a shop I'd be working in one of those supermarkets.'

He spits on to the ground. He hates supermarkets – he says all they care about is driving prices down for farmers and rejecting perfectly good veg if it isn't all the same shape.

'Uncle Monty?'

'Yes, Charlie boy?'

'Will you let me watch you shoot the rabbits, will you really?'

It's very odd how Charlie manages to combine his passion for wildlife with being fascinated by the idea of shooting things. I've tried pointing out how contradictory this is, but he just goes into a long, patronising *Lion King*-type speech about the circle of life.

'Of course I will, do me a favour. Blasted things. But my eyes aren't what they were, you know, I'll have to get old George round with his infra-reds – that's the way to sort them out. Never know what's hit them. Bastards.'

Charlie is watching Monty with a look of complete hero worship on his face. Spitting, saying bugger and bastard, and a gun too. It's all too perfect.

'Actually, I'm not sure about that, Monty. I think he might be a bit young to be around shotguns, don't you?'

'Well, I wasn't going to start him off on a shotgun, for heaven's sake, girl. I've got an old air rifle somewhere – he can have that.'

Oh no he bloody can't. I'll have to nip this one in the bud really sharpish.

'I think six is a bit too young for that, Monty. Actually, come to think of it I think it's probably illegal, isn't it?'

I give him what I hope is a pointed look.

'Oh well, yes, quite probably. All sorts of sensible things are illegal now. Do you know, if a burglar comes into your house and you take a pot shot at him – I heard it on the radio the other day – they can sue you for compensation.'

Oh dear. Not being able to shoot people while they're in the middle of robbing you is another of Monty's favourite rants.

'They say they've got post-dramatic shock or something. It's ridiculous. And the police are all at it too. I mean it's a rotten job being a copper, everyone knows that. Sorting out drunks. Scraping up people after they've driven their cars into trees. But it has its compensations, backhanders and the like. Always a welcome in the local after-hours. A Christmas box from all the shops. That kind of thing. But not any more, oh no. Ask them to do something a bit iffy and they all start suing for compensation for shock. Or retire early with stress. Good Lord, it's a good job they didn't have that in my day, I can tell you. We'd have all come back from the war and put our claims in. And I can tell you, we saw some things, you know, make your hair curl. But you just got on with it. Thanked your lucky stars you still had all your bits and got off home.'

'Right.'

Good. He's off on one of his good-old-days rants now. Maybe he'll forget about teaching Charlie to shoot, and Edna will be in with a chance of getting him into bed tonight without being taken hostage. Excellent.

Charlie sulks all the way home in the car and stomps off upstairs as soon as we get in because I've refused to promise to buy him an air rifle for his birthday. But he cheers up when we start icing the fairy cakes.

'Don't eat them, Charlie. I've got to take them to school later, to sell on the cake stall.'

'But I'm starving.'

'You can have one or two, Charlie, but not all of them.'

'That's not fair. I'm doing the icing and everything. I wouldn't have bothered if you'd told me they were for stupid school.'

'It's for the school fund, Charlie. To pay for trips and things.'

'I don't care. It's not fair. Please, Mummy.'

'Charlie, try not to drop icing on the floor, please. Look, there's another bit, it's gone on my foot now.'

Charlie bends down, wipes up the icing with his finger, eats it, and then he abandons helping altogether and moves on to trying to nick teaspoonfuls of icing when he thinks I'm not looking.

'Mummy, we've got a round table, haven't we? Like Merlin.'

'It was King Arthur who had the round table. And stop doing that.'

'Yes, but Merlin told him to get it.'

'Oh. Right. Well, yes, I suppose it was.'

He gives me another of his pitying looks.

'So anyway, we've got a round table, haven't we, so if we had a dog he could be called Merlin. Or we could have two. And one could be Arfur. That would be great, wouldn't it?'

Great, so now it's two dogs. And one of them will be called a name he can't actually pronounce without sounding like Pauline Fowler in *EastEnders*.

'Dogs are a lot of work, Charlie. They need looking after, and they don't like being at home on their own. They might chew up all your toys while we're out.'

'Well, we could stay in.'

'What about when you go round to play with James?'

'I could take my best things with me. Or they could come too. Honestly, Mummy, where there's a will there's a way, you know.'

I don't know where he gets these handy little phrases from, but Mum and Edna are my top suspects. Sometimes it's like he's morphed into someone's annoying old auntie. All pursed lips and tuts of disapproval.

'Yes. And where there's a dog there's trouble. And anyway, what about Buzz and Woody? It wouldn't be fair on them. Rabbits don't like dogs.'

'Yes, they do, if they're friends.'

'Charlie, for heaven's sake stop eating the icing and let me finish these cakes.'

'Everyone else has got a dog. It's not fair. Uncle Monty says a good dog is worth its weight in gold. He told me. And I've been very ill, you know, and I need a dog.'

I think I'll just ignore the bit about him being ill, mainly because I never really know how to cope with it. It was nearly six months ago now, but he still mentions it quite a lot. Usually whenever he wants something and isn't getting it, like now. When we first got home from the hospital he used to have fairly epic tantrums and I tended to cave in, partly because I was so exhausted, and partly because I was so glad that he was all right I didn't really care about anything else. Although deep down I knew what he really needed was reassurance that he was safe again, not a mother who caved in every time he threw a wobbler.

But that's the thing about meningitis. It's just so terrifying. I still have nightmares where we don't get to the hospital in time and he's lying on the trolley and they turn all the machines off. Then I have to go and check he's still breathing, just like I used to when he was tiny. But lately I've moved on to the more usual kind of bad dreams, which I think is probably a good sign. The kind of dreams all parents have, where you've gone to work and forgotten to take them to school, or left them in a shop or something. But at least they're not the kind of dreams that have you sitting bolt upright at 3 a.m. too frightened to turn the light off, with tears rolling down your face. And I can almost hear the sound of ambulance sirens now without getting flashbacks to sitting holding him unconscious in my arms, desperately rocking him and trying to pretend he was just asleep.

I'm getting much better at coping when he's off colour too, although the first time he got a cold was pretty tricky: trying to balance being normal and just doing the hot drinks and Calpol thing, with wanting to check every thirty seconds to make sure there were no signs of a menacing rash. And that bright lights weren't a problem. And it's not easy to judge whether someone's sensitive to light because they've got a life-threatening illness, or because you've just woken them up in the middle of the night by turning the big light on to check that the red mark on their neck's just from lying on the dagger they insisted on taking to bed with them. But we're getting there, slowly, and when I think of what might have happened, well, I try not to really, but it certainly puts things into perspective.

Would you like a drink, sweetheart? There's apple juice or pear, I think.'

'Yes please, but I'd like Coke. It's in the fridge, behind the lettuce. A whole can. I've been saving it. Edna got it for me.'

'Did she? That was nice.'

'Yes, she's lovely, my Edna. Like my Nana. She gets me Coke too.'

He gives me a meaningful stare to emphasise the point. Decent people like Edna and Nana understand about buying boys Coke and don't insist on water or fruit juice like cruel heartless mothers.

'How about an apple and a bath, so we can get the icing out of your fringe?'

'Cut-up apple?'

'All right.'

'Great.'

He charges off upstairs and starts running the bath, so I'd better be quick peeling the apple unless I want the bathroom floor flooded. But at least I can pretend I've forgotten about the Coke and take some juice up. Suddenly he's back in the kitchen, stark naked, and hopping up and down because the floor tiles are so cold.

'I almost forgot my Coke.'

Bugger. Outmanoeuvred. Again.

* * *

22

The PTA Barn Dance is in full swing by the time we arrive. We're in Sally and Roger's car, and Roger's doing the driving so we'll be able to have a drink. He's wearing a Stetson and has borrowed William's potato gun so he can shoot Mrs Harrison-Black if she tries to make him dance with her like she did at the Summer Disco. He's also talking in a special cowboy voice and keeps saying 'OK, partner'; Sally says he's been doing it all afternoon and it's driving her crazy.

The village hall has been transformed by Ginny Richmond and her helpers: they've brought in bales of hay and put checked tablecloths on all the tables, with candles in glass holders. They've hung lanterns everywhere, and stuck pink crêpe-paper hearts all over the walls and the stage, with balloons and red ribbons tied up in bunches. Mrs Harrison-Black is standing glowering in the gloom in a corner behind the cake stall, and Ginny's gang have made their husbands dress up as cowboys, and they're all looking pretty uncomfortable in their neatly pressed jeans with sharp creases down the front, while the women are in twirly skirts with fringes and tassels, and spangly shirts.

The Harrison-Black contingent are wearing their usual padded waistcoats with navy-blue skirts and smart court shoes. Everyone else has gone for a mixture of jeans and checks, apart from Tina Foley who's gone for a skintight white sequinned catsuit like the ones Elvis Presley used to wear. Actually, I think she might have seen too many Dolly Parton videos, but she's certainly attracting lots of admiring glances.

'Oh good, there's a table over there. Quick, Roger, go and sit down and bagsy it for us while we go and get some booze.'

'OK, partner.'

Sally gives him a Look.

'Roger. Are you going to say that all night? Only it's getting quite annoying.'

'I'm just getting into the spirit of things.'

'Well, stop it. Or I'll shoot you with your potato gun.'

We head over to a table in the far corner and dump our coats, and then I take our cakes over to Betty. Proper mothers have smart Tupperware cake containers, usually in pale yellow, for some reason, whereas we have knackered old biscuit tins with lids that don't fit properly. Sally's made scones and couldn't find a tin at all so she's put them in a plastic bag.

Betty gives them a very suspicious look.

'I'll just pop these on a plate, shall I? Mrs Jenkins has made some scones too, and they're always so light, oh and fairy cakes too. Jolly good.'

She looks at them like they might be toxic and I make a swift retreat to our table before she gets a chance to make critical comments, or suggest foolproof remedies for flat sponge.

Sally and Kate have already got a couple of bottles of red.

'I hope it's all right. That stuff we got last time was lethal.'

'I'm sure it'll be mighty fine, partner. But I might just mosey on over and see if there's any beer. I'm not sure cowboys drink red wine.'

'Roger, please stop talking in that ridiculous voice.'

Sally and Roger always bicker like this, but it's in a nice background sort of a way, rather than an I-really-hate-you-and-I-wish-you-were-dead way that other couples seem so fond of. Sally teaches history at the local comprehensive three days a week, and the rest of the time she's at home with William, who's six and a bit Tricky, and

24

Rosie, who's nine and Not. Roger's the local solicitor and one of the nicest men on the planet. He's just become a Parent Governor at the school because he thought he ought to be doing his bit, and he's having a terrible time getting caught between the two rival camps on the Committee.

Ginny's already spotted him and is coming over.

'Hello, everybody. What a pretty shirt, Sally. Super. Hello, Roger. Isn't it wonderful that so many people have come? I wasn't sure we'd get a turnout like this.'

'Well, you've done a marvellous job with the decorations. It looks terrific.'

'Oh, do you think so? I just wish we'd had more time. I could have done something really special, but the Brownies had the hall until three and there was no budging them. There was some mix-up with the booking, apparently. Although I suspect you know who.'

Roger looks rather blank until Ginny glares in the direction of Mrs Harrison-Black, who's still standing behind the cakes but looking like she'll be bolting over any minute.

'Oh. Right. Well, anyway, it all looks splendid.'

'I hope you'll be dancing later – I've found us a sweet little band, quite famous locally, I think. They play in the Walnut Tree, you know, that super pub in Massing. Have you heard of them? They're called Harvest Moon.'

'Er no, sorry.'

'Well, don't be shy. The dances are very simple once you get going, and the caller shouts out all the steps. It's super.'

Oh dear. Here comes Mrs Harrison-Black.

'Mrs Richmond, were you aware that there's a problem with the urn? Only it is rather temperamental and I did say this might happen. If you overfill it it simply cuts out, and someone seems to have filled it almost to the brim. People do like a cup of tea or coffee, you know. Not everybody wants to drink themselves insensible.'

She gives Kate, who's in the middle of pouring us all some wine, a withering look. But Kate's impervious to withering. I think it's something she learnt at finishing school.

'Hello, Betty. Hasn't Ginny done a fabulous job with the hall? We were all just telling her what a genius she is. Are the cakes selling well?'

'Very well, thank you, our cake stalls always do. They are a lot of work, of course, but, yes, just coming, please excuse me, duty calls, but, Mrs Richmond, if you could just pop into the kitchen and sort out the urn situation I'd be very grateful. I simply can't do everything myself.'

She marches off back towards her stall, and Ginny rushes off towards the kitchen.

'Crikey. Do you think I ought to go and offer to help?'

'Roger, you don't know the first thing about tea urns. It'll be fine.'

'Oh. Well, good. But perhaps I ought to circulate a bit, do the Governor thing. Should I?'

'Yes. Good idea. But I'd leave your potato gun here, if I were you, or one of them might take you hostage.'

He's soon trapped in a corner with a rather relentless woman, who keeps complaining that her son's just started in Reception and isn't reading yet. Apparently, she thinks he's very bright and is being under-stimulated; Sally says she's a textbook example of how to alienate the entire teaching staff in the first term, and her son's doing fine according to his teacher, although he does seem rather Tense. Apparently, he does all sorts of classes after school, and often falls asleep in the home corner after lunch.

'So how did the Still Happily Marrieds do Valentine's Day then?'

Kate passes Sally a glass of wine.

26

'Roger made me breakfast in bed, and the kids did me a card.'

'Oh rub it in, why don't you?'

'Hang on a minute, I hadn't finished. And then William jumped on the bed and knocked my tea over, and Roger shouted at him so he stormed off and slammed our bedroom door and the mirror fell off our wardrobe. I've been meaning to fix it for ages. So that's seven years' bad luck. As if being married with two kids wasn't bad luck enough.'

'Well, as long as it's not just me and Annie living in a romance-free zone.'

'Hardly. The closest Roger gets to romance is offering to take the bin out for me. Like he's doing me a favour.'

Kate laughs.

'No, I'm serious. He does. Usually when we're in the kitchen after supper. He says, "Shall I take the bin out, darling," like it's really my job, but he's offering to help me out. It's infuriating.'

'Yes, but at least he offers. Not like Phil, who never lifted a finger. He was doing it again tonight – he's round looking after the kids, so god knows what state the place will be in when I get back – and just as I was leaving he asked me if there was there anything for supper, only he was starving. I mean you'd think, wouldn't you, after the divorce and everything, that what he was having for supper might not actually be my responsibility any more. But apparently not.'

'I hope you told him to bugger off.'

'Well, I would have done, but the kids were there, so I made him some scrambled eggs. But I didn't put cheese in, and he hates them without cheese.'

Sally shakes her head.

'No cheese. Poor thing. Honestly, Kate, you should just tell him to sod off, you know.'

'I know. But I have to try to keep things civil in front of the kids.'

'True. But still.'

'And I put lots of white pepper in, and he hates too much pepper.'

Sally and I exchange glances.

'And I'm going to get some extra-strong chillies, for next time he's peckish. That'll show him.'

Kate's really moved on in the last year, now the divorce is final, but I think she's still got a fair way to go. When Phil first left she was in a terrible state; he just announced one morning that he was leaving, completely out of the blue, because he'd met Zelda at his art class, and she understood what a deeply creative spirit he was. Despite the fact that he's actually an accountant, and not a very good one at that. Sally and I had to take it in turns to go round and sit with her, and she sobbed for days. But gradually she started coping, and then he told her Zelda was pregnant, which set her right back again. But she's almost over that as well now, mainly because it turns out Zelda has quite firm ideas about who should be left holding baby Saffron, while the other one goes off being Artistic. And it's not her.

Sally pours us all some more wine.

'What's Zelda been up to lately, then? Still keeping Phil on his toes, I hope?'

'She's away for the weekend, at a spa. So she's dumped Saffron on her mother.'

'I've always wanted to go to a spa, All I've managed so far is a weekend away at a bloody school conference, and even then Roger rang me on Sunday morning and begged me to come home early. You've got to admire her, haven't you?'

'Technically speaking, no, not really.'

Sally goes slightly pink.

'Sorry, I didn't mean it like that. I just meant that having Saffron's not exactly holding her back, is it?'

'No. But it's certainly cramping Phil's style.'

We all laugh.

'Is she still unfortunate-looking?'

I know Kate loves it when I ask her this. Both Phoebe and James were very beautiful babies, whereas Saffron is definitely the kind of baby only a mother could love: and even then you'd have to be exceptionally keen. She's got very wispy hair, and not much of it, and a rather prominent hooter.

'She's just started walking, and she screams every time she doesn't get what she wants. He looks completely exhausted.'

Sally and I both say 'Shame' simultaneously, and cackle with laughter.

'Don't look now, but I think the Harvest Mooners are about to start.'

'Oh good.'

Sally's looking genuinely keen. I really don't think she gets out enough.

'Aren't you two dancing then?'

Kate's looking horrified.

'Have you ever done country dancing, Sal?'

She shakes her head.

'Well, take it from me, it's appalling. And exhausting. And Annie will end up dancing with Bob Jenkins like she always does.'

I always get stuck with Bob Jenkins, who's about four foot six and has very sweaty hands. His wife makes a point of sending him over to dance with all us tragic single types, and then she stands there smiling and nodding at you, like she's giving you a real treat, dancing with her fabulous husband, which is so annoying, on so many levels, that it doesn't really bear thinking about.

'Oh. Right. OK then. So definitely no dancing.'

We manage to hold out for about ten minutes, and then nip out for a quick fag, which is another reason we all became friends; Kate caught me hiding out of view of the school gates before collecting Charlie, and said 'Oh Thank God' and promptly lit up too. Sally gave up last year, but she still comes out with us because she says she's buggered if she's going to become one of those born-again types who wave their hands in the air and tut when anyone lights up. Although it's getting beyond a joke now, trying to grab a quick fag without getting a lecture from somebody; I've been reduced to standing outside the kitchen door in the pouring rain with an umbrella in a furtive manner, and Kate sometimes lies on her kitchen floor and smokes out of the cat flap. And of course it is an appalling habit and we keep talking about giving up. Obviously. And we will. Just not tonight.

We go back in and walk straight into a combined pincer movement from Ginny Richmond, and Roger, who badly lets the side down by deciding that country dancing looks like fun, and it's all a bit of a blur after that. There's lots of charging round in circles and stepping forwards and backwards in complicated combinations of squares and circles, and lots of stamping. Ginny Richmond and her groupies have obviously been practising, so part of the hall is dancing in perfect synchronised formation, clapping and stamping on cue, while the rest of us lurch about frantically looking at other people to try to work out what we should be doing. One tune follows another, and we're Gathering Nuts and Mowing Meadows like our lives depend on it. Kate soon gets the hang of it, but Sally and I are pretty hopeless and Roger loses his hat, which gets stamped on by mistake by Tom Forrester's dad.

Just when I think I might pass out with the combination of the wine and twirling, Harvest Moon announce they're taking a short break, thank Christ. So we lurch back towards our table, and Roger comes over with more wine, even though he's not drinking, which seems pretty heroic to me.

'You're a lovely man, did you know that, Roger?'

He goes pink.

'Oh. Well, thank you very much, Annie.'

Sally laughs.

'You've made him all embarrassed now. Roger darling, while you're up, could you get us some cake, to keep Betty happy?'

'What did your last slave die of?'

'Answering back.'

He heads off towards the cake stall.

'I wish I could have a Roger.'

I must be drunker than I thought. Sally sniggers.

'I'll lend you mine, if you like.'

Actually, I think we're all a bit drunker than I thought.

'I didn't mean it like that.'

'No. I know. And I'm quite fond of him myself, actually. Daft old thing.'

Kate nods.

'Well, there's a definite shortage, that's for sure, especially of ones who aren't about to sod off to New York like your Mack.'

She gives me a sideways glance.

'Exactly.'

'So you're still missing him then?'

'No. Well, sometimes. Slightly.'

'Well, I don't blame you. He was absolutely scrumptious.'

'Thanks, Kate. That really helps.'

Sally smiles.

'Yes, but what kind of man goes off to New York when his kids live in London? That's what I want to know.'

Kate nods and gives me an encouraging look.

'And he was a bit demanding, wasn't he? The sort of chap who needs total devotion.'

'Yes.'

'Well, there you are then – lucky escape really.'

I half listen while Kate tells us about her lunch with her mother today; Kate's mother is so right wing she makes Margaret Thatcher look almost sane. She keeps parading 'suitable' men in front of Kate, and today it was her friend Beanie's son Martin, who collects stamps and likes to tell people all about where he found the more unusual ones in his collection.

At least Mack didn't have any unusual hobbies, not unless you count doing James Bond impressions. Not that he dressed up or anything, but he did used to call me Moneypenny, and he had a really great voice, sort of Sean Connery meets Mel Gibson in *Braveheart*. And he had beautiful grey eyes. And he used to raise his eyebrows just before he kissed you, like he was about to try a tricky bit of DIY. And I loved the way he used to put his hand on the small of my back. Damn. That was almost worth going all the way to New York for. Almost. But not quite. I couldn't really drag Charlie halfway across the world, away from everyone he loves, for a man I'd only known for a few months.

And even if I could, I'm not sure I'd have really wanted to. He was just too overwhelming, too demanding. Everything had to be on his terms. And I think I've gone past the total-devotion stage now, where you're up for melting your life into somebody else's and you think it will all be wonderful and you'll live happily ever after. I'm happy with my life the way it is, most of the time, and if someone does come along then they'll have to be into partnerships and joint decisions. Someone who knows how to share, and doesn't have to be the centre of everything all the time.

'And then she said beggars can't be choosers, and if I was happy for James to grow up to be a woofter then that was fine, but everyone knew that boys needed a man around. And when I said it hadn't done my cousin Justin much good, she got completely furious.'

Sally laughs.

'Is Justin the one with the hotel in Brighton?'

'Yes, and he's lovely, but the old guard in the family have practically had him excommunicated.'

'Well, more fool them.'

'I know. But it doesn't stop it being annoying. I mean you could win the Nobel Peace Prize or something and they'd still say yes, but has she got a man yet?'

Roger comes back with a huge tray of cakes because he isn't sure which ones we'll fancy. He's such a hero.

'What are we talking about?'

'Men.'

'Oh. Right. Any particular one in mind? What happened to that Mick chap of yours, Annie? He seemed like a decent sort of bloke.'

'Mack. Honestly, Roger, he was called Mack, don't you ever listen, I told you, he wanted Annie to go and live in New York with him, at Christmas, I told you. But she didn't want to go.'

Sally's giving him a Be Careful look.

'Oh god, sorry. I hope I didn't hit a nerve or anything.'

'No, it's fine, Roger, really. All water under the bridge now.'

33

'It's like that song, you know, "This old man, he played two"?'

We give Kate rather blank looks.

'With a Mick Mack Paddywack, give a dog a bone.'

We shriek with laughter and Roger goes off to get us all some coffee.

Which is probably a good idea.

'Well, he won't be coming rolling home, that's for sure. And that's fine by me.'

Sally's giving Roger a really sweet look as he stands in the queue for coffee being harangued by another discontented parent. And he gives her a little wave. Kate and I make noises like we're about to be sick and Sally laughs.

'So nobody new on the horizon then, Annie?'

'Absolutely nobody. All the nice ones are married, or gay. Or both. And it's not like you can just go out and nick somebody else's.'

Kate stiffens slightly.

'That didn't seem to stop Zelda.'

'True.'

'But then she ended up with Phil, so there is some justice, I suppose. Sometimes I'm just so pleased he's gone, you know, I really am. He took up so much space. What he liked, what he wanted to eat, what he wanted to watch on telly; sometimes I used to sit in the bathroom just to get away from him. But the kids miss him, I know they do, and so do I, occasionally. I know it's ridiculous, but I do. It's so unfair.'

'Well, I'll tell you something else that isn't fair. The Harvest Moonies are getting ready for round two.'

'Oh good Lord, not again.'

We manage to hold out for about fifteen minutes this time, but inevitably we end up dancing again, charging about like mad things, with the music getting faster and faster, and then the zip on Tina Foley's catsuit comes undone and she dances pretty much topless for about five minutes before she realises, which goes down extremely well with most of the dads, especially Bob Jenkins.

By the time I get home I feel like I've just taken part in a marathon, only nobody's given me a tin-foil cape. I try not to appear too drunk in front of Edna, and fail, and then collapse into bed and try to get my jeans off while I'm lying down, which turns out to be trickier than I'd thought. I'm just trying to work out if I've got the energy to get up and go downstairs and turn the heating back on, because it's absolutely freezing, when Charlie stumbles in, and shuffles into my bed muttering something about bad dreams and werewolves. He grabs three-quarters of the duvet and adopts his starfish sleeping position, so I have to nudge him sideways, which isn't easy because he weighs a ton.

I'm just drifting off to sleep when he suddenly goes in for a bit of random arm-flinging and hits me on the head, which makes him surface and accuse me of waking him up.

'I was in the middle of my best dream. With griffins. Why did you wake me up? Honestly, Mummy, you're horrible. Horrible.'

'You woke yourself up, Charlie, and now you're awake you can go back to your own bed. Come on, I'll come in with you and tuck you up.'

He pretends to be asleep, and mutters 'night-night' from under the duvet.

'Charlie, I know you're pretending.'

'I love you, Mummy. To infinity and back again. Nighty-night.'

Oh bugger it.

* * *

35

Oh god. Oh god. I will never drink red wine again. Ever. I wake up feeling appalling, to find Charlie's already downstairs watching cartoons. Bugger. And we've got twenty minutes before we should be at school, all sparkling and shiny and in possession of a nutritious packed lunch. Double bugger. I charge about like someone in a Benny Hill sketch, waving bits of clothing and trying to get Charlie to eat Shreddies, whilst simultaneously trying to turn a stale bread roll and a bit of knackered cheese into an attractive lunch. I wish Jamie Oliver would come up with handy hints for situations like this, instead of clever things to do with roasted vegetables and pecorino.

'What's for my packed lunch today?'

'Hold your arms up, Charlie, so I can get your sweatshirt on.'

There are sounds of muffled whining from inside the sweatshirt. He emerges red-faced, with his hair sticking up in tufts.

'Not cheese. I hate cheese.'

'Don't be silly, Charlie. You like cheese.'

'No I don't.'

'Yes you do. And anyway sometimes you just have to have whatever's in the fridge. And today it's cheese. Or you can have school lunch.'

He gives me a stricken look.

'Stop being horrible, Mummy.'

His lip is starting to quiver. And to be fair he has got a point: the school lunches are completely revolting, and everybody knows it. Even the caretaker brings a packed lunch.

'Cecily Bates had school lunch last week. And then she was sick. In the hall.'

'Oh dear, poor Cecily.'

'Yes. But she's always being sick. Once she was sick on

the stage, when we were doing singing. And some of it went on James's shoe.'

Yet one more reason to be thankful that I'm never going to be a teacher of Mixed Infants.

By the time we get to school I'm feeling like I've got a very tight hat on. I really don't think those Panadol have kicked in yet, and I'm fighting back the urge to do a Cecily impression and throw up on someone's shoes. Luckily we didn't spot any pheasants on the drive to school, but Ted was blocking the lane with his milk float again, and we had to wait until he had a nice chat with Mrs Thomas before I could squeeze past him and rocket off up the lane. I'm very tempted to go home for a nice little lie down, but I've got to get round Sainsbury's, and work out where to buy a cagoule. And then I'd better get home and call Barney and see what other brilliant new ideas he's come up with to make the Northumberland job complete hell. Fabulous.

II

Stormy Weather

IT'S BEEN RAINING FOR days, in a steady, torrential kind of way, and the river that runs past the church is nearly up to the wooden bridge, so all the people who live in the posh cottages along the riverbank have stopped being superior about their lovely views and started shifting sandbags. Driving anywhere is like being in *The Poseidon Adventure*, only without the added bonus of Shelley Winters, and I'm heading up to Northumberland tomorrow, where they've also got sleet and gales.

And to top it all it's Pancake Day today and the PTA have decided to do pancake races in the hall this afternoon for some reason best known to themselves, so Charlie's got to take a frying pan to school, which I'm in the middle of scrubbing so I don't win the Most Sluttish Mother of the Year Award (Kitchen Appliance Division). Charlie's been out talking to the rabbits and charges into the kitchen looking agitated.

'Mummy, they're doing it again.'

'What?'

'Buzz and Woody are doing sex again.'

'No they're not, Charlie, I've told you before. They're just being friendly.'

'We should get them lady rabbits – you're being very mean, you know – and then they could have lots of babies. Grandad says rabbits breed like blazers.'

'Blazes, Charlie, not blazers. And he meant in the wild. We haven't got enough room for baby rabbits too – it would be cruel.'

Actually, I'm starting to think that we might have one of the few pairs of gay rabbits in Kent, because poor Woody's got a bald bit on his back where Buzz keeps leaping on top of him. I'm sure I read in the newspapers about a pair of gay penguins in New York, who tried to hatch a rock until their keeper gave them an egg. Maybe our rabbits are the same. Christ. That's all I need. I'll have to find them a surrogate baby rabbit from somewhere, or be accused of being homophobic. Maybe I should ring the vet and ask him what he thinks.

'When's Nana coming?'

'Tomorrow. She's picking you up from school.'

'Oh good. We can have a feast.'

Mum usually turns up with enough food to cover any eventuality, with a few spare tins of luncheon meat just in case, although she's also quite keen on Fray Bentos steak-and-kidney pies.

'And Grandad's coming?'

Actually, I might ask Dad what he thinks about the rabbits.

'Yes.'

'Good. And, Mummy, will you tell Nana about my cakes? Because Miss Pike says anybody who doesn't re-member to bring their things won't be able to do cooking.'

'Yes, I've already told her, but I'll remind her, I promise.'

Knowing Mum, she's probably got everything weighed out already, clearly labelled and in proper Tupperware containers.

'Yes, and I need Smarties. You can put Smarties on top of your cakes if you like. Or chocolate buttons. But James and me are doing Smarties. Chocolate buttons are just for girls really.'

'Right.'

I've given up trying to decipher the subtleties of what is considered girly and what is not. God knows why chocolate buttons are girly and Smarties aren't. But at least I'm now crystal-clear that no self-respecting six-year-old boy would be seen dead in a cardigan, even if his nana did knit it for him. Mum still thinks I shrank it in the washing machine.

'And I need some stuff for my hair, like the Year Six boys have. James is getting some too. It makes your hair stick up. Look, like this.'

He pushes the front of his fringe up in the air, so he looks like he's just been electrocuted.

'It's really cool.'

'Right. Well, I'll try to get some when I get back, all right?'

But apparently this is Not All Right. In fact it is Absolutely Vital he has hair gel for tomorrow or his life won't be worth living. There's a great deal of stamping about and muttering and he's about to launch into a mega-whine when the phone rings. It's Kate, and she's having a similar I-must-have-gel-or-I-will-die crisis round at her house, so do I want her to get us some when she goes shopping? I say yes please and convey the good news to Charlie, who does a celebratory dance round the kitchen.

⌐ knows what Mum's going to say about Charlie going

to school with his hair sticking up in pointy peaks. But I don't think she's going to be pleased.

Leila rings just as I'm putting the finishing touches to the final budget sheets. Leila's Charlie's godmother and my best friend; we worked together at a huge advertising agency years ago, and she's now MD of a big agency, making bucketloads of money, which she's very good at spending.

'So how's your morning been so far, darling? Mine's been total bollocks.'

'Not much better. I've been doing bloody spreadsheets and emails from Lawrence, and trying to delete all the ones offering me drugs I've never heard of or a larger willy.'

'Forward them to Lawrence.'

'Yes, I thought of that. But I think it might just make him worse. Are you all set for tomorrow then?'

Leila's agency are the clients for the Northumberland job and she's coming up to the shoot.

'Yes. We're flying up late in the afternoon.'

'Well, don't forget to pack warm stuff, because it's going to be bloody freezing. Christ, I've just seen what time it is – I'm going to be late for the pancake races.'

'I beg your pardon?'

'The PTA are doing pancake races at school, and if you don't show up you end up on the lost-property rota.'

'Can't you just send a cheque?'

'Not really.'

'Well, they're definitely missing a trick there. Do you get to eat the pancakes?'

'In theory. If you like cold pancakes that have been trodden on.'

'How lovely. Well, give my boy a kiss from his godmother. And see you tomorrow, sweetheart.'

The pancake races turn out to be far more diverting than I thought they'd be. Ginny Richmond's organised things and there's an overwhelming smell of batter in the hall, and lots of children swarming everywhere trailing frying pans. There's a tremendous sound of clanging metal coming from the playground, where the Year Six boys are re-enacting *Gladiator* by bashing their frying pans together while a supply teacher tries to get them to line up. In the end Mrs Taylor has to go outside with her whistle.

The dads' race is first, and some of them are wearing tracksuits and Peter Marley's brought a wok. He's always very keen on Winning, and catches every single pancake, but is then disqualified for unsportsmanlike behaviour and promptly lodges an appeal with Mrs Taylor.

The Reception class seem to have no idea what they're meant to be doing, and either eat their pancakes or wander off, and then one small boy throws his frying pan into the air along with his pancake and narrowly misses giving himself concussion.

Charlie and James hurl their pancakes so high they haven't a hope of catching them, but I've got a feeling this is the whole point. And for once the children from the poshest families are at a distinct disadvantage – because running with a Le Creuset frying pan is no joke. Georgia Harrington drags hers along the floor making a terrible grinding noise, much to her mother's annoyance.

'Oh god, it's William's turn now. Watch yourself, it could go anywhere.'

Sally takes a step backwards as William's class lines up in teams of four. He starts off really well, but when he gets to the middle bit where he has to stop and toss the pancake he flings it and then trips over and as he's getting up the pancake lands on his head, which the rest of his class think is hysterical. Roger goes over to de-pancake him, and give him a quick cuddle, but he doesn't seem to mind, and is busy eating the bits Roger has peeled out of his hair.

'God, I wish they'd done this when I was at school.'

'I'm surprised none of them have gone for the teachers. Oh, too late.'

The supply teacher now has a pancake on her shoulder.

The final race is the mother's relay, with teams of four, which turns out to be basically between Mrs Harrison-Black's gang and Ginny Richmond's, because nobody else is daft enough to enter. It's a photo finish, except Roger forgot to bring his camera. Oh god, he'll be in for it now. Sally's looking nervous all of a sudden, as well she might. If he gets this wrong he'll be in big trouble.

'It's a draw, absolutely nothing between them. So three cheers for all the mums.'

All the children cheer, and Roger looks very pleased with himself. Neither of the teams is completely happy, but they're not swarming round him complaining either, and Mrs Taylor's looking very relieved, as is Sally.

'Thank god for that. I thought I'd have to smuggle him out the back with a blanket over his head.'

Kate comes over with James and Charlie.

'Miss Pike says we can take them home now – they just need to get their coats.'

The teachers have obviously decided that trying to get everyone back into their classrooms and sitting nicely ready for home time is going to be a complete non-starter, given the current levels of hysteria and general charging about. And they're not wrong. It takes us nearly twenty minutes to find coats and lunch boxes and get to the car. The parents who go for the stop-that-or-I'll-slap-you approach get away in record time, but our more child-friendly let's-go-home-and-have-a-lovely-tea technique means we're left dithering about trying to negotiate our way out of the playground for ages. Roger's still trying to talk William down off the climbing frame as I manage to lure Charlie into the car with the promise of more pancakes at home.

I've decided to bypass my usual fill-the-kitchen-with-black-smoke motif for Pancake Day this year, and gone for the more relaxed buy-them-from-M&S-and-stick-them-in-the-microwave approach. But Charlie's talking about more pancake-flipping when we get home, which might be slightly tricky, and I've got a sinking feeling he'll still manage to get one stuck to the kitchen ceiling like last year.

By the time I arrive in Northumberland at teatime the next day I'm only a smidgen away from complete hysterics due to a combination of last-minute packing, helping Mum unload all her food supplies whilst telling her about Charlie's new passion for hair gel, and explaining why there are still bits of pancake on the light in the kitchen, before spending hours driving in the pouring rain behind lorries who seem to have developed a new technique of pulling out in front of you on the motorway with no signals of any kind, just for a laugh. It's like driving through a series of waterfalls, and when I stopped for a coffee I managed to get out of the car straight into a enormous puddle, which soaked my socks up to my ankles.

But at least I've managed to avoid the botulistic bed and breakfast where Lawrence had booked me a room, after a bit of nifty manoeuvring this morning. So I'm now in the hotel where Barney and the crew are staying. They're all in the bar when I arrive, trying to persuade the make-up woman to play the new game they've just invented, strip karaoke.

Barney's looking very pleased with himself.

'Hello, darling, journey up all right? Good. Well, hurry up and dump your stuff, only I need to run through a few changes with you.'

He's giving me one of his Don't You Start looks, because his changes tend to require all sorts of extra equipment, which blows the budget completely and sends Lawrence into a frenzy.

'Fine. And the client arrives tomorrow, yes?'

'Oh fuck. I forgot about that. Who else is coming?'

'Leila, and the agency producer, Nick, and one of the junior copywriters. They're staying in Newcastle – Lawrence has got all the details. Didn't he tell you?'

'Oh I never listen to Lawrence, you know that. And why is the lovely Leila gracing us with her presence?'

'Because the account's worth a fortune and the client likes to be made a fuss of.'

'Oh does he?'

'Don't start, Barney, I'm sure it'll be fine. Leila's brilliant with high-maintenance men. It's one of her specialities.'

'Well, good for her. But I'm warning you, if he starts kicking off I'm not having it. I've decided. I'm not going to get involved any more. It's a waste of energy. Fucking clients. And the agencies are no better. I'm just going to walk off. Go home and leave them to it.'

'Right.'

Even the faintest whisper that Barney's planning to walk off jobs if anyone annoys him will give Lawrence a heart attack. And if he does march off we won't get paid, which means I don't get paid. So it's good news all round really.

He's done it once before, and the agency producer had to try to finish the job, and they've never worked with us again. Barney's already got quite a reputation for being spectacularly rude to agency people and clients who turn up and make suggestions, although luckily most of them are so stupid they don't realise. And the ones that do are usually calmed down by a frantic combination of Lawrence oiling himself all over them and me sorting Barney out. But the trouble is he's usually right, and he's such a brilliant director it's almost worth it. But not at the time, obviously, when you just want to strangle him.

'Leila will sort it if we have any problems, Barney. I'm sure she will.'

Christ, I'm definitely going to have to ring her and warn her.

'Well, as long as she keeps him off my back, that's all I ask.'

'Yes, I know, we all know, Barney. You're a creative genius who must not be trifled with.'

He gives me a menacing look.

'So tell me about the changes. Are they the kind of thing the client's going to notice, by any chance?'

'Oh Lawrence can take care of that.'

'Is he up for the duration then?'

Lawrence usually stays well clear of shoots. His nerves can't stand it.

'Yes. I think he's hoping he'll charm your Leila into giving us more work.'

'Fat chance of that.'

'Yes, darling, I know that. And you know that. But Lawrence doesn't. So don't tell him, all right? It'll give him something to do. Now hurry up, will you, the lights going and I want you to see the beach. And put more clothes on, it's fucking freezing down there.'

Bloody hell. He's not kidding. I'm half expecting to see polar bears. It's beyond pouring. It's raining in solid sheets, it's like standing in a freezing power shower, except the hurricane-force winds mean you can't actually stand upright, so you have to sort of hunch. Christ. I'm going to be spending the next few days hunching and trying to stave off hypothermia. How lovely.

The sound of the waves is almost deafening and the fisherman's waiting for us in the harbour, ready to show off his boat again. He greets Barney like a long-lost friend, which means he's still on a high due to the enormous sum of money we're paying him to use his bloody boat. But I know from bitter experience that this won't last, and Barney's bound to make him sail round and round for hours in gale-force winds and ask him to do something tricky like sail backwards into the harbour, and the honeymoon period will end with a sickening thud.

He gives me a very cheerful smile.

'Bit nippy for you, pet?'

Bit nippy. Is he Mad? Every time I turn my head I disappear inside my hood because the only way I can keep the bloody thing on is by tying a double knot under my chin. I must look like a complete nutter. Barney's marching up and down talking about what he wants tomorrow, and what the weather's going to be like. Total crap, apparently.

While we drive back to the hotel Barney runs through a few of his top ideas. I'm definitely going to have to ring Leila. Instead of a simple little walk along the beach with a wet umbrella he now wants to get shots of the boat leaving the harbour looking like it's about to capsize in a storm, which if we're really lucky it probably will, and then, and this is the thing he's most excited about, shots from a helicopter coming in from the sea towards the

47

beach. Lawrence has organised the helicopter. I just hope he's booked air-sea rescue too.

'Handy colour, your coat, darling. Bright orange really suits you.'

'It was the only one they had in the shop that was properly waterproof.'

'Well, at least if you get washed out to sea we'll be able to spot you.'

'Oh do shut up, Barney.'

'Sorry, what did you say? I can't hear you, you keep hiding inside your hood.'

'I'm not hiding. I can't get the knot undone.'

We're starting really early tomorrow so we have supper and then the crew head for the bar and I scarper upstairs to make calls. I'm rather worried about our model, who's tiny and doesn't look like she'll be able to walk along a stormy beach carrying a small handbag, let alone an umbrella. And she also looks like the kind of girl who's going to be deeply unhappy if she gets soaking wet. She's already complained to her agent that the hotel doesn't have a swimming pool.

I call Mum, and end up having a long conversation with Charlie about his new hairstyle while call-waiting beeps on my mobile and the crew send me multiple texts asking me to come downstairs and play strip karaoke. Jesus Christ.

'Mummy, tell Nana, will you, she says she likes my hair nice and flat. But Grandad says it reminds him of when he was young. He says he wouldn't have been seen dead without his quiffer.'

I never knew Dad had a quiff. There are some photos of him and Mum before they got married and his hair does look a bit lively, but I always thought it was just a rather breezy day.

'What's a quiffer, Mummy?'

'It's quiff, Charlie, not quiffer. And it's when you stick your hair up at the front like Elvis Presley.'

'Who?'

'Ask Grandad, darling, ask him to sing you some of his songs. Look, I've got to go, but have a lovely day at school tomorrow and I'll call you at bedtime, all right? Can I talk to Nana now?'

'Yes, but I haven't finished yet.'

Oh god. I can't get stuck in a mammoth random-chatting routine with him now, I've got too many calls to make.

'All right, Charlie, but I think *The Simpsons* might be on.'

He drops the phone, and I can hear him running off down the corridor towards the telly, while Mum comes on and says yes she's remembered about his packed lunch and not giving him chocolate, so she's just put a little KitKat in, because they're more of a biscuit really, and she's given the kitchen cupboards a good clean-out, and why on earth am I collecting old jam jars under the sink, because if I'm thinking of making jam they'll need sterilising, only it's the wrong time of year for jam really, so was I thinking of chutney?

After explaining that I was only thinking of recycling, and I hate chutney, so can she please not make me half a ton as a surprise for when I get home, we get stuck in a rather heated conversation about whether I should be allowing Charlie to use hair gel, and why Dad stopped having a quiff, which turns out to be basically because Mum told him to.

Just when I think I'm going to have to adopt my emergency there's-someone-at-the-door technique to get her off the phone Dad saves the day by coming into the kitchen singing 'Love Me Tender, Love Me Do' with Charlie on backing vocals and she says she'd better go.

I call Leila at her posh hotel in Newcastle. She's about to take the client to dinner, and she's Not Happy.

'How was your journey up?'

'Fine. But Jesus Christ, Venice of the North? They've got to be fucking kidding. You don't get frostbite in Venice, and even if you did at least you'd be in the Cipriani.'

'Wait until you get out here tomorrow.'

'Can't wait, darling. So what's old Barney got planned for us then? Few little unexpected changes, are there?'

'How did you guess?'

'Don't tell me. He wants you to hire a sub so he can do the whole thing underwater.'

'Not quite. But almost. So far we've got a fishing boat and a helicopter. And he's decided he's not going to argue with clients any more. He's just going to walk off the job and go home.'

'Is he now? Well, you can tell him from me if he walks off one of my jobs I'll kill him. Bloody hell. You'd better take me through it so I can sell it to Mark at dinner.'

'What's he like?'

'A complete tosser.'

'Oh. Good.'

The next morning we're down at the harbour filming the boat heading out to sea when Leila arrives in an enormous black Chrysler Voyager with tinted windows. Lawrence immediately leaps on the client and takes him off for a coffee, and Leila wanders over and kisses me hello.

'Hello, darling. Are you wearing that coat for a joke or something?'

'Oh thanks very much. Lovely to see you too. Look, it's waterproof and that's all I care about at the moment.'

'Yes, but Christ, Annie, it's bright orange. And trust me, it's not your colour. Does it double up as a dinghy or something? It's big enough. And why on earth are you wearing that tragic woolly hat?'

'Because my hood will only stay up if I do up the ties and then I can't see where I'm going. I'll end up falling into the sea.'

'Well, that might not be a bad plan if it means you'll lose that hat. Take it off, darling, please – I can't talk to you while you're looking like a glow-in-the-dark tramp. It's too weird. Christ, I'm freezing.'

She's wearing a floor-length white sheepskin coat, with matching hat, beautiful leather boots, jeans, and a silky grey jumper and cardigan, which knowing Leila are probably cashmere. She looks fabulous.

'Leila, you've only just got out of the car.'

'Yes, and I'll be getting straight back in again, as soon as possible. Oh god, what's he up to now?'

'Who?'

'Mark. He's heading for Barney.'

'Bloody hell.'

We race over and manage to head him off before he can get to Barney. Lawrence seems very worried, and not without reason, that Mark, who's wearing a very thin suit and seems to have forgotten to bring a coat with him, will have to be airlifted out with frostbite before he realises what a fabulous job Barney's doing for him. So while I persuade one of the crew to lend him a fleece Leila takes him over to watch the monitor and drink more coffee.

We've done our usual trick and turned the colour down on the monitor so the picture's only black-and-white, which makes it harder for people, especially clients, to work out what's going on. But he still spots the fact that we seem to be going in for a lot more in the way of elemental forces than was in the original script. Wait until he sees the helicopter.

Lawrence brings Barney over for a quick hello, and then rushes him off again before Mark gets a chance to ask any tricky questions, and we carry on traumatising the fisherman by making him sail sideways into freak waves because Barney likes the way the light hits the boat at that angle. The First's on board, swearing into his headset and promising to kill us if he ever gets back on dry land, and the crew aren't happy, squelching round in wet-weather gear swearing and texting each other pornographic messages.

But we finally get what we want, and head for the beach, where it takes us ages to set up, and then we break for lunch, which we eat huddled on the catering bus while wind and rain buffet the windows.

The model comes down from the hotel, whereupon she promptly begins sulking in the make-up van; apparently she's up for an audition for *Emmerdale* and shouldn't have to put up with this kind of thing. Barney takes her off for a little chat; he's surprisingly good with models and actors and usually seems to be able to tap into their vanity, or talent, or a combination of both, and get them to do what he wants. But I think he might have met his match this time.

'Fucking hell, she's a complete nightmare. Why didn't someone talk to her before we brought her all the way up here?'

'We did, Barney. We told you we thought she'd be trouble but you said she was perfect.'

'Well, she is, lookswise. It's just a shame she's an idiot. Christ, do I have to check everything?'

He stamps off towards the catering bus, and then marches back looking furious.

'Annie, darling, do you think you could possibly go over to those fuckers and explain that when I ask for a bacon sandwich I want it now, with no chat. Not some camp bastard telling me he's just run out but he'll pop some more bacon on and bring it over in a jif.'

'Right.'

'Thank you. And what the fuck are they doing?'

The crew are having a doughnut-eating competition and Kevin, our electrician, is winning. He gives me the thumbs-up and looks very pleased with himself.

'I don't know, Barney. But it looks like they're eating doughnuts.'

'And who's paying for all the bollocking doughnuts?'

He gives me a thunderous look.

'Five minutes. And I want that bloody girl out of the trailer and ready to go. Got that?'

When we finally get back to the hotel it's getting dark, and I'm frozen solid and caked in salt from all the sea spray. My jeans are actually crackling as I walk. Leila's sent Mark back to Newcastle with Nick and the copy-writer, who's still sulking about the changes Barney's made to his very mediocre script, and she's having supper with us at our hotel. She's busy flirting with Barney and generally annoying him.

'So what's the plan for tomorrow? Only Mark's quite keen to come up in the helicopter with you.'

'Oh is he?'

'Yes. That won't be a problem, will it?'

'No, not at all. I can always push him out the door if he starts coming up with ideas.'

Mark has made a couple of suggestions during the afternoon, mostly about getting more shots of the umbrella with his company logo on it.

'Leila, just tell Mark the insurance won't cover it and

stop winding Barney up, please – he's bad enough without you starting him off. And Barney, stop being so narky.'

'Narky? Me? I'm never narky.'

Leila laughs.

'So when I ask you to come to the awards dinner next month, because that beer film you did for us is up for an award, you'll just be really nice and say of course you'll come, you'll be delighted. Right?'

'Not fucking likely. I don't do awards. Lawrence goes. He loves all that bollocks.'

'Yes, but, Barney, you're up for a Gold, and a big hitter like you ought to be there.'

The big-hitter line has gone down rather well. Barney's smiling.

'Don't think you can smarm your way round me, darling. Big hitter, my arse.'

Oh dear.

'Tom Harris is a judge this year, I think.'

'Why would anyone in their right mind want him for a judge? The man's blind. They should give him a dog.'

'Well, quite, so you've got to come, and then you can put him straight, can't you?'

'I'll think about it, but I'm not promising. Now bugger off and pick on someone else, will you – I've got work to think about. And, Annie, see what they're doing in the bar. I don't want us getting banned from another hotel. And make sure that bloody girl's all right, will you.'

We check in on the bar and find the model sitting in a corner looking quite chirpy, but that might be down to the triple brandies the lighting cameraman is pouring down her neck. He's particularly good with young models: actually, he's got rather a reputation for it. And the strip karaoke's going much better than yesterday. Kevin's already got his shirt off and Cathy, the make-up woman, is in her cagoule and not much else, but the barman says he doesn't mind, because they're only having a laugh and anyway nobody ever comes in during the week and if they do he'll tell them it's a private party.

'Do you want a drink in my room, Leila? Only I need to call Charlie, and my mobile needs charging. We'll have to take our drinks up with us, though – there's no room service.'

'Are you joking?'

'No, Leila. There are hotels that don't do room service, you know.'

'Really? And what exactly is the point of that then, darling? Christ, it's like being catapulted back in time. They'll be asking us for our ration books next. Gin or vodka?'

'Gin, please. A large one, please.'

'Let's just save time and get a bottle. You carry the tonics. Here.'

We clank upstairs like a couple of alcoholics, and call Charlie, who has a nice long chat with his godmother and she promises to come down and see him soon and says his new hairstyle sounds fabulous, and then we lie on my bed, which is a fairly snug double, and get completely plastered.

'So how's the flying Dutchman, then?'

Leila's latest man is a Dutch architect called Frank, who's been redesigning her house, but she's been going off him for the past few weeks.

'Fine, as far as I know. He's off in Amsterdam on some job, so I'm supposed to be going over there. But I might give it a miss.'

'Oh I thought he sounded nice.'

'Yes, but what's the point of being nice when you're stuck in the land of the tulip? And anyway I've got my eye on someone else: there's a gorgeous new yoga instructor, Tor, at my gym, and he's got to be one of the most breathtaking men on the planet. Officially, I mean, he's stunning. His classes are booked solid, full of women in leotards with their legs behind their necks trying to flirt with him. It's hilarious.'

'I thought you hated yoga.'

'Yes, well, I do. But I might change my mind. So I've hired him, for some one-to-one sessions. I told him I was a complete beginner and too nervous to come to class. He seemed to like that.'

'Leila, you've never been nervous in your life.'

'Well, he doesn't know that, does he? And actually he does make me rather nervous. He's so fucking gorgeous I'm nervous I'm going to jump him before I get a chance to learn the lotus position.'

'Have you had your first lesson yet?'

'No. Next Wednesday, at 8 a.m. Not ideal, is it, can you believe it? But he has classes all over the place so it was the only time I could get.'

'Well, good luck. And just think how flexible you'll be.'

'Oh I think I'm pretty flexible already, thank you very much, darling.'

She snorts in a rather rude way.

'God, I love gin. It's such a civilised drink, isn't it? Mother's ruin, that's what they used to call it, isn't it? Do you feel ruined, darling?'

'No, but I'd like to. I just feel knackered. Ruined sounds much better.'

'Talking of which, do you want the latest on Mack the Knife?'

'No.'

'All right. Be like that. Are you sure?'

'Yes. Well, no, actually. Oh go on then. I know, he's met

some fabulous supermodel type and they're madly in love, right?'

'Who told you?'

'Nobody. Fuck. I was just saying the worst thing I could think of.'

'Oh. Sorry, darling. And she's not really a supermodel, not quite. And I bet love isn't on the horizon, just mutual wankage.'

'What's mutual wankage when it's at home?'

'You know, almost as good as the real thing, but no Conversation. She's probably as boring as fuck, and obsessed with how she looks. Nicky worked with her once and he said she was a complete nightmare.'

'Nicky? The one who does fashion? Christ. Who is she then?'

'Vanessa Vanburgh. She does fashion mostly. She's in this month's *Vogue*, I think.'

'Fucking hell.'

'Do you want me to ring reception and get an emergency copy of *Vogue*?'

'No. Mainly because there isn't the slightest chance of them having one. *Woman's Realm*, possibly. She's not in that too, is she? Christ, it didn't take him long, did it?'

'Sweetheart. You don't care. Remember. He asked you to go to the Big Apple and you turned him down. It's over. Onwards and upwards. Plenty more fish in the sea and all that bollocks.'

'Christ.'

'Annie, sweetheart, stop it. She'll be giving him a good run for his money, trust me, and money will be playing a vital role in their relationship, for sure. And serve him right. He'll be looking back and thinking about the real thing. You. Lovely, gorgeous you.'

'Oh of course he will, it stands to reason. I mean I bet

she hasn't even got a bright-orange cagoule, let alone a proper woolly hat. Poor man's probably in a terrible state.'

Leila smiles and puts her arm round me.

'Well, there you go then. Now look, before you start getting all tragic, let's just remember who turned who down. And quite right too. You can't go chasing all over the world after a man. Terrible mistake. He'd probably have dumped you by now and you'd be stuck in New York trying to get Charlie to stop saying "Have a nice day".'

'Thanks, Leila, that makes me feel so much better.'

'You know what I mean – if he didn't dump you then you'd have dumped him by now, for sure. You wouldn't be happy stuck in some flash apartment playing the corporate wife. Sorting out his dry-cleaning and working out what to cook for supper. Now would you?'

'No. I suppose not. I get enough of that with Charlie.'

'Exactly. You've gone past the point where you want to morph yourself into some man's identity. You've got your own.'

'Have I?'

'Yes.'

'Well, what is it then, my identity? Only I've sort of forgotten.'

I'm actually feeling quite tearful now. Oh Christ.

'Darling. You're a grown-up.'

'Right.'

'Not someone's happy helper. You've cut out the middle man and gone straight for motherhood. You've got enough on your plate looking after Charlie. You need someone to look after you for a change. Not some high-maintenance fucker like Mack MacDonald, who needs total devotion and a relocation to the other side of the Atlantic.'

'Right. Yes, that's right.'

'I know. It was you who told me.'

'Oh. Well, good, because it's all true. Good. I feel much better now.'

'So what you need is someone to take your mind off things for a while, a nice little diversion. So here's the plan. I'll have a dinner party and you come and I'll ask all the available men I know and you can take your pick. It'll be great, I'll dress you up, proper frock, cleavage, the works. What do you say, darling?'

'Leila, you know I don't do dinner parties. I've never met anyone remotely nice at a dinner party, or if I do they turn out to be married, or weird.'

'Like Dreadful Daniel.'

'Yes. Exactly.'

'Tell me again, the bit about when he said he wanted to explore every avenue of his sexuality, and then asked you if he could borrow your slingbacks. I love that bit.'

'Shut up. And they weren't slingbacks. They were high heels. Pink suede. They were lovely, actually. But I went right off them after that. I've never worn them since.'

She laughs.

'Shame. Make a change from those bloody sandals.'

I bought a pair of Birkenstock sandals last year, and Leila's still on a mission to persuade me that they're the most revolting footwear ever invented, even if loads of trendy magazines include them in their what-mothers-are-wearing-in-Notting Hill features.

'They're very comfortable. I've told you.'

'Yes, but that's not really the point, darling. Anyway, if you won't do dinner parties then we'll get you flashed up for this awards do. There's bound to be loads of talent at that. Cream of British advertising – there must be someone there who can help take your mind off Mack. Actually, on second thoughts, maybe there'll be a gorgeous waiter. But I really want you to come – it'll be a laugh. Promise?'

'Oh all right, but no dressing up.'

'Yes, dressing up. Everyone dresses up, they really go for it.'

'I could wear my velvet dress, I suppose.'

'Great. Though hang on, isn't that the one we bought for your dinner with Mack? Oh no you don't – you'll spend all night moping. No, we'll go out and get you something new, something that goes with the pink shoes so you can weed out any potential cross-dressers.'

'Leila. I'm warning you.'

'God, this bed's uncomfortable. Good job there's nobody to play with up here. You'd probably slip a disc or something. Actually, you know, I should probably be making a move. My hotel's bloody hours away, and I'm knackered. I'll just ring down and get them to warm up the driver, shall I? Fuck.'

Leila reaches for the phone and falls off the bed. For some reason this strikes us as extremely witty and we both end up in hysterics. By the time we get back downstairs and find Leila's driver, he's seriously pissed off at being made to hang about all day waiting to ferry Leila about.

'See you tomorrow, darling. But only for an hour or so and then we're back down to London with Moaning Mark.'

'All right.'

We walk towards the car. The driver gives Leila a very stroppy look.

'Ready for the off then, are you? Only I was told you'd be finished by early evening, you know, and this isn't early evening in anyone's book.'

'I beg your pardon?'

Oh dear. I think the driver might have picked the wrong person to have a moan at. In fact I know he has.

'I was just saying, it's getting on a bit isn't it, pet? Been busy, have you?'

'Yes, as a matter of fact I have. And I think you'll find I'm not anyone's pet. So cut the attitude. If you don't want the job then feel free to leave, and get them to send me another car. Otherwise I'd like a nice peaceful journey back to the hotel, with no lip, if that's all right with you. And no music, and the heater on full blast. I'm fucking freezing. Do you think you can manage that?'

He looks rather shaken and mutters yes.

'Are you sure?'

'Yes.'

'Good. I'm very glad to hear it, and when we get there I'll give you a fabulous tip. All right?'

He perks up at this.

'Yes, madam.'

'Good. I'm glad we understand each other. Night, Annie darling.'

She blows me a kiss as they drive off, and then points to the driver and makes a very rude hand gesture.

The next morning the weather's almost worse than yesterday. Less windy, but colder, and the really bad news is Barney's fallen completely in love with the helicopter and wants to spend most of the day in it. The pilot's ex-Navy special forces or something and completely round the twist. He says he spent years fishing people out of the sea in gales, and he's not at all bothered if it's a bit breezy. Christ. All we need now is that music from *Apocalypse Now* when they come screaming in over the sea. I mention this to Barney, whose face lights up in very worrying way, which just makes me wish I'd kept my mouth shut really.

And then he gets the helicopter to hover about three feet above our heads on the beach, which produces a mini-tornado that blows over all the chairs outside the catering van, and Kevin trips over and sprains his ankle so he spends the rest of the morning moaning and limping. The rest of the crew think this is highly hilarious and start limping too, and pretty soon everyone's walking with a limp, but Barney doesn't notice because he's too busy trying to get the model to stop pouting.

By the time we finally finish it's late afternoon, and the crew pack up in record time and start heading back to London. Kevin says he'll get his lawyer to contact us about the compensation claim, which sends Lawrence into a complete tail-spin, even though I know he's only joking because he gives me a massive wink when Lawrence isn't looking.

'You'll have to talk to the insurance people, Annie, and warn them, and I'm holding you personally responsible for this. You should have told the caterers to be more careful about where they put those chairs. Honestly. This could end up costing us a fortune.'

'Lawrence.'

'And I'm not going to be the one to tell Barney. I want to make that perfectly clear. You know how he gets into a terrible bate about this kind of thing. Perfectly happy to blow the entire budget on some silly idea he's had, without consulting anybody, but if we go over by even a few measly pounds he goes mad. He was giving me a long lecture about doughnuts earlier. Do you know what that was that all about?'

'The crew were having a doughnut-eating competition.'

'Oh. Were they? And who gave them permission to do that then?'

'Well, nobody, obviously. It's not really the kind of thing you schedule in advance, Lawrence. They were just having a laugh. And Kevin isn't going to be putting in a claim. He was just joking.'

'Oh very funny, I'm sure. Honestly, Annie, you've got

to get a grip on this kind of thing. After all, it is what we pay you for.'

'Less of the we if you don't mind, Lawrence.'

Oh good. It's Barney.

'So what's this all about then?'

'Oh nothing, Barney, just having a chat with Annie about budgets. I was just telling her you were concerned about the doughnuts.'

'I was joking, Jesus. I don't give a fuck how many doughnuts they eat.'

'But you said – '

'Oh don't start, Lawrence. Honestly, you're like an old woman sometimes.'

Lawrence looks furious.

'Annie darling, brilliant job, as usual. See you next week in town?'

'Yes. I'm up on Tuesday.'

'Great. Well, come on, Lawrence, if you want a lift back to the airport. Or are you hanging on here to count doughnuts?'

Lawrence glares at me and stalks off after Barney. And to be fair, Barney is being mesmerisingly annoying, as usual. He does have a habit of going completely tonto about something when he's in the middle of a job and not quite sure what to do next, and then pretending he doesn't know what you're talking about if you refer to it later. But he's always been like that and Lawrence ought to be used to it by now.

The journey home isn't much better than the journey up. I should have flown back with everybody else but I usually quite like the drive home after a job; it gives me time to unwind, and get back into Charlie mode before I get home. But this time I wish I hadn't bothered. The rain's been replaced with dense fog, so everyone is crawling along, apart from the BMW drivers who all seem intent on testing out their airbags by driving into the back of lorries.

I stop and buy a copy of this month's *Vogue* and get a look at Vanessa Vanburgh. Which turns out to be a Big Mistake, and I end up having a mini-meltdown in Caffé Nero. She's absolutely gorgeous, in an ice-maiden kind of way. Pale blonde, with giraffe legs and big blue eyes. She can't be more than a size eight, but with great skin and not a hint of the usual anorexic pallor that so many models have. Actually, she's pretty classy all round really, although she does look like the kind of girl who'd fall into a dead faint if you offered her a doughnut. Bugger.

I spend a disconsolate half-hour eating a double chocolate muffin and trying to work out how much plastic surgery I'd need to look like that, because I think it would definitely take more than a few dabs of Clarin's Beauty Flash Balm if I'm ever going to have to go head to head with her, that's for sure. Not that I am, of course. Hopefully I'll never clap eyes on her. But still. Bugger.

* * *

Lizzie comes down for the weekend, without Matt, who's busy overseeing a building they're doing where the client keeps changing his mind, which is driving them both mad. We spend ages pouring over *Vogue* and Lizzie announces that she thinks Vanessa looks too plastic and should be renamed Vapid Vanessa, which I think is an excellent idea. And then we talk about baby plans and how to get Mum to Calm Down. Actually, this birth plan thing is really starting to worry me; Lizzie's still very keen on the birthing-pool idea, and going the homeopathic route, and apparently arnica is very helpful. But I've got a funny feeling she's going to want more than a couple of pellets of arnica when things really kick off. And I'm not sure how I'm going to handle seeing her struggling away in a paddling pool. And I can't work out if I'll need to be in a swimsuit, or just lurking at the edges.

I'm trying to be encouraging and positive, and we work out a complicated routine where Mum will belt round here to look after Charlie and I'll race up to London at the first contraction, and every so often it dawns on me that she's really going to be having a baby soon, which is pretty amazing. Charlie's already given her his top names, although I'm not entirely sure Merlin or Mab are going to make the shortlist; Matt's quite keen on Bessie, apparently, but Lizzie thinks he's just being rude about how big she's getting, and she likes Orlando, but I think that's just the hormones.

Kate comes round for tea on Sunday with James. Phoebe's off at a party, and James bolts straight out into the garden with Charlie, to play pagans.

Lizzie's just been out to check on them.

'They're fine. They're doing spells to make sure the baby's a boy, and Charlie wants to know if you've got any sacred hawthorn handy.'

'Not on me, no. God, I wish they'd get over this pagan thing.'

Kate pours us all some more tea.

'Me too. They're boycotting assembly completely now. Did you know? And Miss Pike had a word with me on Friday, and said it's probably just a phase but could we tell them to stop trying to convert the other children, only it's upsetting the Vicar.'

'Oh Christ.'

'Quite.'

Lizzie smiles.

'Well, I think it's great. It's so much more intelligent than being mad about trains or something.'

'Just you wait until yours is busy boycotting assemblies. It won't be long, you know. What are you now, six months?'

We all stare at Lizzie's stomach.

'Nearly seven. But it still doesn't seem real.'

'I was like that with Phoebe. It gets real, don't worry.'

'I'll never forget when Charlie was born, Annie was so brilliant. I'm hoping I'm going to be like that too.'

I don't remember being brilliant. All I remember is being terrified.

'You'll be great, Lizzie. I know you will.'

'Yes, well, I hope so. I really want to keep it as natural as possible. Just doing my breathing, and listening to my music. I think I'll be able to cope if I feel in control.'

Kate and I exchange glances.

'And if you change your mind you can always grab the drug trolley and refuse to let go. That's what I did.'

Lizzie gives Kate a rather anxious look.

'Yes, but I'm feeling pretty positive about it, and I feel prepared, you know, well, I think I do. I'm doing all the classes, and Matt helps me do the breathing and everything. And the water's supposed to really help.'

Kate smiles.

'I'm sure it does, although I still think the wake-me-up-when-the-hairdresser-comes-round routine is the best, but you have to go private for that, I think.'

Lizzie stiffens slightly. She's very passionate about the NHS.

'Yes, and then you get fabulous food and flower arrangements, but no Intensive Care if anything goes wrong. Not that it will, of course.'

She strokes her bump and looks even more anxious.

'Well, the midwives were all great with Charlie.'

Kate finally twigs that I'm trying to be reassuring.

'Oh yes, of course, mine were too. And I'm sure it'll be just how you want it. And it's good you're doing all the classes. I never went to mine, and I wish I had. I'm sure it would have made a big difference. Heavens, what are they doing out there?'

James and Charlie are running past the kitchen window waving sticks and shrieking.

'I'll go and see, shall I? Get a bit of practice in.'

Lizzie heaves herself up off her chair and goes out into the garden.

'You don't think I've worried her, do you? I just wasn't thinking.'

Kate's looking mortified.

'No, she's fine, I think everyone gets a bit nervous at this stage. I know I was.'

'Me too. Poor thing. Well, I just I hope I haven't made it worse. Only I really do think drugs are the only way.'

'Yes. So do most of us when we actually get to the sharp end. But it's nice to start off all chirpy, isn't it? Paddling pools and candles, and a bit of deep breathing, and Bob's your uncle.'

'Are you sure you're really up for this birth-partner thingy?'

'Oh yes. Well, I definitely want to be there. But I'd quite like to be out in a corridor, walking up and down or knitting or something. I just hope I can handle it. Do what she wants, you know. Be the right kind of support. She was so great when I had Charlie. I don't know what I would have done without her. She was just so calm, and

67

she held my hand, and stroked my back for ages. It was so reassuring. Actually, she was the first person to hold him, after the doctor.'

I can still see her standing holding him. And then she put him in my arms and he opened his eyes and locked his gaze on to mine, and it was the best moment ever. I don't think anything's ever going to top it. Like being hit by some sort of invisible, loved-up tidal wave, where everything's perfect, but you know nothing's ever going to be the same again and you're hoping you'll make it back to the surface before you run out of air.

Kate smiles.

'I'm surprised she's not going for a home birth.'

'Oh she was, but Matt got nervous.'

'I don't blame him.'

'Neither do I. But some people do manage it, you know.'

She gives me a very sceptical look.

'They do.'

'Oh I know. My cousin Georgina had both of hers at home, and she was up an hour later sorting out the dogs. But she's mad.'

'She sounds it.'

'Half my family are mad – you know that. But anyway, I've got something I want to tell you, and I can't do it in front of Lizzie. So quick, before she comes back in, brace yourself.'

'Oh god. Am I going to like it?'

'No.'

'Is it about school? Hair gel? Do they want perms now or something? Mullets?'

'No. It's worse than that. It's just . . . well . . . I'm sort of having a thing with Phil.'

'A thing?'

'Well, an affair sort of a thing.'

68

'You're having an affair. With your Phil? Bloody hell, Kate. Oh. Sorry.'

'I know, I know. It's too awful, isn't it? I'm actually having an affair with my own ex-husband. How pathetic is that?'

'Kate. You can't be.'

'Well, I am. You remember Valentine's Day, when we went to the Barn thingy, and he was babysitting. And you remember we all got tiddly and you fell over in the car park.'

'Yes.'

Actually, I'd forgotten the bit about falling over in the car park.

'Well, when I got home he was just sort of there, and being really nice and everything. And it was so familiar, I just sort of forgot. About the divorce, I mean.'

'Sort of forgot?'

'I know. But I did. And anyway it was like we were finishing off the circle.'

'What circle?'

'You know, being friends, getting married, hating each other. Now we're sort of back to being friends. And before you say it, yes I know friends don't have to, you know. But it makes me feel like I'm not completely hopeless. I mean I know he's a terrible fool, but it really got to me, you know, being chucked on the scrap heap while he waltzed off with Zelda. Like I was an old sock or something. It's just nice to feel that you're not completely revolting after all.'

'Oh Kate. Why didn't you tell me?'

'Well, I thought it was a one-off, and I wasn't very proud of it, to be honest. But I have to say, it's one in the eye for old Zelda, isn't it? What goes around comes around.'

'Yes, but, Kate. You don't want him back, do you? Do you?'

'Oh no. God forbid. But I like having the upper hand for a change. And he's being great with the kids, popping round to see them more, quick spot of flirting when they're not looking, that kind of thing.'

'He really is unbelievable – you know that, don't you?'

'Yes, so I need you to tell me what to do, bring a voice of sanity into things. Because I can't hack it on my own. I keep thinking I'll put a stop to it, and then he comes round and somehow one things leads to another and he ends up staying.'

'But what does Zelda think he's doing when he stays with you?'

'Well, he goes home, of course. Later.'

She's gone rather red.

'Oh Kate.'

'I know. So you've got to tell me what I should do. Be my voice of reason.'

'You should tell him to fuck off.'

'I know. And I keep trying, honestly I do. But it's just so nice, not feeling useless.'

'You've never been useless, Kate.'

'That's easy for you to say, you weren't married to Charlie's dad. He didn't leave you for another woman after ten years of being married.'

'No. He just went back to his ex-wife after a few weeks.'

'Yes. But they'd split up, while you were seeing him. You weren't to know he was going to go back to her, were you?'

'No.'

'So you see, it's different, and I know it's not good, and I'm not proud of myself, but – '

Lizzie opens the kitchen door looking rather red-faced and panting slightly.

'Sorry, but I think I need back-up. The rabbits have got out of their run and they're eating all your plants.'

70

'Christ, who let them out of the run?'

'Take a wild guess.'

We spend a rather fraught half-hour racing round the back garden trying to corner Buzz and Woody, who are having none of it. Bill's going to be furious: he comes in to do the garden once a week for a couple of hours, and takes a very dim view of recalcitrant rabbits mucking up his flowerbeds. We finally get them back in their hutch, and Lizzie takes Charlie in to wash the mud off his face because he's ended up lying in a flowerbed trying to coax Woody out from under a bush, and then Kate realises she's already late for picking up Phoebe.

'Look, I'd better be off, but not a word to anybody, on the Phil thing. OK?'

'Totally secret squirrel, I promise.'

'Not even Lizzie. I don't want her thinking I'm a complete sap.'

'Of course not.'

'Shall I ring you later?'

'Great.'

'And thanks, Annie.'

'What for?'

'For not making me feel like a complete dimwit.'

Christ. I do understand. I really do. But bloody hell. She must be mad. And it's bound to end in tears. I just hope they aren't going to be hers. Because she's only just got back on her feet after the last time.

Lizzie and Charlie are watching a wildlife programme, and Charlie's telling Lizzie all about sharks, even though the programme is actually about penguins.

'Yes, and they can swim right up rivers, you know. We saw it, didn't we, Mummy?'

'Yes, but that was in India.'

'Yes. But they might do it round here. We should ring Grandad.'

Lizzie laughs. 'Well, that would be a nice surprise for Grandad and his friends, wouldn't it? When he goes on one of his fishing trips. One minute they'd all be sitting there having a chat about chub and then they'd suddenly find themselves on the wrong end of a great white.'

'Yes, and I bet Nana would be pleased when he brought that home for the freezer. She makes enough fuss about the trout.'

Lizzie and I both get the giggles at the idea of Mum trying to fillet a great white, but Charlie gives us a very contemptuous look.

'It's not funny, you know, Mummy. A shark can bite you right in half.'

This sets Lizzie off again, and we take refuge in the kitchen so Charlie can watch his programme in peace.

'More tea?'

'Please. And then I'd better be off. I want to be home before it gets too late. I tend to flake out really early now.'

'I'm not surprised. Well, get all the sleep you can.'

'I know, I know. Don't say it. People keep saying that to me. Sleep while you can because you won't get much chance once the baby's born. It's really annoying. Actually, the whole thing's starting to annoy me. Being pregnant, I mean. It goes on far too long. You haven't got anything to eat, have you? Only I'm starving again.'

'Sure, toast and honey? Or I could cook you something – macaroni cheese?'

'Oh yes please, macaroni. Yum.'

Macaroni cheese has always been one of Lizzie's favourites.

'Pass me the butter then, and I'll start on the sauce. So what else is annoying you then?'

'I hate the way complete strangers think they can touch you. You know, pat you on the stomach. A woman did it to me on the bus the other day and I nearly hit her.'

'That would have been nice, getting arrested for assault while heavily pregnant. Mum would have a fit.'

'I know, but I'm much more aggressive now – did you get like that? I'm so bloody uncomfortable most of the time, it makes me bad-tempered. Matt says it's like living with a very grumpy Teletubby.'

'Actually, now you come to mention it, I do remember feeling a bit stroppy. When I wasn't in floods of tears.'

'Yes, but that was mostly down to Adam.'

'True.'

'No news on that front, I suppose?'

'What front?'

'The appalling fuckwit Adam front.'

'No. Not since his email last year.'

'Which he only sent to check you weren't going to start suing him for all the money he owes you. Bastard.'

'Probably. But he doesn't owe me anything, Lizzie.'

Lizzie hates Adam, and he's not exactly my favourite man on the planet either. We'd first met at college, but we split up fairly amicably and he went on to marry a Canadian woman called Denise and moved to Canada. But then he turned up a few years later saying he was getting divorced and I was the one he really wanted. We had a few blissful weeks and we were talking about buying a flat together when it all started to go wrong. He decided he'd made a terrible mistake and Denise was the one he really loved, and he got a new job in Toronto and left.

Which was all a bit of a shock, to be honest. And then

73

I realised I was pregnant. Which was even more of a shock. Adam had always been adamant that he didn't want children. And he seemed particularly worried about how Denise would react if she found out. Like I gave a fuck what she'd think. But in the end I realised it didn't matter, because I knew, without a second's hesitation, that I wanted the baby. Really, really wanted it.

'I still don't see why you let him get away with it. I know what you always say, but I just don't.'

'Lizzie, we've had this conversation. And I don't want his money.'

'Yes, but did he ever offer?'

'No.'

'Well, there you are then, he's a bastard.'

'So is Charlie, technically.'

Lizzie laughs.

'You know what I mean.'

'Yes. So why would I want such a crap dad for Charlie? Just think how much he could screw Charlie up. And I couldn't bear that.'

'True.'

'I'd have to kill him or something.'

'Or maybe he'd climb up something and fall off.'

'What? Pass me the cheese out of the fridge, will you.'

'You know, like those nutters that keep climbing up Tower Bridge dressed as Superman and won't come down, campaigning for Families Need Attention-seeking Fathers or something. The traffic was screwed up all day. It was on the news.'

'Just the kind of father every child needs, one who dresses up in weird outfits and infuriates London motorists.'

Lizzie laughs.

'Yes. A bit like Ken Livingstone, only more annoying. Well, at least we won't be seeing Adam on the news, since he doesn't pay you a penny. He wouldn't have a leg to stand on.'

'Well, he bloody wouldn't if he started embarrassing Charlie with stunts like that. I'd get Leila to sort him out. She's always threatening to kneecap people.'

'But I still think he shouldn't get away with it. It's like if you smash into someone's car, you can't just say you didn't mean it and walk away.'

'We're not exactly a car crash, Lizzie, me and Charlie.'

'I know you're not, but it's the same principle.'

'No it's not, not really. The principle has to be that Charlie's happy, Lizzie. That's all that matters. And he is. I keep waiting for him to give me a hard time about it, or show some sign of being deprived or something. But he doesn't. He's never met Adam, and he knows Adam's never seen him, so he doesn't feel rejected and I think that's the vital bit. And I know it might be an issue at some point, and so far he's not been bothered. I think he's fine about it, I really do.'

'Of course he is, he's great. And you're doing a brilliant job bringing him up. But why should you have to cope with everything on your own?'

'Because I love him, Lizzie, more than anything, and having him is the best thing I've ever done, for sure. You'll see. It's just amazing, how much you love them. And anyway I'm not on my own – I've got you and Matt, and Mum and Dad, and Leila. And on top of that it was my choice, Lizzie. I chose to have him. And Adam chose not to. And I know who lost out on that one.'

She smiles.

'True.'

'I was thinking about it the other day, you know, about when Charlie was ill. I always thought, when he was tiny, that I wouldn't be able to cope if anything serious happened. I mean I knew I wanted to try, but I thought that if he was ever really ill or anything, then that would be the time I'd mind not having someone to share it with, and I wouldn't be able to handle it. But it wasn't like that. It was just so terrifying that there wasn't room for anything else. When you've stood there watching them, not knowing if they're going to make it, you realise nothing else matters. Nothing. And watching you and Mum and Dad in pieces, well, it was all I needed really. We weren't alone. And even if we had been it wouldn't have mattered, as long as he got better.'

'I felt so useless. That's the thing I'm most scared of really, that there'll be something the matter with the baby and I won't be able to fix it.'

'I know. That's the hard part, sweetheart. But I'm sure everything's going to be fine.'

I put my arms round her and give her a hug.

'But what if Adam changes his mind, or she does, and they have kids. How would you feel then?'

'I don't know, but I don't think it's likely. He's too selfish. They're getting into huskies, well, that's what his last email said. Denise breeds them and they race them, I think.'

'You'd have to run pretty fast to beat a husky.'

'With sledges, you twit. He's in Canada, don't forget, up to his neck in snow for most of the year.'

'Good. Well, I still think he's a selfish bastard fuckwit.'

'He's a sad bastard, that's for sure. He's missing out on Charlie. So in the end I haven't really got anything to complain about, have I? I get to be with my lovely boy and he gets a load of old huskies.'

'All right, Pollyanna, have it your way. But I still think it's not fair. How long's that macaroni going to take? It smells great.'

'Here, have a bit of cheese to keep you going. About

half an hour in the oven. Go on, go and sit by the fire and see what Charlie's up to, will you. Make sure he's not rewiring anything.'

Charlie decides that macaroni cheese is in fact his least favourite supper ever, and will only deign to eat it if there's a sausage lurking somewhere on the plate. And then he throws a fit because I won't let him have Coke.

'Nana always lets me have Coke.'

'No, she doesn't, Charlie. And anyway we haven't got any.'

'Well, will you get some at the shop tomorrow then? Because I need some, I really do. I feel as weak as a kitten.'

Lizzie inhales macaroni in an effort not to laugh, so we have to pat her on the back and get her a glass of water.

'Charlie, you're the exact opposite of a weak little kitten.'

He smirks.

'I can almost lift my bed up.'

'Yes. But you're not meant to, Charlie, I've told you. You'll snap the leg off.'

'No I won't. I'm building up my muscles. Look.'

He holds out his arm for us to feel his muscles. Which are tiny. But he's very proud of them.

'Great. Now finish your macaroni. That'll help you build up your muscles too.'

We spend the evening watching telly after waving Lizzie off, and I gradually zone out and sit looking at the fire and thinking about Mack and Vanessa, and whether you could train a husky to bite people on command, and what on earth Kate's going to do about Phil. And then it's bath-time. Charlie's exhausted but still finds the energy for a fairly major random-chatting routine. We cover electricity and why putting a hairdryer in the bath would not produce a nice whirlpool effect, and whether it's possible to make a laser gun out of things you might find lying around the house.

And then I suddenly feel inspired to reassure myself on the missing-dad front after my conversation with Lizzie earlier.

'Charlie. You know we don't have a dad in our family, because Adam lives in Canada and we stopped being friends before you were born?'

'Yes.'

He carries on splashing.

'Well, do you ever mind about that?'

'No. I think it would be a lot of bother.'

'Why?'

'Well, I wouldn't get to sit in the front of the car. And I wouldn't get more presents, because you'd just share them out. And he might shout at me, like Jack Knight's dad does. He's always shouting. If I had a nice one, that might be good, if he liked dogs and stuff. I might go and see him in Canadia, when I'm bigger, I might. It might be interesting. But I haven't decided yet.'

'Oh. Right. It's actually called Canada, darling. And that would be fine, if you wanted to meet him, when you're bigger. I'm sure we could arrange that. We could go together, if you like, or you could go by yourself, or with Aunty Lizzie, or Leila or someone else if you wanted. It would be up to you.'

Actually, I'm pretty sure Adam would throw a fit, but sod him. If that's what Charlie wants, then that's what'll happen. But I don't think I'll mention anything about the huskies. I don't want Charlie turning him into some fantasy dog-lover when the reality would be such a disappointment.

'Yes. I can decide. And I might go to Australia too, and see the sharks. The big ones.'

'Right.'

'And you know how I'm a pagan, Mummy.'

'Yes.'

'Well, pagans don't go to school, you know.'

'Oh.'

'Yes. I can't be a proper pagan with Miss Pike fussing on all the time.'

'Everyone has to go to school, Charlie. Even pagans.'

'No they don't. You can have home school. Milo's mum told him. He's going to have home school, his mum says.'

Milo's mum is a bit of a hippie who floats about in lots of home-weaving with flapping sleeves.

'Oh. Right. Well, that's nice.'

She must be completely bonkers.

'We could do home school too.'

Oh no we bloody couldn't. I did briefly flirt with the idea of an alternative education for Charlie and went and looked round the local Steiner school. But they were all wandering about in felt slippers using thick crayons and looking like members of a cult. All the pictures on the walls were in orange or mauve, and the man who took me round was so patronising and smug you just wanted to slap him.

'Charlie, you love Miss Pike. And you'd miss all your friends.'

'They could come too.'

Excellent. So I'd have thirty mixed infants milling about in my living room looking for learning opportunities. It would be like being in a nightmare where you never wake up.

'And also, Mummy, I need to go to Scouts. Me and James want to. We think it could come in very handy.

79

They teach you how to make fires, you know. And you do stuff with ropes and you get badges.'

'Oh, well, that sounds good. Come on, out of the bath now, Charlie.'

If it's a choice between home school and the Scouts I think we can safely say he can start practising his knots now.

'I'll see what I can find out about the Scouts, shall I?'

'Yes. And home school.'

'No. Not home school, Charlie. We are not doing home school.'

'I hate you, Mummy. I really do.'

III

Strangers in the Night

LIZZIE'S BABY IS DUE any day now, and every time the phone rings I have a minor cardiac moment. We've already had one false alarm, when I raced up to town after dropping Charlie off with Mum, only to have Lizzie call me just as I got to the hospital to say they'd sent her home, and it was probably only indigestion and she's got at least another week to go. Maybe ten days.

Mum's on permanent standby, and has bought herself a mobile phone, but the salesman obviously mistook her for a top executive because he's sold her one that does hundreds of things that no normal person can actually understand. So now she keeps taking pictures of the inside of her handbag, and sending epic hieroglyphic texts to her entire address book, which is basically me and Lizzie, and Aunty Brenda.

She's just sent me another mega-text, so I'm trying to call her whilst simultaneously de-Shreddying Charlie's school sweatshirt, and putting the finishing touches to a particularly tragic packed lunch when my mobile goes.

It's Leila.

'Hello, darling, who on earth are you talking to at half-past eight in the morning?'

'Mum, but she's engaged.'

'No news from Lizzie yet?'

'No.'

'Well, tell her to get a move on, will you – I've got her a fabulous present. Baby Dior, even the box is gorgeous. What time are we meeting up later? Around six, I thought.'

I'm staying with Leila tonight, after the awards dinner.

'Fine.'

'And what are you planning on wearing?'

'I haven't decided.'

'Look, just tell me, darling, and I want a full run-down – shoes, the lot.'

Bugger.

'I'll call you later, all right? I promise. I'm late for the school run.'

She makes a disbelieving sort of noise and says she'll talk to me later.

Charlie's disappeared upstairs for his pre-school hair-gel session, and I'm just finishing packing his bag and congratulating myself on remembering his PE kit when there's a piercing scream from the bathroom and the sound of thudding footsteps as he races downstairs.

'Mummy, my quiffer's gone all pointy. Look.'

It's pointing sideways. He looks like one of the more challenging entrants for the Eurovision Song Contest.

'It'll be fine. Come here and I'll fix it for you.'

A very tense ten minutes follows, where I get yelled at for ruining his hair and we have to de-gel – which requires a great deal of vigorous flannel action – and then reapply before the desired effect is reached. He wants a series of little tufts rather than one major peak. Christ, I'm exhausted already and I'm not even out of the house yet.

'There, you look lovely now.'

He gives me a scowl and stalks off. Actually, I wonder what would happen if I just pat him on the head quite firmly as he gets out of the car and flatten the whole thing.

'What's for my lunch?'

'Put your shoes on, Charlie. Come on, we're going to be late.'

More scowling. I think I'm definitely going to try the patting thing soon, and serve him right. By the time we've got in the car we're on the verge of being late, and there's definitely no time for chats with pheasants.

'Mummy, go slow past the field. I want to see if the badger's out.'

'It won't be out in the daytime, Charlie.'

'It might be, or there might be hedgehogs, or a vole. Or anything.'

'Yes, but not lions.'

He tuts. Sometimes he falls for this diversionary tactic and we spend the journey listing lions and tigers and other animals we're not terribly likely to see wandering the lanes of Kent unless the nearest zoo has had a particularly bad night. But not today, apparently.

My mobile rings inside my handbag. Bugger. I haven't got my headset thing plugged in, and I don't really want to risk being arrested for using a mobile phone whilst driving, because apart from anything else the PTA would be bound to hear about it.

Charlie answers it. He loves answering phones, especially my mobile.

'Hello, Nana. Yes. Mummy's driving. We're going to school.'

Oh dear.

'Yes. Yes. I don't know. Mummy, what's in my packed lunch? Nana wants to know.'

Damn.

'Tuna.'

'I hate tuna.'

'Talk to Nana, Charlie, and tell her I'll call her back.'

'She says she'll call you back – and, Nana, tell her, will you, I hate tuna, I really do. Yes. Yes. I loved the sausage rolls you made me. Yes. I did. Mummy never makes sausage rolls. Never. No. Oh yes. I forgot about that. But that's because you were there. She never makes them normally. Yes. Bye, Nana. I love you. Bye. Nana says you've got to ring her straight back. Once you stop the car. All right?'

'Did she say anything else?'

'Yes, she said I can have sausage rolls for my lunch tomorrow, and she'll make me some. She says she'll bring them when she picks me up later. So I can have a snack on the journey. Won't that be lovely, Mummy? I love Nana. I really do.'

Great. I've been trying to stand firm against Charlie's sausage obsession, but I'm definitely fighting a losing battle. Edna made him some emergency sausage rolls last week, and Mum saw them; she loves popping in when she knows Edna will be around, and I'm sure they have nice long bonding conversations about the tragic state of my kitchen floor. And of course as soon as she saw Edna was breaking the sausage embargo it was only a matter of time before she followed suit. Actually, I'm surprised it's taken her so long.

There's a long line of parked cars outside the school as usual, so we end up parking practically in the next village and then sprinting back towards the school gates just as the bell is ringing, and attracting superior glances from Mrs Harrison-Black and her group of padded-waistcoat mothers, who've all been here for ages, no doubt, trapping people and putting them on rotas for the Easter Fair.

I'm still puffing and panting while I kiss Charlie goodbye and then I head over to lurk at the back of the playground with Kate until the rota mafia give up and go home, and we can escape without being put down for a gross of fairy cakes.

'Your hair's looking very nice.'

'Thanks, I'm off up to town for the awards thing tonight.'

'Oh right, of course. Well, lucky you, I'm on the bloody reading rota today.'

'Christ, I'd forgotten about that. I'm not down for today, am I?'

'No, you're all right, you're Friday. It's me that's got the short straw. I'm in Reception and guess who I've got.'

'Travis Willis.'

'Yes.'

'Oh dear.'

One of Ginny Richmond's new missions involves everyone taking part in some complicated literacy scheme where each class gets legions of parent volunteers, or mums as they're known round here, who sit in the PE cupboard in the hall every morning to help with reading practice. On small chairs that do your back in. Surrounded by soft rubber mats and plastic balls.

'Well, good luck.'

She's going to need it. Travis may be very tiny and not quite five yet, but he still managed to break a window in his classroom last week during a rather energetic sand-and-water session, and rumour has it that he told one of the dinner ladies to piss off and get a life. Somehow I don't think reading all about Roger Red Hat is going to be quite his style.

'Is Charlie still on about Scouts? Because James is driving me demented.'

'Yes, but only because he wants to learn how to start fires, and I'm not sure I'm that keen, to be honest. He's enough trouble as it is.'

'Phoebe tried Brownies, you know, but she hated it. Too much bossing about. She only went for a couple of weeks, so they'll probably be the same. Shall I find out the times and everything? Only Phil says he loved it, and he got loads of badges.'

'How is he?'

'Fine.'

She looks rather uncomfortable. Damn. I didn't mean to bring it up like that. We haven't really talked about how things are going, but I saw his car there the other night, on my way back from seeing Lizzie. I didn't say anything the next day, and neither did she. It's all rather tricky. On the one hand I don't want to be annoying and judgemental, but at the same time I think she's making a big mistake.

My mobile rings.

'That's bound to be Mum – she rang earlier. I'd better take it.'

Kate waves goodbye, and goes into school.

It is Mum, and she's got a cunning new plan on the sausage-roll front, involving goat's cheese and sun-dried tomatoes.

'I saw it on *Delia*, and they looked lovely. You make little ravioli shapes in pastry, so I thought I could make a few and see if he likes them.'

'Fabulous, Mum, that sounds great. Look, I'd better go. I've got to drive up to town and I'm already late.'

'Yes. And she puts oregano in, but does he like oregano? Only I thought I could use chives instead. Do you think he'd prefer chives?'

In the end I plug in my headset thing and put the phone back in my bag while she talks about pastry and why Aunty Brenda couldn't make a decent sponge if her life depended on it, although in which of Mum's parallel universes your ability to make a light sponge would determine your life expectancy I'm not really sure. I walk past the PTA mafia talking away into my headset like some city trader who's busy with copper futures and can't stop to chat, which works rather well. I must remember to try it again.

By the time I arrive in Soho I've had an exhausting combination of calls from Barney, who doesn't want to go to the awards thing tonight and is on the verge of cancelling, and Lawrence, who's desperate to go and wants me to make sure Barney doesn't cancel. Leila rings and says she wants me to come shoe shopping with her at lunchtime, and by the time I've finally persuaded her that I haven't got time to go shopping, especially with a woman who can take an entire day to choose the perfect lipstick, let alone a pair of shoes, Mum calls me back to say she's having second thoughts about the goat's cheese and wonders if Cheddar might be better.

And then the car park's full and I end up driving up the bouncing metal ramp and parking on the sodding roof. Bloody hell. I feel like I need a lie-down already, and I haven't even made it into the office yet. If only you could rent hotel rooms by the hour, for a nice little rest. Working-mother mini-breaks. Bugger all that pampering lark: all you really need is a bed that somebody else has to make after you've ruffled it all up, thick curtains and maybe a nice pot of tea when you wake up from a child-free sleep. Perfect. They'd make a fortune.

The office is particularly lively: we've got a couple of scripts in for floor polish, which Barney wants to turn down because they're crap, but Lawrence wants us to do because they're both only a couple of days in a studio with a very generous elastic budget.

Stef, Barney's PA, warns me that Ron is going through the expenses on the Northumberland job in the meeting room, and wants my help. Great.

'Do you want coffee?'

'Thanks, Stef. Any calls?'

'Nothing major. There's a few messages on your new desk.'

'New desk?'

'Yes. Lawrence has been moving things round again. And you're in the basement. Look, he's done you a memo.'

She raises her eyebrows and hands me a piece of paper.

Oh great. This isn't going to be good.

'And your friend Leila called, and she says she'll meet you at Liberty's at three-forty-five, because it's on the way back from her lunch, for fifteen minutes. And she's in a meeting all morning, so she said don't bother calling her back to cancel.'

Christ.

Lawrence's latest theory is that keeping the furniture in the same place makes things static and unproductive, so he's decided to adopt hot-desking, which basically seems to involve me working at a computer trolley in the corner of the basement while everyone else stays exactly where they are. He's out at a meeting, so I sit at his desk, and Stef has just brought me a cup of coffee when he comes back in.

'Why are you sitting there? Didn't you get my memo?'

'Sorry, Lawrence. I thought the whole point of hot-desking is that people sit where they like.'

'Yes, but not at my desk. There's a work station for you downstairs.'

'I don't need a work station, Lawrence. I need a desk. With daylight. And this is fine.'

Stef sniggers.

'No it's not, it's my desk.'

'But, Lawrence, how can it be your desk if we're doing the hot-desk thing?'

Barney comes downstairs.

'For Christ's sake, what are you two bickering about now?'

'Lawrence's new office-furniture plan. Where I end up in the basement with no desk.'

'What? Oh for heaven's sake. Get over it, will you. Use my desk – I'm off out.'

Lawrence is furious. I don't think the plan was that I'd end up in Barney's palatial office upstairs.

'Okey-dokey. Thanks, Barney. See you later then, Lawrence.'

Round one to me then, I think. I wonder what he'll try next week. A tea trolley in the kitchen, maybe.

I spend most of the morning with Ron trying to decipher Barney's scribbles and crumpled receipts, and sorting out Lawrence, who's come up with another new plan for re-organising the office: I get my old desk back, but it's moved into the back room by the photocopier. Then I meet Leila for her express shoe-shopping session, which involves a frank exchange of views when she tries to make me buy two pairs, and I try to make her understand that whilst spending nearly four hundred quid might seem like a good idea to her my bank manager is unlikely to share her view that this is in fact a tremendous bargain. Then she decides she'll buy them for me as an early birthday present, and we spend another ten minutes bickering before a compromise solution is reached: I will buy one pair of shoes and she will shut up and leave me alone.

Lawrence is in a filthy mood by the time I get back to the office, because he's just tried on his purple-velvet dinner jacket and Barney's told him he looks like a waiter and keeps trying to order Martinis from him. So he's decided now would be the perfect moment to run through the budgets for the soup job we did ages ago, and nitpick over every tiny detail. I'm on the point of ordering a large Martini myself, when his friend Tristan, an agency producer, turns up to talk about a new script and they disappear into the meeting room being all important and ordering teas and coffees and generally annoying Stef.

By the time I get to Leila's house in Notting Hill to get changed it's nearly half-past six, and she's in her bedroom surrounded by piles of clothes, with her hair in enormous foam rollers. She makes me one of her killer vodka tonics, where you fill a tumbler full of ice and vodka and then hold it quite close to a bottle of tonic for a moment before necking it back, and I try to practise walking in my new high shoes. Actually, the vodka seems to be helping.

When we're finally in the taxi heading for the hotel I'm feeling quite floaty in my velvet dress, and Leila's looking amazing in lilac silk with beaded silk shoes.

'Now remember, darling, please stop looking at your feet.'

'I can't help it. I'll fall over if I don't keep looking down.'

'No you won't.'

'This dress feels too tight. I'm probably going to pass out at some point. You won't forget and go home without me, will you? If I'm slumped in a corner somewhere?'

'Annie, stop it, you look great.'

'Well, so do you. All that yoga must be good for you.'

Leila is continuing her pursuit of Tor, and now has three yoga sessions a week. I think she's really getting into it, but she won't admit it.

'It's the magic knickers.'

'I beg your pardon?'

'You know, the ones that pull your stomach in and shove all the fat somewhere else.'

'Where?'

'God knows. Your ankles?'

We both look at Leila's ankles, which are just as elegant as usual.

'Well, thank god I'm not wearing them. I'd end up looking like my legs were on upside down.'

Leila laughs.

'Oh fuck, we're here – and there's Barry, he's one of our creatives. Total tosser, but his wife's nice.'

Leila sweeps through reception and meets and greets countless people, while I trot along behind her trying not to trip over. You could parachute Leila into the middle of the rainforest and she'd still meet three people she knew, and an ex-lover. And she'd remember all their names, and the names of their partners and children. And pets. It's sort of impressive and kind of scary at the same time. Barney's standing by the door to the bar looking very smart in his dinner jacket.

'Well, this is a fucking joke, that's all I can say.'

'Good evening, Barney.'

'Evening, Leila. Listen to this, they're giving a Gold to that prick Howard Riley for that terrible campaign with the horse. Christ. All he ever does is nick all the best bits from everyone else's jobs.'

'Thank you, Barney. I do look rather lovely, don't I? And as for Annie, well, you're absolutely right, she looks fabulous.'

'What? Oh yes. Sorry. You look terrific, both of you.'

'Thank you. I'm off to check out the table plan but I'd love a vodka.'

'Oh would you? God, I hate pushy women.'

'No you don't, Barney. With ice please.'

Barney smiles, and Leila heads off in search of the table plan. It's pretty vital that we're near the front; Leila's agency are bound to be, because they've bought three tables this year, but we've only paid for one, and if we're relegated to the back of the room with the also-rans there'll be major ructions.

'Come on, then, let's go and mingle, shall we? Isn't that what you're supposed to do at these things?'

'Yes, Barney, but mingle, all right? Don't start a fight with anyone.'

'I don't know what you're talking about.'

'Yes you do. Last year. Lawrence has only just got over it.'

Barney smirks. Towards the end of the party last year, when everybody was tired and emotional, Barney ended up having a blistering row with one of the judges, who he said ought to be taken outside and sorted out, because he'd voted for a soap powder ad that Barney had taken particular exception to.

'I promise. Peace, love and understanding. All right? I shall be charm personified. Great dress, by the way. Not sure about the shoes, though. Aren't they a bit Cruella for you?'

'Thanks, Barney. They're new. Leila made me buy them.'

'Oh right. Well, that explains it then.'

'Christ, you make it sound like I usually wear wellies.'

'Well, I wouldn't put it past you, darling. But that's what we love about you.'

Great. Now I feel like a country lumpkin in town for a big night out. Actually, I think I might be slightly drunk already. I think I'll switch to water or something and try and pace myself.

Leila comes back and announces that our tables are gratifyingly near the front, and then introduces me to countless people, and I end up talking to Maggie, an agency producer I've worked with a few times, who's a real sweetheart. She's telling me all about a recent job where they had such bad weather she had to call four weather days on the trot and one of the crew got alcohol poisoning and ended up in hospital, and I'm starting to quite enjoy myself, trading horror stories with Maggie, and I'm in the middle of telling her about the job last year where we had a studio full of St Bernards and two of them had a fight when we have to move into the ballroom and sit down for dinner.

The food's pretty awful, as it always is for some reason at these kind of things, all fussy garnishes and lukewarm sauces, and Lawrence has packed our table with agency people who he's busy fawning over. Barney's insisted on inviting Andy, his favourite lighting cameraman, and they're having a fabulous time chucking back the booze and trading insults. By the time the judges appear on stage and the ceremony actually begins nearly everyone is plastered and there's a fair bit of heckling going on.

The only awards that really count are the Golds, and the competition's pretty fierce. Last year they refused to award a Gold in cosmetics because they said all the entries were too average, which went down really well with the agencies who'd got films shortlisted. But apparently this year was a bumper crop and they've even come up with a couple of new awards for outstanding contribution to new branding or something. I couldn't hear properly because the waiter was coming round with the puddings and Lawrence was throwing an epi because he'd ordered fruit salad and got a rather substantial portion of lemongrass trifle instead.

They've hired a few celebs to dole out the awards and Julian Clary turns out to be very witty although Jordan seems to be slightly out of her depth. But the mystery of how her dress is actually staying up is so compelling that she's greeted with rapt attention; there's got to be some sort of heavy duty wiring in there somewhere, otherwise she's completely defying the laws of gravity.

Barney wins a Gold for the ad we did with the piano coming down a staircase, which is great, and as he makes his way towards the stage, to wolf whistles from the team from TBB, a small man I've never clapped eyes on mounts the stairs at quite a pace and is at the podium smiling before Barney has even reached the steps. Everyone claps and a few people cheer and then Barney comes back to the table.

'Who the fuck was that?'

'The art director from the agency, I think.'

Lawrence nods.

'Yes, he's called Brian.'

'Well, I've never clapped eyes on him. Fucking cheek. You'll have to go and get it back off him, Lawrence. I'm not having some polisher having it away on his toes with my fucking award.'

I'm not sure exactly how Lawrence is going to approach wrestling the award off Brian, but I hope I get to watch.

We win a couple of Silvers, which Barney makes

Lawrence go up to collect because he says it's a total insult, and two Bronzes, which get sent out in the post because the alpha males in ad land aren't very good at coming third, and then Leila appears on stage with a rival director to collect a Gold for a shampoo ad.

'What's she doing up there with that wanker?'

'It's Hi-Shine Barney, don't you remember? The one where the client said we could shoot in one of their salons but he didn't want any damage. And you promised it would be fine and then took the whole of the front window out.'

'Oh yes.'

Barney grins.

'Won a Gold, that one too, didn't it?'

'Yes. And he said he'd never work with us again.'

By the time all the awards have been announced the noise-levels are rising, and there's a lot of heckling and general hilarity going on. Quite a few people are making fairly regular trips to the loos and coming back doing the hokey cokey with mad grins on their faces, and the people on the table next to us are having a competition to see who can drink the most tequila slammers without passing out.

Leila is waving at us and making her way towards our table.

'Don't look now but you'll never guess who's here.'

'Jordan's emergency support team?'

'No.'

She makes Barney move, and sits down next to me.

'Mack the Knife. I've just spotted him, sitting over on the Prentice Palmer table. He must have arrived late and come straight into dinner. And Vanessa's with him.'

'Fucking hell.'

'I know. But don't panic. Oh fuck. Too late. He's coming over.'

He is. I suddenly see him, and even though it's ridiculous the rest of the room seems to fade into a background of noiseless faces and all I can see is Mack, weaving his way through the tables. He's wearing a dinner jacket and looking very polished and slightly tanned. And he's had his hair cut. Living in America obviously agrees with him. He looks like George Clooney. Fuck.

Leila grabs my hand and squeezes. Quite hard, actually.

'Chin up, darling. And remember, you look absolutely gorgeous.'

Mack walks towards us.

'Hello, Barney. Just came over to say congratulations.'

Barney stiffens slightly as he realises who it is.

'Hello, Nick.'

He's done it on purpose. And Mack knows he has.

'Great ad, but how did you get the piano to come down those stairs?'

'Oh it's a mystery, Nick. A total mystery.'

'Well, good to see you, and congratulations again.'

He turns and hesitates.

'Leila.'

Leila glares at him.

'Evening.'

He smiles.

'Having a good time?'

'Fabulous, thanks.'

'Great.'

He smiles again, and turns to walk away. But just before he does he turns to me.

'Hello, Annie.'

'Hello.'

God. My voice has gone all nervous, just like the rest of me. He looks at me for a moment, and then sort of nods. And walks off. Like I'm some vague acquaintance or something. Not the woman he was asking to come and live with him in New York a few months ago. Bloody hell. I feel like I've just tripped over and fallen flat on my face in front of hundreds of people.

While I'm trying to work out whether I'm actually going to be sick with humiliation, or just feel like it, Leila suddenly puts her arm on Barney's shoulder and bursts into hysterical laughter. Barney gives her a puzzled look, but she carries on.

'There's nothing worse than when you hear people laugh like drains as you walk away from them, don't you think, Barney?'

'Oh. Right. Fine. God, you had me worried there for a minute.'

Lawrence is looking especially gleeful.

'Oh, was that Mack MacDonald?'

Barney gives him a threatening look.

'Don't start, Lawrence, I'm warning you. Annie, sweetheart, are you all right?'

'Fine, thanks, Barney.'

All four of us watch Mack as he walks back towards his table. Vanessa is draped across her chair looking every inch the supermodel. I can't really see what she's wearing but it looks like a black dress in some sort of slinky material.

'Well, that was fucking rude.'

Leila's looking furious.

'I've got a good mind to go over there and tell him.'

'Leila, please.'

'I know, let's find someone gorgeous to come over and stick his tongue down your throat. That'll show him.'

'Leila, I feel sick enough as it is.'

'Well, if you change your mind just let me know. Now, let's get another bottle of champagne and get plastered, shall we?'

'Good plan.'

She manages to find a waiter and get a bottle of champagne in about thirty seconds flat. Leila's always completely brilliant in emergencies. She pours us both a glass.

'Wanker.'

'Wanker.'

'Is this some sort of girls-only toast, or can anyone join in?'

It's Leila's friend Steve; everyone's playing musical chairs now and huge amounts of mingling and networking are going on.

'We're just saying what a wanker Mack MacDonald is.'

'Oh, right, well, I'll drink to that. Although actually it's slightly worrying news, since it looks like I'm going to be working for him soon.'

Leila cross-examines Steve, who reveals that Mack's company are buying a London agency, and he's got his eye on Prentice Palmer, where Steve works. It's all unofficial at the moment and supposed to be top secret. So of course half of London knows. Damn. That means he'll probably be back in London some of the time. It's been so much easier coping with not seeing him when I knew he was over the other side of the Atlantic.

Vanessa walks past on her way to the ladies, and the black dress turns out to be navy blue, in chiffon or something, and she looks even more stunning than she did in *Vogue*. Leila gives me a sympathetic look, but she's busy sending rude texts to people on nearby tables.

And then my phone starts flashing. It's been on silent alert so the awards weren't interrupted by Mum calling to discuss goat's cheese, and I'm just about to check the voicemail when a little flashing envelope appears on the screen. It's a text from Lizzie. 'Come now. Not joking. Love Lizzie.' Fuck.

I tell Leila, who leaps up and says she'll get me a taxi; we've got a car booked for later, but it's not here yet. She's yelling into her mobile that we need a car now, and nearly knocks a waiter flying on her way out, and I'm trying to call Lizzie but her phone's off – she's probably already at the hospital. And then we get outside to find it's pouring with rain and there are no taxis in sight. Christ. I'm suddenly feeling completely sober.

'They say they'll have a car here in five minutes, so if a taxi hasn't turned up by then you'll be on your way. It'll be fine. Just breathe deeply.'

'It's Lizzie that's in labour, Leila, not me.'

'And don't forget to call me, all right? As soon as something happens. God, I'm feeling quite tearful.'

'Me too.'

'Oh darling, she'll be fine. I know she will.'

'No you don't. You hope she will. And so do I. But nobody knows. Christ, I don't think I can do this.'

A dark-grey Jaguar glides into view, and Leila walks towards it still talking into her mobile. But no. Obviously life can't be that simple. And who's the person I most don't want to see at this precise moment? Oh good. Here he comes. With Vanessa. Even better. Who I now see is not wearing a slinky dress at all, but a short skirt with an inch or two of tiny brown midriff on show, and a halter-neck top. This is just getting better and better.

I'm standing by the doorman feeling desperate, and Leila's pacing up and down shouting into her phone.

'Listen to me, this is an emergency. She's got to get to hospital. Her sister's giving birth. Do you understand? And I'll see to it that our account with you is cancelled first thing tomorrow morning if you don't get me a car here in the next thirty seconds. How complicated can it be, for fuck's sake? Just get me a car now.'

One of the doormen gives me a sympathetic look and grabs an umbrella and says he'll go out into the street and see if he can find a black cab, and the chauffeur from the Jag gets out and walks round to open the car door. There's a sort of lull for a few seconds and then Leila's phone rings and Mack turns and looks rather quizzically at her, while Vanessa walks towards the car, looking very poised and slightly supercilious. Leila turns her back on him as an enormous white limo screeches into the hotel driveway, and comes to an emergency stop, right in front of Leila. It must be for Jordan. Wrong again. The driver leaps out and Leila says 'Thank Christ' and ushers me into the back seat. I think I've gone into a sort of trance.

'What hospital is it, Annie?'

'What?'

'What hospital?'

'Oh. The Royal London, in Whitechapel.'

'Do you know where that is?'

Leila gives the driver a very steely look.

'Yes, madam.'

'Are you sure? Because if you take her on a tour of London you'll never hear the end of it. Trust me. Am I making myself clear?'

'Perfectly, madam.'

'Right. Well, don't just sit there. Go. Go.'

I find myself muttering 'Go Go Power Rangers' to myself and thinking about how much Charlie would love this car. I think I must be really cracking up now. Leila waves as the car drives off, and I finally come to my senses and ask the driver if he's sure he knows the way to the hospital, but he ignores me completely, and then I realise there's a glass partition between him and the back of the car. Bloody hell. There's a telly, and what looks like a bar as well. This is ridiculous.

The phone in one of the armrests starts discreetly beeping.

'Good evening, madam. I just wanted to check that you have everything you need.'

'Yes, thank you. It's just, well, I'm in a bit of a hurry.'

'Yes, madam. They did tell me. Don't worry, I'll get you there as soon as I can. Just relax.'

Relax. Right. Actually, I'm not sure I can. I'm sitting bolt upright, and the seats are made of some extra-slippery sort of cream leather so every time we go round a corner I slide sideways. I'm trying to brace myself into a corner when my phone rings. Christ. What now? It's Leila.

'All right, darling?'

'Yes, fine, I think. And thanks, for sorting out the car and everything.'

'You're welcome, darling. It's their C-list celeb limo. I know it's tacky but they didn't have anything else. But I thought you'd like to know, Mack just asked me what was going on. So I told him. And he said he hopes everything goes well, and then, and this is the best bit, he said he wondered what we were doing out in the rain, and you could have had his car if he'd known, and why didn't we say. And Vanessa did not look happy. Almost the complete opposite of happy, actually. She just stood there with a face like thunder, tapping her foot, looking deeply pissed off. Fabulous shoes, though. Prada, I think.'

'Oh.'

'Yes. And then he went all funny. Sort of stammered something about how he'd better be going and got in his car.'

'Right.'

'Anyway, I'm sure you don't care in the slightest, but I thought you'd like to know. Safe journey, darling, and call me as soon as there's any news.'

Actually, all I care about at this precise moment is getting to the hospital. God, I hope Lizzie's all right.

The driver manages the journey in record time, and even though I end up slipping right off the seat and on to the shag-pile a couple of times he's been brilliant to get me here so quickly. I'm already halfway out of the door scrabbling in my bag for a tip for him when he sprints round to hold it open for me, and wishes me luck.

He's parked right by the main doors, and we're attracting a fair bit of attention. This isn't the kind of hospital where people turn up in limos. Police cars possibly, but not limos. I get out and thank him, and then suddenly I can't bear tottering about on high heels any more, so I take them off and start running, which isn't one of the best ideas I've ever had because the floor's filthy and I'm sort of skating now. All I need is a triple toe loop and I'll be straight into A & E. Actually, I think I must be what is officially known as Losing It Completely now.

The sign says Maternity is on the second floor, and I find the lifts and surreptitiously take my tights off as soon as the doors close. I just hope there aren't security cameras in the lifts because if there are someone is in for a laugh tomorrow morning when they check the tapes.

After what seems like hours of running down corridors and being directed up to the fifth floor to Labour and Delivery I'm suddenly faced with a pair of locked doors with a buzzer. I buzz. Nothing happens. I buzz again, and end up buzzing for what seems like hours before a young nurse wanders over and lets me in and says, 'Oh yes, she's in Room Four,' and then wanders off. So top-level security then. Great.

As I walk towards Room Four I'm suddenly not sure if I should just barge in or try to find somebody. But the place looks deserted, so I nudge the door open. I don't know what I'm expecting to see, but it's not Lizzie rocking backwards and forwards balanced on a large pink rubber ball with Matt rubbing her back.

'Oh Annie, you're here. Thank god. Ow.'

She begins a low sort of moaning, and then she suddenly stops and carries on as if nothing had happened.

'Why have you got bare feet?'

I explain about the shoes and try to ask her how she's feeling and what's been happening, but she gets so obsessed by my bare feet she can't concentrate, and starts trying to persuade me to wear her slippers. Fabulous birth helper I've turned out to be. Turn up late in a posh frock and slightly pissed, and then nick her slippers. We eventually compromise on socks with those rubber gripper things on the soles, because she's got a spare pair that Matt bought last week. They're bright pink with flowers on, and she says she hates them and won't wear them even if her feet drop off. Poor Matt. He looks exhausted, and now he's having his socks rejected. But she's adamant about things like that, my little sister. She once made me take some perfectly nice white bath towels back to John Lewis because they had a tiny sea horse embroidered in one corner.

Once I'm safely in my socks she sends Matt off for a coffee, and as soon as he's gone she bursts into tears. And it's not that easy putting your arms round someone who is perched on a giant beach ball. I don't want her ending up on the floor, so I sort of crouch and do some light patting and stroking, which finally calms her down, although the contractions seem to be coming every couple of minutes so she has to keep stopping to do the groaning thing.

'Sweetheart, what's the matter? You're doing so brilliantly.'

'Yes, but it's just I've been wanting to cry for so long

and I didn't want to upset Matt. He's been so brilliant, and oh god, here comes another one.'

She grips my hand. Christ. I wish I'd taken my rings off. Bloody hell. I might be ending up in A & E tonight after all, having my hand reconstructed.

'Tell me right from the beginning what's been happening. And where's the midwife?'

'On her break. And she's horrible.'

She starts to cry again. Oh god. I'm being completely useless. And my hand really hurts now.

Matt comes back in with a polystyrene cup of coffee and passes it to me, and I take a sip and remember just how revolting hospital coffee is. Actually, it's so revolting I almost like it. It's sort of familiar, which is somehow reassuring.

The midwife appears and says she wants to check on the baby, so we help Lizzie on to the bed and then listen to a little pounding heartbeat on the monitor. Which makes the whole thing more real, and reduces us all to complete silence.

'Lovely. Well, that all seems fine. Now do you fancy having another little walk? It often helps.'

'Can't you just check me again, to see how many centimetres I am?'

'Not yet. You're due for another check in an hour, and first babies do tend to take their time, you know. You were only two centimetres last time so I think you'll be a fair while yet. Just keep moving, that's my advice.'

Oh how very bloody encouraging. Lizzie looks tearful again. Time for the bossy-big-sister act, I think.

'Yes, but you can go from two centimetres to ten in half an hour, you know, Lizzie, so if you feel things have changed then you just let us know, sweetheart, and I'm sure they'll check.'

I give the midwife an encouraging smile.

'You're doing so well, Lizzie. I can't believe how well you're doing. Isn't she, doing well, I mean?'

I leave a gap for the midwife to tell Lizzie how terrific she is. She's probably an excellent midwife, but I think she must have missed the day when they did communication skills.

'Oh yes, excellent. Just keep up the good work.'

Lizzie smiles briefly, before another contraction hits. The midwife waits until it's over, and seems to soften slightly.

'Well done, that was a big one, wasn't it? Would you like to try some gas and air?'

Lizzie nods and the midwife shows her how to use the tube and the plastic mouthpiece, and then says she'll be back in a little while, but she's got another woman next door she needs to check on. Lizzie gets up for a walk around the room, and clings on to Matt, who looks even more exhausted now. She keeps returning to the bed for a quick puff on the gas and air, but she's coping really well. I can't work out if this is really active labour, in which case she's being completely stellar, or if this is still the early stages, in which case it's going to be a really long night. It's nearly one o'clock in the morning already, and she's looking pretty tired to me. And I'm not sure at what point we're meant to be doing the paddling-pool thing, but I'm really hoping I don't have to get in, because I think I'm too knackered for underwater action. Maybe I can just lean over the side or something. Lizzie is puffing on the gas again.

'God. I don't think I can do this.'

Matt strokes her back.

'Yes you can, angel, of course you can, you're doing it.'

He's being so sweet; you can see him creasing his fore-head every time she has a contraction, and sort of wincing when she holds his hand, but he's hanging on in there being supportive. Although he's probably going to need splints and a support bandage by the time this baby arrives.

Gradually, in between puffing on the gas and air and walking round the room, she tells me what's been happening so far, and it turns out they've been here since lunchtime, only they didn't call me in case it was another false alarm. They've been in the pool for most of the afternoon, and she says it was great although her feet got really wrinkly and Matt says she's been completely amazing, and even managed to have a bit of a sleep.

Then she decides she'd quite like to try a walk down the corridor. Matt's holding her arm as they walk towards the door, but then she suddenly changes her mind and says what she really wants is to lie down, so we help her on to the bed again, and she curls up on her side and grips the gas-and-air thing and goes very quiet and determined-looking. And I know. Somehow, I just know that something has changed. She's always been like that; whereas I tend to make an enormous fuss about things she just goes all steely and determined. And silent.

She looks at me for a moment, briefly, and she's very distant now, and I know I'm right. She's making a different noise now, a noise she hasn't made before.

'Oh god. I can't. Do. This.'

'Yes you can. Just hang on. Matt, is there a bell for the midwife or something?'

'Yes, it's that button there, I think.'

I press it, and Matt gives me an anxious look.

Lizzie groans again and changes position. Now she's kneeling, slightly rocking backwards and forwards and holding on to the metal rail at the head of the bed.

'I. Want. A Fucking. Epidural.'

106

'I know, darling, and we'll get you one, in a minute, but just breathe now, all right? Breathe.'

I press the button again. For longer this time.

'Matt. Matt.'

She grips his arm, and I see him wincing and trying to make reassuring noises as she grips even harder. And then she yells. A long powerful deep yell, just as the midwife comes into the room looking rather irritated. She takes one look at Lizzie and says 'Oh', and wheels a trolley over that's been standing in the corner of the room, and starts putting on her plastic gloves and apron. Christ, I think this is really it. I'd quite like to have a moment to pull myself together, but there's no time.

Lizzie starts making a new kind of low growling noise, and the midwife tells her she's doing a great job and reminds her to breathe, and Matt and I exchange terrified glances. He's gone a pale-grey colour, and I notice my hands are trembling. Lizzie grips my shoulder and presses downwards really hard, and I'm really glad I took those heels off or they'd be permanently embedded in the lino. I move closer to the bed and she grabs Matt's hand again.

She's closed her eyes now and disappeared into some elemental world of breathing and pushing and the midwife's tone of voice suddenly goes from calm to slightly panicky and she says something about panting and not pushing and then all of a sudden there's a baby, making tiny little noises, lying on the bed on a square of green cotton, covered in blood and a few traces of waxy white. A baby girl. And she's absolutely perfect, with the same dark hair Lizzie's got in her baby pictures. One minute there were four of us in the room, and now there are five. It's totally staggering. Like magic. An invisible person suddenly made visible.

107

She goes slightly pinker as the midwife wipes her with a sheet and then she opens her eyes and they're that fabulous newborn navy blue, and the midwife takes hold of Matt's hands and he cuts the cord and then Lizzie picks her up and holds her to her chest, and everyone smiles. Lizzie's crying, and so is Matt, and he's got his arms round them both, and they look completely exhausted and ecstatic at the same time. I feel a sudden overwhelming urge to have Charlie here.

Another midwife bustles in, who looks much older than the others and is wearing a dark-blue uniform, so I think she must be sister or something, and takes the baby off to weigh her and then hands her back to Matt. She looks even smaller in her dad's arms.

'Eight pounds five ounces – well done.'

The older midwife smiles at Lizzie.

'What are you going to call her?'

'Ava.'

'That's a lovely name. Well, many congratulations. Would you like a cup of tea and some toast? It's the best we can run to, I'm afraid.'

'Oh yes please.'

'Would you like some too, Daddy?'

Matt ignores her.

'I think she's talking to you, Matt.'

Lizzie smiles.

'Oh god. Sorry. Yes please.'

She smiles.

'Do you need a hand or anything?'

I'm thinking it might be good to leave them alone for a bit, just the three of them.

'That would be lovely. Thank you.'

We go down the corridor and into a tiny little kitchen, and I suddenly feel very tired. And freezing cold.

'You look like you could do with some tea yourself, love.'

The next couple of hours pass in a blur of toast and tea. Matt phones the new grandparents, and Mum gets so hysterical Dad has to take the phone off her, and Lizzie gives Ava her first feed, and they both cope really well, although I can tell Lizzie feels slightly self-conscious.

'I never realised, when I watched you with Charlie that first night, how weird this all is. It seemed like the most natural thing in the world, and you seemed so calm.'

'I think that was the drugs, sweetheart. I was pretty spaced out.'

'Yes, but you seemed so natural. It's almost scary, isn't it?'

'What?'

'How much you love them. From the first minute you see them.'

'Terrifying. But it's brilliant, isn't it?'

'Yes. Terrifying and brilliant.'

She smiles.

'Do you want to try to get some sleep now?'

'No. I just want to look at her.'

Matt's fallen asleep, with one hand holding on to the empty plastic crib.

'I think I might go and make some more tea. Do you want one?'

'Oh yes please. And thanks, Annie, I meant to say earlier. For being here and everything. It made such a difference.'

'I don't think it did, you know. You two were amazing. Well, you three, actually, she did her bit too, and I wouldn't have missed it for anything. She's so beautiful.'

'She is, isn't she? I can't wait for Mum to see her.'

'I know. It's like it isn't official until Mum sees her, isn't it? You know she's going to go totally over the top, don't you?'

'Yes. And Matt's mum's really nervous about it, she was telling me. She says it's years since she held a new baby.'

'She'll be fine.'

'That's what I said. Oh look, she's starting to wake up again.'

Ava surfaces and starts making snuffling noises like she might be building up for a cry, but settles back down again after some crooning and cuddling from Lizzie.

'See? You're obviously a complete natural.'

She smiles.

'But I can still ring you in the middle of the night, if I'm worried. Can't I?'

'Of course you can. Any time.'

We're settling down for a doze after another cup of tea when the doors swing open and Mum arrives, with Dad and Charlie in her wake. It's only half-past seven in the morning, so she must have hoiked them out of bed at dawn. Charlie hasn't even had time to get his hair gel on. We have a long cuddle and I reacquaint myself with just how soft the nape of his neck is and do that mother thing of patting him and stroking his hair, which he puts up with far more calmly than usual, mainly because he's still half asleep.

Mum gets her first cuddle with her new granddaughter, and gets very tearful, and Dad has a cuddle too, and says she reminds him of us when we were little, and then he goes all gruff and hands her back to Lizzie. He puts his arm round Matt and says well, this is the start of all your troubles now, she'll lead you a right old dance if her mother's anything to go by, and Matt smiles and says he hopes so.

'Isn't she going to open her presents?'

Charlie can't stand the suspense any longer. Mum's got two carrier bags with her, obviously full of presents, but she's been so overwhelmed by looking at the baby she hasn't actually given them to Lizzie yet.

'Oh yes, I nearly forgot. Jim, go and get the other thing from the car.'

Dad says he'll be back in a few minutes. My God, how much stuff has she brought?

'It's only a little Moses basket, and a few sheets. I saw it in Mothercare and I couldn't resist. And there's a few more things here.'

'Oh Mum, thanks.'

Lizzie starts opening one of the bags while Matt sits smiling and proudly holding Ava.

'That's from me and Mummy. It's a vest and trousers.'

Actually, it's two vests and matching sleepsuits with ducks on, from Baby Gap. I showed them to Mum last week, and she must have found the bag in my wardrobe and remembered to bring it. She's so brilliant sometimes.

'And these are from me and your dad.'

An avalanche of small pink girly things descends from a giant carrier bag.

'God, this is brilliant, Mum, but how did you know? That she'd be a girl, I mean.'

'Oh, I just had a feeling.'

Mum smiles, one of her mothers-know-best smiles. Actually, I already knew about the pink starter kit, because she's got another bag full of blue things, and she's kept all the receipts so she can take it all back and exchange it. But I'm not going to tell Lizzie that. I'm still under a bit of a cloud for telling her that Father Christmas didn't exist when she was six and I was eight. And anyway, mothers do know best. Most of the time.

111

'Oh god, look, Matt.'

Lizzie holds up a small pink cardigan, with flowers and velvet ribbon. Which just goes to show how bloody clever those hormones are. My minimalist sister, who would normally refuse to have any garment with ribbons on it within a five-mile exclusion zone, has been transformed into a pastel junkie.

'And look.'

She holds up a tiny pair of white tights.

'I tried to choose a few simple things, because I know you don't like anything fussy.'

Lizzie smiles.

'It's all fabulous, Mum.'

Dad reappears with a Moses basket, lined in white cotton with pink ribbon threaded through the sides and wrapped round the handle, and pink blankets.

'Yes, and look, she's got a teddy.'

Charlie lifts up a small white teddy by one ear, and shows it to Lizzie.

'It should be brown really, because bears are brown. But it could be an artic one, I suppose. From the North Pole. Then it would be a polar bear.'

Lizzie smiles.

'Right, well, I'm sure she'll love it, Charlie, and you can tell her about polar bears when she's a bit bigger. But actually, do you know what I'd really like?'

'What?'

'A cuddle. From my best boy.'

'Oh. OK.'

He wanders over to the bed for a quick cuddle, and a closer look at the baby.

'She can't do much yet, can she? Because she's only little.'

'That's right.'

'Yes. You did sex and then she was born.'

112

'Um, yes.'

Oh god.

'And when she's bigger, then she'll learn how to walk and stuff. Jack Knight's baby sister is learning how to walk.'

'Is she?'

'Yes. And his mum says she's a little bugger.'

'Oh.'

I think now might be a good moment to go and see when the canteen opens.

By the time we get home I've gone past the being-tired stage and am floating on some sort of ethereal energy reserve that I didn't actually know I had. Mum and Dad brought us home, and I've left my car in the NCP. It's going to cost a fortune but I'll charge it to work, and give Lawrence a heart attack. Barney won't mind.

And at least I haven't got a hangover, which is something of a miracle given how much booze I necked back. Maybe the adrenalin soaked it all up, which is rather brilliant. Not that you could really market it as a hangover remedy: go on a bender and then attend a birth. Not unless you got a job with the NCT or something.

I ring Leila and say how much Lizzie liked her present, although I still can't work out how she managed to get a bouquet of pink roses and a box of Baby Dior gorgeousness delivered within two hours of my call. The motorbike messenger did look pretty nervous though, so I'm guessing she handled it personally.

'And is she lovely?'

'Beautiful.'

'And Lizzie's all right? Bloody amazing of her to do it drug-free.'

'I know.'

'Has she got stitches? I always think that sounds so revolting.'

'Only two tiny ones. Nothing major.'

'Oh don't. It makes me feel sick just thinking about it.'

'She's still on such a high, she doesn't seem to care.'

'I'd need to be on a Class A high not to notice something like that. Christ. Anyway, how are you?'

'Completely knackered. But happy.'

'Jealous?'

'No. I thought I might be, but no. Just pleased. Deep-down, seriously pleased.'

'Good. So you'll be my partner then, if I ever sprog?'

'Of course I will. Why, is there something you haven't told me?'

'God no, Tor's still being very enigmatic. It's driving me crazy. And I haven't got anyone else lined up yet. But in theory, I might. I can't decide. There's part of me that really wants to but it's a huge commitment, isn't it?'

'Epic.'

'And you can't change your mind and send them back, can you?'

'Not really, no.'

'So there's a crap returns policy, and endless sacrifice. Not very well thought out, is it, motherhood? And there's all that dancing-at-dawn bollocks. I'm not sure about that either.'

Charlie used to wake up at around four in the morning when he was a baby, for months, and we used to end up downstairs dancing to sixties soul music, basically because it was the only way I could shut him up. I still can't hear 'I Heard it Through the Grapevine' without saying a little prayer of thanks that he's sleeping through the night now.

'Well, you don't have to decide now – you've got ages yet. Loads of people have babies in their early forties.'

'Yes, I know, but still, I wish I was slightly closer to knowing what I really want. Sometimes I think I really want one, but then I worry that I'd be hopeless, and I couldn't bear that. I'd want to be great, like you are with Charlie. Maybe I'll just get a dog, and see how that goes.'

'Well, don't bring it down here, for god's sake, or I'll never hear the end of it.'

'Maybe we could do a dog share. I could have it for some of the time.'

'No.'

'It might work really well. And you only have to – '

'No. Double No. Absolutely not. Are you getting my drift here, Leila?'

'Oh all right. Although I think it's a really good idea.'

'It's a terrible idea. It's one of your worst ever, in fact.'

'I wonder if Tor likes dogs?'

'Leila, I'm serious. If you – '

'Calm down, it was only an idea.'

'Yes, but I know you, Leila. One minute it's an idea, and the next minute you'll have twin Great Danes and be dropping them off with me for the weekend.'

'God, you're bossy.'

'I know. My best friend taught me. You might know her, actually. She's the one who made me drive for nearly ten hours in a heatwave, just to go to a party in Manchester, only it was the wrong weekend.'

'It was fun though, wasn't it, when those policemen stopped us, and ended up asking us out for a drink. Actually, there's a great party on next week you should come to.'

'No thanks.'

'You haven't even heard who's having it yet.'

'No, but I still won't want to go.'

115

'You can't spend the rest of your life moping about Mack, darling.'

'I'm not.'

'She looked really pissed off, you know, Vanessa, when he was talking to me. Somehow I don't think he's going to be very happy with her for long. I bet he'll ring you. He definitely had a look on his face, before he got in the car. You never know.'

'Oh yes I do.'

'She looks like a limpet-mine girl to me.'

'A what?'

'You know, hard to shake off, and explosive if you make a wrong move. But he can be pretty determined when he wants to be, can't he?'

'Oh yes. Steely.'

'Well, there you are then. Let's just see. And in the meantime let's have lunch next week. And you can show me the photos of Ava, and I'll bring the puppies. I'm really liking the idea of Great Danes. Bye, darling.'

After lazing about with videos and watching Charlie fling Lego all over the living-room carpet, I opt for a line-of-least-resistance fish-fingers supper and decide to forget about bathtime because I'm so tired. We read books and generally wind down, and it's all going rather well. He's in bed in his pyjamas, and not kicking up in the slightest. He's actually lying down, looking sleepy, as I back out of the door. Yes. There is a God.

'Night, darling, sleep well.'

'Mummy.'

He sits up.

Oh bugger. This could be the start of an epic random-chatting routine and I'm just too tired. I try to look resolute.

'I'm too tired for chats tonight, Charlie.'

'Yes, but, Mummy. Baby Ava is my aunty now, isn't she?'

'No, Lizzie's still your aunty, darling. Ava's your cousin.'

'Yes. And I'm still Nana's best boy.'

'Yes, of course you are, darling.'

'So who does Lizzie love most now? Me or Ava?'

In other words, Am I, or Am I Not, still the top boy? Fuck. I always end up feeling like I never know the right thing to say at moments like this. But I think honesty is probably the only way to go.

'Ava, because she's her baby. You always love your own baby most.'

'Most in the world?'

Oh I get it. This isn't about Lizzie at all.

'Yes, more than anything.'

He gives a satisfied little nod.

'I love you, Mummy. To infinity.'

He pauses and looks at me, just to check that I still know the words.

'And I love you too, Charlie, to infinity and back again. Now go to sleep.'

He lies down with a smile on his face and snuggles into his pillow.

'That's right. To infinity and back again.'

IV

Springtime in Paris

AVA'S ONE WEEK OLD today, and I've just finished singing 'Happy Birthday' on the phone to Lizzie when Sally rings. Ginny Richmond has really outdone herself this time. Charlie brought an emergency PTA communiqué home with him yesterday:

Marhurst Primary School PTA are pleased to annouce that following interest expressed at the recent meeting details of the forthcoming trip to Paris have now been finalised. All parents who would like to know more should attend the meeting after school tomorrow, in the library.

He's very keen, mainly because he thinks the Eiffel Tower is twinned with Alton Towers and you shoot up it at a hundred miles an hour strapped into a special seat.

Sally's just been to the meeting to find out what's going on. She's still trying to make it up to me and Kate for her tragic blunder of landing us with doing the bathroom-baskets stall at the Easter Fair next weekend. She stood too close to Mrs Harrison-Black in the playground without back-up, and her emergency counter-rota kit failed to deploy. So now we're bulk-buying talcum power and trying to jazz up the load of tatty old baskets recycled by the PTA every year, and Easter Fair Commandments are coming home practically every day. They've moved on to 'perishables' this week, so if you're not down for baking you've got to bring in fruit for the healthy-eating version of the lucky dip, although I'm still not sure how the kids are going to react after they've fished around in a bran tub, only to be rewarded with a banana. But I predict quite a lot of fruit-flinging.

'So how was the meeting then?'

'I felt so sorry for Ginny. I mean she'd done a sort of brochure, but the Harrison-Black brigade were all in the front row giving her the evil eye, so when she came to the bit about needing to know how many people were interested there was this awful silence, and I just had to say something.'

'Had to what? Oh don't tell me. Not only are we doing bathroom bollocking baskets, now you've volunteered us for the Paris mission too.'

'I didn't promise, honestly I didn't, but I said I'd go with Rosie. William's a bit young for trips, and anyway he'd be a nightmare, and then I sort of said you and Kate were bound to be keen too. She looked so grateful. She's spent ages on it, you know. Her husband works in some travel firm, I think, so he can get us a really cheap deal on the coach. And they're going to start a French club after school.'

'Hang on a minute – did you say coach? Tell me you're joking.'

'Well, coach or minibus, depending on how many people

sign up, and we only have to pay for the hotel, so it's a real bargain.'

'It would have to be, given that we've got to go on a coach full of kids.'

'Yes, but just think cultural awareness, and language skills. It'll be so good for them.'

'Right.'

'And I'll have all the kids one evening, if you like, and you and Kate can go out and hit the town.'

'Now you're getting desperate.'

'I know. But please say you'll come. I don't think I can face it on my own.'

'When is it?'

'Quite soon. That's how she's got such a cheap deal – it's a sort of last-minute thing, I think. It's in the Easter holidays, we go on Friday night and come back late on Sunday.'

'What does Kate say?'

'I thought I'd start with you first.'

'What, with me being the total pushover, you mean?'

Sally laughs.

'No. But if you say you're coming Kate will too.'

'Well, show me the stuff and I'll think about it.'

'*Merci, Madame.*'

'Bugger off. Or *va te faire foutre* – I think that's how it goes.'

'What does that mean?'

'Take a wild guess.'

'Thank you so much for finding out about this fabulous learning opportunity for our children?'

'Close, but it's more like get stuffed. I think. Or it might be something to do with bottoms. I'm not sure. A French crew taught us all sorts of rude phrases a few years ago when we did a shoot in a vineyard.'

'Well, that might be useful.'

'Oh I'm sure it will.'

Dear god. This just gets better and better. I've spent most of the day on the phone because we've got a last-minute job on at work: two days in a studio surrounded by tubs of margarine, and when I'm not immersed in low-fat spread I'll be touring bus depots with Barney because we've got a script in that calls for stunt drivers and lots of double-decker buses. And on top of bathroom baskets and a potential trip to Paris with assorted Mixed Infants Charlie's got his first Scouts meeting tonight. Christ. This week is turning into a complete nightmare, and it's only Monday.

The noise coming from the village hall is deafening as we walk up the path, and Charlie and James are hopping up and down with excitement at finally being inducted into the wonderful world of Scouting. Inside it's even worse. It's like *Lord of the Flies* in green sweatshirts and comedy shorts. The Scoutmaster, Trevor Nason, is blowing his whistle and trying to get them all to line up, and his wife Penny is attempting to get the younger ones into the far corner of the hall, and failing.

According to Kate, there are actually three stages to this Scouting lark: Beavers, for six- to eight-year-olds, whose motto is 'fun and friends'; Cubs, from eight to ten, who 'do a good turn every day'; and Scouts, from eleven to fifteen, only they don't seem to have a motto. It's probably 'Piss off', or 'What?'.

Mr Tillingham usually takes care of the Beavers, but he broke his ankle tripping over a plastic bollard while he was doing a cycling proficiency course with them a few weeks ago, so it's down to Penny to hold the fort. She's busy pouring out beakers of orange squash and lining them up in the kitchen for half-time; she says they like a drink and a biscuit, only we have to keep the biscuits hidden, so we lurk in the kitchen on biscuit patrol and watch the proceedings through the hatch, while Charlie and James are taken off to bond with the Beavers.

They already know most of the boys from school, so they're soon running round pushing each other and generally annoying Trevor, who finally gets his Cubs lined up and walks up and down inspecting uniforms, while the Beavers lurk at the back sniggering. It's a bit like *Dad's Army*, but without the rifles.

One of the older boys collects the subs, and then they all start chanting that they promise to serve their Queen and Country and God and do a good turn while Charlie and James go visibly pale and look generally horrified. Technically they're meant to be Beavers, but I think they see themselves more as Cubs and have crept forward during the pledging thing. And are now busy creeping backwards again. I hope Charlie doesn't make one of his Comments. Somehow I don't think Trevor's going to take a tolerant line with a pagan would-be Cublet. He'll probably hoist him up a flagpole or something.

'Good Lord, what's he doing now?'

Kate's looking slightly alarmed.

Trevor's setting up a Calor-gas stove in the middle of the hall, and he's surrounded by a group of boys clutching paper bags.

'They're doing Fire Balloons. The boys always love it.'

Penny has nipped into the kitchen for a pair of scissors.

'Oh. Right. Lovely.'

Bloody hell, she came in really quietly. Maybe it's some Scouting trick you learn when you go camping: how to creep up behind people and frighten the life out of them.

She smiles and returns to her Beavers, who are making kites with bamboo sticks and lots of tissue paper and are busy gluing tissue paper to the trestle tables. But gradually her group starts to shrink as the boys gravitate towards the Fire Balloon extravaganza, which turns out to involve holding a paper bag above the flame so it fills with hot air and then wafts up to the rafters for a minute or two, before falling back down on to the hall floor to be trodden on by a stampede of small boys.

Just when it's all going rather well one of the bags catches fire and there's a great deal of running and yelling while Trevor tackles the blaze.

'I do the stamping, it's Health and Safety. I've told you before. Stand back.'

He stamps on the bag and makes sure it's completely out before a small boy rushes forward with a beaker of squash and tips it all over Trevor's shoes.

'What did you do that for, Harry?'

'There was a fire.'

'Yes. But I'd put it out.'

He sighs and mutters something about stupid boys under his breath, and then squelches into the kitchen in a Captain Manwaring-like fashion, clutching a bent old frying pan and a packet of chipolatas. Somehow I don't think Trevor has entirely grasped the meaning of the phrase 'Quit while you're ahead'. While he instructs the boys in the basic techniques for their Sausage-burning Badge the frying pan sits on the gas cooker getting hotter and hotter, and then he grasps the metal handle firmly, says 'Bloody Hell' really loudly and charges over to the sink to run his hand under the cold tap.

Kate offers to take over sausage-surveillance duties, while I stand there wincing and trying to look sympathetic. The boys take no notice at all of poor Trevor with his third-degree burns, so clearly nobody's doing their First Aid Badge. But if I was Trevor I'd definitely get them started on the rolling-crêpe-bandages routine pretty sharpish.

They stand about eating their sausages while other boys drift by the hatch and say 'Give us a bit' and are firmly told to Go Away, including Charlie and James who wander over and are told that Beavers don't do sausages. Oh yes they do, I think they'll find. Charlie's looking deeply shocked.

After everyone's had a beaker of radioactive-looking squash they all start playing a weird version of basketball, where they stand in a circle and throw balls at each other until the last one still standing up wins. It's like human skittles, but nobody seems to mind.

Kate and I are agog through the hatch but gradually convince ourselves that minor concussion isn't actually life-threatening, and nip out for a quick fag while nobody's watching.

'Do you think the other parents know there's quite so much fire involved?'

Kate's looking rather worried.

'Maybe we picked a bad night. But he did say we should stay and watch.'

'I've got a feeling the pledging thing didn't go down too well. Or the lack of sausage-sharing.'

Kate smiles.

'Maybe they'll decide they don't want to do it again.'

'Well, I bloody hope so, or we're going to have to bulk-buy Savlon.'

'I got the soap, by the way, for the baskets. Boots have got a special offer on.'

'Great.'

'And Sally's got some ribbons and stuff, so we should

124

be fine. And she told me about the Paris thing, and I think it sounds great.'

'You're up for it then?'

'Yes, why not? It might be fun. We can go and see my Aunt Celia – she's fabulous. And it can mark the start of the new me, off to Paris for the weekend with the children. Because I think the worm has finally turned.'

'What worm?'

God, I hope this isn't about Phil moving back or something.

'Me. It all started to feel rather undignified.'

She looks slightly embarrassed.

'So I've told him, he'll be welcome to see the children any time, but that's it.'

'Oh. Well, that's great. Good for you.'

'I know. I feel I'm finally in the driving seat for a change. And then I really got into my stride and said I wanted him to turn up on time when he came to see the children, not be late like he usually is, and not always with Saffron – they need to see him on their own sometimes. And if he promised to do something he had to do it, and not ring up at the last minute and cancel. He's always doing that.'

'And how did he take it?'

Not well, I'm guessing. He has a terrible knack of wriggling out of things.

'Well, he got all huffy and said his life was very complicated and he had to try to balance things.'

'And whose fault is that then? I hope you told him.'

She's smiling now.

'Do you know, I actually went one better than that. I said I could always have a word with Zelda, woman to woman, if he thought that would help. He went as white as a sheet.'

We both laugh.

'I think blackmail's going to turn out to be very useful. At least it might make him sharpen up his act with the children. And that's all I really want.'

'Brilliant.'

She's still smiling, and it's the way you smile when you realise you've gone past the doormat stage and on to something better, and slightly less horizontal.

'I mean I don't want to talk to Zelda, obviously, but I don't think it'll come to that. I'm just going to get on with it, and as long as the kids are happy then that'll be fine. And I'm going to tell my mother to stop lining up rejects for me, and harping on about what a failure I am just because I haven't got a man around the place. It's about time I stood up to her. And we're going to go to Paris and have a ball. Right?'

'Right.'

'Great.'

Blimey. Well, good for her. I thought that getting tangled up with Phil again would make everything worse, but it seems to have been just what she needed. Sort of like the final stage of her getting over him. Which is brilliant. I just wish I could have seen his face when she threatened to have a nice little chat with Zelda.

The day of the Easter Fair arrives after a pig of a week. I've been locked in a studio for hours with Barney trying to stop him throwing tantrums, or tubs of marge, and it looks like we've got the bus job, so I'm trying to track down stunt drivers, and work out how many buses we're really going to need. Far too many is the basic gist, and Barney's busy rewriting the script, which is always a bad sign.

And it looks like Mack's agency are definitely buying

Prentice Palmer, and Leila says she saw him at lunch in Claridge's the other day. So it's probably only a matter of time before I bump into him, which is completely freaking me out, and I bet I'll be wearing my cagoule.

At least I managed to see Lizzie and Ava on the way home yesterday. They're still completely blissed out, and Ava's already changed. She's got fat little cheeks now and is much more lively. Lizzie's abandoned her plans for nice long sleeps and calm routines because it turns out Ava's much keener on very short sleeps and bursts of frantic feeding, just like Charlie was. In fact she's following in his footsteps almost entirely, and seems to have decided that the middle of the night's the ideal time to have a go at a bit of hand–eye co-ordination practice, and gets close to hysteria if anyone tries to lie her down. So Matt's taken to driving round Tesco's car park at 2 a.m. and Lizzie's perfecting the night-time shuffle. Two steps forward, one step back, with a slight rocking motion. God, I can remember it like it was yesterday.

Mum's gone up for a few days to give them a hand. She's been itching to get there and start hand-washing woollens, and she finally got the green light yesterday. So she's decreed that tomorrow is the ideal time for me to combine my weekly mercy mission to Monty's with giving Dad Sunday lunch. Only he likes a proper Sunday lunch, so she's dropped an enormous joint of beef round, and a short note on how to make decent Yorkshires and cook Dad's favourite vegetables. So no pressure there then.

Actually, the only really useful thing that's happened all week is Charlie deciding he's not going to Scouts any more because they don't share out their sausages. And I think he and James reckon pagans aren't meant to pledge allegiance to things, at least not unless its midsummer and they're balanced on a bit of sacred ash.

By the time I've got Charlie in the car surrounded by the sodding bathroom baskets, after persuading him that Buzz and Woody don't want to enter the Small Pets competition, we're already late.

'Everyone else will be bringing their rabbits.'

'No they won't, Charlie. Put your seat belt on.'

'Natasha said she was bringing her tortoise. I want a tortoise. I really do. They're so prehistorical. You could get two and then they could have races. It would be like the tortoise and the hare, only it would be the tortoise and the tortoise. That would be fairer really, wouldn't it?'

'Do your seat belt up.'

He fixes me with a very determined look.

'Can I have a tortoise?'

'What, before you do your seat belt up? Don't be silly. Do it up right now, or we'll be late for the Fair.'

He mutters, but does the seat belt up. In the spirit of trying to avoid arriving at the Fair with him in High Dudgeon mode I offer a compromise.

'Maybe you could have one for your birthday.'

Actually, come to think of it I don't think you can buy tortoises any more, not unless you've got a note from the RSPCA. But I'll cross that bridge when I come to it.

'No thank you, Mummy. For my birthday I'm having an Irish wolfhound.'

Bugger. I walked straight into that one. His new tactic in the I-must-have-a-dog-or-I-will-die campaign is to pretend there's a new rule governing birthdays, and all you have to do is make it clear to your nearest and dearest what gift is required and it will be automatically delivered. Which is a good idea in theory, I've got to admit, although if it applies to adults George Clooney might find himself in rather more demand than usual. He's even

128

started writing notes, 'I Want A Dog Please,' and putting them in my handbag – Charlie, that is, not George, who sadly has never clapped eyes on my handbag, let alone popped a little note in.

'We are not getting a dog, Charlie, I've told you. Not until you're bigger.'

He kicks the glove compartment and starts muttering again.

We arrive at school to find Roger's volunteered to keep the kids out of trouble while we set up the stall, and is rather bravely organising an impromptu game of football on the field. He's even brought his whistle, and is soon joined by hordes of screaming children and looking very close to panic. I've often noticed this before: if you do anything even vaguely amusing with your own child in public you're inevitably joined by hordes of somebody else's, while their parents look on indulgently and occasionally give you a congratulatory smile, like you must be thrilled to be spending so much quality time with their outstanding offspring.

Kate's very good at shaking other people's children off, but Sally says it happens to her all the time, but she's a teacher so I don't think that counts. If she sees any group of kids milling about anywhere she seems to feel compelled to organise them. Even quite big ones. On the beach last year she went over and made a couple of enormous teenagers, who were playing beach volleyball, move and play in the sea, away from the sandcastle-builders and paddling toddlers. They kept glaring at her, but she seemed oblivious. She says you get used to it after a few years of teaching history to adolescents, who couldn't really give a toss what the Tudors were up to.

There's quite a queue building up outside the gates, but

that's probably down to Mrs Harrison-Black putting notices up everywhere announcing the appearance of a mystery television celebrity. The tension mounts until a man nobody recognises appears, and Mrs Harrison-Black introduces him as Colin Chapman, who she's sure we all recognise from his excellent weather reports on *Newsroom South East*. He declares the Fair officially open, to a round of rather bemused applause, and says he's sure it's going to be a lovely day, with just a hint of cloud moving in from the east by teatime, and then everyone surges round the stalls.

Kate's getting nervous about Phil and Zelda arriving, because she's managed to avoid having them at school things so far. She's got a lovely new jumper on, in pale cornflower blue, which really suits her, and her hair's loose instead of in her usual ponytail, so I think she's made a bit of extra effort. I offer to lend her my new scarf, which looks like cashmere but is actually M&S, and in shades of blues and greys. We've got pretty similar colouring but her hair's slightly darker than mine, and the scarf really suits her.

Sally lends her a lipstick for a quick dab and then Phil arrives, with Zelda and baby Saffron, and comes straight over to complain that he's had to park miles away because the car park in the field is full up. Kate's especially friendly and upbeat with Zelda, who looks slightly uncomfortable, like she knows something has changed, only she can't quite work out what.

We all compliment her on her new hairstyle, which is a very short peroxide crop.

'I know, I'm rather pleased with it, actually, and it's so much easier with Saffron. Babies do take up so much time, don't they? And it's so easy just to give up and sink into being all mumsy, isn't it?'

Bloody cheek. Is she trying to say we're all looking mumsy?

Kate smiles, but I can tell she's annoyed.

'Well, it really suits you. Oh, here come the children. Phil, would you mind taking them for a drink and something to eat, only I'm a bit stuck here.'

'Oh. Haven't they had lunch then?'

'No. You don't mind, do you?'

Phil hates having to pay for anything. I bet he'd have brought a packed lunch for them all if he'd known.

'No, of course not.'

'Take Charlie too, would you, only I promised him a burger earlier. The barbecue's really good this year – a bit expensive, but worth it. You don't mind, do you, Annie? I did promise.'

'No, that's fine.'

Phil looks furious. What a shame. He wanders off, trailed by Charlie and James and Phoebe busy debating how many burgers they can eat.

'Not hungry, Zelda?'

'Not really. I'm a vegetarian now – it's so much better for you. No, I think I'll just go and look at some of the stalls.'

'See you later then.'

She's not looking happy either. Excellent.

The bathroom baskets seem to be going down quite well, although I didn't actually know they still made Yardley bath cubes. We've had to add things to quite a few of the baskets to make them look less pathetic, and as usual it was the posh mothers who sent in giant bottles of Tesco Economy Bubble Bath. But all in all I think we've done rather well, and at least we've exceeded the target issued by the PTA High Command.

We take it in turns to tour the stalls and I buy a

chocolate cake for lunch tomorrow with Dad and Monty before Charlie drags me off to Small Pets, which is basically three trestle tables covered in cages full of hamsters and guinea pigs, and yes, the occasional rabbit, although I do point out how cross they look. In fact, one large white one looks positively furious.

Natasha is nowhere to be seen with her tortoise, so perhaps it's putting up a bit of a fight. Lizzie and I had one when we were little, but it disappeared through a hole in the back fence and Mum and Dad told us it had gone on holiday, which we believed, gullible fools that we were. Telling lies seems to be a pretty vital part of parenting, when you come to think about it. Nice ones obviously, like tortoises going on holiday rather than snuffing it, or how you look like a fairy in your ballet outfit, rather than a piglet with bunches.

I'm in the middle of trying to remember what colour my ballet shoes were when an astonishingly handsome man starts opening cages and picking up hamsters while various small children look on anxiously as their pets are hoisted into the air for closer inspection. He's so breathtakingly Adonis-like that I just stand there with my mouth slightly open, hoping he's not some weird kind of pervert who likes fondling rodents.

Charlie starts making an enormous fuss of a dog that's appeared out of nowhere and is busy licking his hands and face and generally wagging itself into a frenzy, and on closer inspection turns out to have only three legs, and just when I'm about to retrieve Charlie in case he knocks it over, the hamster-fondling Adonis clicks his fingers and the dog hops towards him.

'Sorry about that, but she's very friendly.'

'No, that's fine.'

He smiles at Charlie.

'Is this one yours?'

He points to a particularly manky-looking guinea pig and Charlie shakes his head.

'No. I wanted to bring our rabbits, but Mummy said they wouldn't like it.'

He pauses for a quick glare at me.

'Why has your dog only got three legs?'

A sorry saga unfolds about the dog being a rescue dog, during which Adonis introduces himself as Gabriel Jones, the new vet at the local surgery run by Mr Willett. He's been sent along to judge the show as one of his first jobs.

'Mr Willett thought it would be a good way to get to know people.'

In other words Mr Willett didn't fancy it.

'We could rescue a dog, Mummy, couldn't we? We could rescue Tigger. Mrs Brooks is always leaving him outside the shop.'

Charlie looks to the vet for back-up. Tigger is Mrs Brooks's chocolate-brown Labrador, and she's completely besotted with him. She even takes him for walks in the rain, because he likes it, apparently. She'd be mortified if he was 'rescued', and I'm explaining this to Charlie as firmly as I can when the vet finally cottons on and starts muttering about what a big commitment dogs are.

'Awful lot of work. I'd stick to rabbits, if I were you – for a while, anyway.'

'Yes, but they don't play with you. Dogs play with you.'

Charlie pauses to look suitably tragic.

'And they keep doing sex and Mummy won't get them a girl rabbit, so they can have babies. That's very cruel, isn't it? You should tell her.'

Oh dear.

'Well, not necessarily. Um . . .'

He's gone rather pink now, and the mention of Sex has

133

got the rapt attention of all the children standing behind their cages.

He turns to me.

'It's probably just hormones. They do tend to get a bit keen – separate hutches might be a good idea. Or they might start fighting. Or get depressed.'

Great. That's just what I need. Depressed rabbits. Or bunny wars.

'Bring them into the surgery if you'd like me to check them over, but I'm sure they're fine.'

Actually, if there was a sexy vet competition he'd definitely be in with a chance. He's blond and tanned with blue eyes, and lovely hands, and even though you know he's probably been doing something revolting with them fairly recently I think you'd probably forget about that after a while. Maybe I should be taking the rabbits in for a quick nail-clipping moment or something.

He smiles.

'I've never really done much judging before. I hope nobody gets upset.'

Two small girls are staring at him. They're wearing their party dresses and standing proudly behind what look suspiciously like rats in cages.

'Well, good luck.'

He smiles again.

'I think I might need it.'

Despite Colin Chapman's forecast for perfect weather the slight cloud turns into a torrential downpour, so we all get soaked packing up the stall. But at least we've sold most of the baskets. I tell Sal and Kate about the gorgeous new vet and they wander over for a quick look in the hall, but he's still surrounded by rodents so they don't linger.

We see him getting into his car as we're driving off, and

he gives us a cheery wave, and then Charlie falls asleep really early after supper, so all in all it's been rather a cracking day, and not nearly as annoying as I thought it was going to be. Now I've only got Sunday lunch to sort out, and a huge pile of ironing, and I might be able to have a nice doze in front of the telly.

I'm pondering a low-profile trip to see Gabriel in the surgery while I'm peeling carrots the next morning ready to take to Monty's for lunch when Leila rings. She's finally managed to get Tor into bed, and is feeling euphoric.

'He's a complete marvel. Christ. Who knew doing yoga could make you such a top shag.'

'Fiona Fisher does yoga in our village hall and she wears pastel leggings.'

'Well, Tor doesn't, and I can't wait for the action replay. Actually, I think I might have to call him for an emergency session this afternoon.'

'Well, I'm very pleased for you.'

'Not half as pleased as I am – trust me. How did the school thing go yesterday, by the way? Any potential new talent lurking?'

'Well, actually . . .'

As soon as I've finished telling her about Gabriel I realise I've made a fairly major tactical error because she gets wildly over-excited.

'Ooh he sounds perfect. Or totally mad. Both probably. Anyway, hurrah, something to take your mind off Mack the Knife.'

'Leila, I only met him briefly, for about three minutes, surrounded by kids and hamsters. And for all I know he could be married with six kids.'

'Don't be so defeatist – you need do to some more research. So listen, this is what you do. Get round there sharpish, wearing something casual but not orange, and take a rabbit and make up a mystery ailment. He wasn't looking longingly at your shoes, by any chance, was he? You weren't wearing those bloody sandals, were you?'

'Of course not. I always wear my stilettos when I'm doing a PTA stall.'

'I'm only trying to help you weed out any more potential shoe fetishists.'

'Thanks for reminding me.'

'Oh this is great. Tor's finally succumbed to my charms and you've got a vet to play with – with a three-legged dog for Charlie – and he's willing to help you work out if you've got straight rabbits. What more could a girl want? And a trip to Paris on the horizon. Fabulous shops, cheap booze, and you can smoke in public without being arrested. Can I come?'

'Sure. It's a coach trip, with the kids. Shall I get you a ticket?'

'Oh. Right. Well, maybe not then.'

Call-waiting starts beeping on my phone.

'Look, I've got to go, but I'll call you later, and I'm pleased Tor was such a success.'

'Me too. Bye, darling.'

It's Mum, calling to tell me that Dad doesn't like swede, and to say Ava's had them up half the night, and do I think Charlie would prefer a chocolate bunny or a Harry Potter Easter egg. Since we both know she'll end up buying both of them I don't really know why she's bothered calling, but at least it gives her an excuse to remind me that Dad likes his beef well done, and isn't very keen on custard.

Lunch goes rather well in the end, although we eat quite late because Monty's Aga is completely mystifying. I normally just take something round for him to heat up, but this time I'm actually cooking the whole thing and two of the ovens are completely hopeless: the top one nearly incinerates the potatoes, before I manage to rescue them and put them in the slower one. And the bottom one has either gone out completely, or is only to be used for warming up your wellies. I end up spending ages grovelling about on the floor trying to work out what the various ovens are doing, and then I forget about the horseradish until we're halfway through lunch.

Beef turns out to have been an excellent choice though, because Monty suggests a walk after lunch to see the sheep and I can vividly remember being reduced to tearful quiverings after snorking through Aunty Florrie's roast lamb and mint sauce and then being taken out to see the sheep with their new baby lambs. Actually, I think that might have been why Lizzie went vegetarian.

Monty says he wants to move the sheep into the next field, so he does the whistling thing with Tess, who rounds them up very efficiently, while we loiter on the sidelines waving our arms and generally getting in the way. The lambs are charging about, which Charlie loves, and all in all it's going rather well and the sheep are trotting quite happily towards the gate when two fighter jets suddenly scream in from nowhere, flying incredibly low and making a phenomenal noise. God knows what kind of top-secret mission requires low-level flying over sheep on a Sunday afternoon but they scatter in all directions. Charlie's delighted, but Monty's furious. Apparently it's happened a lot lately.

'Practically every afternoon they're up there, showing off. Bloody RAF. They've always been good at showing off. To hear them talk you'd think they'd won the war all by themselves. Battle of Britain, my arse. They should have tried it down in the mud with the rest of us.'

Dad smiles. Monty's views on the RAF being a load of snobby show-offs who take far too much credit for Winning the War are well known to all of us, and there's no point arguing as it only encourages him.

'Practically shake the slates off your roof, they do.'

'You should ring them up, Monty, put in for some compensation if they damage anything.'

'I wouldn't give them the satisfaction. Well, we'd better get this lot sorted out. Look at them, daft things, you'd think they'd be used to it by now.'

We finally get them into the new field and the lambs all rush straight over to a fallen tree trunk and try to climb up on to it. Monty tells Charlie that lambs have some sort of in-built instinct to get to the highest bit of ground available. He says it's probably something to do with spotting wolves.

'Werewolves?'

Charlie looks slightly nervous and stands a bit closer to Dad.

'Grandad, have you ever seen a werewolf? They come out at night. And bite you. On your neck.'

'No, Charlie, but your nana would give you a nasty nip if you tried to wake her up after midnight. She likes her sleep, your nana does.'

We start walking back to the house while the lambs push each other off the tree trunk and generally have a lovely time playing a lamby version of I'm the King of the Castle. Charlie starts complaining of exhaustion and tries to persuade us to give him a piggyback, but none of us are falling for it, and then before I can stop him Dad rootles round the pockets of his coat and finds a massive chunk of Kendal Mint Cake for him.

'Here you are, Charlie boy. This'll perk you up a bit.'

It certainly does. He's fully recharged in a matter of

minutes. He starts to run ahead of us waving a stick, battling invisible wolves.

'So you'll be giving him his bath tonight then, will you, Dad? Now he's fully perked up on a massive sugar high?'

'Oh don't fuss, he'll be fine. Bit of sugar never hurt anyone.'

'No, not if you were stuck up the wrong end of a mountain, it wouldn't. I'm sure it would be really handy. But I was hoping for a nice cup of tea and a doze in front of *The Antiques Roadshow* when we got home.'

We both look at Charlie, who's now leaping into the air doing kung fu.

'Oh. Right. Well, that might be a bit tricky, I'll give you that.'

'Why've you got Kendal Mint Cake in your pockets, anyway? What's wrong with Fruit Polos all of a sudden?'

Dad always had Fruit Polos in his pocket when we were little if we were going on a walk. And he's sort of carried on the tradition with Charlie.

'Your mother got it for me, for fishing. She's got this theory that Pat Maynard's going to keel over and need sugar, because he's just been told he's diabetic.'

'Oh, poor thing.'

'He seems fine about it to me, but you know your mother, she's been talking to his wife Pauline, and they've decided he can't be trusted, so she keeps filling my pockets up with biscuits and stuff every time we go fishing, just in case.'

'That's sweet of her.'

'Oh yes, very thoughtful, I'm sure. Although it's not you that's got your pockets full of bits of biscuit.'

'True.'

Monty makes a cup of tea when we get back to the house while we try to calm Charlie down, and fail, and then we all troop out to search through one of the barns for the old rabbit hutch Monty says we can have for Buzz and Woody, although he's very sceptical about the advice of vets.

'Most of them are terrible villains, you know. Never come out without giving you a hefty bill. We had a good one a few years back, he had a real feel for it, but he left, and the new one's terrible. He'd charge you if he met you in the street and said good morning. He's so mean he's probably still got his christening money.'

Getting the hutch home turns out to be a total palaver, since it won't fit in Dad's car. Monty has to lend us an old trailer, which is so rickety it looks like it'll collapse as soon as we go round a corner. We have to drive really slowly, and people keep flashing at us before finally over-taking.

Eventually we get it home and install Buzz in it. It looks a bit ramshackle but it's actually much bigger than the one we bought in the pet shop. Buzz looks very pleased with himself and appears to be smirking at Woody through the wire netting.

'We'll have to swap them round so they both get a turn.'

Dad smiles.

'They'll be fine.'

'Yes, but I don't want Woody getting jealous.'

He gives me a look and shakes his head.

'Well, I'd better get the trailer back to Monty, because if I pick your mother up at the station with that thing still on the back of the car tomorrow I'll never hear the end of it.'

'True. Oh god, what's he doing now?'

Charlie is marching round the back garden with a metal colander on his head yelling 'Terminate, Terminate' at the top of his voice.

'Playing trains, is he?'

'I don't think so, Dad. Not unless it's Thomas the Very Loud Psycho Engine. Come on, Charlie, it's nearly bath-time. Let's go in and see if there are any cartoons on.'

'I'm not having a bath tonight. They're bad for you. A sheep told me.'

Great. Who knew Kendal Mint Cake could be quite so lethal.

Easter's a blur of melting chocolate; Lizzie and Matt bring Ava down for Easter lunch at Mum's, and she's invited Monty too. When Charlie and I arrive to collect him he's wearing his best suit and is sitting waiting for us with his coat on, holding a little parcel wrapped up in pink paper. It's a present for Ava, a tiny silver bracelet, just like the ones Aunty Florrie got for us when we were little. I've still got mine somewhere. He's even had her name engraved on it, which almost reduces Lizzie to tears.

We take loads of photographs of everyone cuddling the baby, including Monty, who holds her very carefully, and even Charlie has a go, although he's rather disappointed that she's not walking yet. But she has bought him an Easter Egg, which he's very impressed with.

We're off to Paris for the school trip on Friday, so I'm borrowing Mum's black suitcase with wheels, and I even remember to ask her to re-set the combination lock to four zeros, because last time I forgot and had to phone her from Italy for the numbers before I could get the bloody thing open. Lizzie's particularly jealous about Paris because she says she can barely make it round Tesco's at the moment, let alone a trip abroad, so I promise to buy Ava something chic from Paris to add to her already extensive collection of frocks.

* * *

The journey to Paris isn't quite as bad as I thought it was going to be and after an initial burst of over-excitement as the coach drives into the train compartment and we enter the tunnel most of the kids falls asleep, and only start to surface when we're in the outskirts of Paris. Phoebe and Rosie are sitting together giggling quietly and generally amusing themselves, and James is dozing next to Kate. Charlie's been asleep on my lap for most of the journey, so I end up with very hot thighs, which is rather unpleasant, but at least he doesn't wake up in Attila mode. He's even quite chirpy when we arrive at the hotel.

It's turned out to be a gratifyingly large group for Ginny: fifteen parents and twenty-three kids. More parents put their names down on the list initially, but took them off again when they realised they had to come too. But even a couple of Mrs Harrison-Black's cronies have broken ranks and come along, so Ginny's very pleased, although checking into the hotel takes a while.

She's done a brilliant job organising everything, and she's come up with a timetable of trips to museums and galleries and the Eiffel Tower, with quiz sheets for the kids, and the hotel's even got satellite telly, so the kids watch cartoons while we unpack. There's no room service, which is probably a good thing given Charlie's secret plan to wake up in the middle of the night and order chips and ice-cream, which he confessed to me earlier, so Sally goes down to the bar and brings us all up gin and tonics, with Coke and crisps for the kids.

'What's the plan for tomorrow then?'

Sally looks at Ginny's notes.

'Well, it's downstairs for breakfast by eight-thirty ready for the coach to the Eiffel Tower at nine, and then you can go to your aunt's for lunch and I'll take them on to the Louvre.'

'Are you sure?'

'Yes, honestly, I've never been, and I want to see *The Mona Lisa*, and they've got a Vermeer too, I think.'

Kate nods.

'They have, but if I remember rightly it's at the other side of the museum to *The Mona Lisa*, so wear really comfy shoes because you walk miles.'

'Has your aunt always lived in Paris?'

'Pretty much. She was excommunicated by the family years ago, for being Fast. She'd got in with a very arty set, painters and film types. She knows everyone. Gerald Dooby Doo, all of them.'

'Do you mean Gerard Depardieu?'

Kate nods and Sally makes a sort of squeaking noise.

'Oh he's so lovely, don't you think, Annie?'

'He always looks slightly sulky to me. Like he'd sleep with one of your friends and then tell you off for being bourgeois if you minded. I think Inspector Clouseau's probably more my style if you're talking French movies. At least you'd have a laugh.'

It turns out that Kate adores Pink Panther films and can do a very good Peter Sellers impression, and when I come back from the bar with more gin they've moved on to doing impressions from *'Allo 'Allo!*, and Sally's practically collapsed on the bed by the window and keeps saying 'Lissen, I will zay zis only once' and going off into fits of giggles. We play cards with the kids, who all try to cheat, and then charades, and Charlie does a brilliant impression of an elephant. I just hope nobody is trying to get to sleep in the room below us.

The Eiffel Tower's a huge success the next morning, despite the enormous queues, and the weather's perfect, all bright sunshine and warm enough to stand in the lines for the lifts whilst being bombarded by slightly menacing-looking men trying to sell you Eiffel Tower key rings.

The queues are huge, and we're treated to a fascinating snapshot of different parenting styles. The Italians seem to go in for the most cuddles and stroking, with occasional bursts of ferocious gesticulating and shouting and the odd slap or two. And the French all seem to dress their little girls in posh coats with velvet collars and their hair in pigtails, and then ignore them, whereas the Germans seem keen on sensible sandals and lots of reading guidebooks and earnest chats, with the occasional cuddle thrown in, and the Americans are the loudest, and wear the most amusing trousers.

Kate refuses to come up to the top of the Tower because she's not keen on heights and says she'll probably faint or something equally embarrassing, so Sal and I take the kids up in the lift. It's mostly glass and it turns out I've been quietly developing a fear of heights too, only I didn't realise it until now, and Sally has to help me out of the lift, and I have to use all my willpower not to cling on to the door and scream to be taken back down again sharpish.

Once I manage to pull myself together it turns out that the top level is completely enclosed in a sort of plastic screen rather reminiscent of a seventies Wimpy bar, with a wall display to match. But at least you don't find yourself being pulled over the edge by the invisible threads of vertigo, which is good news for the people standing down on the ground in the queues.

Charlie doesn't seem the slightest bit bothered by being stuck up at the top of an enormous pole that definitely feels like it's swaying slightly, but he and James are very annoyed about the plastic windows, because they were planning to drop a coin and see if it went right inside somebody's head down in the queue. We take photographs and buy ice-creams for everyone who isn't feeling wobbly, and then we're thankfully back on the ground and Sally takes the kids off on the coach to the Louvre while Kate and I walk to her aunt's apartment, after stopping in a nearby café for a restorative café crème, and a quick fag.

Just as we're congratulating ourselves on being somewhere where you don't get glared at for smoking, two American women sit down at the table behind us and start waving their hands and talking in very loud voices about how much they mind all the cigarette smoke in France. Maybe they should just bugger off back to Baltimore then. They ask the waiter if there's a no-smoking section but he pretends not to understand them, and just brings them an ashtray and a box of matches and then winks at us on his way back to the bar.

Kate's telling me all about Celia being a communist as we arrive at the apartment, which is extremely posh-looking from the outside, and turns out to be even posher once you get inside. The door's opened by a maid in a pale-grey uniform, so Celia's clearly the kind of communist who doesn't mind having Staff. She was obviously a great beauty in her day, and still has the manner of a woman who's used to getting her own way simply by giving people dazzling smiles and flirtatious looks. But whereas this usually gets a bit tragic once you're the wrong side of fifty, and still opening your eyes just that little bit too wide and talking in a slightly breathless girly voice when you've got a neck like a turkey, Celia is somehow much grander than this, and doesn't simper at all.

She tells us that parts of *Last Tango in Paris* were shot in the apartment opposite, makes some rather disparaging comments about Marlon Brando and then pours us all a glass of champagne and takes us into a tiny dining room with a view of the river where the maid serves us lunch.

It's all incredibly elegant, with delicious omelettes and green salads with perfect dressing.

'So, Katherine my darling, how's your sex life now you've finally managed to get shot of that ghastly husband of yours?'

'Aunt Celia!'

'You must take a lover, darling, they keep you young. Although how you'll find one buried away in the country I don't really know – English men are so hopeless at that kind of thing. But go for youth, that's my advice. They're so very grateful.'

'I'll bear that it mind.'

'Do, darling, do. I think lovers are so much more useful than husbands, all in all. And far less trouble to get rid of. Don't you, my dear?'

She fixes me with a very beady look.

'I think it probably depends on the husband.'

'How very true.'

Kate smiles.

'Not Uncle Bernard, though. You should have married him, he was lovely.'

'Yes, he was my favourite, I think. But it would have spoilt things. He would have taken me for granted, and that's always fatal. He was very good to me, though. And so rich. Which always helps. I know it's not fashionable, but it's true. You need a certain style, a few little things, just to make life bearable.'

She waves her hand vaguely around the room, which is stuffed with quite a few serious-looking pictures and the sort of china figurines that you can't buy in the Sunday colour supplements. She obviously likes collecting things, but unlike Uncle Monty's collections these all look like they're worth a small fortune.

'But I'll tell you something marvellous, darlings, shall I?

It all seems so important at the time, but actually the only thing that matters is that you have as much fun as possible. Kick up your heels. And your tastes change, you know. It's like champagne. You absolutely adore it when you're young, but as you get older you want something with a bit more staying power, don't you? But of course you're still both champagne girls, aren't you? Quite right too. Let's have coffee in the drawing room, shall we?'

We sip very strong coffee from tiny little cups, and Celia moves on to telling us about the galleries she thinks we should visit, but gradually grows quieter until we realise she seems to have nodded off in her chair.

'God, you don't think she's had a stroke or something, do you?'

Kate looks rather anxious.

'No, she's just asleep. Look, you can see her breathing.'

'Well, thank heavens for that. Let's creep out then, before she wakes up, and I'll leave her a note, or we're going to be late for Sally.'

Kate gives Celia a kiss as we're leaving, but she's fast asleep, and doesn't stir. What a lovely way to spend your afternoons, sleeping off a lovely lunch and reliving your glorious past while someone else does the washing up. Perfect.

We meet up with Sally at the Musée d'Orsay, which is fairly near by, and look at their amazing collection of Impressionists, which seem completely dazzling to me, but that might be the champagne. In fact, going round art galleries when you're slightly tipsy is my new top plan, especially if you're going to be followed by children trudging along behind you telling you how bored they are every twenty seconds.

Charlie's rather taken with a statue of an alligator being

pierced with a spear, but the real success is the café, which has a terrace with a great view of the river. Charlie and James settle down to play with their Gameboys, clearly grateful to be sitting down with a lemonade at last, and desperate to keep a low profile in case they're marched round another museum, and Rosie and Phoebe seem quite happy to wander about outside on the terrace, and vaguely circle around a group of French boys and then come back in to sit down at our table and whisper to each other.

We tell Sally all about how marvellous Celia was, and she says the Louvre was great, apart from the enormous crowds around *The Mona Lisa*.

'Honestly, you could hardly see it. They should come up with some sort of queuing system or something. The kids couldn't see at all – well, not until I pushed them to the front, they couldn't. Anyway, you could spend days there, it's so vast. Actually, I thought we might have to at one point, because Ginny lost Olivia. We found her in the end, in the shop, but Ginny was beside herself by then.'

'I don't blame her. None of ours tried to give you the slip, did they?'

Kate pours Sally some more tea.

'Oh no, I'm used to it from school trips. I threaten to tie them to my handbag if they go out of sight. It always works. No, they were fine. And Charlie said a great thing about *The Mona Lisa*, when we finally got to see it. He said she looks like she's going to tell you a rude joke. Wasn't that clever? She does too.'

'It wasn't just an excuse to tell a joke about willies, was it?'

'No, he just stood there pondering for a bit. It was really sweet.'

Secretly, I'm rather pleased that Charlie has shown a small flash of artistic instinct, but of course I play this down because apart from anything else he's just as likely to have said she looks like she needs to do a wee, which is what he said earlier when we were looking at a portrait of a rather anxious-looking woman in a black dress.

'So your aunt was on top form then, was she? She sounds great.'

'She is rather. I adored her when I was younger, it drove my mother demented, and she always had wonderful clothes, and amazing jewellery. She used to make all her men buy her diamonds, or paintings. She told me once it was her pension plan.'

Sally smiles.

'Well, it's much better than a direct debit to Scottish Widows, that's for sure.'

We wander back to the hotel to laze about before supper, and then go out for steak and chips and drink too much wine and have an early night because we're all knackered. Charlie falls asleep almost instantly, and I lie awake thinking about Celia and how I want to be like her when I'm old, sitting reliving my past glories. Although a flat next to the Eiffel Tower might be pushing it a bit. And there hasn't been an exactly overwhelming amount of glory so far. So I'd better get cracking. Drink more champagne and be braver.

I bet Celia wouldn't wimp out if a gorgeous new vet came on to the horizon. I'm going to be bolder and more brazen. I've always wanted to be brazen. And if I bump into Mack somewhere I'll just say 'Hello, darling' in a nonchalant fashion, give him a blistering kiss and then walk off. Actually, on second thoughts maybe I should build up slowly on the brazen thing.

The next morning we're all on a Bateau Mouche before I've had a chance to work out just how bad my hangover really is, and strangely enough being on a boat bobbing round Paris and trying to stop Charlie being rescued by the river police turns out to be rather a good way to take your mind off a fledgling headache. Everyone is very disappointed not to see the Hunchback of Notre Dame clinging to the steeple, but apart from that the trip's a big success, and then the coach drops us off on Boulevard Haussmann for a nice bit of shopping and an early lunch. How very civilised.

We've got a choice of a trip to the Pompidou Centre or more free time this afternoon, but we reckon the kids are already way past their museum quota so we take them to the Tuileries Gardens while Sally has a bit of child-free shopping time to make up for her one-woman Louvre patrol yesterday.

The weather's still perfect, and it's hot enough to sit in the Gardens on the metal chairs, which unlike their British equivalents turn out to be extremely comfortable with slightly sloping backs and sturdy legs, just perfect for a cuddle when Charlie trips over and drops his ice-cream. There are donkey rides, and an old-fashioned roundabout, and after checking that nobody they recognise is watching them all four of them clamber on for a ride.

But the real treat for Charlie is all the dogs we meet on the walk back to the hotel. For some reason a fairly significant number of Parisians appear to be completely mad about dogs, and Charlie seems to meet and greet most of them, including a particularly snooty-looking man, who turns into charm personified when Charlie makes a tremendous fuss of his enormous sheepdog, who turns out to be called Gugu and is very keen on licking people's faces. The man practically gives us his phone number in case we're ever in Paris again and want to take a sheepdog for a walk.

After an early supper and lots of frantic packing, the journey home turns into a nightmare of epic proportions, because everyone's tired and Mrs Palmer manages to leave her passport in the hotel safe, so we have to go back for it. And then Tommy Williams is sick, just as we enter the Tunnel. The children amuse themselves by playing their new game of asking questions, and then answering in French by saying 'Oh Wee', and then falling about laughing, and by the time we're home and I'm putting Charlie to bed we're both so exhausted we can hardly stand up. But he's still got enough energy for a little chat.

'You know I'm going out with Emily now. Well, it's great. And James is going out with Georgia. And Emily gave me a bit of her Twix in the museum and she kicked Jack Knight for me.'

God. One minute he was tiny like Ava, and suddenly he's got a girlfriend who kicks people in museums. I'm not sure I'm ready for this.

'Well, that wasn't very nice.'

'Yes it was.'

'So what does it mean then, if you're going out with someone?'

He gives me one of his why-are-you-such-an-idiot looks.

'You play with them at playtime, sometimes. And stuff like that. We don't do kissing. You don't have to do kissing.'

'Oh, right.'

Thank god for that.

'When I get my hormones I might do. But not now. And then when you don't want to go out with them any more you just say "You're Chucked".'

'Right.'

Well, that sounds nice and simple. And at least it doesn't involve saying you need some space.

'I love Paris, Mummy.'

'Do you, darling?'

Maybe he really is developing an artistic nature after all. How lovely.

'Yes. We should go again. I liked the chips. And all the dogs.'

V

Welcome to Cricklewood

I DON'T KNOW WHO came up with the brilliant idea at the local Education Authority of touring round schools telling children that it's vital they take more exercise or they'll become completely spherical and be unable to wear normal trousers, but if I ever find out their name I'm going straight round to poke them in the eye. Instead of concentrating on telling everyone to lay off the Penguins and eat more fruit, the main focus of the Healthy Assembly last week seems to have been brainwashing them about the evils of using cars to get to school. Apparently, good mothers should be cycling or walking to school, no doubt in pristine tracksuits and trainers with just a touch of lipstick and a light foundation because there's no need to let standards slip. Bastards.

Charlie's been desperate all weekend for us to cycle to school, no doubt whistling a merry tune and ringing our bells in chorus, so I've been praying for rain on Monday, but it's a lovely sunny morning with not a cloud in the sky, and even though he's still in his pyjamas Charlie's already got his cycling hat on and is out annoying the rabbits. I'm assessing my trousers for maximum comfort while perching on saddles, and minimum flappage potential round the ankles so I don't find half my trouser leg disappearing into my bike chain at some point during the journey.

To be completely honest I'm not what anyone would call a natural cyclist. I hate the hats, for a start; I was talking to Leila about it last night and we reckon that it's pretty much a golden rule that if something requires a Special Padded Hat you probably shouldn't be doing it in the first place. It's completely obvious when you think about it: horse riding, mountaineering, hang gliding. Special hat. Special kind of person. And apart from the hat issue I've never really mastered the gears on my bike, which is silver with a wicker basket. It's a sort of racing shopper, and by the time I've changed up a gear it's usually time to change down again.

'Come on, Mummy, hurry up. Do you think we'll see a pheasant in the woods? I bet we will. They won't hear us on our bikes, will they? Not like in a horrible car.'

Actually, the sound of him ringing his Dennis the Menace bell and me puffing along behind him is pretty much guaranteed to alert any wildlife for miles, I'd have thought, but knowing my luck we'll be deluged with pheasants lining up along the verge laughing.

'Maybe, but you'll have to get dressed first, Charlie.'

He races off upstairs while I finish his packed lunch. And there's been an annoying development here too, because instead of the usual campaigning for sausages both he and James have now moved on to demanding sushi, ever since one of the Year Six boys brought some in with a mini bottle of soy sauce last week. I've tried suggesting a tuna roll, but this was met with a very cool response, so now I'm reduced to making speeches about how when I was young we were happy with a Dairylea triangle and a custard cream so could he please just eat what he's given and be Grateful. And whilst this approach has its merits, it's also slightly too close to the Victorian Workhouse School of Parenting to be entirely successful with Charlie. But if I ever find out the name of the mother who sent her child in with sushi I'm going to poke her in the eye too. Maybe with chopsticks.

We leave for school twenty minutes earlier than normal to allow time for someone to cycle into a bush and still not be late for registration. Charlie sets off at a cracking pace, swerving slightly every time he rings his bell but generally keeping to our side of the road. I'm riding alongside him to stop him veering wildly whenever he spots anything interesting, and it's all going rather well until we get to the road that passes through the woods. Suddenly he yells 'Pheasant', and performs a very impressive emergency stop, hurls his bike on to the grass verge and disappears into the hedgerow while I sail past him and then have to cycle back and stand peering into the undergrowth like a nutter, issuing a series of increasingly dire ultimatums.

I can hear him crashing through the bracken, and somewhere in the distance there's also the unmistakable sound of a pheasant doing that croaky clicking thing they do. Monty says they're marking out their territory and impressing the girls, but it seems a pretty stupid sort of noise, if you ask me – you'd think they'd go for something a bit more low-profile so that foxes and people with shotguns couldn't track them down quite so easily. But I suppose if you've got a bright-red head with neon-blue flashes there's not much point in trying to keep a low profile.

'Charlie, if you don't come back right now, we're never cycling to school again. Ever.'

He completely ignores me. People are driving past on their way to school giving us little toots and waving. How very bloody annoying.

'Charlie. I'm going to count to three. And if you're not back by three then there'll be no cartoons tonight. And no nice tea. And I was going to make sausage and mash. One . . .'

I leave a longish gap.

'Two . . .'

He thunders out of the bracken.

'I saw one, I did, and I nearly got him.'

Bits of fern and leaves are clinging to his sweatshirt, and he's got a twig sticking out of his cycle helmet.

'And what would you have done if you had got him? He'd have been really frightened.'

'I would just have talked to him. Honestly, Mummy. You can't keep wild creatures, you know. It's very cruel and they don't like it.'

He gives me a pitying look while I de-twig him.

'Yes, I did know that, Charlie, thank you. And they don't like being chased through woods first thing in the morning either.'

'Oh yes they do. They love it. They know I'm a pagan. We're kindled spirits.'

'It's kindred spirits, Charlie, and you're not. Not if you chase them. Now come on, get back on your bike or we'll be late.'

Arriving at school turns out to be an obstacle course of people parking, car doors opening and assorted Mixed Infants milling about in an entirely random manner which means one of them is bound to get tangled up in your wheel spokes sooner or later. I make Charlie get off and walk, propping my bike up against the fence while I help him wheel his towards the bike shed, much to his annoyance because I think he quite liked the idea of cycling across the playground and mowing down half of Reception.

'You're not allowed to ride your bike in the playground, Charlie, you know that.'

'Yes you are. When they put the cones out you are. Mrs Taylor said.'

'Yes, but not when everybody's lining up.'

A couple of big boys whizz past us, and screech to a halt at the bike shed, and Charlie gives me one of his martyred looks.

'See?'

But Mrs Taylor has spotted them, and comes over in Harassed Headteacher mode. Hurrah.

'Gary Wilkes, I've told you before, you must get off your bicycle and walk – that's very dangerous. And I'm surprised at you, Oliver. You're normally such a sensible boy.'

There's a chorus of muted 'Yes, Mrs Taylor's, and I can't resist giving Charlie an I-told-you-so look, which he ignores completely.

'Hello, Mrs Taylor. I've come on my bike, look, I've got a bell.'

He rings it. Twice.

'And I saw a pheasant, and I went over and talked to it, I did. Really. It was fabless.'

Mrs Taylor smiles.

'How lovely, Charlie. Well, that was a lovely start to the day, wasn't it? Maybe you can write about it in your news diary.'

Never one to miss a learning opportunity is our Mrs Taylor. Charlie gives her a thoughtful look.

'I might. Or I might do a picture. Shall I do you a picture and bring it to you in your office? You could put it on your wall. To cheer you up when people are being Silly.'

He gives her one of his best smiles.

'Well, that would be lovely too, Charlie.'

She drifts off towards Travis, who's sitting down in the corner of the playground and making a start on a family-sized bag of smoky-bacon crisps. I really don't fancy her chances if she's going to try to wrestle them off him.

We're still trying to get Charlie's bike to stay upright on the stand when one of the Fit Families arrives; they cycle along most mornings wearing matching helmets and fluor-escent armbands, and even do hand signals in unison in a rather smug kind of way. The dad's in the Territorial Army and fiercely competitive, and he wears special running shoes for the fathers' race on Sports Day.

He gives me a condescending look and makes some comment about how it's good to see people not using their cars for a change. I've noticed this before, it's one of the main drawbacks of Fit People: they all seem to think that being able to run up six flights of stairs without requiring oxygen transforms them into some sort of superior being, instead of just someone who wears much smaller shorts than the rest of us.

I smile and say isn't it a lovely morning, but apparently he's not finished.

'It's quite a good way to keep fit, cycling. I try to do at least five miles a day. Find it keeps me in trim quite nicely.'

He pats his non-existent stomach and starts jogging on the spot, doing leg stretches as if he were an Olympic athlete warming up for the final.

'You might want to start off with something a bit more gentle than five miles, though. If you're trying to tone up, that is.'

He gives me another superior look. Bloody cheek. If I need tips on personal fitness, and god knows I probably do, I certainly don't want them from a man wearing a bright-orange cycling hat.

'Oh no, nothing so laudable, I'm afraid. No, I just realised that if I bike to school I can go home and eat a whole packet of Hobnobs and not be any worse off than when I started. It's brilliant. I bet that's why so many people are taking up cycling.'

And I walk off, leaving him standing with his mouth slightly open, towards Kate, who's just arrived on her bike too and looks completely knackered, but perks up when I tell her my line about the Hobnobs.

'That's just what I need, a quiet half-hour with biscuits; we're bloody driving to school tomorrow, I can tell you. It's been like a Wacky Races cartoon with James dawdling along and Phoebe racing ahead.'

'Maybe you should get them a tandem.'

'I don't think they build one strong enough to hold the two of them when they're bickering. They'd probably snap it. Your place or mine for coffee?'

'Mine's nearer.'

'You're on. I'll race you if you've definitely got biscuits.'

'Oh no you bloody won't.'

By the time Kate and I get home I've gone past the puffing stage and I'm on to the rasping gasp. When I get off my bike my legs have gone all wobbly and I practically collapse into the flowerbed by the garage. I've barely got the energy to get my shoes off. Oh dear. Maybe I should be trying to get a teeny bit fitter after all. And I've got to do it all again this afternoon when it's home time. Bugger.

* * *

By Wednesday the weather has turned and you'd need a snorkel to cycle to school, so we're back in the car again, thank god, but pretty much everything else is going from bad to worse. The job in the bus garage starts next week and I'm frantic with phone calls and budget bickerings with Lawrence, and when I finally get up the nerve for a trip to the vet's in the hope of meeting Gabriel I get stuck wrestling with the rabbits for nearly an hour while Mr Willett does the nail-clipping routine, because Gabriel's out on a call somewhere.

But at least the village grapevine has yielded a few nuggets of information: apparently Gabriel trained in Yorkshire in a James Herriot-type fashion, and some woman broke his heart up there so he's come down here for a new start. Kate overheard Mrs Harrison-Black telling Mrs Jenkins; she's got such a booming voice you practically have no choice but to eavesdrop. And he's very Shy and reads the *Independent*, according to Sally who saw him in the village shop. So at least I know he's single and literate, if elusive. It's a start, I suppose. Although I'm definitely going to have to reconsider using the rabbits as decoys, because it's amazing how strong one small black rabbit can be when he doesn't want his toenails done.

I'm in the middle of another round of work calls when Leila rings.

'Guess what? You know Mack's agency was buying Prentice Palmer?'

'Yes.'

'Well, they're not. They've just bought Chalfont Standish.'

'Blimey, they're huge.'

'I know, and he handled it really cleverly too, because everyone thought it was Prentice Palmer they were after.

Even Prentice Palmer. Anyway, he's back over here for a while, according to Tanya. She's an account director there now and she says he's putting the fear of god into them all. So you'd better be prepared.'

'What for?'

'Hello? Your big bus job. For DriveLine. And the name of the agency is is?'

'Oh. Fuck. Chalfont Standish.'

'Exactly. Come in, number twenty-seven. Your time is up. And the DriveLine account's a huge one for them, so he's bound to want to do the big-boss thing and turn up for the shoot at some point, don't you think?'

'Christ.'

'Well, at least you know, so you can be prepared. Wear something smart and then you'll be able to completely ignore him, but in a stylish way. That's always nice. And wear the leather jacket, please. Not that disgusting orange anorak.'

Leila has 'lent' me a beautiful black leather jacket that she bought at vast expense and then had to jettison because she saw another one she liked even more.

'Yes, but, Leila, it doesn't do up, I told you. You're at least two sizes smaller than me and you know it.'

'Darling, it's not meant to do up. I've told you until I'm sick of it, Stop Doing Things Up. And wear a decent white shirt or something.'

I think I'd better change the subject sharpish or she'll be into one of her fashion-police rants in a minute and start lecturing me about shoes.

'How's Tor?'

'Fabulous, thanks. I'm really liking having him around. Actually, shall I bring him down so you can give him the once-over? Sunday lunch or something?'

'Yes, or you could bring him to Charlie's birthday party, if you like.'

'Perfect. We can bring my surprise present. You did say Great Dane, didn't you?'

'Very amusing, I'm sure.'

'And will we be getting a glimpse of the new vet?'

'Shouldn't think so. He's very shy, apparently.'

'Oh shy isn't a problem. Just get him drunk, that always works. It's amazing how the quiet types can shock the life out of you after a couple of vodka Martinis. Remember that man in accounts at the DPP Christmas party?'

'Pete?'

'He was brilliant when he got going.'

'Yes, but stopping him turned out to be a bit of a problem. Didn't he turn up at your office?'

'Oh yes, I'd forgotten that. I had to get security to sort him out in the end. But that doesn't mean your vet will turn out to be a stalker.'

'He's not my vet – I've only spoken to him for about ten seconds. And anyway, he'll probably turn out to be busy stalking someone else. Or have a wife and secret twins somewhere.'

'Well, don't give up yet, darling, because having a vet on standby's going to be really useful when I give Charlie the puppy, isn't it? Shall I wrap it, do you think, in a big basket or something?'

'A basket would be perfect, but make sure it's a big one. Because Tor's going to have to carry you home in it if you turn up with anything remotely canine.'

I'm just settling down with a nice cup of tea and a modest pile of digestives and trying to work out if I can risk sounding out Lawrence to see if he's heard anything about Mack turning up on the shoot when Monty calls.

He's got a special voice for the telephone. And it's very Loud.

'LOVELY BIT OF FISH, THAT WAS.'

'I'm glad you liked it, Monty.'

We took him a fish pie on Sunday. He's taken to ringing up at some point during the week to tell me how nice the food was, which is very sweet, obviously, but does tend to leave you slightly deaf in one ear. I'm holding the phone at arm's length and then moving it back when I need to speak.

'SO HOW'S CHARLIE BOY, THEN?'

Monty and Charlie have taken a real shine to each other over the past few months. They disappear off for walks in the fields while Charlie explains the finer points of *The Lord of the Rings* to Monty, and Monty gives him wildlife snippets.

'He's fine, Monty, looking forward to seeing you on Sunday. And are you still sure you're all right about the birthday party? Really? Because it's fine if you've changed your mind, you know.'

'NO. LOOKING FORWARD TO IT.'

Monty's said we can have Charlie and James's joint birthday party at the farm this year; last year's extravaganza was a joint swimming party at the local pool where they did the tea and all the clearing up. But this year they want a *Lord of the Rings* fancy dress, with a barbecue, thank you very much. When we found out that the village hall was booked solid it was looking very much like we'd have to have it at our house, because Kate's garden's even smaller than mine, and I was seriously wondering if the GP would give me some Valium for the Big Day when Monty stepped into the breach. He says we can use the barn if the weather's bad, and he seems quite excited about it. Which is typical of Monty: just when you think he's some barking old nutter he comes up with something really kind and thoughtful and you remember how nice he is.

And the really brilliant bit, the bit that's going to send

Charlie into orbit for weeks, is Monty's plan for Charlie's birthday present. He's going to get him a pheasant. Well, two, to be exact, poults or whatever they're called. His friend Curly Jago breeds them and Monty says he'll sort out a pen for them, and they only need a bit of seed and he'll feed them during the week if we're too busy to get over to the farm. Actually, I've got a feeling that's why he's so keen on the idea. I think he gets pretty lonely, and us popping over to see the pheasants during the week will be a nice change for him. Which is fine by me, because I've got enough trouble looking after Charlie and the rabbits without adding two pheasants to the mix. God knows whether pheasants get surging hormones like rabbits and start plucking each other or something, but at least it won't be me who has to work out what to do if we end up with two bald pheasants.

The first day of the Cricklewood shoot goes fairly well, mainly because we spend most of the time setting up. The really tricky stuff with the buses is down for tomorrow. Barney's getting very nervous and we're all keeping a low profile in case he makes us lie in front of a double-decker so he can work out the shots he wants.

The job's for car insurance: Sometimes the Unexpected Happens. It's Good to Know People Who Understand. We've got a woman driving along in her car singing when she realises her brakes have failed, at which point, for some reason that's still not entirely clear to me, she veers round a corner and ends up driving straight into a bus garage. Luckily her superior driving skills are revealed in all their glory as she plays dodgems with an assortment of buses and passengers, and manages to avoid them all, but only just, and she brings the car to a stop a few milli-

164

metres from a pile of old planks and paint pots piled up against a brick wall. She gets out smiling, and as she's walking away from the car some complicated chain reaction amongst the planks tips a pot of white paint all over her car bonnet.

So nothing tricky there at all really. Jesus Christ. I told Barney not to do this job. Someone's bound to get run over or covered in white paint, and I just hope it's not going to be me.

The stunt drivers are all as mad as buckets, especially the two ex-SAS types, who spend their time talking in Alpha Zero Bravo code bollocks and pretty much live on another planet to the rest of us. They amuse themselves by doing handbrake turns in the car park, and spend most of the day moaning about the coffee and not getting a proper cooked breakfast, because apparently bacon sandwiches don't really count as far as they're concerned. But nobody's brave enough to tell them to shut up, because we've all got the sneaking suspicion that they know how to do that thing where they creep up behind you and kill you by pressing a secret bone in the back of your neck. The crew give them both a very wide berth, and spend their time muttering about how this is never going to work, in between laying track and whining about how nobody told them they'd have buses winging all over the place.

And just to finish off a perfect day my car decides to conk out on the way home. One minute everything's fine and the next minute there's an appalling grinding noise like I'm dragging a large metallic object behind the car, which it turns out I am. And it's the exhaust. Excellent.

After an interminable wait for the AA, where because I'm so hungry I'm reduced to eating a whole packet of those extra-strong mints that make your eyes water, the AA man finally arrives and it turns out that despite having signed up for the intergalactic-home-start-gold-star-pick-your-dry-cleaning-up-on-the-way-home membership option, this doesn't actually include spot welding people's exhausts back on to their cars, however fresh their breath might be. No. Apparently I will be towed home. And there's no need to call out a special truck since I'm only a few miles from home: he'll just tow me along on the back of the van.

So while he's busy clanking things I sit in my car having a mini-meltdown about what happens if you brake suddenly whilst being towed. Maybe to avoid a squirrel or one of Charlie's flaming badgers or something. What if I've suddenly developed Stunt Driving by Proxy or something? We'll end up in a ditch, that's what.

I manage to calm myself down by the time it actually comes to doing the steering thing, but to be frank I was expecting something a bit more high-tech for my enormous annual membership fee than being attached to the back of a van with a bit of rope and hurtled round country lanes by the fastest AA driver in Kent. Actually, I think he's probably some sort of weekend rally driver in his spare time. Or maybe he thinks being part of the Fourth Emergency Service means calling out the other three at the earliest opportunity to compare fluorescent jackets while they dig you out of a hedge.

By the time I get home it's nearly ten, and after booking a cab for the morning with our company firm, who practically require an Ordnance Survey Grid Reference before they'll take the booking, I get into a hot bath with a large gin and a packet of Maryland cookies. Perfect. Although waking up nearly an hour later in a bath full of tepid water and soggy biscuits isn't quite so fabulous. For a minute I thought I was having my Titanic dream again.

* * *

The next morning's not much better, and by the time I make it to Cricklewood I practically need sedating. The cab driver turned up late muttering about country lanes and no signposts so I had to give him directions in between fielding calls from Barney, and simultaneously haranguing the service manager at the local Peugeot garage, whose initial reaction to the exhaust dropping off my car two weeks after they'd serviced it is to mutter something about motor mechanics not being psychic, which, as I point out, is not exactly helpful. But he finally ends up agreeing to send someone out free of charge to pick up the car as a special favour to a long-standing customer, as long as I pay for a new exhaust, because they take customer relations very seriously, especially with the kind of customers who are not going to shut up and get off the phone and give a man a bit of peace, thank you very much. Madam. You always know you've got them on the run when they call you madam.

After a bit of undercover work with Lawrence yesterday it turned out that yes, there has been some mention of Mack MacDonald popping along to the shoot at some point, but Lawrence didn't find out any details or mention this to me, because he didn't think I'd be interested. Which, as Stef says, is Just Typical really. So I put my best white shirt on this morning, just in case, and then managed to dollop raspberry jam all down the front while I was eating toast. Dabbing away with a damp cloth only produced a huge damp circle and a wet bra, which reminded me of the early days of breast-feeding, which wasn't entirely the look I was aiming for, so now I'm in my second-best shirt, which is too tight, and my second-best bra, ditto. But at least I've got Leila's leather jacket, which is great, although it is a bit shorter than I remembered and perfectly highlights just how little attention I've been paying to those

167

magazine articles on how to firm your bottom up. Oh well. He probably won't even turn up. And even if he does it doesn't really matter. But I bet bloody Vanessa never dollops jam all over her shirts.

Barney's in a foul mood when I arrive, which is always a sign that he's not exactly sure how he's going to pull this one off. The stunt drivers are all standing around drinking coffee again and talking about the most terrifying stunts they've ever done, and what things went wrong and how many ambulances were required, which doesn't exactly fill you with confidence.

The crew are busy setting up for the first shot while Barney talks to Claire, the woman stunt driver, who like most women who've made it in a male-dominated world is completely brilliant and really knows her stuff, but is quiet and charming with it, except when she's talking about work when she goes all steely and determined. When Barney suggests one of his little changes on the spur of the moment she just gives him a firm look and says no, that won't work. Which he accepts without a murmur.

I must try it sometime. I wonder if she'd show me how she does it. Or give me a few stunt-driver parking tips for Sainsbury's car park. And I bet she'd have given that AA man a run for his money last night. She'd have done something clever where she ended up towing him, if only for a moment. That would have wiped the smirk off his face.

Things are going surprisingly well, given how many buses we've got screeching around in circles, and we break for lunch without requiring an air ambulance or armed assistance to sort out the Alpha Zero Bravo boys, so our luck seems to be holding. The crew have all been watching *Welcome to Collingwood* on DVD in between takes and keep replaying the bit where one of the characters gets flattened by a bus, which they seem to find very amusing, and then they spend most of the afternoon talking about Bellinis and Mollinskis, and repeating their favourite bits of dialogue. Two of George Clooney's best lines appear to have been 'You're a total idiot' and 'As a film it's a total disaster' and they come in really handy all afternoon. And they're predicting that the end of the job's going to be just like the ending of the film: where everyone is left standing in the street waiting for a bus with tufts of their hair singed off and their clothing in shreds, with one of them wearing a pink dressing gown. I'm not sure who they've got in mind for the dressing gown, but I'm really hoping it's not going to be me.

Things go slightly pear-shaped after lunch when one of the stunt drivers manages to hit a concrete pillar with his bus, but with fairly minimal damage, thank god, apart from a hideous scratch and a few small dents, and he's one of the SAS ones so nobody risks telling him what a prat he is. The man from the bus company is pretty irate, but soon calms down when I offer to give him cash for the repairs if he could just shut up and let us get on, and we've pretty much got what we need by the time we're breaking for tea.

I'm standing by the catering truck when a large black Mafia-type Mercedes arrives and a chauffeur leaps out and tries to get to the back of the car to open the door, but it's already opening, and sure enough Mack gets out and starts walking towards me. Right. Here goes. Ignore, ignore. Be cool and calm. He's looking very smart in a dark-grey suit, sort of like Tom Cruise but taller. Bugger.

'Hello, Annie.'

'Hello, Mack. Oh and congratulations, by the way.'

My voice has gone slightly squeaky. Great.

'What for?'

He looks rather panicky. Christ, maybe he and Vanessa are getting married or something.

'For the Chalfont Standish thing.'

'Oh, right. Well, more luck than skill, I promise you. Look, I hope me turning up like this is OK. Lawrence said it would be fine but I know what a complete wanker he is. I tried to ring you. Have you changed your mobile?'

'Yes. The old one got dropped in a river.'

'Charlie?'

'Yup.'

He smiles.

'How is he?'

'Fine. And Daisy and Alfie?'

God, I can't believe we're standing here talking about our kids, like we're old friends and we've just bumped into each other in the street. And I don't buy all that trollocks about my mobile, because my home number's still the same, so he could have easily rung if he'd wanted to.

'They're fine too. They're in the back of that ridiculous car, actually.'

He waves an arm in the direction of the Merc.

'Laura's got some homeopathy crisis on so I said I'd pick them up tonight. Is it OK if I get them a drink or something?'

'Sure.'

Laura's Mack's ex-wife. They were already divorced before I met him, and they seem to have sorted things out fairly amicably. He's off being a master of the universe and she's busy saving the world with bits of belladonna. But she doesn't usually dump the kids on him at short notice, and definitely not on a school night. I suddenly have a flash of inspiration and realise that maybe he's feeling slightly nervous about seeing me again and the kids are some kind of security blanket. It was only a few months ago he was asking me to go to New York with him, after all, and somehow I don't think he's very used to being turned down. How very bloody gratifying; if he has brought them as a kind of diversionary tactic then at least it's not just me who's still feeling rather wobbly about it all. But then again, maybe Laura really did have some sort of crisis, or maybe she's just pissed off with him for buggering off to New York.

There's a weird beeping noise from the pocket of his suit and he retrieves one of the *über*-mobiles. I think it might be a raspberry, or a blackberry, or whatever the new trendy ones are called.

'Fucking thing. It's got some alarm programme that keeps telling me I'm late for a meeting.'

'And are you?'

'No. But I don't know how to switch it off, and somehow I never seem to be able to find a spare day or two to read the bloody manual.'

'Can't you just turn the phone off?'

'The office sends up distress flares if I'm out of radio contact. I think they'd wire it into my pulse if they could.'

'Maybe you should just drop it into a river.'

'Actually, that's not a bad idea. Charlie's not around anywhere, is he?'

He's smiling, his special crinkly-flirty smile. Damn.

'Do you want to come and say hello to Barney?'

'Please.'

We walk over to Barney, who's deep in conversation with the lighting man, and gives Mack one of his who-the-fuck-are-you looks.

'Hi, Mick. Come to see how your money's being spent, have you?'

'Something like that, Benny. Going well, is it?'

Barney smiles. He likes people who fight back.

171

'So far, so good, but next time could you get your creatives to go for something a bit more manoeuvrable than double-deckers, by any chance?. They're a complete fucking nightmare.'

'I'll have a word. Actually, there's another job I wanted to talk to you about while I'm here. No buses, but it's an idea we've been working on this morning, with a windmill. Be right up your street, I'd have thought. Needs a genius touch. But it could be great. Anyway, what changes have you made on this one then? Only I'm thinking you've probably improved things here and there. Am I right?'

Barney's rather swayed by this, and starts telling him how he's turned a very mediocre script into something that might just be worth watching if we don't lose any more buses in reversing incidents. We walk over to the monitor, where the rest of the agency are busy in a huddle, and Mack immediately gets surrounded by eager young members of his team all keen to impress the boss. He looks slightly hopelessly towards the car.

'Do you want me to get the kids out and give them a drink?'

'Oh please. Would you? Thanks, Annie.'

Damn. I don't know why I said that.

'I've promised them Pizza Express later, but they're probably starving.'

He turns back to the monitor.

How very bloody annoying. I'm a very busy professional-type person, with a hundred things I should be doing right now, but somehow I've ended up playing Mary Poppins to his flaming kids. Well, a spoonful of sugar it is then.

Alfie seems particularly pleased to see me when I open the car door, and is busy telling me all about his new school and what he did in PE today, which basically seems to have involved wall bars and a sticky moment with a rope, but Daisy's not quite so effusive. We all went on holiday to Cornwall together last summer, and she wasn't terribly keen on me then either, and kept sharing useful bits of information like how much bigger my bottom was than Laura's. Alfie's a year younger than Charlie and perfectly happy as long as you feed him regularly, but Daisy's much more complicated. The only really successful moment I had with her was when I lent her some nail varnish.

I bring them over to one of the tables outside the catering truck and get them Cokes and a doughnut each, and even Daisy manages a small smile, and then we invent a competition to see who can do the best drawing of a bus. They both start scribbling away with the two pens I find at the bottom of my bag, and Daisy goes back to the car to get her pencils from her school bag, and they sit happily colouring in and eating a second doughnut, while I try to work out what the prize should be for the best bus. I know. More doughnuts. It's not going to be my problem if they're both on massive sugar highs when Mack's trying to get them to sit nicely in Pizza Express.

Mack gives me a very grateful look when he glances over, but doesn't notice Alfie practically inhaling his doughnut. I really don't fancy the chances of anyone who's going to be stuck in the back of a car with him in the next half-hour. I sit drinking tea and pondering why it is that when a woman brings her kids to work she looks badly organised, but when a man does it it's somehow rather endearing, when Mack wanders over and says it's time they were off.

'Say goodbye to Annie, and thank you for your drinks.'

'Oh, aren't you coming for pizza, Annie? We're having ice-cream. Daddy said we could.'

I've obviously earned Alfie's undying devotion for being so generous on the doughnut front.

'No thank you, sweetheart. It's very kind of you but I've got to work.'

Mack looks slightly uncomfortable.

'Yes, well, come on, you two. You've taken up enough of Annie's time as it is.'

Daisy comes over and gives me a hug. Crikey. Those doughnuts must have really gone down well. Actually, I've just remembered, Laura's pretty fierce about that kind of thing. Rice cakes and banana chips are more her style. Oh dear.

'Tell Barney I'll get that windmill script biked over to him tomorrow.'

Windmill? Bloody hell. I thought he was joking.

'OK.'

'And thanks again, Annie, for looking after these two for me.'

'No problem.'

'You're looking fabulous, by the way. Love that shirt.'

I look down, and see that I've got far fewer buttons done up than when I left home this morning. Oh bugger.

Mack grins and does his crinkly-flirty look again. Double bugger.

It's all bloody Leila's fault. I'd never have had this trouble in a nice comfy T-shirt. He'll think I did it on purpose. Not that it matters. At all. Not in the least. But still.

'Come on, you two, back to the car.'

The Merc glides away with the kids waving out of the window, and Barney comes over to start running through what he wants to do next.

'All right, are you?'

'Sorry?'

'About Mr MacDonald and his flying visit.'

174

'Oh yes, fine. No problem.'

'You've gone a bit red.'

Oh excellent. Not only have I been marching round flashing my second-best bra to all and sundry, but now I'm bright red as well.

'Well, my shirt sort of came undone, while I was saying goodbye to the kids.'

'Subtle.'

'I didn't do it on purpose, Barney.'

'It's been like that most of the day, actually, sweetheart. I thought you were just trying out a new look.'

'What, the slut-producer look?'

Barney laughs.

'Sweetheart, it was nowhere near slut. You're just not the type.'

'Well, good. I think. Now shall we get on, or we won't be finished until after midnight and that'll screw my budget completely. And you know how upset Lawrence gets.'

'Like I care.'

We finally call it a day around nine, and in the cab home I call Leila for a debrief on my mobile.

'Sounds like Vanessa might be on her way out, to me. And he might be up for round two with you.'

'And how do you make that one out then?'

'Look, darling, he'd have just cut you dead if he wasn't bothered. Men like him do that, they just look right through you. Once they've gone on to pastures new you become invisible.'

'Oh. How very charming.'

'And it doesn't sound like you were very invisible to me.'

'No. I'd rather not think about it, actually. Bloody shirt.'

'That's not necessarily a bad thing.'

'Not if you're wearing a satin Wonderbra and you're out on the pull. But I was trying to be cool and professional.'

Leila's sniggering now.

'I think you might have blown that one slightly.'

'I bet Vanessa's shirts never come undone.'

'Not for less than twenty grand, anyway.'

'Alfie's really grown, though.'

'What else did Mack say?'

'Nothing. I told you. He just said goodbye and that was that.'

'Well, we'll see, shall we? Fifty quid and a bottle of something nice if he rings you.'

'You're on.'

He won't ring, I know he won't. It's not his style. And even if he did there'd be no point. I haven't changed my mind: I still don't want to live in New York, and play happy helper to his corporate wizard. But at least now we've broken the ice it won't be so tricky if I do run into him in town somewhere. And that's fine. It's just a shame he had to be looking so fabulous, that's all. But that's probably down to Vanessa. She probably whisked him into Armani after their first date. Or maybe she hired one of those stylist people who come round and throw all your jumpers away, although I can't see Mack putting up with that. No, she probably handled it personally, and got a discount because she's in the business.

Anyway, it was nice seeing the kids again. I bet that's one area where Vanessa isn't taking such a hands-on approach. Somehow I just don't see her being very happy with sticky fingers and long stories about ropes and wall bars.

* * *

Edna's full of Charlie's latest adventures when I get home. She cycled to school with him today; she goes everywhere on her bike because her son Peter tends to borrow her car, selfish bastard that he is. She's always baling him out with money, and dealing with people who turn up on her doorstep and try to take her telly away as payment for some loan he's taken out.

'And he pedals along really nicely, doesn't he? Bless him.'

'Yes, unless he sees a pheasant.'

'We stopped on the way home and he had a look for a badger.'

'Oh.'

'Didn't find one, though. Good job too, nasty dirty things.'

I can just see Edna bringing a badger home in the basket of her bike for a good wash and brush-up. It wouldn't stand a chance.

'And he's so excited about his party, isn't he? He was telling me all about it. Now don't forget, just you let me know if you want me to make anything. Because it's no trouble, cakes or anything. I'm more than happy to help, you know that.'

She pedals off into the night, and I realise that I'm more tired than I thought when I find myself putting my car keys in the freezer. Maybe a nice cup of tea would be a good idea. And Edna's made me a sandwich, like she always does, bless her. She's done all the ironing again, even though I've told her she doesn't have to. I'd hidden it behind the Hoover in the cupboard under the stairs, but she's obviously tracked it down because there's a pile of neatly folded T-shirts on the top of Charlie's chest of drawers when I go in to check on him.

He's asleep, with the duvet on the floor, and one leg hanging over the edge of his bed. I risk covering him up, and tiptoe out, and as I'm closing the door he kicks the duvet off again, but doesn't wake up, thank god, because however much you love them when they're awake, you always love them just that tiny bit more when they're fast asleep.

Christ, I've just remembered. I'm supposed to be making a birthday cake for Charlie and James, in the shape of Stonehenge. Kate's doing jelly and fairy cakes, and sausage rolls, and I said I'd do the cake. It seemed like quite a good idea at the time, although god knows how I'm going to make grey icing. Damn.

I sit by the fire drinking tea and eating my sandwich and end up thinking about Mack, and how nice it was seeing him again. And then I make a huge mistake and listen to the Frank Sinatra CD he bought me, and get very tragic over 'When Somebody Loves You'. Actually, I think maybe the crew were right. And the person in the pink dressing gown feeling a bit frayed around the edges is going to be me after all.

If I ever win millions on the lottery I won't be splashing out on extra houses with swimming pools or fast cars, I'll be having a housekeeper, thank you very much. And then when I wake up on a Saturday morning to find that the fridge is empty it won't be down to me to trudge round Sainsbury's trying to summon up the enthusiasm to plan another endless round of meals and packed lunches; I'll sit reading the papers and having my nails done by someone in a pastel overall, and at some point the housekeeper will appear and we'll discuss the menus for the day.

I've almost convinced myself that I'm actually living in this parallel universe, and I'm beginning to wonder where the imaginary housekeeper has got to and whether I should risk a mild rebuke for her being late, when I'm painfully wrenched out of my twilight zone by Charlie marching into the kitchen brandishing a plastic dagger ready for our Sainsbury's marathon. Oh dear. He watched his *The Lord of the Rings* video with Edna last night, and he's in full Frodo mode again and wearing his brown cloak.

'I can't find Sting.'

Sadly he means his sword, not the Tantric Former Rock Star.

'It's on the sofa, Charlie, and you can't wear your cloak to go shopping.'

'Yes I can. Frodo wears his all the time, and he must have gone shopping sometimes.'

'Yes, but not to Sainsbury's.'

He's got a very determined look on his face, and I'd really like to avoid a drama before we even get in the car, but it's also pretty vital that Sting remains on the sofa unless I want to be repeatedly jabbed in the bottom in dairy produce. Maybe it won't be that bad having a Frodo trotting round pushing the trolley.

'All right, but not your sword.'

An uneasy compromise is reached and he wears the gold ring that Mum found for him in the Oxfam shop, which is actually brass and makes his finger go green after more than half an hour, but never mind. He's sitting in the front seat of the car muttering 'My precious, my precious' as we drive off. Christ. I hope he's not going to take all his clothes off and start writhing about being Gollum.

'So what's James going to be at the party? Has he decided?'

'Gandalf. Or Sauron. He's the Evil Lord of the Orcs. And he's got a big sword. But Gandalf's got a stick. And Georgia's going to be Galadriel – she's the Elven Queen of the Forest.'

'Has she got a sword?'

179

I'm thinking the fewer pointy objects the better, to be honest.

'No, but she can do magic. You could have been Galadriel, Mummy, if you were going to dress up.'

He gives me a sideways glance because the birthday boys still aren't happy that Kate and I won't be dressing up. We only managed to negotiate a last-minute reprieve when Kate threatened to come as one of the queens in a silver see-through nightie.

Sainsbury's is even more hideous than usual. I try to avoid Saturdays and now I've remembered why. There are far more kids here than usual, and whole families seem to have chosen this as the ideal way to spend a Saturday morning, traipsing round screeching 'Get off her, Wayne', combined with occasional bursts of vigorous yanking.

If the NSPCC really want to do something useful maybe they could stop running those horrible television ads that mean I keep having to change channels in the middle of programmes or feel sick for the rest of the evening. They could spend the money on setting up emergency training booths in supermarkets instead, and give out earpieces to anyone with kids as they walk through the doors and then trail along behind you with a walkie-talkie, prompting you to say, 'How nicely you put that baguette into the trolley, darling, well done, have a sticker,' instead of screeching, 'Put that back right now, I've already got the bread.'

'Mummy, that man's looking at me. Why's he looking at me?'

Oh god. We've attracted a nutter. I bet he'll be some kind of tragic hobbit expert.

'Probably because you've got your cloak on.'

I turn to check out who's staring at Charlie, on full loony alert just in case, and find myself face to face with Gabriel the gorgeous vet. Oh. Terrific. Charlie twirls his cloak.

'Hello, I thought it was you. Great cloak, by the way.'

Blimey. He's even more good-looking than I remembered. And more tanned now – he must have been working outside. Probably doing unmentionable things to cows. But he certainly looks good on it. And of course it's absolutely typical that I decided to wear my tragic old denim skirt and a knackered old T-shirt today. And I think the manky old flip-flops add a particularly elegant touch.

'Are you being a Friar Tuck?'

God, I hope he doesn't mean me. But Charlie's still twirling.

'No. I'm Frodo. From *Lord of the Rings*. See.'

He holds his ring up for inspection.

'Oh. I see. How does it go again?'

He pauses and adopts a very deep whispery voice.

'"One ring to rule them all, one ring to find them. One ring to bring them all, and in the darkness bind them."'

Charlie's dumbstruck with admiration, as are quite a few of the other shoppers. Gabriel goes slightly red.

'I loved the *Lord of the Rings* books when I was little.'

Clearly.

'It's Charlie's favourite at the moment. We've practically worn the video out.'

'Yes, and I'm having it for my party. You can come, if you like. Grown-ups don't have to dress up. But they can. If they want to. You could be Gandalf, if you like. He just wears a white dress.'

'I think I'd rather avoid a white dress, what with my name being Gabriel.'

'Why?'

'Well, people might think I was pretending to be some sort of angel.'

Gabriel raises his eyebrows and Charlie laughs.

'Come on, Charlie, we're blocking the aisle. We'd better let Gabriel get on with his shopping.'

I don't really want to trap the poor man into a mammoth random-chatting routine with Charlie, especially not when I'm so badly dressed.

'We don't do angels at our school. Because me and James are pagans.'

Oh here we go. He'll be starting on about the summer solstice in a minute.

Gabriel smiles.

'Are you?'

Charlie nods.

'Yes. Where's your dog?'

'Outside in the car.'

'Did you leave your door open? Because you have to do that, you know. I saw it on *Pet Rescue* with Edna. You can cook your dog right up if you leave them in a hot car. Did you know that?'

Gabriel's smiling again. He's got a really nice smile.

'Yes, I did. We've got signs up in the surgery reminding people not to cook their dogs, but I left a window open, so I think she'll be all right. Actually, I left all the windows open a few inches. If I leave them open too much she jumps out. She's very silly.'

Is there no end to this man's talents? Not only can he do pretty impressive *Lord of the Rings* impressions, but he's got a dog that jumps out of car windows.

'She can come to my party too, if you like, and she can play with Tess, that's Uncle Monty's sheepdog. We're having a barbecue and everything. She can have a sausage, can't she, Mummy?'

'Charlie, stop badgering people.'

Gabriel's looking rather embarrassed. Maybe he thinks I'm not keen on him coming to the party.

'If you're around you're more than welcome, but I'd give the children's tea party a miss, if I were you, unless you like being covered in jelly. We're having a barbecue in the evening though, after most of the kids have gone home, just a few friends, so do come along to that, if you'd like to.'

I think I'm starting to gabble slightly, and I can feel myself going red.

'Well, that's very kind. I haven't really met many people yet in the village, so that would be great. If you're sure?'

'Oh yes, definitely. We'd love it.'

Oh God. I think I might have gone slightly overboard on the warm-invitation front now. We're blocking the aisle with our trolleys and causing a fair bit of tutting as people manoeuvre past us.

'Look, I'd better let you get on, but should I bring anything? Bottle of wine or something?'

I give him directions to Monty's farm and write down our telephone number, and then we carry on shopping, and keep seeing each other at the end of aisles and smiling and doing that half-nodding-waving thing, which frankly is getting to be rather a strain, especially with a small Frodo twirling about and trying to slip things into the trolley when he thinks I'm not looking.

I'm already starting to panic about what I'm going to wear, whilst simultaneously trying to decide what bread we want, and what exactly is the difference between wholemeal and granary and wheatgerm and which one has the bits in that Charlie hates. Maybe I could change into something glamorous after the children's tea, because my chances of looking even vaguely attractive in the evening, and without something stuck to my sleeve, are pretty much non-existent unless I have a change of clothes. What I really need is a show-stopping casual outfit that can cope with musical chairs and a tea party and still look nice for the barbecue, but the only thing I can think of is something you can wipe down like PVC, which isn't really my style. And anyway the only PVC item I own is a floral tablecloth.

Actually, I might as well just admit defeat now because my chances of looking anywhere near decent at the end of a children's party are completely non-existent without the back-up of professional wardrobe and make-up assistants, and even then I'd be pushing it. I'm resigning myself to jeans and trying to concentrate on the bloody bread when I suddenly realise that there's a Frodo-shaped hole by the trolley, and Charlie has disappeared.

I can feel myself starting to panic as I scan the bakery aisles, but he's not standing looking longingly at the amusingly shaped biscuits with neon icing like he usually does. Oh. My. God. I'm suddenly plunged into a complete nightmare vaguely reminiscent of *Don't Look Now*, except instead of being tormented by glimpses of a red dwarf hurrying around corners I keep thinking I can see a small brown cloak.

I'm walking towards the customer services desk, frantically searching as I go and wondering what the chances are of them calling the police when I tell them I'm looking for a small boy in a brown cloak answering to the name of Frodo, when I suddenly see him, standing by the barbecue and picnic stuff, mesmerised by the water pistols.

'Look, Mummy. Isn't this one fabless? I really need a supersoaker.'

I actually can't speak I'm so angry. And relieved. And still replaying bits of *Don't Look Now* in my mind, and holding my breath. Christ.

'What's the matter, Mummy?'

'What's the matter? What's the matter? I'll tell you what's the matter.'

My voice gets increasingly shrill as I run through the routine about not wandering off and staying close to me when we're out, whilst simultaneously half smothering him by putting my arms round him and holding him really tight. God in heaven, I'm not cut out for this much adrenalin on a Saturday morning. My heart's racing. He was only out of sight for a couple of minutes, five at the most, but when you can't find them five minutes feels like an eternity.

And of course the worst thing about it, now I've actually found him, is that it was all my fault. Because everything calamitous always is. I wonder if it ever stops. If they fuck something up completely when they're forty-five, I wonder if you still think, Oh god, that's down to me and my terrible parenting skills. Probably. How very bloody encouraging.

'You mustn't wander off, Charlie, you know that. I'm really angry and I was frightened, Charlie. I really was.'

He makes muffled sorry noises, and tries to wriggle around so he can still see the water pistols.

'I really need one of those, Mummy.'

'No way, Charlie. Maybe if you hadn't wandered off. But not now.'

I'm being slightly disingenuous here because there's absolutely no way I would have bought him a supersoaker, under any circumstances. If I really want to get soaked by freezing-cold water at unexpected moments I can always just turn the garden hose on with the dodgy nozzle.

'Please, Mummy, please. It'd be great for my party, and I promise I'll hold the trolley, all the time. I will.'

He's adopting his new I-know-I've-really-blown-it-but-please-let's-make-friends posture, with his best pleading look.

'No, Charlie.'

'But . . .'

'No, Charlie, and that's final. You don't wander off in shops. Ever. Now come and hold the trolley and let's go and get some apples and then we're done.'

Now he's doing his special my-life-is-an-appalling-tragedy trudge. With the drooping shoulders. And serve him bloody well right.

The car park's full when we get back to the car, and people are circling round in desperation, which makes me feel rather guilty since we're in one of the parent-and-child spaces, which technically I think are meant to be for people with babies in buggies rather than hobbits.

As I'm putting the bags in the boot there's a tremendous screeching of brakes and a young-executive type in dark glasses and an open-topped sports car reverses at high speed and stops just past my car. He sits drumming his fingers on his steering wheel with his stereo turned up so loud the bass is reverberating up through my flip-flops, and he's clearly far too busy to be kept waiting by the likes of me and Charlie, and the woman in the Fiat Tipo who's been patiently waiting further back to give me room to reverse out. She sort of slumps in her seat and looks like she's losing the will to live; she's got two baby seats in her car, and what looks like a very lively toddler in one of them, since I'm sure I heard the unmistakable sound of 'The Wheels on the Bus' from her car earlier. Technically there's still room for me to pull out and go past him, but I know as soon as I do he'll shoot into the space and leave Tipo mum stranded. I don't think so, as Leila would say. I don't bloody think so.

I walk towards his car, and he looks up at me like I'm a waitress about to take his order and turns the music down slightly.

'Yes?'

Oh good. He's a complete wanker.

'Um, I just wondered, did you realise, these spaces are for people with children?'

'Oh.'

'Yes. And that woman behind you has been waiting. For quite a while, actually. With her children. So the space is hers really.'

He gives me a look of utter contempt, but makes no sign that he's about to move.

'So I'll just wait here, shall I? Until you move your car. Thanks.'

I walk back to my car and he roars off in a fury, so fast that he misses the turning into the second half of the car park. Fiat Tipo woman's delighted and gives me a look of total devotion and a cheery wave as she drives into our space as we're leaving. Christ. I bet Jamie bloody Oliver never has this problem when he pops in for a couple of limes and some pancetta. I bet he has his own special Jamie space.

Now if I can just work out how to make a nice little party outfit from my PVC tablecloth, and exactly how I'm going to make grey icing for the bloody cake, I think we can definitely say this was one of our more successful trips to the supermarket. Gabriel's coming to the barbecue, Charlie's Houdini moment didn't quite reach the cardiac-arrest stage, and Mr Sports Car has had a Sisterhood Is Powerful moment. And there are sausages for tea. Top result really.

VI

Gone With the Wind

CHARLIE'S BIRTHDAY PARTY HAS turned into a major production, and the wallpaper scripts from Mack's agency arrived at work last week, so in between panicking about balloons and paper plates I've been frantically trying to budget for a two-day shoot in Holland while Barney and Lawrence race off to Amsterdam to look at sodding windmills. And I spent most of yesterday up to my elbows in grey icing trying to make the Stonehenge cake at Mum's house. She's got every size of cake tin and icing nozzle ever invented and was so full of helpful suggestions and handy hints that I nearly hit her with my spatula.

We've got twenty-seven kids coming to the party, and Kate appears to have invited half the village to the barbecue in the evening, including Ginny Richmond and Mrs Harrison-Black, by mistake, so that should be fun. Roger's been volunteered to poke things with tongs because he's very keen on barbecuing, and as Sally says, we might as well let him get on with it because we get enough of standing, burning sausages at home. Which reminds me, I must get new batteries for our smoke alarm.

In between pencilling in crew and picking grey icing out from under my fingernails, I've spent the rest of my time on the phone, with Monty bellowing about whether we want party lights and telling me all about his adventures on his new lawnmower. It's one of those enormous ride-along ones that look like mini hovercraft, which used to belong to one of his old-codger mates until his wife banned him from using it because he mowed over all her daffodils. Monty's never off the bloody thing now. He even went up to the local shop on it last week, which I'm pretty sure is illegal, so I'm half expecting a call from the local constabulary asking me to come and bail him out. And when he's not waxing lyrical about the bloody lawnmower he's banging on about fireworks for the party, and don't I think a few rockets would be nice. Dear god. Maybe we should have booked the village hall after all.

By the time party day actually arrives Charlie's so excited he's in full Frodo kit by 7 a.m., and gives me a very nasty turn by marching into my bedroom while I'm still half asleep with the hood of his cloak up screeching 'Get up, get up, you need to get up'. And whilst it's true that most burglars don't usually do their burgling in fancy dress, for a minute or two I thought I was in real trouble.

The weather's supposed to be sunny all day, which means it's bound to tip it down at some point, so we plan to have tea in the barn just in case. Monty's mad squirrelling of assorted bits of manky furniture all over the farm has finally come in handy, but Mum's not convinced by the collection of rickety tables we've lined up in the barn, and one of them does have a particularly dodgy leg, which has had to be nailed back on again by Dad and me.

Monty's out mowing the grass again, but the barn's looking lovely, and we've moved the piles of rusty old bits of tractor and things with spikes into the old stables. Monty's festooned the beams with strings of fairy lights and we've put bales of straw along the back wall, so apart from an old mangle and a couple of iron girders that were too heavy to move it's all looking very *Little House on the Prairie*. We've even got red-checked tablecloths.

We're indoors having a quick cup of tea before everything kicks off when Monty comes in carrying a huge box that he puts on the floor next to Charlie.

'Here you are, Charlie boy, this is for your birthday.'

Everyone smiles, because we all know what's in the box. Except for Charlie. He walks towards it and there's an unmistakable sound of cheeping, and as he lifts the lid there's a ruffling of feathers and a small brown head appears. Charlie nearly passes out with a combination of shock and sheer pleasure.

'Oh, oh, it's a baby pheasant, it is, oh, and there's another one. Oh Uncle Monty, thank you, thank you.'

He hurls himself on Monty, who staggers backwards but looks very pleased.

'Well, let's get them outside and into the pen I've made you then, or they'll make a terrible racket.'

We carry the box to the stables where he's rigged up a pen with chicken wire and what looks like bits of old trellis, and the pheasants rush up and down flapping for a while and then settle down to eat the grain Monty's scattered on the floor.

'They'll be fine in here, but you'll have to come and feed them regular like. They take a lot of looking after, birds do.'

Charlie's lying on the floor, peering through the wire netting, watching them.

'Oh yes, I will, I promise.'

'That's a good boy.'

Mum's busy taking photographs.

'Are you going to give them names then, poppet?'

My money's on Gandalf or Merlin, but you never know with Charlie.

'No, Nana, they're wild creatures. You don't give names to wild creatures. And when they're big we can let them go in the woods, so they can be free and have babies.'

Yes. And get shot at by all the local snooters, but I think I might not mention that just yet.

'Yes, and Monty says if they stay in the woods nobody will shoot them dead, because he doesn't have pheasant shooting any more – they make too much mess, driving their cars in all the fields. That's very naughty, isn't it? Driving your car right in a field. And then they can live for ever. But Monty says if they go on the road they'll have to take their chances. So I'm going to teach them. Like we do at school. Look and Listen. Do you think that's a good idea, Nana?'

'A very good idea, sweetheart.'

Maybe they can have a crack at the Green Cross Code while they're at it.

Kate arrives with James and Phoebe, and they're intro-duced to the pheasants and make suitably impressed noises, and then Kate and I start putting paper plates and cups out while Mum's in the kitchen tutting at the state of Monty's old cracked work surfaces and making sand-wiches.

Kate's really getting into this *Lord of the Rings* theme. It's slightly worrying, actually.

'I've done a pass the goblin, and I've put a plastic thing in each layer so they all get something, and you can do musical hobbits. Did you bring your CD player? Only I forgot ours.'

'Yes, and I got a children's party compilation, so we should be all right with the games, although one of us will have to do the music because Mum and Dad can't work my CD player – they'll just keep pressing the eject button. And I've got loads of sixties stuff for later. That should be all right, shouldn't it?'

'Perfect, and what time's your vet arriving?'

'Around seven, I think, and I wish people would stop calling him my vet.'

'People?'

'Well, you and Sal. Oh and that reminds me, not a word to Mum; I don't want her giving me the third degree all night.'

Kate laughs.

'Fair enough. But he might be, you know. Your vet, I mean. You never know. I'm still completely off men for the moment, but you're not, and honestly, Annie, if you spot a chap who doesn't actually make you want to vomit then I'd say go for it, and good luck to you. What's that thing they say? Suck it and see. Oh no, that doesn't sound quite right.'

'No. It doesn't. And definitely not at a family barbecue.'

We both snigger. Actually, I'm feeling rather nervous about Gabriel turning up, but at least with lots of people around it won't feel like a first date or anything sick-making like that. Unless Leila turns up. She can be incredibly unsubtle when she wants to be.

'Crikey, that sounds like the first of them arriving.'

A car is driving slowly up the lane, which has quite a few potholes. It's full of eight-year-olds in hobbit outfits, and a hideous half-hour follows where we try to stop Charlie and James practically knocking people to the ground in their excitement to get at the presents. We're going for the thank-you-nicely-we'll-open-it-later approach, but it's touch and go until Mum and Sally take over, and turn out to be much better at imposing a bit of order on the proceedings than either Kate or I, which doesn't really bode terribly well for the rest of the afternoon since we're supposed to be in charge of the games. And then Edna arrives on her bike with her basket full of fairy cakes with Smarties on top, which are Charlie's favourite, just as Lizzie and Matt arrive with Ava, and I lose track completely.

Ava's nearly four months old now, and absolutely thrilled at finding herself surrounded by hordes of screaming children in hobbit mode, with Tess racing round barking and Monty whizzing past on his lawnmower. She obviously thinks we've laid it all on for her amusement.

We all take it in turns to walk round with her, and Lizzie says that if we could lay something similar on at three o'clock in the morning she'd be very grateful, only Ava tends to get a bit bored around then and there's only so much you can do with a glove puppet when you're half asleep. God, I'd forgotten about the bloody glove puppets. I used to have to spend hours wiggling my fingers and making animal noises. Sometimes in public, which was always especially humiliating. Thank Christ Charlie's past all that now.

Matt offers to have a go at doing the music for musical hobbits but frankly he's hopeless. He doesn't leave enough gaps between the music and the rushing to sit down on chairs, so most of them just stay firmly seated, which leads to a fair bit of shoving and tipping people off chairs until Kate takes over.

For some reason that completely escapes me I get stuck with taking small people who need a wee into the loo in the house, because the one in the stables is full of planks and cobwebs. And then Cecily very cleverly manages to pull the handle off the cistern so the loo won't flush, and I'm reduced to standing with a pair of pliers gripping the top of the cistern handle, while Monty goes off in search of an old chain he's squirrelled away somewhere.

By the time I've finished my loo patrol they're playing What's the time, Mr Orc, and Jack Knight falls into the duckpond by running backwards and then suddenly disappearing down the bank. Thankfully the pond turns out to be not very deep, but full of mud and weed, so he emerges dripping with green slime, which he seems rather pleased with. Edna takes him into the house to give him a quick rub down with a flannel, while Dad and Matt stand guard round the pond, because naturally most of the boys are now desperate to be covered in slime too, and keep edging closer and closer when they think we're not looking.

We move on to blind man's hobbit, with Charlie and James being blindfolded, and then the rain starts. Everyone races into the barn screaming while we dash backwards and forwards across the farmyard carrying trays of food and drink like demented caterers on an especially dodgy job. But somehow the rain just makes everything even more exciting and they sit chomping their way through hundreds of sausage rolls and fairy cakes, and making a staggering amount of noise, which is magically absorbed by the cavernous expanse of the rafters. The lights are twinkling away and Monty says it reminds him of when he was younger and they used to have the harvest teas in here. Only they didn't have jelly. Or paper hats.

The Stonehenge cake is a big success, and we sing 'Happy Birthday' while Charlie and James sit wide-eyed and go very pink, and they blow out the candles with so much enthusiasm that another one of my standing stones falls over. Sally organises games they can play while they're all still sitting at the tables, including a version of Chinese whispers with boys versus girls, which leads to huge amounts of hilarity because pretty much all of the boys' messages have the word 'willy' in them, and the rain finally stops and they run round outside yelling as parents start arriving for home time and try to get them back into cars. Thank god. No major incidents, no tears from the birthday boys, and only one duckpond moment.

We dole out slices of cake and are thanked very politely by a series of small girls, including Emily and Georgia, Charlie and James's erstwhile girlfriends, who according to Charlie are now no longer girlfriends because it was Boring. But nobody seems the slightest bit bothered about this, and Charlie is in the middle of a fairly good-natured sword fight with Emily, who has three brothers and is very handy with anything pointy, when her dad arrives to collect her. She waves very sweetly as they drive off, and pokes her sword out of the car window. My kind of girl really.

'Can we open the party presents yet? Can we, can we?'

Charlie's hopping up and down with excitement.

'Not yet, sweetheart. Wait until everyone's gone. Did you have a lovely time?'

'Yes, and we're going to have ice-cream later, aren't we?'

'Yes.'

'Strawberry and chocolate. Nana told me. And you can have a bit of both if you want.'

'Right.'

'And me and James are going to feed my pheasants in a minute. I said he could help. That was nice of me, wasn't it, Mummy?'

'Very nice.'

'Yes, it's sharing. We do it at school. Miss Pike's always

going on about it. But Monty says they don't like cake. So we just have to give them seed.'

'OK.'

'This is my best birthday ever, Mummy.'

He throws his arms around me and I get a quick cuddle before he races off to find Monty.

'He's having a lovely time, isn't he, bless him.'

Mum's been watching us.

'Yes.'

'And it was very kind of Monty to get him those pheasants, you know. I think he's got a bit of a soft spot for him. It's such a shame Florrie isn't here – she'd have loved this.'

'Yes, she would. And thanks, Mum, for helping with all the food and everything. And he loves his spaceship.'

'Oh I know, he was shooting the cannon at your father earlier. Got him in the back of his neck, but he didn't seem to mind. Now shall I make some more tea? I think everyone could do with a nice cup of tea, don't you?'

'Yes please. And I'll start clearing up. Have we got enough clean cups?'

'Edna and I did some earlier. And we've started on the salads for later.'

'Thanks, Mum.'

She might be a bit too forthcoming with the handy hints when you're trying to ice your standing stones, but I don't know what I'd do without her, I really don't.

Roger's already lit the barbecue by the time we're finished clearing up, and I go into the house to change into my clean shirt. I've gone for trendy floral with a cornflower-blue cardigan if it gets cold, and my jeans are still fairly respectable, mainly because I kept well clear of Jack when he fell in the pond. The sun's come out again and it's a perfect summer's evening, so we move the tables out from the barn and put them under the trees at the front of the house, which is slightly too close to the pond to be sensible but it's the prettiest part of the house.

Matt takes the kids off into the barn to make a castle with the bales of straw and Kate opens a bottle of wine. I'm sitting having a quick cuddle with Ava, who's still being the perfect baby and grinning away like mad. You get such great cuddles from them at this age. No pointy elbows. She's so gorgeous it almost makes you long for another baby of your own, just for the cuddles.

'Who's that?'

Lizzie's nodding towards a car that's parking down the lane by the gates.

'Phil. Kate's ex. And Zelda. Who we all hate. So don't be nice to her. And their baby.'

'And what did they call the baby again? Savlon?'

'Saffron. Zelda's very artistic. Her real name's Sandra.'

'Oh right. I get the picture. Poor Kate. She's looking great, though. That skirt really suits her.'

It does, actually. Kate usually wears slightly tweedy country-lady outfits, it's probably the lingering influence of her mother, but today she's gone for a Laura Ashley floaty number.

'So when's this vet person due to turn up then?'

'Any time. Oh Christ, there's Mrs Harrison-Black. Trust her to be early.'

She's making a beeline for Roger. She's probably got some urgent committee business she wants to harangue him about.

'Where's Uncle Monty got to? He's not on that bloody mower again, is he?'

'I'm not sure. Probably.'

'He's looks years younger than when I last saw him, you

know – I think you and Charlie must be good for him. And I'd forgotten how beautiful it was here, I mean apart from the house obviously, but you could do it up, you know, make it stunning. Take the back wall down and extend it.'

'I don't think Monty's really up for stunning. Not unless it includes more room for old hatracks and chairs.'

Lizzie smiles.

'True. Are you all right with her for a minute? Only I need to nip indoors to the loo.'

'Sure. But watch the chain, the pliers are by the sink.'

Ava decides she's bored with giving people cuddles, and starts revving up for a bit of shouting. I'm carrying her over to the barn to check on the kids when Gabriel arrives, clutching a bottle of wine in blue tissue paper, and looking very gorgeous in a pale-green shirt and jeans. He's closely followed by Ginny Richmond and her husband, and Kate's friend Bunny, who's a bit of a nightmare County type, but Kate's got a soft spot for her after years of Pony Club when they were younger. There are cars parked all the way down the lane now, and more are arriving. Christ, I didn't know we'd invited quite so many people. I should probably be belting into the kitchen and making more salad but I really want to chat to Gabriel and be the attentive host, only it's not exactly easy what with jiggling Ava and trying to welcome Bunny and Ginny.

'Hello, Angie, gorgeous night for it.'

For some reason Bunny always calls me Angie.

'Evening, Bunny.'

Ava decides she's had enough of being the perfect Social Baby, and bursts into tears. Bunny laughs a rather braying, hooray sort of laugh, which makes Ava cry even harder.

'I always have this effect on infants. Can't stand them, to be honest. Thrilled when I could pack my two off to

198

school. Can't tell you. Didn't know you were sprogging again, Ange. Congratulations and all that. Now, where's the booze, I'm dying for a drink.'

Gabriel's looking rather overwhelmed as I shepherd everyone towards the tables, and I explain as casually as I can that Ava's not actually mine, and then Lizzie rescues her while I belt indoors in a blind panic to find Kate's already frantically making more salad.

'There's loads of people coming up the drive.'

'I know. I was sure I asked people to bring food.'

'Well, nobody has so far.'

'Mrs Harrison-Black did. Some sort of cold-chicken thing. It's bright orange. And Phil's brought crisps.'

'How generous – one bag or two?'

'One, and they're salt and vinegar, which he knows the kids hate. He's so bloody mean, I forget how much that used to annoy me sometimes. There, that looks all right, doesn't it?'

'Delicious. I think we've got some more tomatoes in the fridge. I'll do another bowl, shall I?'

Ginny appears.

'Hello, I thought I'd just pop back to the car and bring this in. Good heavens, you've been busy.'

Good old Ginny. She's carrying two enormous Tupperware containers, one with a rice salad and the other full of strawberries and peaches in some sort of juice.

'It's my special fruit salad, and just a teensy bit boozy, so not for little people. I'll just pop it down here, shall I? Super evening, isn't it? I must have a little chatette with Roger – I've had a lovely idea for the end-of-term play. I thought we could do a musical medley, you know, tunes from all our favourite musicals. You'll help, won't you? I know I can count on you two, especially you, Annie, being a professional and everything. And Mrs Pemberton has got all the music from the Dramatic Society. They've done such a huge range over the years, and she says she'll play the piano for us. It's all going to be absolutely super.'

And before we can stop her she's rushed outside to lobby Roger.

The PTA have volunteered to organise the Christmas concert this year, since the teachers are frantic about the looming Ofsted inspection next term. They're all in a complete frenzy of wall displays and laminated lesson plans.

'Bloody hell. Have we just been volunteered to do a concert?'

Kate nods.

'I think so, but it'll only be a few songs. Things from *Oliver Twist*, that kind of thing.'

'Well, it'll be more like round the twist if we've got to get our lot singing in tune.'

Kate starts humming.

'Somehow I get the feeling this isn't the first time you've heard about this.'

She's looking rather sheepish.

'Well, she did mention something about it the other day.'

'You haven't started taking some special new tablets you haven't told me about, by any chance, have you?'

'No. But I had a hangover, and she just sort of crept up behind me in the playground. And there are some great songs, you know. I really loved the film *Oliver*, didn't you?'

'What?'

'You know. "Who Will Buy This Wonderful Morning?" "Consider Yourself At Home".'

She carries on humming.

'Consider yourself totally buggered.'

'Shall we put this wine in the fridge?'

'Yes, and then let's get this lot outside and start our

counter-manoeuvres, or we'll be making Victorian urchin costumes before we know it.'

'Oh god, I hadn't really thought about costumes.'

'Well, unless you want to be up to your neck in calico ruffles you'd better start.'

'Good point.'

I'm scrabbling about on the floor trying to rearrange the contents of the fridge so I can fit the wine in when Leila suddenly appears in the kitchen as if by magic, wearing absolutely dazzling pink wedge sandals and a very tiny silk dress.

'Darling, what on earth are you doing down there? Christ, this place is fabulous, and I just saw the birthday boy, babbling on about pheasants, only I hope I don't have to go and stroke them or anything, because I'm not too keen on birds. Anyway, here's something to start us off. Was I meant to bring food? Bollocks. I forgot. Oh well. I'll just drink. Tor, Christ, where is he? Oh god, I think I left him in the car. Tor, oh no, here is, this is Annie. My best friend in the entire world. And her lovely friend Kate.'

A tall, blond, athletic-looking man hands me a bottle of champagne and smiles. Good god in heaven. He's absolutely breathtaking. Kate and I stand gazing and Leila smiles.

'Tor, do you think you could find some glasses, darling? I think these girls need a drink.'

'Sure.'

He's got a really deep sexy voice. Lucky, lucky Leila. No wonder she's been so perky lately. Kate picks up a plate, and he asks her if she needs any help.

'Yes please.'

Kate's nodding and seems to have gone into a sort of trance. Actually, I think I have too. I'm still kneeling on the floor in front of the fridge, having temporarily lost the use of my legs.

He goes off with two bowls of salad, followed by Kate carrying a tray of plates.

'Blimey, Leila.'

'I know. Sometimes I have to pinch him to make sure he's real. Actually, he gets quite annoyed about it sometimes. He says it's inner beauty that counts, and all that bollocks, which is always so much more convincing coming from a demi-god.'

'Well, it doesn't seem to have made him go all pretty boy. I mean in the five seconds I've seen him so far, he doesn't do that thing like he's doing you a huge favour even deigning to talk to you.'

'I know. Although he does take his yoga really seriously. He spends hours doing his breathing and stuff. Which is fine by me. All he needs is a mat, and I get to look at him while he's zoned out cleansing.'

'I bet you do.'

'Has the vet turned up yet?'

'Yes, just arrived.'

'Well, what the fuck are you doing in here playing with the fridge then? Get up and brush your hair, and put some of this on and let's get out there.'

She hands me a tube of lip gloss, the really expensive stuff that actually stays on, and opens the champagne, and we go outside to find more people arriving and more salads emerging from cool bags.

Gabriel's talking to Bunny and looking rather trapped, but Leila soon sorts that out by marching over and giving him a blistering kiss on the cheek and greeting him like a long-lost friend. He looks rather shaken but relieved to have been freed from the barking Bunny.

'Sorry, only you were looking rather desperate and we

202

want you to come and talk to us. We're much nicer, I promise. Glass of champagne?'

'Please.'

'Now who do you know? I'm Leila, and you know Annie, I think?'

'Yes.'

'Good. Oh there's Lizzie with the baby. I must go and say hello. I'm having a go with other people's babies whenever I get the chance at the moment, just to see if I'm getting broody. Nothing so far but it's worth checking, don't you think?'

She gives him one of her dazzling smiles, and waltzes off.

'So – '

'This – '

'Sorry, you first.'

'No, go ahead.'

Oh god. This is tragic. We're like a couple of awkward teenagers.

'I was just going to say I'm glad you found the farm all right.'

'Oh yes, fine. And it's a lovely place, isn't it. Your uncle's, you said?'

'Yes. He's the one on the lawnmower.'

'Oh. Right.'

Charlie appears, covered in bits of straw, wanting to show me the castle. But as soon as he claps eyes on Gabriel he's straight into his where-is-your-dog routine.

'She's at home I'm afraid. She doesn't really like parties.'

'Are you sure? Because sometimes people are shy, but then they like it when they get there.'

'Yes, but in her case she really isn't keen. She gets all excited and starts barking.'

Like that would be a problem.

'And then she gets silly and starts running around in circles and falling over.'

That'd be down to only having three legs, no doubt. Charlie's looking Very Keen. I'd better nip in quick.

'Charlie, why don't you tell Gabriel about your pheasants.'

'Oh yes. I've got two, actually. Of my very own. They're only babies, but they'll be big soon. They're boys. With tails and everything. Would you like to see them?'

'Yes please.'

'Maybe after supper, Charlie? I think the sausages are nearly ready. Why don't you go and get James?'

He races off, just as Roger announces that the food's cooked. He's done a brilliant job with the barbecue and everyone gathers round in the twilight, while Kate puts some jazz on the CD player and it all starts feeling very mellow. Monty's finally got off his lawnmower and joined us, and is giving Gabriel the benefit of his views on vets, while Mum holds Ava with Charlie sitting next to her snorking back sausages. She's looking completely blissed out with both her grandchildren within reach.

Tor's attracting quite a few new fans, particularly Mrs Harrison-Black, who seems completely smitten and is busy telling him all about her holiday in the Norwegian fjords last year, presumably hoping that since he's Swedish this will earn her extra points on the I Love Scandinavia front. He's got a fabulous accent, and I've finally worked out who he reminds me of: he's like an early Boris Becker but without the towelling headbands, and before he started having unfortunate moments in cupboards and his hair went all tufty.

Leila's deep in conversation with Matt about architecture, which is one of her many passions, and Kate's busy with Ginny having a rather half-hearted go at getting us out of the musical extravaganza.

Gabriel copes rather well with Monty, and is obviously quite good at being harangued by mad old farmers. He says Yorkshire was much worse, particularly because they'd go off into dialect to try and confuse you.

'At least round here I can usually work out what they're saying.'

'Yes. Although with Monty that's not always a good thing.'

'Oh he's all right. I agree with him really – there's far too much reliance on drugs and not enough on good practice.'

'So are you keen on everyone going organic then?'

'Oh definitely, yes. It takes longer, but it's better in the long run, it's got to be. Just look at BSE. Never would have happened if things had been done properly.'

'Right.'

'Same with scrapie.'

I'm nodding, although I'm not entirely sure what scrapie is. I think it's something revolting to do with sheep.

Kate comes over.

'Sorry but I need back-up. Ginny's desperate for us to do it and you were right about the costumes. She's thinking pinafores for the girls and she's already bought the material. Metres and metres of calico.'

We explain to Gabriel about the plans for the school play and agree that yes, 'Consider Yourself At Home' is a nice song, but not necessarily with our kids singing it, and then Mrs Harrison-Black comes barrelling over.

'I gather from Mrs Richmond that you've volunteered to help out with the end-of-term play.'

She's giving me a very pointed look.

'Um . . .'

'And whilst I commend your good intentions I did just wonder if you realised quite how much work something

205

like this involves. I know how busy both of you are, and it's very important that you're sure you can really commit to something like this. Because it would be no good changing your minds halfway through.'

Bloody cheek. As if we'd get halfway through rehearsals and then bale out. Well, that's decided then. Oliver Twisting here we come.

'Oh no, I'm sure it'll be fine. We'll gather a team together, like you do with the cake stalls and things. We'll put a notice up and people will help: I'm sure we'll be able to cope.'

She gives me a furious look.

'Well, if you're sure.'

Bugger. Ginny's delighted, and Sally says she'll do her bit too, but I still can't help thinking we walked right into that one. Gabriel seems to find the whole thing highly amusing, and is now humming 'I'd Do Anything' and volunteering to lend us his dog.

'Why would we want a dog?'

Let alone one with only three legs. But Kate seems far more clued up than I am.

'For Bill Sykes. I loved that song. "As Long As He Needs Me". What was her name again?'

Gabriel frowns. He's obviously a fan too.

'Nancy.'

Kate smiles.

'Yes, that's it. Nancy, it was so romantic. Apart from the bit where he clubs her to death under the bridge.'

Gabriel laughs and they go off into a medley of favourite songs from the film. They're both humming 'Who Will Buy This Wonderful Morning' when Gabriel's shirt suddenly starts vibrating, which is slightly alarming, and I'm half wondering if he's actually much older than he looks and he's got some sort of dodgy pacemaker when he stops humming and retrieves a tiny mobile phone from the pocket.

'Sorry, I'll have to go. I'm on call tonight. It's always the way. If you're at home with nothing on the telly no one ever calls. But if you're out having fun, well it's the sod's law of being a vet. But thanks so much for inviting me, Annie, it was lovely.'

His phone starts vibrating away again.

'Yes, yes, I'm on my way.'

He waves as he starts walking towards the gate.

Kate's still humming.

'Wasn't he nice? I bet he'll ring you, and he's perfect for you. Oh no, here comes Zelda. Help me out, will you? She keeps trying to bond with me about the kids and it's really annoying me.'

We move back into the house, pretending to gather up plates, and Leila follows us in.

'Where's he gone off to then?'

'He's on call tonight.'

'Oh. How annoying. Well, you looked like you were enjoying yourselves anyway, and, Jesus Christ, what was that?'

There's a loud explosion from behind the house.

'Monty and his fireworks, I expect. It's his surprise for the party.'

'Well, you could have warned me, bloody hell, I thought a bomb had gone off. It's all very well for you country types, us London girls are on high-terrorist alert, thank you very much.'

'In advertising? I don't think we're exactly a top target, sweetheart.'

'Well, no. Probably not. But still.'

'I didn't know he was definitely going to do them. I spent most of last week trying to persuade him not to.

Look, we'd better get round to the barn sharpish and watch the kids. I wouldn't put it past Monty to have them lighting the bloody things.'

We retrieve the children, who've created complete chaos inside the barn with their straw castle, which has now degenerated into a series of straw heaps all over the floor, and we stand watching the fireworks while Monty and Matt race up and down lighting rockets and a Catherine wheel that Monty has nailed to an old plank by the gate. Matt's very sensibly got a bucket of water on standby, which Monty clearly thinks is ridiculous until one of the rockets goes up about three feet and then lands back on the grass and starts a small fire. The children are thrilled and William says he wants fireworks at his party too, and everyone claps and Monty says it's not a proper party without fireworks and looks very pleased.

We make endless cups of coffee as people start drifting off home. Leila says she'll call me tomorrow. Tor gives me a hug goodnight, which attracts lots of envious glances, and Mum starts tidying up until Dad frogmarches her off to the car. Kate and I do the best we can with black bin bags and a brush with most of its bristles missing, but Monty doesn't seem to mind in the slightest. He's sitting down to watch telly with a beer and a bowl of crisps as we're leaving. We promise to return after lunch tomorrow, with mops and buckets, and he waves crisps at us and says there's no need to bother.

'Best night I've had in ages.'

Kate's looking tired as we're walking towards our cars.

'Good party, I think.'

'Yes. But let's not do it again soon, though.'

She smiles.

'You're on.'

'See you tomorrow then, around three, for the clean-up? And we can start panicking about the concert.'

'Fine. Phoebe, stop teasing him. And James, stop that, just get in the car.'

By the time we're home I'm completely shattered and so is Charlie, but he's too dazzled by his day to fall asleep. He's in bed, but still jabbering.

'It was my best party.'

'I'm glad, darling, but it's sleep time now.'

'Yes, and can we go and see my pheasants tomorrow? I have to go every day, you know, to feed them.'

'Yes, fine, but not if you don't go to sleep. Come on, lie down.'

'Stroke my back in circles, Mummy. Pleeese.'

'Lie down then.'

'Yes, but proper circles. Not lines. Lines are itchy.'

'Charlie. Lie down. And be quiet. Or I'm going downstairs.'

He lies down and I do the circle thing until his breathing slows down and he's falling asleep. As I'm tiptoeing out he turns over.

'Night, Mummy. Thank you for my lovely day. And you know the play at school that you're doing, well, I'm not singing, all right? Definitely. Me and James have decided. And we're not dressing up either. Unless we can have swords. Proper ones. With metal. Not plastic.'

Excellent.

I'm still in my pyjamas looking at the Sunday papers and waiting for the grill to set the smoke alarm off as a prelude to the toast being done, because someone helpfully poked a bit of Lego down the toaster a few weeks ago and I can't

209

get it out, when the phone rings. Blast. I'm not terribly good at having proper phone conversations if I'm not wearing actual clothes; somehow I always feel the other person can see you.

It's Gabriel, and he launches straight into telling me how much he enjoyed the party and how sorry he was he had to leave early, which is nice, and rather keen really, calling first thing the next morning. Possibly. Ooh. He might be calling to ask me out for a drink or something. I stand up a bit straighter.

'Anyway, thanks so much, and I was wondering, um, I'm not very good at this sort of thing, but I was just wondering . . .'

Oh bless. He sounds really nervous.

'It's just . . . your friend Kate. Is she seeing anyone at the moment? Only I thought I might call her. We got on so well last night. But I thought I'd better check. I've got a terrible habit of putting my foot right in it. I'm sort of like the Rain Man of romance. Completely clueless. I've asked out married women by mistake. And on one memorable occasion a plain-clothes nun.'

I can't help laughing.

'A plain-clothes nun?'

'She was in training. But still. So you see what I mean. It's not like I can really rely on my gut instinct. And I thought since you were so kind asking me along, well, I thought I could ring you up and you'd put me straight. If she's engaged elsewhere. Well, not engaged, but you know what I mean. Or maybe she is – engaged, I mean.'

'No, not at all. She's divorced. But not engaged.'

'Oh right. Good. So that Phil chap was her ex then, was he? I wasn't sure. So it would be all right, would it?'

'Absolutely. Do you want her number?'

'Yes please.'

Bugger. Double bugger. I mean I'm pleased for Kate, obviously. Of course I am. It's just what she needs, someone nice ringing her up for a change, especially after all the nutters her mother keeps fixing her up with. But still. Damn. And I'll have to ring her up and warn her, make sure she doesn't think I mind. Which I don't. Not really. Apart from a faint twinge or two. I mean he's definitely as nice as I thought he was when I first met him, there wasn't anything that put me off him last night or anything. Apart from him knowing all the bloody tunes from *Oliver*, which is rather suspect if you ask me. And he's very relaxing to be with, in a low-key sort of way. Almost the opposite of Mack really, who tends to dominate everything wherever he goes. Not that it matters how he compares to Mack. Not at all. He's just nice and relaxing. But perhaps a tad too relaxed for me. A bit too quiet, possibly. And anyway, he's interested in Kate. So that's that. I'll have to convince her that I went off him last night, mildly, so the field is completely clear if she fancies going out for a drink. But still. Bollocks.

Kate took a fair bit of convincing that I didn't mind about Gabriel ringing her, but she was terribly flattered, which was sweet, and agreed to go for a drink with him, which went really well, despite her initial reluctance, and they're going out for supper next week. She's still not completely convinced that I don't mind, which is slightly tricky, because I can't exactly say I think he's hopeless or anything in case she decides she really likes him. And if I'm honest I am still a tiny bit put out that my efforts at seduction have been such a roaring success. Not so much that he prefers Kate, but that my flirting technique is obviously so pathetic that he didn't even notice I was flirting with him.

Leila thinks it's highly amusing, and says it just goes to show how stupid men are, and really it would be easier if we just bought large pieces of white card and wrote instructions on them, because subtle signals are a complete waste of time. But I can't help thinking that if I tried it they might just write rude messages back. Things like 'Not on your life', or 'Are you joking?' That kind of thing. But at least I've been so frantic with last-minute preparations for this bloody windmill job that I haven't really had time to get too depressed about it. And anyway I'm really pleased for Kate. I really am. It's just what she needs. Something to take her mind off Phil, who keeps turning up with Saffron and whining about how expensive children are. Silly sod.

Mum's coming over to stay with Charlie and I'm off to Gatwick tomorrow for the flight to Amsterdam. And I've got a horrible feeling that the combination of Barney and windmills isn't going to be a good one, so I'm having my customary pre-job moan with Leila.

'And on top of everything we've got this fucking musical.'

'Yes, but it's just a few songs, isn't it? How tricky can that be?'

'I beg your pardon. Have you ever tried getting twenty-nine seven-year-olds to sing a song in tune and all finish at the same time? Ginny's beside herself, and we've only done one rehearsal so far. And then we tried Year Six out with a song from bloody *Oliver*. And it was a complete disaster.'

'And how old are Year Six then?'

'Ten and eleven, going on fifteen. And all the girls wanted to be Nancy and all the boys wanted to be out in the playground. Except for Justin, who'd quite like to be Oliver. Or Nancy. He doesn't really mind. It's really tricky.'

Leila laughs.

'So you want me to cancel the press launch and you'll just go straight to video then?'

'That's another thing. The PTA want to video it, and sell it to raise funds for the new library, so it's going to be preserved for all posterity.'

'Well, never mind, darling. I tell you what, I'll come down and do the play for you, if you'll do my pitch to Trident. Deal? The boys on the sixth floor are getting so hysterical about it they can hardly breathe. Nat nearly passed out in the meeting today. We had to do that thing with a paper bag. He's such a drama queen.'

'Is it a big account then?'

'Beyond big. Massive. Epic. And we won't get it. Rumour has it that it's a done deal and your bloody Mack the Knife's already got it in the bag. Bastard. So now we've got another reason to hate him. Talking of which, any more news on the wet-vet front? How's he getting on with Kate?'

'You said you thought he was really nice.'

'Yes, but who needs a man who's going to keep charging off at vital moments to resuscitate someone's hamster? It would be a total nightmare. No, you're definitely better off out without him. Oh Christ, that's my bat phone, I'd better go. Nat's probably hyperventilating again. Ring me from Amsterdam and give my love to Barney.'

I knew this job was going to be tricky, but as usual I've underestimated just how tricky. We've got the perfect windmill, with a stuntman pasted to each sail, but no bloody wind. The flaming thing's standing completely still, and the crew are all trying to keep busy and out of Barney's way. We've done the shots from the crane, and nobody

213

fell off, which was good, and shots of the actors being pasted on to the sails, but what we haven't got is the bloody things actually twirling.

Although why you'd want to buy a brand of wallpaper paste because you can use it to paste people on to windmills is still beyond me. But it's part of an ongoing campaign. They've had a man pasted to the side of a lorry and hurtled round the M25. I'm particularly pleased we didn't do that one. And someone pasted on to a board and dangling off a rope from a helicopter over Miami. So I suppose the windmill thing was only a matter of time really. And it's just typical of Mack and Barney to have expanded on the idea by having four of them stuck fast to the sails and going round and round. Or staying completely still, which is our current version. Christ.

'Let's break for lunch and see if the wind picks up, shall we?'

Barney nods.

'But tell them if it starts getting breezy – I want to be ready to go, pronto. Understood?'

'Sure.'

It takes us nearly half an hour to hand-crank the sails around slowly and get the stuntmen down, and none of them are too happy, especially the one that's been upside down for most of the morning. The crew are all making *Gone With the Wind* jokes and asking to be sent back to Tara, and Barney's getting more and more tetchy.

'Oh Christ, that's all we need. Here comes the bloody client.'

They were only supposed to be coming over tomorrow, for the last hour or so. After we'd got all the tricky stuff sorted.

'Oh great, and Mack bloody MacDonald too. Excellent.

214

Anyone else likely to be turning up to watch me filming a totally fucking stationary windmill?'

'Don't ask me, Barney. Lawrence said they were only over for an hour tomorrow, just meet and greet.'

'Well, ring him up and find out what the fuck's going on, would you. And keep them out of my way, I'm not in the mood. And check on the weather and start ringing round for wind machines. Big ones.'

'Barney, you know the museum bloke's not going to let us do anything like that.'

'Well, let's not tell him then. All right?'

He gives me a furious look.

'Christ. Just sort it, will you?'

He storms off to talk to the lighting cameraman.

I'm having a quick sandwich after failing to track down Lawrence. The man from the museum who owns the wind-mill is explaining to me, for about the tenth time, how vital it is that we stop filming if it gets too windy. Chance would be a fine thing. But apparently the reason there aren't wind-mills dotted all over the place is because most of them actu-ally burn down at some point. If it gets too breezy you have to put the brake on really sharpish before the sails start turning too quickly or you have two choices: one, you can let the sail keep twirling, whereupon it will eventually fly off the spindle thing and trash everything within five miles, which given that we've got four stuntmen pasted to the sails is probably best avoided. Or two, you can try to put the brake on using the huge wooden drum thing, which then bursts into flames and burns the windmill down. Excellent. So that's something to look forward to.

We've promised to stop the minute he says we have to, so he can put the brake on and turn the sails out of the wind. And the stuntmen are rather keen we get it right too. But I'm still feeling faintly sick with the tension of it all. And Barney's started talking about hiring a fleet of helicopters, to hover just out of shot and really get the bloody thing going.

We spend the rest of the afternoon doing the best we can with a few puffs of wind, which barely move the sail at all, and the crew continue with their *Gone With the Wind* motif and are now whistling the theme tune pretty much constantly.

Even Mack's starting to get worried. He's kept a pretty low profile so far, talking to the client and Barney, but he now he comes over to me with a plastic beaker of coffee.

'So what's the plan then? If the weather doesn't change.'

'Panic.'

'Right. Well, that's very reassuring.'

'There's always tomorrow.'

'I'm assuming you're talking in a non-*Gone With the Wind* kind of way here, right?'

'It's bound to be windy tomorrow.'

'Yes. But if it's not, Miss Scarlett. What then?'

'Mack, relax. We're professionals. We'll come up with something.'

'Right.'

He's smiling. Damn.

'I'll leave you to get on then, shall I?'

'Please.'

He winks. And walks off, whistling the bloody theme tune. Cheeky sod. I think I preferred it when he was all cool and distant.

'When do you want to break for tea, guv? Only they're getting pretty pissed off up there.'

The first is nodding towards the stuntmen, who've been

whining into their radio mikes over the past half-hour and saying they need a break.

'What?'

'Tea, guv. Any thoughts?'

'Fine, we're not getting anything. You might as well get them down.'

We start cranking the sails round again to get the stuntmen down, when it starts getting breezy, so they're quickly zipped back into their overalls as the sails slowly start to turn. And they're not happy.

'This is more like it.'

Barney's starting to relax.

'Just a bit more and it'll be great.'

'Um, guv, the windmill guy's getting pretty nervous.'

'For Christ's sake, it's only just started moving.'

The breeze picks up and the sails keep turning, and the museum guy's getting really twitchy but Barney wants to keep going. And then suddenly there's a huge gust of wind and the sails whizz round. Only a couple of times, but it's amazing how fast they go. They're almost a blur of pale-green faces. There are muffled groaning noises from the stuntmen, and the museum guy's definitely had enough. He puts the brake on and starts frantically turning the sails out of the wind, and then we get the stuntmen down, who are all deeply unhappy, staggering round trying to get their balance back, and one of them's busy being sick. Barney and Mack are huddled by the monitor.

'Fucking brilliant.'

Thank god for that. I seriously don't want to be the one who has to tell them we want to go again. Mack's smiling now.

'So can I bring the client over?'

'Sure.'

'I knew we could count on you, Barney.'

'No problem.'

Barney's very pleased with himself.

'I don't know what all the fuss was about. We just need a few more shots tomorrow of them arriving on their bikes, and we'll be done.'

'Bikes? What bikes? Nobody told me anything about bikes.'

'No, well, Mack and I were talking, the opening's a bit flat, and we thought they could all arrive on bikes. Like they're out for a day in the country and just sort of decide on this on the spur of the moment, for a bet.'

'Decide to paste themselves to a windmill? Like you do, you mean?'

Sometimes I wonder what planet these people live on.

'There's bound to be somewhere to rent them round here – the whole country's as flat as a fucking pancake. They must have hundreds of bike shops.'

Bloody hell. So now I've got to find a selection of bikes ready for tomorrow morning.

'And we're talking bicycles, right, not motorbikes?'

They both look at me like I'm mad.

'Yes. Bicycles. With pedals. And nothing too flash. Proper old-fashioned ones. All right?'

'Sure you don't want tandems? Or what about a penny-farthing? Make it a bit more of a challenge, why don't you. Honestly, Barney, I've told you before, you can't just suddenly decide on stuff like this.'

'Oh yes I can.'

'Why didn't you tell me earlier?'

'Actually, that was my fault. I was meant to tell you, Miss Scarlett, and I sure am sorry I forgot.'

Mack's talking in a weird Southern accent now and grinning, and Barney gives him a vaguely puzzled look. He's been completely oblivious to the *Gone With the Wind*

218

motif the crew have been building. He zones out totally when he's working, and then tends to tune in again suddenly and demand to know what's going on.

'What the fuck is he on about? Miss Scarlett. Is this some weird Cluedo thing you've got going?'

'Just don't ask, Barney, all right? Now, have you got any more new ideas you should have been sharing with me before I start my bicycle quest? Nothing else you forgot to mention?'

I give Mack what I hope is a very pointed look.

'No, that's it.'

And Mack winks at me. Again. Only I pretend I haven't noticed.

By the time I get back to the hotel, after combing the countryside and tracking down an assortment of manky-looking bikes that I hope will satisfy Barney's not-too-flash brief, everyone's in the restaurant having a lovely time and making a phenomenal amount of noise. Mack's in the middle of telling one of his stories, and everyone's laughing. Actually, I think I'm just too tired for this. All I want is a bath and some room service. A toasted sandwich. Or maybe some chips. And a very large gin.

But I'd better check with Barney first.

'If it's all right with you I'm off up for an early night.'

'Fine with me, darling. Did you find the bikes?'

'Of course. Would I be here if I was bikeless? Chris is collecting them first thing tomorrow.'

'Great. Sure you don't want a drink, sweetheart?'

'No thanks, Barney, I'm pretty knackered. But I'll see you first thing tomorrow, yes? The car's coming at eight.'

'Christ. Why?'

'Because you said you wanted an early start.'

'Oh. Right. Well, good. See you then.'

'Night, Barney.'

He blows me a kiss as I walk out of the door.

I've just had a quick shower and I'm draped in towels because the hotel bathrobe seems to have been designed for an anorexic dwarf. I've ordered my food and called Charlie, when there's a knock on the door. Blimey. Room service is obviously very speedy here. Great.

It's Mack. Christ. I pull my towel a bit tighter.

'Aren't you coming down for a drink?'

'Dressed like this?'

He smirks.

'I'm pretty tired, Mack, and I've got stuff to do for tomorrow.'

'It's not because of me, is it? Only I can go back to my hotel, if you'd prefer. I've left the client there with one of the juniors, and I should probably be getting back there anyway. We're off at the crack of bloody dawn to get back for a big pitch.'

God, he smells wonderful. He's leaning against my door frame, smelling wonderful.

'Trident?'

Damn, I shouldn't have said that.

'Yes. How did you know? Oh I get it, your friend Leila's going for it too, is she?'

'No, it was somebody else said something about it. And I just sort of assumed you'd be up for it.'

'Well, you were right. We are. And we're more than up for it. We're completely fucking desperate. It's huge money.'

'Great.'

'What's that supposed to mean?'

'Nothing.'

'Good. Anyway, I just wanted to say it's been great seeing

220

you again. And all that bollocks. And thanks for today. Great job.'

'Night, Mack.'

I start to close the door.

'I hadn't finished, actually.'

'Oh. Sorry. But could you possibly speed it up, only I'm getting rather chilly.'

He frowns slightly.

'Well, I just wanted to say I'm sorry I was such a prick. When I saw you at the awards thing. Only I wasn't expecting you to be there.'

'It's fine, Mack. How's Vanessa, by the way?'

'Great. As far as I know. I haven't seen her for weeks.'

'Oh.'

He smiles.

'Yes. It turned out I wasn't quite what she had in mind. No real taste. And not quite biddable enough.'

'I bet.'

'And she was completely obsessed with fashion.'

'A fashion model being obsessed with fashion. Isn't life shocking sometimes?'

'Shut up.'

'You can't just knock on people's doors and tell them to shut up, you know. You're being very annoying. Go away, I'm getting cold.'

'Shut up.'

'Look, Mack. Much as I'd love to stand here trading insults with you all night I've got things to do. Clothes to put on. And room service is on its way. So why don't you go and play with the boys downstairs.'

'I've missed you. Did I say that? I've really missed you.'

Oh. God. He's really being flirty now. I think he must be drunk or something.

'Goodnight, Mack.'

He leans forward to kiss me on the cheek but changes his mind at the last moment, and it turns into a different kind of kiss entirely. I'm standing there like a complete lemon clutching my towel and trying to work out what the fuck's going on.

'Mack?'

'Yes.'

'What's this all about?'

He looks at me and smiles.

'Frankly, my dear, I don't give a damn.'

And as it turns out neither do I.

VII

Ten Green Bottles

'Bloody hell, so what time did he leave?'

'About half an hour ago – he had an early flight. They've got some big meeting with Trident.'

Leila makes a snorting noise. 'Has he, indeed? What a shame. And did he say anything about Vanessa, or were you too busy shagging to actually speak?'

'Leila!'

'I'm sorry, but it's half-past six in the bloody morning, so let's cut to the chase, shall we? Is he still seeing her, or not?'

'Not, apparently. I think he threw an epi in Armani or something when she was making him try on loads of suits.'

'I bet he did. English men just don't get that kind of thing, unless they're gay of course, which he's not.'

'Not as far as I've noticed.'

'And did you have a great time? Headlines only, please, I'm still half asleep.'

'Lovely. Absolutely brilliant. He did his – '

'Enough already.'

'I was just going to say he did the James Bond thing, his Sean Connery voice, calling me Moneypenny. I'd forgotten how much I loved that.'

'No you hadn't.'

'True.'

'So go on then – what's the plan now?'

'Um . . .'

'Don't tell me you didn't talk.'

'Not really.'

'But you haven't just let him walk off into the dawn saying he'll call you, have you? Jesus Christ, haven't I taught you anything?'

'It was all a bit of a surprise, to be honest.'

'To you, maybe. I've been telling you for weeks this would happen.'

'You have not.'

'Well, I said he'd call you. And you owe me fifty quid and a bottle of vodka.'

'Yes. But this was a bit more than a phone call.'

'Clearly.'

'Anyway, it'll probably just be a one-off.'

'Oh yes, Little Miss Optimistic, and how do you work that one out then?'

'Well, I still don't want to move to New York, and he's still busy being Mr Transatlantic, isn't he?'

'Yes, but just think of the air miles you'll collect. You'll be able to go to Barbados for the weekend and not even notice.'

'Trust me. I'd notice.'

'Well, try to relax, darling. Have a large brandy or something – that's supposed to be good for shock. Although personally I'd go for vodka. Or tequila.

That always takes the edge off for me. Have you got any limes?'

'Oh yes, Leila, I always pack limes when I'm off on a job.'

'A minibar?'

'Yes.'

'Well, bloody use it. And remember, for all we know this is just his way of paying you back for not moving to New York, so if he does call for an action replay then just try to be cool, will you, or he'll bolt.'

'Right.'

Actually, come to think of it, I wouldn't mind a bit of bolting myself. God knows how I'm supposed to work this morning.

'Oh and Annie?'

'Yes? Although if this is you starting on about shoes again, I don't want to hear it, all right?'

'Don't go into one if he doesn't call today. Which he probably won't. He'll be trying to be cool too.'

'Right.'

'So call me later, when you're home.'

'You can count on it. And I'm sorry I woke you up, but I waited as long as I could.'

'No problem, I'm always happy to wake up for good news. Thank god you've finally come to your senses and realised that there's no point wasting your time with daft vets when you can be playing with the big boys. Bye, sweetie.'

Playing with the big boys. Actually, I quite like the sound of that. Although on second thoughts. Oh god. Maybe I should help myself to something from the minibar after all. I need to calm down and get dressed because I've got to work this morning, and there's still a strong chance we'll manage to set fire to that bloody windmill.

But while I'm trying to detangle my hair and put on enough make-up to stop me looking like the living dead, but not so much that I look like I'm about to appear in *Cabaret*, I can't help thinking that there is one huge advantage to daft vets: they're so much simpler. And they tend to live on the same sodding continent as you.

I'm sitting at the airport what seems like days later, but in fact is only a few hours, and I'm beyond knackered. Way beyond. It's all starting to feel slightly weird; it's almost like it hasn't really happened. Actually, maybe it didn't, and I've made the whole thing up in some twilight zone in my head because I'm finally officially cracking up. One minute he's in New York living with a supermodel and the next he's knocking on my hotel door. And that's another thing: I think I probably should have been a teeny bit more restrained, tried to show a bit more self-control or something, because the words brazen and slut keep coming into my mind, and I'm not entirely sure that's the image I want to be going for. I haven't got the right kind of underwear for a start. And I've been having freeze-frame moments all morning whenever I close my eyes, and none of them are suitable for daytime television. And if he does call it's going to get very complicated very quickly. And if he doesn't I'll be mortified.

Thank god the job went well this morning, because I really don't think I could have handled anything major. We had a tricky moment with the crane, and one of the stuntmen fell off his bicycle into a drainage ditch, and got covered in vast quantities of evil-smelling mud, but apart from that we got finished really early, and I managed to get Barney and the crew on to an earlier flight to Heathrow. Which was a very lucky break, because sitting in airports with them whingeing and whining is definitely to be avoided at the best of times, let alone if you've only had about ten minutes' sleep.

I'm booked on a flight to Gatwick because it's nearer to home, so I'm stuck here at the sodding airport and desperately trying to stay awake long enough not to miss my flight, trying to make a lukewarm cappuccino last as long as possible because I've nearly run out of Euros.

I decide to call home to check in with mission control, and Mum puts Charlie straight on so he can launch into a tirade about his horrible day. They've had music and movement this afternoon, which he hates, with Mrs Beamish, who's a nutter. She only comes in two afternoons a week to float lots of chiffon scarves about and get them all to be elements. It was wind last time. Which I thought was rather brave of her, to be honest. Today it was sunshine, apparently.

'You've got to tell her, Mummy. Me and James hate dancing. We really do.'

'Don't be silly, Charlie.'

'And she made us have bare feet. We might have got splintered.'

'It was in the hall, wasn't it? Where you do PE, Charlie. And you have bare feet for PE, don't you?'

'Yes. But that's different. That's got wall bars.'

Time to change the subject, I think.

'Is Nana doing you a lovely tea?'

'Yes. With a cake. A proper one. From Marks and Spensives.'

'Great.'

'And when will you be home, Mummy?'

He's using his special wheedling voice, which with the help of my handy in-built motherhood translator I quickly decode into when exactly will I be getting my present.

'You'll probably be asleep, sweetheart. But I'll come in and give you a kiss goodnight, the minute I get home.'

'Oh.'

In other words, fat lot of use that will be, what about the present?

'And there might be a little surprise in the morning.'

Bingo. That's more like it.

'I love you, Mummy.'

'Only a little present, mind.'

'I know, bye.'

I wonder if he's going to be quite so chirpy when he sees just how little we're talking. It's already wrapped up and on top of my wardrobe; it's a small box of Lego, a horse with a knight. But he's got a silver sword so I'm hoping there won't be appeals to Childline. Although you never know; he was threatening to call the United Nations in last week because I was violating his human rights by washing his hair and getting soap in his eyes. Actually I'd quite like to have seen how the boys in the blue helmets would have coped with a small person covered in soap bubbles throwing a strop. I bet they'd have ended up using the water cannon. Anyway, I'm hoping the silver sword will do the trick, because he's a sucker for anything with a sword.

But the having-a-present-whenever-I'm-working-away-from-home routine is definitely getting out of hand. Obviously it's great that he doesn't lie in front of the car screeching or clamp himself to my leg as I try to leave the house, but I thought the present thing would have faded out by now. Maybe I should just buy more boring presents, like jigsaws. Or one of those horrible maths books where you learn your times tables with cartoon characters and really annoying rhymes. Because if I don't start downgrading on the gift front soon I'm still going to be buying him little surprises when it's him going off on business trips.

Mum comes on the line and updates me on the progress she's made with reorganising the garage, which she discovered was in a shocking mess when she was putting the rake away, although why she had the rake out in the first place is still a complete mystery to me. She spent half of yesterday untangling bits of hosepipe and garden twine, and Dad was round at B&Q first thing this morning buying shelving.

'It's looking much better. You can find things now without something else falling over.'

'That's great, thanks, Mum.'

'And I thought we'd use up that tin of white paint. You weren't keeping it for anything, were you?'

'No.'

'Good. Because your father's already done one coat on the back wall, although it could do with another one.'

She'll be hanging curtains at the windows next.

'Thanks, Mum.'

Call-waiting starts beeping on my phone.

'I've got to go, Mum, I'll see you later.'

'All right, but be careful. And don't drive too fast on that motorway.'

I don't recognise the number but it's bound to be one of the crew ringing up for a whine about something. Lost luggage probably, since they'll be in Heathrow by now.

'Good afternoon, Moneypenny. And how are you? Not feeling quite as knackered as I am, I hope.'

Christ, it's Mack. I sit up a bit straighter and accidentally knock my coffee cup over.

'Fuck.'

'How charming.'

'Sorry. But I've just spilt my coffee.'

'Shaken but not stirred, right?'

'It's gone everywhere. Oh Christ.'

I must look like a particularly urgent candidate for lady-incontinence products.

'Where are you?'

'At the airport.'

'And are we talking an entire cup of coffee, head to toe sort of thing?'

'Pretty much. Soaking wet in Schiphol. Christ. It's gone everywhere.'

'Sounds like the title of a very dodgy movie to me.'

He's laughing. How annoying.

'What time's your flight?'

'Another couple of hours.'

I'm dripping on the floor now. Actually dripping.

'Go shopping then. They've got some quite interesting shops at that airport. Maybe you could get a little rubber outfit. Very good for spillages, I'd imagine.'

He's still laughing. Bastard.

'Mack. Try and rearrange these words into a sentence. Off. Right. And Fuck. Have you got it yet?'

'I think so. Almost. Can I have another consonant and a couple of vowels?'

'You think you're being very clever, don't you?'

'I'm not the one who's wearing a beverage, sweetheart.'

I think I'm just going to ignore him.

'Moneypenny. You still there?'

'Yes. But not for much longer. There's a puddle forming now.'

'Well, before you go I just wanted to say hello.'

'Hello.'

'And I'll call you later, when you're home and dry, shall I? But it might have to be tomorrow, because I've got a work thing tonight, and I didn't want you to think I was playing it cool, or any of that bollocks. I think we're beyond all that now, and anyway I'm not cool. Never have been. I can't be bothered with all that game playing.'

Crikey.

'Oh. Well, that's good.'

'So maybe dinner, later in the week or something?'

'That would be lovely.'

'Bye, darling.'

The phone goes dead. I'd forgotten he does that; cuts the phone off the minute he's finished speaking. But still. Darling. He called me darling. And he rang. And he's not Cool. How very brilliant. I'd quite like to enjoy the moment for a bit longer but people are giving me rather odd looks, so I think I'd better squelch off towards the loos and get changed before someone alerts the airport staff that there's a nutter in the café. And then I'll call Leila for a debrief.

It's nearly ten by the time I get home, and Mum insists on practically spoon-feeding me shepherd's pie after I've completed a short but very detailed tour of the garage, which is looking fabulous, and much tidier than it's ever looked before. In fact I could enter into a That's My Garage competition, if they have them. I'd be sure to win.

'Well, at least you'll be able to find things now.'

'Thanks, Mum.'

'Oh and some man rang earlier, said he'd call back. Wouldn't give his name.'

She gives me a very piercing look; her antennae are pretty finely tuned after years of constant practice with me and Lizzie, and she's definitely picking up on something, only she's not sure what.

'So he'll have been someone from work then?'

'Yeah.'

231

'Don't say yeah, Annie. You're not a cowboy.'

She's been saying this for so long now I almost don't hear her.

'Well, he sounded very nice anyway.'

She's still digging.

'They are nice, Mum, the people I work with. Well, apart from Barney.'

She tuts. She doesn't approve of Barney. Too much swearing. She came into the office once and heard him yelling down the stairs to Stef after he spilled tea all over the white rug in his office and she's never forgotten it.

'Do you want a hot drink before bed? And a digestive?'

'Yes please.'

Mum and Dad are staying the night, even though they only live half an hour's drive away, because Mum won't let Dad drive in the dark. As far as she's concerned head-lights are for emergency use only.

'I've done his packed lunch for the morning. A nice pasta salad.'

'Great.'

'And I put a couple of sausage rolls in too, because a salad's not going to keep him going all day, is it, bless him. And a Penguin. And yes, I know, there's no need to look at me like that, I know they're supposed to have fruit, so I've put a satsuma in as well.'

'Thanks, Mum.'

Dear god. He'll need an extra rucksack just for his lunch. Beam me up somebody, quick. Maybe I'll just go and have a nice long bath.

I'm in my bedroom unpacking my bag and generally dithering about when the phone rings.

'Annie?'

'Hello, Mack.'

'Got home safely?'

'Yes, fine, thanks.'

'Did you get the rubber outfit?'

'No, they didn't have anything in your size. So I put you on the mailing list, and they'll send you their catalogue. I gave them your work address. That was right, wasn't it?'

He laughs.

'Anything to liven them up a bit in that office. Jesus Christ, I've just had the most fucking boring client dinner ever. Total waste of an evening.'

'Oh dear.'

'Yes. And nobody spilt anything, or set fire to their hair or anything. Boring bastards.'

I once slightly singed the ends of my hair on a candle at a drunken dinner party and I seriously wish I'd never told him about it.

'And then they all wanted to go to some hideous lap-dancing club.'

'Like Spearmint Hippos?'

'I think you'll find it's rhinos, sweetheart, but yes, that's exactly the sort of thing.'

'So is that where you are then, in a rhino?'

'No, Christ, give me some credit. I stuck them in a cab and said I'd see them tomorrow. The juniors have gone with them, poor sods, to make sure none of them get arrested or anything. Anyway, I've checked the diary and I'm in Frankfurt on Friday.'

'Oh.'

'Yes, but I'll be back by six. So we could meet around eight, give air traffic time to fuck up.'

'Great.'

'My office?'

'Sure.'

'Night, darling.'

The line goes dead.

I wonder if there's any way I can get him to stop doing that.

Kate and I are having lunch the next day round at her house and fast-forwarding through our various collections of musical videos and DVDs. It's amazing how many you accumulate without noticing it when you've got small people in the house. We've done *Mary Poppins* and *Oliver* and we're about to start on *Chitty Chitty Bang Bang*.

'Tell me again why we're doing this?'

Kate reaches for another Hobnob.

'To remind ourselves of the songs.'

'Right, and then we come up with a shortlist?'

'Yes. Do you think we should include something from *Annie*? "The sun'll come out, tomorrow." That one?'

'Over my dead body. Anyway, we've got to give the kids a chance. It's really high, that song. They'd never make it.'

'True. See, I knew you'd be great at this. So tell me about Mack again. It's so romantic, flying back from Frankfurt just so you can have dinner. Will you two be getting back together again, do you think? Properly, I mean.'

'I don't really know. It was all such a surprise. We didn't really talk much. But it was only one night in a hotel. So who knows. Do you think that's a bad sign, that we didn't really talk?'

'Don't ask me – it's decades since I had a night in a hotel with anybody, except for my mother, at that wedding last year. And that was a total disaster.'

They'd ended up sharing a double bed because there

were no twins available, and Kate's mother spent the whole night telling Kate exactly where she'd gone wrong with Phil. Kate says she was seriously considering suffocating her with her pillow.

'But he's called you, hasn't he, and that's got to be a good sign.'

'I hope so. We'll just have to see how Friday goes. How was Gabriel, by the way, last night, talking of good signs? Still keen?'

'I think so, but it's driving me crazy. Every time we start to get going, you know, where it looks like something might happen, his bloody phone starts ringing.'

'What was it this time? Not the mad goat again?'

When they went out for supper Gabriel had to leave early to sort out a goat that had eaten a fairly substantial amount of wire fencing.

'Some horse, I think. Although it's probably a good thing really. It's like swimming, isn't it? When you haven't been for ages, that moment before you dive in, when you know you're going to sink straight to the bottom.'

'Maybe you could wear armbands.'

'Yes, and that's another thing.'

She's gone very red.

'What?'

'The condom thing. It's too ghastly. I mean when are you supposed to mention that kind of thing? Do you wait until you get going and then run the risk of losing the moment or do you just blurt it out early on? I mean not that it was on the cards last night, obviously, it was just a drink, but still, I can't help thinking about it, and I know I'll end up blurting. Anyway, I drove into Tonbridge yesterday, just in case, so at least I avoided Jane Phillips. But still. It makes me feel panicky just thinking about it.'

Jane Phillips lives in our village and works in the

pharmacy at our local chemist's. She wears white clogs and a white overall and sometimes wears her uniform when she drops her daughter off at school. And she's a terrible gossip. So everyone has to trail into Boots in Tonbridge if we don't want our more confidential purchases bandied about the playground.

Kate reaches for another biscuit.

'It takes the spontaneity out of it, doesn't it? Not like when we were young – you only had to be on the pill and you were fine. But I don't know why I'm getting myself into such a bother about it really, since we're probably doomed to be interrupted by mad animals hurling themselves on things. I've probably got more chance of winning the lottery. Release the balls is such a good phrase, isn't it?'

We both snigger.

'You could always try saying that.'

'I think he's quite shy, you know. It's what I like most about him. So different to Phil. He was always lungeing at me, you know. Sometimes with absolutely no warning. I was always losing my G & T down the arm of the sofa. Horrible man. Although if Gabriel doesn't get a move on soon I think I'll have to do a spot of lungeing myself.'

We do a bit more sniggering.

'Well, lunge away, I'd say. I'm sure he'd like it.'

'I'd have to be very drunk. And then I might miss.'

'Well, give it a try, ask him round to supper and get plastered. I'll have the kids for the night.'

'Oh would you, really?'

'Sure. You're having Charlie on Friday, so it'll be my turn anyway. That's if you're still sure it's OK?'

'Oh yes, James loves it when Charlie stays. He's already planning what they're going to be doing. What will you wear, something new?'

'I don't know. Leila's practically ordering me to go shopping, but I'm not sure. I don't want to look like I'm trying too hard.'

'Wear what you'll feel comfortable in. Honestly. I wish I had. I could have had a pudding yesterday if I hadn't been wearing my new skirt.'

We've got fifteen songs for the shortlist by the time we drive off in convoy to collect the kids from school, and I'm still campaigning to add the suffragette song from *Mary Poppins* to the list, if only to see Mrs Harrison-Black's face when we get the kids marching round on stage demanding Votes for Women. And if Lizzie's coming down to see the show I'd quite like to try to get something from *Bedknobs and Broomsticks* in, because it was her favourite when we were little. She used to spend ages sitting on her bed tapping her headboard in the hopes of being transported off somewhere magical. I've still got a few more films to check through tonight. I'm thinking maybe we could slip something in from *The Rocky Horror Show*. Or *Cabaret*. I'm sure Year Six would love that. '*Willkommen, Bienvenue* . . .' So multicultural. And the girls would love the outfits.

Charlie's had a good day at school, with an epic game of It on the field at lunchtime, so his shirt's covered in grass stains and his hair's sticking up in tufts. Apparently the dinner lady had to resort to blowing her whistle to get them to calm down, and since she pretty much saves this for emergency situations only it must have been pretty lively out there.

We read the prescribed three pages from his reading book, without the usual diversionary tactics, and then end up having a mammoth random-chatting routine while he eats his supper, and after a quick burst of cartoons I persuade him to watch *Bugsy Malone* on video, which I'd forgotten I taped at Christmas. Maybe we can find a budding Tallulah from the ranks, or maybe Justin might fancy it.

Charlie loves the foam-spouting machine guns, and is particularly taken with the pedal cars, but as far as he's concerned the ending's a complete travesty. He stares horrified as the final battle deteriorates into a custard-pie fight, and when everyone gets up and starts belting out 'You Give a Little Love and It All Comes Back to You' he can't stand it any more and grabs the clickers and switches the telly off.

'That film's total crap.'

'Charlie!'

'Why can't I say crap? It's not that rude. Bugger is much ruder. And you say that all the time. And bloody. That's much ruder. Jack Knight said bloody in choosing time today and he had to stand in the home corner.'

'That's enough, Charlie.'

'And I'm not having a bath tonight. Definite. You don't have to have a bath every night, you know. There's no actual law.'

He gives me a furious look.

I start humming 'My Name is Tallulah'.

'Stop singing that song. I hate that film.'

'I'll stop when you're in the bath.'

He carries on scowling, but starts walking towards the stairs. How brilliant. Maybe this concert thing is going to come in handy after all.

I'm having lunch with Leila on Friday for last-minute outfit approval for my dinner with Mack, and for once she hasn't insisted on racing me round countless posh shops. She thinks my black linen suit is fine, but announces that I'm

238

not allowed to wear my new slinky vest under the jacket or I'll look like a store manager for M&S. Apparently I must wear nothing at all, and do a clever trick with some special kind of tape that sticks your jacket to your chest so you don't inadvertently flash people when you're walking along the street. She's got some in her office, apparently. I don't bloody think so.

Just when I think I'm going to have to throw zabaglione at her to get her to shut up she relents and says the really vital thing is to have fun and not take it too seriously. And I'm welcome to stay with her later if I need to, only she might be out, but Tor will be in, and I'm not to panic if he takes a while to open the door because he might be in a cleansing trance.

'Thanks, Leila.'

'And call me, all right, if he comes up with any stunts. Go to the loo and call me. And I'll talk you down from there.'

'Right.'

'Oh fuck, my meeting's turned up early.'

Her phone is vibrating round the table.

'I'd better go. So tell him I said hello, and I hope Trident are being a total fucking nightmare. Actually, I pretty much know they are. So tell him I said it serves him right.'

'Will do.'

When I get back to the office Lawrence and Barney are still bickering about our office summer drinks party. Lawrence's decided we've got to have one for all our agency clients, and he's holding out for a posh club while Barney's insisting on having it at the office with a few bottles of Tizer and a packet of crisps. By half-past four Barney's finally had enough and decrees that we'll be having a small gathering in the office, in a few weeks' time, in a low-key kind of way, and Stef and I can ring round everybody and organise the whole thing, thank you very much. And we're not to spend a fortune or he'll be taking it off our wages. Brilliant.

And then Lawrence decides to have another go on the moving-the-desks-around front with me, since I've refused to be in the basement, or the room in the back. His new plan is to move my desk so it's facing the wall in the darkest corner by the stairs, and he wants to know if I really need a filing cabinet, because they take up so much space.

'And where am I supposed to keep all the job files then, Lawrence?'

'In the archive files in the basement. Didn't you read my memo?'

'What memo?'

Actually, I threw it away.

'All paper relating to completed jobs must be stored in the archive files.'

'Right. So every time we want to check anything we have to go downstairs then? That's not very efficient, is it? And anyway, you've got two filing cabinets by your desk. What's in them then, the non-archive files?'

Lawrence likes to keep his paperwork secret, and only let you see it when you've put in a written request. Which is bloody annoying when you're trying to do a budget in a hurry.

'I can't talk to you when you're being like this, I think you do it on purpose, Annie. You just like making things difficult. And what are you doing, Stef? Aren't you meant to be making calls about the drinks party?'

He glares at Stef, who's been standing behind his back making faces.

'That's what I want to talk to you both about, Lawrence.

They're all booked. So we're knackered. Annie might be able to come up with someone else but not if you piss her off all afternoon.'

Lawrence goes off to sulk, leaving Stef and me frantically calling round the caterers who do food for us on shoots, but they're either booked or don't do drinks parties. Bloody hell.

By the time I'm in my taxi Stef's still making calls, and I'm already running late. I haven't heard from Mack so I'm assuming he's back from Frankfurt, but when I get to the office the receptionist says he's still on the way in from Heathrow, and I'm to go up to the fifteenth floor where one of his assistants is waiting for me.

It's all very designerly, with acres of pale marble, in fact just the kind of marble that makes you slip and fall flat on your face when you're wearing new pointy slingbacks. I walk very carefully towards the lift, which is all glass and mirrors, and swooshes me up to the top floor at a tremendous rate. I'm busy checking my make-up when the doors suddenly open and a stunning young woman in a much smarter suit than mine and fabulous high heels steps forward.

'Annie, hi. Mack said would you mind waiting a few moments, only he's caught up in traffic. Would you like a drink?'

She's smiling, but in a rather icy kind of a way. I wonder what she'd do if I said I'd quite like a triple vodka. God, I'm feeling nervous.

'No, I'm fine, thanks.'

'Sure?'

She doesn't look too pleased. Oh good. It's going to be one of those moments where you have to have a drink or they get all huffy.

'Actually, a water would be great.'

241

'Sparkling or still?'

'Sparkling, please.'

'Mimi, could you get a Pellegrino for Annie, please.'

A woman appears from the other side of a door at the far end of the room and nods.

Crikey, this office is enormous. Full of trendy denim sofas with unusual cushions and huge pale wooden desks.

'What a great office. Lucky Mack.'

I smile at her. Which is a complete waste of time. She does her icy pursed-lips thing again.

'Thanks. We like it. Now, if you'll just follow me, Mack's office is just through here.'

Oh. Great.

She opens a door and leads me into another enormous room, with more sofas and a huge flat-screen television, and a large circular table covered in paper and what looks like bits of newspaper and pages ripped out of magazines. Nice to see Mack is still wildly untidy.

'Do sit down. I'm sure he won't be long.'

She's watching me very closely, like she thinks I might nick something. Actually, she's really starting to piss me off.

'I'm fine, thanks.'

Mimi glides in with my glass of water. She's wearing incredibly high heels too. I walk towards one of the windows and the view's amazing. Miles of rooftops and trees, and the streets shimmering with evening traffic.

Suddenly there's the sound of the lift doors opening again and Mack marches in, jabbering into his phone.

'I've got to go now, but we'll talk later, George, OK? Great.'

He snaps the phone shut.

'Fucking hell, what a day. Hello, Annie, how's it going? Knocked over any coffee yet?'

Lovely.

'Hi, Tina, don't tell me, I've got nine hundred people who need calling, but I'm not here, OK? I'll sort it in the morning.'

'It's Saturday tomorrow, Mack, and New York want to – '

'I'll sort it on Monday then. OK? So off you go, both of you. You must have better places to be than here.'

Mimi's lurking in the doorway.

'Well, if you're sure.'

'Sure.'

They both fade back through the doorway and the door closes.

'Are they on castors or something?'

'What?'

'Is there some sort of office dress code, where the women have to wear six-inch heels and glide around like they're on castors? Because if there is I think I might be in trouble.'

Mack snorts.

'No. It's just some girls know how to walk in high heels. And some girls know how to tip coffee all over the place. Have they got you a drink, by the way?'

'Yes.'

The door opens again. It's Tina.

'Mack, the car's downstairs and everything you asked for is ready for you at home, in the kitchen. But call me if you need anything, OK? Anything at all.'

'Thanks, Tina.'

The doors close again. Something tells me Tina might have a tiny crush on her boss.

'That was meant to be a surprise. Sorry. I thought I'd cook for us tonight – make a change from another bloody restaurant. But I don't think she reckons I'm up to it – she's been fussing about it all day.'

I bet she has.

'Oh right. Well, that sounds lovely.'

'Now there's something I've got to say to you. And you need to listen, OK?'

Oh dear. This doesn't sound good.

'It's about the car. There's a chauffeur. With a hat. And it wasn't my choice. It just sort of comes with the job. And I know it's bollocks. But if you could restrain yourself from pointing out what a total wanker this makes me look while we're actually in the car, I'd be really grateful, because I haven't had time to sort anything else out yet.'

'Fair enough. He isn't called James, by any chance, is he?'

'Who?'

'The chauffeur. So you can say "Home, James". Isn't that what you're supposed to say?'

'Yes. You see, this is what I thought might happen.'

'Is there a glass partition? So you can tap on it and say pull over here for a moment, I need a muffin from Starbucks.'

'Shall we go?'

'Love to.'

'And, Annie?'

'Yes?'

'There's also an eject button, for annoying passengers. So I'm warning you.'

'Like the key to the executive bathroom, you mean? One of the perks of being the top boy.'

'Maybe you should just sit in the boot.'

A big black gleaming Mercedes is waiting outside with a very smart-looking chauffeur, complete with a hat with a shiny brim. He leaps out and runs round to open the door for us.

'Good evening, sir. Madam.'

'Evening, Stewart.'

'Home, sir?'

'Yes. But madam wants a muffin from Starbucks on the way.'

He doesn't even flicker.

'No problem at all, sir.'

The car whisks us to Mack's house in Notting Hill in no time at all, almost in complete silence. Somehow we both seem to have suddenly got rather self-conscious. I think it must be all the black leather and tinted windows. But at least I've now got a double chocolate-chip muffin in my bag if things get complicated.

It's pretty weird being back at Mack's house after so long. Last time I was here we ended up cooking supper for all the kids, with Alfie and Charlie chopping vegetables, and planning a major shopping moment in Hamleys, which is where I'm assuming Mack bought the racing-car set that is now spread all over the living-room floor.

'Nice race track.'

'I had the kids over at the weekend and I haven't got round to putting it away yet.'

'You play with it when you get in from work, you mean.'

'I do not.'

'So which is your car then?'

'The red Ferrari, of course.'

'Right.'

He smiles.

'Shall I start on supper?'

'Lovely. Do you want a hand with anything?'

'You could do the salad, if you like.'

I end up making the salad, mixing up some dressing, setting the table, emptying the dishwasher and hulling the strawberries while Mack stands by the griddle pan and waves a spatula at the steaks. I'm even thinking about giving the work surfaces a quick wipe down, but manage to restrain myself. It must be some recessive gene from Mum, surfacing at last. She'll be so pleased.

The steaks are perfect. Just the right side of cooked, so it doesn't feel like you're conducting an autopsy.

'Fuck. There were potatoes. I forgot about the potatoes.'

'Never mind. I thought you must be on the Atkins diet or something.'

'Take that back or I'll throw salad at you.'

'Lots of people are, you know.'

'Nutters maybe. Not Special Agents.'

'True.'

'They're all totally obsessed with it in New York, perfectly ordinary-looking people, blokes too. They all know the fat content of practically every substance ever invented. And the other half of the country are the size of fucking trailers. And as for smoking, Christ, it almost makes me want to take it up.'

'Leila said she practically got arrested for smoking a cigarette outside her hotel last time she was in New York.'

'I'm not surprised. How is she, by the way, still terrifying everybody?'

'She only terrifies you, Mack. Because you tried to steal her client that time. Everybody else thinks she's lovely.'

'Oh no they bloody don't. I was talking to an account director who used to work for her a while ago, and he was still terrified of her. Did you know she sticks notices on people's heads in meetings, if they annoy her?'

'Does she?'

'Yes. With those yellow sticky note things. They have to sit there with a bit of paper stuck to their head saying "Wanker".'

Actually, I can just see Leila doing that, but I'm not telling him that.

'I bet he just made it up.'

'It's not that bad on idea, you know. I might give it a try at our next creative brainstorm.'

We eat the strawberries, which are delicious, and talk about work, and then I make a rather major mistake by asking him how Daisy and Alfie are doing and he gets rather tense.

'They're fine. Why?'

'No reason, I just wondered.'

'Well, they're fine.'

'Good.'

There's an awkward silence.

'Well, Daisy's been a bit difficult, I suppose, but nothing major. I think she's pissed off with me for going to New York, and she didn't really get on with Vanessa. They came over for a week at half-term and well, it didn't really work out. Actually, it was a bit of a nightmare.'

'Oh dear.'

I knew it. I knew Vanessa wouldn't be up for too much in the way of child-centred activity. Hah.

'Well, I don't think I handled it very well, I sort of left them to it. I was working, you see, so I thought they'd go shopping, that kind of thing. But it was a disaster. Vanessa got frantic, and even Alfie got bolshie.'

'Did he?'

Good old Alfie.

'That's when I knew really, that it wasn't going to work out, not that she was pushing or anything. She was pretty cool about it all. Pretty cool girl altogether really, apart from the obsession with clothes.'

'Right.'

Great. So now we can have a nice little chat about how cool Vanessa is.

He smiles.

'Anyway, that's all history now. What about you? Been seeing anybody? Since, well, you know.'

'Oh hundreds of people.'

'Hundreds?'

'Yes. They've had to form a queue.'

'Naturally.'

'It's been hell.'

'Keeping track, that kind of thing?'

'Exactly.'

He's still smiling.

'And how's Charlie?'

'He's fine. He got a pheasant for his birthday. Well, two, actually. From Uncle Monty.'

'I bet that went down well. And Monty's still round the twist, right?'

'Completely.'

'Good for him. There's no point being that far past your sell-by date if you can't be round the twist. Coffee?'

'Please.'

While he's in the kitchen making coffee I realise I'm feeling pretty tense, and I don't really know why. Or how to fix it. Maybe another glass of wine might help. Or maybe I should just try to be cool, live for the moment, and not rake over the past. Yes, that would probably be best.

He comes back in with the coffee.

'Do you want milk? Only I don't seem to have any.'

'Black's fine.'

'Sure?'

'So what's going on, Mack?'

Bugger. Bang goes being cool.

'I'm pouring you a cup of coffee?'

'No, I mean – '

'I know what you mean, Annie.'

He's walking towards me now, with the coffee.

'Can we not do this? Not right now.'

'What?'

'The Big Conversation thing. Can we do it later?'

He's smiling, and doing his raising-his-eyebrows thing. Bugger.

'Only I think I've got a better idea.'

And yes. I suppose it is technically my fault that he then spills the coffee all over the floor. And yes. It is highly amusing that I don't seem to be able to cope with anything remotely resembling a hot drink when he's around. Highly amusing.

'Maybe we should try you out with tea?'

'It was your fault.'

'Maybe it's some special force-field kind of thing, like Uri Geller. Do you ever notice forks bending?'

'Mack.'

'Yes.'

'Shut. Up. Or I think you'll find I'll be leaving and drinking my coffee elsewhere.'

'Oh no you bloody won't.'

We finally do the talking thing at about half-past two in the morning, while I'm making toast and Mack's leaning against the fridge wrapped in a sheet and trying to persuade me to give him his dressing gown back. He's off to New York next week, but talking about us going away for a weekend, like we're now back to being an official couple. Which is nice. Although just a tiny bit overwhelming; I think I'd quite like to stay at the new-affair stage for a little bit longer. But then I'd far rather he was being all keen than doing the I'll-call-you thing.

'Maybe we could try getting all the kids together again, have a week away somewhere. Like we did last year. What do you think? You could book somewhere for us, or shall I get one of the girls in the office to do some research, see what's available? Hawaii's supposed to be good this time of year.'

Bloody hell. I'm not sure I'm quite ready for family holidays just yet. It's all going a bit fast suddenly, just like last time.

'Maybe we should take things a bit more slowly.'

'Is this some sort of hot sex-tip you've picked up from *Cosmopolitan* or something?'

'No.'

'*Marie Claire?*'

'Mack, I'm serious.'

'I know. And yes. We can take things slowly. Whatever that means.'

'It means we just take our time, and see how it goes, and don't rush into any big changes. No big plans for racing off to Tahiti or wherever's next on your list.'

'I haven't got a list.'

Oh dear. He's looking rather tense. I think I've gone a bit too far.

'You know what I mean, Mack.'

'Is this you trying to tell me you've got someone else on the go? Because I'm not up for that.'

'No, of course not. But that's the point really. It's more important than somebody else. It's me. My life, and Charlie's. Friends, family, Monty, that kind of thing. I can't just drop everything and be available every weekend for jaunts – it's just not that simple, Mack – and neither can you. You've got the kids to think about as well. Let's just take it slowly, not fast-forward and then crash and burn again like last time.'

'Weekend jaunts sound good.'

'I know.'

'OK. Slowly it is. With jaunts. Isn't that bloody toast done yet?'

'No. Your grill's really slow.'

'That's probably because it's not a grill.'

'Ah.'

'The toaster's over there.'

'Well, why didn't you say?'

'I wasn't really concentrating. I did kind of wonder what you were doing with the oven, but I thought it was probably some secret girl-thing. Broiling or something. Actually, what is broiling?'

'I've got absolutely no idea.'

'Do you want some more tea?'

'Yes please.'

'Well, put the kettle on then, and I'll go and see if I can find some plastic sheeting. I think there's some in the cupboard in the hall. Save on the cleaning bills.'

I'm so happy driving home on Saturday morning I could almost tie a bow in my hair. Mack's already called me on my mobile to say he's got one of my bracelets and he's keeping it hostage, and I haven't even made it out of town and on to the motorway yet. I've talked to Leila, who thinks it all sounds brilliant, and I've spoken to Kate, who says Charlie's fine and he and James are building a camp in the garden. I'm really looking forward to getting home and just savouring how well things are going for a change. I'm singing along to Aretha Franklin and the sun's shining. And there's no school run tomorrow morning, so I can have a lie-in. Perfect.

I'm feeling so chirpy I don't even mind the long queue of cars dawdling along on the motorway; there's probably a police car up in front somewhere. They're all driving at just under seventy, which is always a bit of a give-away, and I'm singing along to the music and feeling very mellow. While I'm overtaking a lorry a man in a white transit van comes belting up behind me, headlights blaring, even though the outside lane is empty, and starts flashing his lights. He flashes a few more times, and makes rude hand gestures and then moves into the outside lane and races off, leaving a black trail of smoke from his exhaust. I say a little prayer to the gods of motorway justice, but I'm not holding out much hope: they're usually too busy making lorries break down so there are fifteen-mile tailbacks.

But then a police car decloaks from the inside lane where it's been hiding between two lorries, and turns the blue lights on. Yess. A couple of minutes later I drive past them on the hard shoulder. The policeman's looking very pleased with himself, wearing his fluorescent jacket and walking very slowly towards the van. I'm almost tempted to wave as I drive past. Somebody give that officer a medal, or at least extra custard in the canteen at lunchtime. Brilliant.

Charlie's not terribly pleased to see me when I get to Kate's, because he's having far too much fun building the camp, so we end up staying for lunch, and Kate and I drink gin and tonics in the sunshine, which is highly diverting, but it does mean Charlie and I have to walk home.

I'm feeling even more mellow now, and Charlie's running ahead of me, down the lane, bashing things with his stick, and lobbying for a lolly from the shop.

'I'm really hot. I need one.'

'There are lollies in the freezer at home, Charlie.'

'Yes. But only stupid juice ones. I want a proper one. An ice-pole one.'

The ice-poles are a neon turquoise colour and look just like you imagine antifreeze would look if you made it into lollies, only with more chemicals. Last time he had one he almost went into orbit. I think I'll try changing the subject.

'We've got to make a cake for Uncle Monty's birthday this afternoon.'

'We could buy one in the shop.'

Actually, that's not a bad idea.

'All right. But only if you promise not to be silly about the lollies. You can have a proper one, Charlie, not one of those horrible pole things, they're full of rubbish.'

'OK. I'll have a Magnum. A white chocolate one. Oh thank you, Mummy, you're the best mummy in the entire world.'

Bugger. I've got a sneaking feeling I've just been outmanoeuvred, again.

'How many candles will Uncle Monty have on his cake?'

'Oh just a few.'

'No. You have to have one for every year.'

It'll have to be a bloody big cake then. I was thinking more along the lines of a small sponge.

'And balloons. We've got to have balloons.'

We spend most of the afternoon covered in a thin but persistent layer of white icing, after Charlie insists on buying a Mr Kipling Country Cake, which he says is Monty's favourite, and then icing it. It looks pretty ridiculous, covered in candles and with the icing dribbling down the sides in a non-Nigella kind of way. But I'm rather hoping Monty belongs to the it's-the-thought-that-counts school on birthday cakes, and anyway I was just too knackered for a full-blown shelf-rattling frank exchange of views in the village shop. Mrs Denton was on the till, and she always makes me feel like she's judging me, and isn't terribly impressed. She belongs to the slap-and-tell brigade of parenting, and has two rather aggressive boys to prove

253

it. They're both at school with Charlie, though thankfully not in his class.

Charlie spends ages balanced on a stool in the kitchen doing the writing with a blue icing pen, and gets so much icing everywhere that I'm seriously worried that the only way I'm going to get him off his stool is with a chisel.

He finally finishes by giving himself a round of applause.

'It looks lovely, doesn't it, Mummy?'

'Lovely.'

'I'm quite good at writing now, aren't I?'

'Brilliant.'

I just hope Monty's going to understand why we're giving him a cake that appears to say 'Happy Bathdog Mandy'.

While Charlie's upstairs de-icing, I go off into a reverie about Mack. I'm trying really hard not to fast-forward but I can't help it. If we are back together again, and it looks like we might be, then I'm still not sure how it's going to work. I don't want to just bob along behind him, like one of those little dinghies people drag behind their cruisers. And there's Charlie to think about: he really got on well with Mack, before. But Mack wasn't really around for that long, so he never encroached on Charlie's territory. And I'm wondering, if things get more permanent this time, whether Charlie might start to get rattled.

Kate says Phoebe and James are already giving Gabriel a fairly hard time, whenever he arrives to pick her up. But she thinks that's down to them feeling more alert to parental dramas: they've both felt supplanted by Zelda and Saffron, and seen Kate really devastated, so she thinks they're sort of looking out for it. Whereas Charlie pretty much assumes he's the centre of everything and always will be. Because he always has been. So maybe it'll be fine. But then there's Daisy and Alfie to consider. Oh god.

I'm busy planning Christmas lunch and wondering what to buy for Daisy, despite resolving to stop obsessing about it, when I hear Charlie turning the bath taps on. Which isn't a good sign. I'd better go up and investigate.

'Turn the taps off, Charlie.'

'The water's run out.'

'That's because it's all over the floor.'

'I was just playing.'

'Charlie. Look at the mess. Come on. Out. Now.'

'But – '

'No, Charlie. No buts. Out. And help me dry the floor. And then there might be time for a story. Or maybe even a film. But not if you sit there being silly.'

He gets out grumbling, and wafts a flannel about in a vague attempt to mop up.

'Go and put your pyjamas on. They're on your bed. While I finish this.'

'Are you very cross, Mummy?'

'Yes.'

'Shall I stroke your back?'

'No.'

'There's no need to be rude.'

He stomps off. Maybe another little gin and tonic with supper might be a good plan.

Monty's delighted with his cake the next day, and says it's the nicest one he's ever had, which just goes to show that even barking old codgers can be very good liars. Charlie's outside irritating the pheasants, who tend to huddle at the far end of the pen and give him supercilious looks while he regales them with his latest adventures. But he doesn't seem to mind.

Monty and I are having another cup of tea.

'I can't remember the last time I had a proper birthday cake.'

'Well, happy birthday for tomorrow, Monty.'

'It's a terrible thing, you know, getting old. Waking up and realising that you're an old man all of a sudden. And you don't feel any different, not until you forget and try to shift something, like when you were younger. Brings you up sharp, I can tell you. It's a terrible business.'

'You're not that old, Monty. Well, you don't seem it, anyway.'

'Oh yes I am. Some mornings I am. Sometimes I think I'm getting a touch of that alka-seltzers.'

'What?'

'You know. When you forget what your name is and put your dinner in the washer. Sometimes I'll be going upstairs, or across the yard to the barn, and by the time I've got there I can't remember what I was after.'

'I do that all the time, Monty. Especially in shops. If I don't have a list it's hopeless.'

'Your Aunty Florrie always had to have a list. She'd spend ages writing one, and then leave it on the kitchen table. Daft as a brush. Always was, right from when I first met her. She was learning to ride a bike, and in them days women didn't ride bikes much. Kept falling off, she did. I used to have to run along beside her ready to catch her. We used to go miles.'

He smiles and looks into the distance.

'I always thought I'd be the first to go, you know. Selfish really, but I did. And it's not the same without her, even though she was always fussing, and always washing things. Wash the shirt right off your back if you let her and leave you sitting in your vest. But I miss her.'

He looks faintly surprised by this, and rather embarrassed.

'Maybe if we'd had children it'd be different, not so much like the end of the line.'

I've never really heard him talk like this before. He occasionally mentions her name, but nothing more than that.

'We tried, you know, for a baby. Nearly broke Florrie's heart. But there was nothing doing. And I didn't really mind, not then, well, apart from how it upset Florrie. Too selfish, I suppose. And now here I am, and she's gone. And I always thought I'd go first. I was counting on it really.'

His voice has gone very quiet. Oh god, please don't let him start getting upset. I don't think I could cope with that. But of course he doesn't. He just shakes his head slowly and carries on staring into the distance.

'Well, you've got me and Charlie, you know. You won't shake us off that easily.'

'You're a good girl, Annie. But I don't want you feeling you have to come round here to keep an eye on me. You've got better things to be doing with your time.'

'No I haven't. We love coming here. Honestly, Monty, we do.'

He coughs and gets up from the table.

'Well, that's all right then. But you're not to feel you have to come. If you don't fancy it or anything.'

'All right, Monty. But we won't. You're stuck with us now.'

He smiles.

'Shall I make some more tea?'

'Lovely, and then we'd better see what Charlie's doing with his pheasants.'

The office drinks party has turned into even more of a production than I thought it was going to be. Stef finally found someone to do the food, after Lawrence threw a complete fit at our idea of just having posh crisps and a few dips, and Stef's friend Cara is doing it for us; she's a brilliant cook, apparently, and just starting out in catering so she's cheap, which has cheered Barney up. She's going for seventies retro food, so I'm thinking mini prawn cocktails and Black Forest gateaux, but at the last minute she has some sort of major crisis with her cooker, and she ends up having to do the whole thing in our tiny kitchen in the basement.

She's almost in hysterics by the time she arrives, so we have to help her out. Stef's on filling vol-au-vents, and Jenny, who's usually on reception, is helping too. I'm on melon balls with Parma ham. Who says being a producer isn't glamorous. What did you do at work today, Mummy? I helped arrange things nicely on plates. I've got melon pips all over the floor and juice up to my elbows. Christ. I'm really hoping she's not going for fondue, because the combination of molten cheese and drunken clients is not going to be a good one.

Lawrence has completely disappeared, and it's nearly five-thirty and we've told people to arrive from six onwards, so any minute now the really neurotic types who like arriving early will be turning up.

And Barney's not pleased, because Stef's just asked him to tidy up his office.

'Why? People won't be upstairs in my bloody office, will they?'

'Well, they tend to wander about, don't they?'

Stef's looking slightly worried.

'Well, it's your job to stop them then, isn't it? I don't want a load of pissed freeloaders wandering around upstairs trashing my office. Keep them all down here. Wankers.'

'Yes, Barney.'

She's looking even more worried now. Time for me to step in, I think.

'Lovely party spirit you've got going there, Barney. Will you be making a speech tonight, by any chance? Only "freeloading wankers" might not work as a toast.'

He gives me a filthy look.

'What the fuck are they?'

'Melon balls.'

He raises his eyebrows, but Cara's hovering anxiously.

'Does everything look all right?'

'Oh yes, you've done a great job.'

I wave my melon baller at him and he retreats slightly. Stef smiles.

'Anyone want a drink?'

Finally. A sensible question.

By half-past seven the place is heaving with a combination of agency types and our favourite people from shoots. Stef's invited all the single men she can think of, because Jenny's just split up with her boyfriend again. And Barney's holding court upstairs in his office with some of his best mates, including his favourite lighting cameraman and two directors.

Cara's arranged for two of her student friends, Nick and Xavier, to be waiters for the evening, and Nick's been great, working really hard pouring champagne and trotting round with plates of food. Although Xavier seems to be slightly confused, and has spent most of the evening quaffing back booze and flirting madly with Jenny. But since it's the first time we've seen her smiling in ages, we're sort of putting up with it.

The kitchen's like a disaster zone, and Stef and Cara are frantically opening bottles and trying to find space to stash the empties, while I'm upstairs collecting empty glasses, and trying to persuade Tim Martin from WPLD that I don't want to dance with him, not least because we're not actually playing any music, when Leila arrives.

'Great party, darling, not too many women and loads of young men. Ideal really.'

'That's down to Stef.'

'Well, good for her.'

'You're not in the market for a new man, are you?'

'No, but there's no harm in a bit of window shopping.'

'True.'

'He looks nice, who's he?'

'Friend of Lawrence's.'

'Oh. Shame. You didn't say Mack was coming tonight.'

'That's because he's not. He's in New York.'

'No he isn't, not unless he's got a secret twin.'

She nods towards the door, and sure enough Mack is just arriving.

'I only talked to him last night, and he said he'd got wall-to-wall meetings.'

'Well, he must have decided to go in for a bit of demolition.'

He's fighting his way through the throng and attracting a fair bit of attention. Lots of young junior creative types seem very keen to shake his hand and remind him of just how talented they really are, just in case there are any jobs going in the new transatlantic empire.

He gives me a blistering kiss hello, which slightly stuns me. He's looking fabulous in one of his corporate-wizard suits. And he smells divine. Ooh. How lovely.

'Don't I get a kiss too then, Mr MacDonald?'

Leila's smiling.

'Evening, Leila, and how are you? You look terrific, as usual.'

'Thank you. Although I'd be even more terrific if some

260

bastard hadn't nicked the Trident account right out from under me.'

'You wouldn't be saying that if you'd spent yesterday in meetings with them. Trust me.'

'On a scale of one to ten?'

'Five hundred and twenty-nine.'

'Good.'

Mack laughs. 'So, it looks like you've got half of London here. Going well?'

'Yes, and no punch-ups. Yet.'

'Where's Barney?'

'Upstairs, holding court.'

'Great. Well, I'll just nip up for a quick word. I've got an idea I want to talk to him about. Just a couple of minutes, and then I'm all yours.'

God. I really hope it's not another job with a windmill.

'Don't you want a melon ball first?'

'I beg your pardon?'

'I spent most of the afternoon making melon balls.'

'Did you, darling? What a fabulous life you lead.'

'They're very nice.'

'I bet. Well, put me down for a gross then. But I just need a quick word with Barney first. See you in a minute.'

And off he goes. Meeting and greeting as he makes his way towards the stairs.

Leila helps herself to another glass of champagne.

'That was a rather significant moment, don't you think?'

'What was?'

'He's just gone public.'

'Gone public with what?'

'You, you fool. Half of London knows now. So it's official. You'll get asked out to dinner parties as a couple now. Just you wait.'

'I'm holding my breath already.'

'Oh good, here comes Lawrence, trotting over at quite a pace, I see. There you go, what did I tell you? Now he knows Mack's back on the scene he'll be smarming all over you, hoping you'll bring in loads more work.'

I'm in mid-bicker with Lawrence when Mack comes back downstairs, and is instantly trailed by a couple of juniors from his agency, eager to see that the boss has everything he requires. He's totally ignoring them, which seems a bit hard. But they don't seem to mind in the slightest.

'Come on then, let's be off, darling. I've booked a table for nine – I thought I'd take you out to dinner. Celebrate us both being on the same continent for a change.'

'Oh Mack, I'd love to. But I can't really leave now, not in the middle of all this.'

Lawrence is practically hopping up and down in an effort to ingratiate himself with Mack.

'Of course you can, Annie, don't be silly. You go off and have a lovely dinner. We can manage here, of course we can.'

He's doing his special sickly grin, which Leila seems to be finding particularly amusing.

'There you go, Annie. Lawrence can be so helpful when he tries, can't you, Lawrence?'

He gives her a furious look, but keeps smiling at Mack. Oh sod it. Maybe I'll just bugger off to dinner instead of hanging about here turfing out drunks and making sure we've locked up properly like I usually do. Lawrence can pull his weight for once. The Merc's waiting outside, with Stewart at the wheel. Great.

'Evening, madam. Nice to see you again.'

I could definitely get used to this.

We're sitting in the back of the car, and it's raining now, which makes the whole thing seem even more luxurious.

262

'All right, darling?'

'Yes thank you, very all right.'

'Good. Look, do you really want dinner? Only I was thinking, maybe we could just go home. There's bound to be something to eat – well, actually there might not be. But we can ring for pizza. And we can try out the new shower again. See if you can't press a few more buttons and flood the place entirely. And there's champagne in the fridge.'

'Well, in that case.'

'Yes?'

'Home, James, please.'

VIII

In the Heat of the Night

IT'S THE LAST WEEK of school before the summer holidays and everyone's knackered. The teachers have pretty much given up, and are resorting to sitting the kids in the hall in front of videos, and Ginny Richmond's made an executive decision after the last concert committee meeting nearly ended up in a fight about whether 'The Birdie Song' actually counts as a song from a musical, and we're just going to do songs from *Mary Poppins*.

And Charlie's decided he really needs a ferret.

'That new boy in Year Six has got one, and they can go right up drainpipes, you know, Mummy.'

'How clever, but put your socks on or you'll be late. Kate will be here in a minute.'

My car's on the blink again, so Kate's picking Charlie up. I've got a cab due at any minute to take me to the station, so I can catch the train up to town ready to be driven to Wales with the crew, for a night shoot. On a hillside. And the forecast is for torrential rain. So it just gets better and better really.

'Yes. And they can climb up on your shoulder, did you know that? Ferrets love climbing on people.'

'Charlie, I think we've got enough animals to look after, with the rabbits and the pheasants. Don't you?'

Stupid question really.

'They're very friendly.'

They'd have to be, since they look so revolting. And they've got very sharp teeth, I think; I'm sure I remember watching a *Blue Peter* presenter trying not to scream when one attached itself to his hand.

'I think they bite, you know, Charlie.'

'Yes, but they only bite people who are horrible.'

'Charlie, enough about ferrets. I don't like them, and we're not getting one. And that's that.'

He glares at me. I'm not usually quite so forthright in the mornings, but I'm still annoyed about the cooker: he's been pressing buttons again, and this time he's managed to programme the alarm so it goes off at unexpected moments. So I keep waking up in a blind panic thinking the smoke alarm's going off and the house is on fire, which is particularly amusing at two o'clock in the morning, obviously. I'm going to need someone with a degree in electronics to sort it out because I've tried reading the booklet and spent ages twiddling knobs, but all I've managed to do so far is reset the clock so it's half an hour fast.

'Look, here's Kate. Put your shoes on, quick.'

The cooker alarm goes off as she walks in through the back door. Great.

'Morning. Ready, Charlie? Why's your cooker making that hideous noise?'

'Mummy's little helper's been fiddling with it. Just don't ask.'

'Fair enough. Do you want me to pick him up this afternoon?'

'No thanks, Mum's going to be here.'

'Oh yes, damn. I'd forgotten.'

'Why?'

'Oh nothing. I just thought you might come with me, to choose an outfit for this bloody wedding.'

Gabriel's asked Kate to go to a family wedding with him, one of his cousins or something. She'll get to meet his entire family. So no pressure there then.

'We could go later on in the week, if you like.'

'Great. Get back in the car, James, I won't be a minute.'

James walks back to the car scowling.

'Is he on about ferrets by any chance?'

'Desperate for one.'

'And?'

'I've said over my dead body.'

'Good. Me too.'

It's nearly nine o'clock at night, and I'm halfway up a Welsh hillside and it's just starting to get dark. But it's not raining, and it looks like we might be finished before midnight, so things could be worse. It's a last-minute job before we all go off for the summer holidays, and Barney's been fairly relaxed so far. He's off for three weeks to his villa in Umbria, which he and his wife Sandy have been doing up over the past few years. I haven't got any Tuscan interludes planned, but I'm off this weekend for two days in a new *über*-country-house hotel with Mack, which his company have booked for their summer brainstorm, and I'm really looking forward to it. Well, not the brainstorm thing, obviously. But Mack says we can avoid all that, and he'll just tip up at the occasional meeting. And Kate and I are taking all the kids to Devon for a week, to stay in a hotel by the sea, because Charlie and James are desperate to try surfing. Which I'm not looking forward to quite so much if I'm completely honest, but at least it'll make a change from loitering around the house making endless snacks and trying to persuade Charlie that I don't want a ferret.

Mack's gone off the idea of us all going away together, thank god, because there's a limit to how many weeks you want to spend in a seaside hotel with under-tens, unless you're on proper medication. He's on a new top-secret plan at the moment that involves him flying backwards and forwards from New York like a man possessed, and I've got a horrible feeling he's got another cunning plan up his sleeve. But I'm not pushing him on it; I've decided he'll tell me when he's ready. I just hope it's not all five of us on a boat, or mountaineering, or anything else that's likely to involve the emergency services.

The job's a new tea campaign, and we did the studio bits last week, so we've already got the doctor answering the phone and rushing out, and we've got him coming back in looking knackered and making himself a nice cup of tea. And now we're doing the car leaving the cottage. It might not be exactly thrilling, but at least it makes a change from those bloody chimps.

We've nearly finished setting up, and Barney's about to get in the helicopter with the cameraman, who's not looking too happy. I don't think he was counting on too much in the way of aerial activity, but Barney's still got a passion for helicopters so there's no way out of it.

'Can't somebody shut those fucking sheep up. They're really starting to piss me off.'

'And how do you suggest we manage that, Barney?'

'I don't know. Haven't you got one of those whistles, like they have on *One Man and His Dog*?'

'Not on me, no. Sorry. I left it at home. And anyway, the whistles are for the dogs, not the sheep.'

Barney smiles.

'Do a spot of Bo-Peeping in your spare time, do you?'

'No. But my Uncle Monty's got sheep.'

'Well, get on the phone to him then, and ask him if he's got any top tips on shutting the fuckers up.'

The helicopter's in the field behind the cottage, and Barney's already had a quick tour round, which is what started the sheep off, and now he's eager to get started again, so the actor drives the car up and down the hill and we get the shots we want, and then he makes the bloody thing hover just above our heads while he waves out of the door like a maniac and gabbles instructions into the radio.

The first's looking very worried.

'He says he wants us all to form a circle and wave torches, and he'll land in the middle. Do you think he's joking?'

'Probably not. But ask him if we can break for supper while he's busy buggering about, will you.'

I wonder if there's anywhere you can buy a rocket launcher round here at this time of night. That way I could just shoot him down and save us all a lot of trouble.

We're halfway through supper, and Barney's standing bonding with Steve, the pilot, with me listening in to make sure he's not planning anything too tricky, when Kev comes over.

'Um, guv. I think we might have just lost Dan.'

'What?'

'Well, he's just jumped over that wall. Only we've moved the van, haven't we. From earlier. When it was down by the house, by that field. Where it was nice and flat. So now, well, it's at least a twenty-foot drop down that hill-side. And I don't think he realised, when he jumped over the wall for a quick slash.'

Christ. We all stand peering over the wall into the darkness.

'Are you all right Dan?'

There's a muffled groaning noise.

'Look, he's down there, by that tree.'

'No, I'm fucking not. I'm over here, and I think I've broken my ankle.'

Bloody hell. It takes three of us to get him back up the hill, and we nearly lose Kev in the process, who trips and is only saved from rolling all the way down the bank by a large bush. Dan's looking very pale, and he keeps groaning, but that might be the torch Kev keeps shining in his face. Barney offers to put him in the helicopter and take him to the nearest casualty but he refuses, and I don't really blame him, and he says he doesn't want a fuss. So in the end we get Kev to drive him to the nearest hospital and get him checked out, and then he'll take him home from there. We're nearly finished here anyway. As they drive off we all stand waving, and trying to look concerned, and then as soon as they're safely out of earshot half the crew start falling about laughing.

Andy, the cameraman, tries to look serious.

'You see, that's what happens, guv, when you push people too far. Is that a first then?'

'Is what a first?'

'People taking dives off cliffs on one of your jobs.'

Barney smiles.

'Yes, so far. Why, do you fancy it?'

'Well, if it's a choice between that and going up in that fucking helicopter again, then I'll give it a go.'

We get the last bits we need of the car driving up the

hill, after endless faffing about with filters so we don't get reflections of headlights where we don't want them, and then we start packing up, and we're almost ready to leave when Barney announces that Steve's flying back to London, and is happy to give him a lift, only Barney's brought his car.

'And I was thinking. Your car's on the blink again, isn't it?'

'Yes, it's in the local garage. Why?'

'Right. Well, why don't you take mine?'

'What?'

He's got to be joking. Drive his silver Porsche back from Wales. Like I need more challenge in my life at half-past eleven at night. But he's not giving up that easily. Apparently, he can't leave it outside his house while he's in Italy, because despite paying a fortune for a huge house in Islington he hasn't got a garage, and passers-by tend to write their initials on the bonnet with rusty nails. So he'll have to leave it in Soho in the NCP, which will cost an arm and a leg, and the parking attendants take their girlfriends out for spins in the fanciest cars, or have races on the top level of the car park. Actually, I know this is true because sometimes when I'm picking my car up you can hear the squealing of brakes and they're all up there placing bets.

'So you'll be doing me a favour really.'

'Yes, but I'm not insured, Barney.'

'Doesn't our insurance cover you to drive anything then? Lawrence told me you were both covered to drive anything.'

'Well, yes, technically, but I bet they didn't mean Porsches.'

'It doesn't say that, though.'

'No, I suppose not. But, Barney, what if I scratch it or something?'

270

'Then you're fired.'

'Oh. Well, that's very persuasive.'

'Darling, just go easy and you'll be fine. I'll take you through it all before you leave. Just drive it home and enjoy it. And if you scratch it, I'll take it off your wages. Should take you about ten years. That'll be all right, won't it? Anyway, at least you'll get a taste of what a proper car's like.'

Barney's always very rude about my tragic old Peugeot whenever he's in it. He looks for the elastic band that drives the motor, or asks me if I mind being overtaken by road sweepers. That kind of thing.

'And you'll be home in no time, which has got to be better than going back with this lot.'

Actually, that bit's true. We've got cars booked back to the office, and then I've got another car booked from there, which will all take hours and hours.

'You'd really be helping me out, Annie.'

He's doing one of his pleading looks. A bit like Charlie does when he wants something.

'Oh all right then. Thanks, Barney. I think.'

'You'll love it. Right, I'll just go and tell Steve, and then I'll show you what buttons you shouldn't be pressing.'

Oh god. I wonder if it's too late to change my mind. Why on earth did I say yes? I think I've just about worked out a way to get out of it when Kev rings to tell me that Dan's only got a sprain, but he's whining so much he's left him at a motorway service station, and could Barney pick him up in the chopper.

'They've got a massive car park. It'll be fine.'

There are muffled sounds in the background of Dan trying to grab the phone.

'Thanks, Kev. Well, just give us a grid reference and I'll get it sorted.'

He laughs.

'Are you sure he's all right? Really?'

'Yes. Stop worrying. Honestly, I promise, he's fine. We called his wife, and she couldn't stop laughing, so we're going to rig him up with some bandages and ketchup, make him look like he's been through World War Three. Stop at a chemist or something, when we get closer to town. Give her a nice surprise.'

'How kind.'

Barney comes back over, with a coffee.

'Here, drink this. I don't want you falling asleep at the wheel.'

'Thanks. But I've been thinking, and I'm – '

'Have we heard any more on how Dan's doing?'

'Yes, Kev's just rung, and he's fine, and about the car Barney, I – '

'Thank fuck for that. Well, you'd better warn Mack, you know. I don't think he realises.'

'Warn Mack about what?'

'About people chucking themselves down hillsides in the middle of jobs.'

'It was only one person, Barney. And anyway, why would Mack need to know?'

'No reason.'

He's looking very uncomfortable.

'Barney.'

'What?'

He's trying to look all innocent, but I know he's hiding something.

'Tell me.'

'I don't know what you mean.'

'Oh yes you do.'

'Look, oh bugger it, I sort of assumed he'd have talked to you by now. I think it's just an idea. He was probably

272

going to talk to you about it when he'd got it worked out.'

'Barney. Tell. Me. Now.'

'All right, all right, don't get hysterical. I hate hysterical women. Christ. Look, he just mentioned something to me about coming to work with us, making a move into directing, that's all. He had a word with me at the party, and we've spoken on the phone a couple of times. But nothing's definite yet. All right?'

'Oh. Right.'

'You don't look very pleased. Hasn't he mentioned it at all?'

'Only vaguely. You know, "One of these days I'd like to direct," that kind of thing. I should have realised. When he's got an idea, it tends to happen shortly afterwards. Only he never said anything about wanting to work with us.'

'No. But I don't blame him for that. I mean where else would he want to work? And he wouldn't want to muddy the waters, would he? Have you lobbying for him.'

'Fat lot of good that would do him.'

'Don't be daft, sweetheart. If you'd come to me and said you wanted me to talk to him, well, it would have been tricky, wouldn't it? You can see that, can't you? You carry a fair bit of influence with me – surely you know that by now.'

Oh. How sweet. He's gone all red.

'Thanks, Barney.'

'And it's not a bad idea, you know. I've been thinking about it for a while.'

'Have you?'

'Yes, take some of the load off me. There's more work out there, you know. Tom Hill's just taken on that bloke from WPB – you know, the one that did that vodka

273

campaign, Sam something. Anyway, he's not bad. And he's working, all the time. They must be raking it in. And the more I think about it, the more I think I'd have done the same. Sounded things out before I made a decision, I mean. So you're all right about it then, are you, if it comes off?'

'Yes, it's just a bit of a surprise, that's all.'

'So you're not going to ring him up and give him a bollocking then?'

'Oh probably.'

'That's my girl. Give him hell. Well, come on then, don't just stand there – let me show you round the car and I'll be off.'

Bugger. I never got a chance to back out on the car idea, and now it's too late. Bugger.

This car's a complete nightmare, and I stall twice as I'm trying to turn the bloody thing round, in front of the entire crew. So that's completely humiliating. And despite adjusting all the mirrors, I can still only see about two inches out of the back, but I suppose Porsche drivers don't really need to see where they've been, because they're going so fast it's all just a blur anyway. The brakes are extraordinary. You only have to touch them and you come to a complete stop. And stall, if you're not concentrating. And I'm a bit worried about the spoiler thing on the back, because Barney says another mini-spoiler pops up on top of it if you go over seventy-five miles an hour. Which sounds ridiculous to me, and anyway, what if it doesn't, or just drops off or something? I think I'll stick to sixty-five, just in case.

Actually, once I get going it's not as bad as I thought it would be, and we're not far from the motorway, so I'll stop at the first services and try to calm down. I could get used to this. And the leather smell is lovely. I wonder if I can risk putting some music on. Maybe when I've stopped. Just in case I press the wrong button and turn the satellite navigation on. Barney said not to touch it, because it's a nightmare and keeps shouting instructions at you.

Fucking hell. The satellite navigation's come on all by itself. I didn't touch a thing. It keeps telling me to Turn Right, and when I don't you can almost hear it getting pissed off. So I press what looks like the on/off switch. Only it isn't, so it's gone into Teutonic mode, and is bossing me about in German.

By the time I get to the first motorway service station I've had enough. I'm fed up with being barked at in German, and I'm really pissed off with Mack. He should have bloody told me. This is just like last time, when he suddenly announced he was off to New York, and assumed I'd just leave everything behind and follow him, dragging Charlie along too. It's bloody typical. No big changes. Take things slowly. That's what we said. So how come he didn't think to mention he might be about to change careers and come and work in my bloody office? I'll get a coffee and call him. It's only late afternoon in New York. And then I'd better get some petrol, because this bloody car will probably need at least four tanks to get me home. Actually, I'm not sure where the petrol flap is. Christ.

The café in the service station's pretty deserted, just a few knackered-looking lorry drivers, and a very bored-looking assistant behind the till who gives me the wrong change. But the coffee's hot, and I'm sitting by the window so I can check nobody's nicking the car, only I keep seeing my reflection staring back at me from the darkness, which is rather distressing since I'm not exactly looking my best.

When I finally get through to Mack, after going through legions of assistants, he's sounding pretty busy.

'Hello, darling. What's up?'

275

'What do you mean what's up?'

'Well, unless I'm very much mistaken, it's half-past one in the morning where you are, so I'm kind of assuming something's just gone pear-shaped.'

'Yes. You could say that. I've just had a little chat with Barney.'

'And?'

'And he told me about your idea, how you might be entering the wonderful world of directing. And of course I told him he must have got it wrong. Because you'd have talked to me about it, before you talked to him. Obviously.'

'Well, the thing is, I can't really talk now, but – '

'So I told him it was just one of your jokes. He's pretty annoyed about it, actually.'

'Oh Christ, I was going to talk to you at the weekend. Honestly. I just wanted to sound him out first. Is he really pissed off?'

'No. But I am. And on top of all that he's made me drive his car home, and I couldn't get out of it, because I was too busy unpicking your latest masterplan, and – '

'Fuck me. Not his 911 Turbo. What's it like?'

'It's silver.'

'Maybe I can get home a bit earlier. We can take it to the hotel for the weekend, it'll be – '

'Mack. Enough about the car. I'm really annoyed – you should have talked to me first.'

'Yes. But I'll make it up to you, I promise. And it's great about the car. Just go easy, all right, darling. You're not used to that kind of – '

'Will you just shut the fuck up about the bloody car. It's fine, actually.'

'Have you got out of third gear yet?'

'Mack.'

'Look, darling, much as I'd love to chat I'm kind of in a meeting.'

'Well, can't you send everyone off for a break or something, because I really want to talk to you about this. I'm not sure it's a good idea, you know, Mack. I mean the directing idea's great, but maybe we should talk about whether Barney's the ideal person to start with, because – '

'Well, it's not that kind of meeting, actually.'

'Well, what kind is it then?'

'A board meeting.'

'And the chairman's looking at you right now, waiting for you to hang up. Right?'

'Yes. Kind of.'

'Well, why on earth didn't anyone tell me that?'

'Because I've told them to always put you through.'

'Oh. Right.'

'So can we talk later? Would that be OK?'

'Yes, I suppose so.'

'And, darling?'

'Yes.'

'Go easy with the car, all right? You've got just a whisker under a hundred grand's worth of motor there, and I want a go at the weekend. So don't wrap it round anything with sharp edges. Promise?'

'Promise.'

Oh my god. I knew the car cost a ridiculous amount of money, but I never realised just how ridiculous. And I'm still annoyed with Mack, although I've got to admit I can see why he talked to Barney first. But still. I like keeping my work separate. My office. My Barney. That kind of thing. And this is one dilemma I can't share with Leila, because you can only tell her stuff you don't mind half of London knowing. She'd be bound to tell someone he's thinking of moving, however much she promised she wouldn't, because being discreet isn't exactly one of her strengths.

By the time I'm nearly home I've started to relax slightly. I'll talk to Mack tomorrow, but if he's really set on directing then there must be a way to make it work without it being a problem, as long as it's clear that I'm not working for him. Because that would be a step too far. It's bad enough running around after Barney, sorting out his strops, but I'm bloody well not doing it for Mack too. Too many blurred boundaries. But it'll be great having him back in London all the time.

I'm still driving fairly slowly, because it's amazing how much traffic there is on the M25 even at this time of night. The only real problem is that the car seems to be some kind of magnet for anyone with even a tiny trace of testosterone in their bodies. I'm trying to ignore it, but I've just been overtaken by a man in a Fiat Panda, who actually raised his fist in a kind of salute as he went past.

I'm a few miles away from home when I start getting hassled by a man in one of those annoying black jeeps with extra-large wheels and bars on the front for denting rhinos. He keeps overtaking and then slowing down so he can overtake me again, and when we get to the dual carriageway where there are three sets of traffic lights, one after the other, he races away at the first two sets and you can almost hear him laughing.

Actually, fuck this. There are no other cars in sight, and I've had enough. Let's just see what happens if I put my foot down. I know the road really well, and it's dead straight. What could go wrong?

Oh. My. God. The car practically takes off, you can feel it almost lift off the ground and then settle back again, and the black jeep becomes a small dot in the mirror. Ooh.

How nice. Now all I need is a police car to race and it'll be perfect. I can star in the next *Police Camera Naughty Drivers* special and refuse to stop until I get to Dover and the road runs out, by which time half of Kent constabulary will be on my tail. Because somehow you just know that a woman driving a Porsche would be one of their top targets even if every other car on the road was doing a hundred and twenty. I'd better slow down. But still. God. What a great car.

Charlie's delighted the next morning when he sees the car Mummy's brought home for the school run. He actually strokes it before he gets in.

'Is this our new car then?'

'No, Charlie. Barney's just lent it to us, that's all. While ours is being fixed. And keep your feet on the floor. And don't touch anything.'

Maybe I should sit him in the back on a bit of bin liner or something. And if he turns that bloody satellite navigation on I'll have a nervous breakdown.

'Well, can we get one? Only I like it. It's cool.'

'Not unless I win the lottery, no.'

'Well, can I have a ferret then? Only I really want one, you know.'

He launches into a list of all the benefits of the wonderful world of ferret-owning, which I decide to ignore by pointing out that James is just arriving at the school gates.

'Well, stop the car then, Mummy. Stop now.'

'I can't just stop in the middle of the road, Charlie.'

'Yes you can. Quick.'

I'm very tempted to put my foot down and then brake sharply, just to show him how quick we could be talking, but we'd be in the next village by the time we'd slowed down, and anyway Mrs Taylor is on duty, wearing fluorescent armbands and standing by the gate making sure people are crossing the road properly, and I don't think she'd approve. And then I spot that one of the organised mothers is leaving. She always arrives really early and parks just after the yellow zigzags, so I nip into her space with a gratifying roar, and Charlie trots in with James, planning the next stage in their campaign to become ferret-owners.

Kate comes over looking very impressed.

'Crikey. Where did this come from?'

'It's Barney's. He's lent it to me, while he's away.'

'Well, it's beautiful.'

'Are you into cars then?'

'Oh yes. I even watch *Top Gear*.'

'Do you? Really?'

'Yes. I think I'm in love with Jeremy Clarkson.'

'Steady on.'

It's amazing how even people you know really well can have mad little secrets up their sleeves. We're attracting a fair bit of attention from the other parents dropping their kids off, especially from Gabriella Hadlow-Tennant's mum, who drives her Mercedes sports car with the top down, even in winter, and has been the queen of the posh-car set until now. She's looking very put out. Kate's delighted.

'Coffee? I'll race you back to my place, if you like. Just give me a half-hour start, to make it fair.'

By the time I'm driving up to London on Friday for my weekend away with Mack I'm totally knackered, and my linen trousers are so badly creased I don't know why I bothered to iron them. I took a cold chicken over to Monty this morning, since we won't be around on Sunday, and then raced round cleaning so Mum won't spend the whole weekend tutting, and then she arrived with a collection of tiny frocks for Ava that she couldn't resist when she was in Brighton last week with Aunty Brenda, for me to take to Lizzie, who I'm seeing for lunch today. And then she went into Spanish Inquisition mode about Mack, and his plans for moving back to London, because she's been cross-examining Lizzie, and got wind of the fact that Mack might be moving jobs.

Lizzie's very pleased with the frocks, and seems to have abandoned her anti-pink ruling pretty much permanently, and Ava's eating lunch when I arrive, and covering herself and Lizzie in mashed carrot, and occasionally clapping her hands to celebrate the fact that she's eating, which is one of her favourite activities.

We go for a walk in the local park after Ava's bolted down her second carton of baby yogurt, and is clamouring for a third. And, since she's pretty keen on animals at the moment, our walk quickly turns into a meet-and-greet session with anyone with a canine friend. We've had two Labradors, a spaniel and a weird-looking poodle so far, and now we're sitting down having a coffee in the café while Ava eats rice cakes.

'I meant to say, Lizzie, thanks so much for telling Mum about Mack moving jobs and everything. She's really on the case now.'

'Oh god, sorry, but you know what she's like. She sort of tricked me into it. She went into a whole routine about how she thought he sounded like bad news after last time, and you shouldn't be seeing him at all, let along going off on weekends with him, and so I sort of had to say that I thought it was serious, and if he moved back to London you'd have even more of a future together, and that was that.'

'Yes. She's clever like that.'

'And anyway, it's true, I do think it's good news, about him moving back and everything. Isn't it?'

'Oh yes, now we've talked about it properly, and he knows I don't want to work for him on jobs, I think it'll be really good, but I didn't want Mum at battle stations just yet. She'll start buying those daft brides' magazines like she did when you started seeing Matt.'

Lizzie laughs.

'Was Mack all right about it? You not wanting to be his producer and all that.'

'Fine. He completely got it.'

'Good. So when's he going to tell them he's leaving?'

'Pretty soon, I think. He's done all the things he promised them he'd do, sorted out the New York office, and bought the London agency, and he's bored now, I think, and he's not really cut out for all the executive stuff.'

'Well, it all sounds great then, although I still think he should have talked to you first.'

'Yes I know, but it's a boy thing, I think. He wanted to be sure Barney wasn't doing him a favour.'

'Where's this hotel you're off to then, you lucky thing? I wish I was going. Do you want another coffee, by the way?'

'Great, but then I'll have to be off. I'm supposed to be at the office by three.'

Mack's in a meeting when I arrive, so I'm ushered into his office and my trousers are subjected to very close scrutiny by Tina, who doesn't seem terribly impressed.

'Shall I give you the directions to the hotel? Only Mack said something about you driving.'

'Please.'

'Mack's driver would be more than happy to take you, so there's no need for you to drive.'

'Oh no, it's fine.'

'Well, we have got a fairly tight schedule, so I don't want Mack going missing or being late – he's doing the keynote address before dinner. It's vital you're there by eight at the latest, if that's all right.'

'Sure.'

'That way I can brief him again. He always forgets people's names and we've got quite a few of the Americans over. I'm really looking forward to the dinner, actually. The food's meant to be amazing there, and everyone really dresses up.'

She looks at my trousers again.

Christ. Mack said it was fairly low-key. Not an intercontinental event. And I didn't realise Tina would be lurking all weekend, ready for last-minute briefings. Bugger. I wonder if I've got time to call Leila for an emergency wardrobe summit.

'Hello, darling. Car downstairs, is it?' Have you had lunch? Only we can stop on the way, if you like, but let's be off, yes? The quicker I get out of here the better, or some bastard's bound to drag me into another meeting.'

Mack's looking very chirpy, in jeans and a navy T-shirt.

'I was just going to get Annie a copy of the schedule, Mack, and the directions. I can order you a sandwich, if you like. It won't take a moment.'

'No thanks, Tina, I know where it is, vaguely. And we won't need the schedule. I've told you. I'll tip up at a couple of things and that's it. The rest of the time they can just piss off. Come on, darling, let's go.'

Tina's not looking pleased as we're getting into the lift. Shame.

'Where's this car then?'

'In the cark park over the road.'

'Great. I've been thinking about getting one, you know,

once I'm sorted and back in London. I've been looking at my contract again, and there's a fairly hefty pay-off, if I play my cards right.'

'But isn't that only if they ask you to go, not if you resign?'

'Well, I'll just have to persuade them to ask me to go then, won't I?'

He smiles.

Oh I see.

'So you might as well let me drive, as a sort of test run.'

He's been trying to persuade me to let him drive the car for most of the week.

'Nice try. But no.'

'Barney wouldn't mind.'

'Maybe not, but I would. I can drive, you know. I've been doing if for years.'

'Yes, but, well, it's just – '

'What? You're not going to say something about it being a man's car, are you?'

'No. But – '

'Good. Because it would be a shame to start the weekend off with you being a total prat, wouldn't it?'

He sighs and shakes his head.

'You can be very annoying, you know, Moneypenny. Has anyone ever told you that?'

'Yes. All the time. Now tell me, what have you got in that bag?'

He's carrying a leather holdall.

'Just a suit and a couple of shirts, why?'

'No dinner jacket? Only Tina said something about dressing up for dinner.'

'Oh the Yanks have said something about dinner jackets, but they've got to be joking. Christ. It's fucking gorgeous.'

He's looking at the car.

'Wait until you get in.'

'Isn't there anything I can say to make you let me drive?'

'No.'

'Nothing at all?'

'No.'

'Damn.'

'Annie, put your foot down.'

'Mack.'

'Sorry, but for god's sake. Can't we go a bit faster?'

'No. And don't touch that. It's the satellite navigation, and it's a total nightmare.'

'I was just going to change the music. All this Wagner's doing my head in.'

'Fine. It's a CD multi-changer thing, they're all in the boot, you just press this button. And get more Wagner.'

'Please put your foot down. Annie. Sweetheart. For pity's sake.'

'Mack. Shut. Up.'

'All right. Well, pull over then. I want to get in the back. That way I can lie under a blanket and I won't have to look at all those smug bastards overtaking us in their Ford Mondeos.'

'Mack. Do you know how pathetic you're being? I'm doing nearly eighty.'

'You just don't understand.'

'Anyway, you'd never fit in the back. You'd have to have your kneecaps removed.'

'Well, if you carry on driving like my granny, that might not be a problem. Please just put your foot down, darling, I'm begging you. You're making a grown man beg now.'

'I know. This car just gets better and better.'

'Oh Christ.'

'What?'

A man in a BMW has slowed down in the outside lane, and his passenger appears to be waving at us.

'It's Martin. One of our account directors. How fucking brilliant.'

'Well, wave back then.'

'I'll never forgive you for this. You know that, don't you?'

'Shame.'

'The bastards are slowing down now. Look, there's plenty of room, and there's nothing in front of them – you could easily pull out.'

'Mack.'

'Yes.'

'Are you sure?'

'Sure about what?'

'That you want me to show you just how fast this car can go.'

He's making squeaking noises now.

'Sure? Am I sure? I'm fucking begging you.'

'OK.'

I put my foot down.

'Jesus Christ.'

'I know.'

'This is a truly great car.'

'I know.'

'I want one.'

'I know. But what about the kids? Do you think they do an estate version?'

'No they bloody don't.'

The hotel's fabulous, and the spa's even better. All wooden floors and slate walls, with plunge pools full of rose petals, and a waterfall you can swim through. It's like being cata-pulted into a parallel universe where the only decision you have to make is what kind of facial you want, and it's trickier than you'd think because there are over forty choices. While Mack's busy brainstorming I'm exfoliated and buffed and massaged to such an extent I go into a kind of spa-shock, and can't decide what shade of pink I want my toenails painted. I've imbibed so much lavender oil I don't think I'll ever get more than mildly excited about anything again. Now I know why groomed women are always so vacant: it's all those oils.

I fall asleep on my padded lounger in the chill-out zone, which is all little candles and low blue lighting with whale music in the background, and have to be woken up by Amber who's come to do my hot-stone therapy, which basically involves rubbing warm pebbles up and down your back. And yes, it does sound weird, but it turns out to be divine.

All the young executives from the agency are busy bonding in the bar in between meetings and calling their girlfriends babe. Which Mack seems to find particularly amusing. I'm still floating about in creased linen, but I simply don't care any more. Who knew half a gallon of lavender oil would solve all my fashion dilemmas.

'Good time in the spa, babe?'

'Mack, I've told you, don't call me babe. It makes me think of piglets.'

'Well, you don't smell like a piglet.'

'That's the lavender.'

'Nice.'

'So what's the plan for later then? Only I'm not sure I'm up for another formal dinner.'

Last night was bad enough. Lots of women in proper frocks, and me doing my best in a beaded cardigan and my smartest black trousers. There were endless speeches and rallying-the-troops moments from the Americans.

'Too chilled out, are you, babe?'

I think I'm just going to ignore the babe thing and hope he gets over it.

'I might just have a bath and watch telly, give room service a go. You can do the dinner though, I'll be fine, if that's OK?'

'Not bloody likely.'

'Oh. Sorry. I didn't mean it like that, it's just – '

'Annie?'

'Yes.'

'Why don't you go on up and start running that bath. And I'll just make our excuses, and be with you momentarily.'

He's talking in his joke transatlantic accent and smiling his special flirty smile. Raising his eyebrows in a very suggestive manner.

'Momentarily?'

'Yes, ma'am.'

'Sounds like a good plan to me.'

'I was hoping you'd say that. Babe.'

The journey home is much more relaxing than the journey down, due to a combination of the lingering effects of all that lavender and the fact that I cave in and let Mack drive. He goes off to New York the next morning, and I'm back down to earth with a fairly hefty hump because Kate and I are off to Devon at the end of the week, so I spend hours washing and packing, and buying new shorts for Charlie, who's suddenly had a growth spurt.

The drive to Devon's a complete nightmare. We're in Kate's old Renault, which is enormous and has room for all the luggage, but it also has three kids in the back and no air conditioning. I briefly thought about taking Barney's car, but I couldn't face being tarred and feathered in Soho Square when Barney discovered I'd filled the boot with sand.

The hotel has turned out to be much nicer than I expected, right on the cliffs with a path down to the beach. It's got too many plastic wall lights and swirly carpets to make it really trendy, which is rather relaxing since it means the other guests are all wandering around in polyester leisure wear rather than the kind of clothes that make you want to go straight back up to your room to get changed.

We've got a balcony overlooking the sea, and two interconnecting rooms with a huge bathroom, and the kids are in bliss, trotting up and down to the beach with fishing nets and buckets. It's like being in one long *Famous Five* adventure. We even bought them some ginger beer yesterday, but they hated it, and demanded Coke. And Phoebe's found a new best friend, who's a year older than her, so they're spending hours sitting on the beach looking longingly at the lifeguards and all the surfers.

I'm down on the beach with the boys, while Kate's taken Phoebe into the village for postcards. We've already done the rock-pool thing, and they've caught lots of tiny crabs in their nets, and tried to organise them into having races, but they kept burying themselves in the sand. So now we're building sandcastles, and I'm longing for the tide to come in so we can go back to the hotel, but it seems to be stuck. I'm starting to wonder if there are days when the tide just hovers, like it can't be bothered, when it suddenly starts racing in. One minute we're sitting about thirty feet from the sea, and the next the castle moat is filling up.

Charlie's thrilled.

'Look, Mummy, look. Take a picture. The moat's filled right up.'

I take a photograph of them both proudly standing pointing at their magnificent creation as the waves lap over their feet.

'We're going to build another one, further up. Where the sea can't get it.'

Oh. Great. I thought we'd done the sandcastle thing for today.

'Don't you want to have a swim?'

'Yes, but later.'

I'm relegated to sitting on the blanket while they make a start on another creation, so I amuse myself by watching the lifeguards, who are having a lovely time marching up and down in red shorts and blowing their whistles. They keep climbing up on their jeep and shouting through their megaphones about how important it is that people only swim between the two marker flags they've placed on the beach, and not in the bit where the surfers are likely to land on your head, and then just to keep everyone on their toes they move the flags. One of them starts walking backwards, scanning the horizon, but then he trips over a plastic bucket and is so furious he blows his whistle and makes a group of small boys come out of the sea.

One of their dads marches over and a shouting match follows, and the boys return to the water and the lifeguard sits in his jeep sulking, but suddenly springs into action and races into the sea to retrieve a very fat man who's perched on a Lilo and heading for France. The man is very grateful and clutches the lifeguard to his chest once he's finally hauled out of the water, which just goes to show that it must be quite hard to remain patient with the Great British Public when they insist on entering notoriously treacherous waters perched on Lilos and inflatable bananas.

Kate comes back with the postcards and joins me on the blanket.

'Nice time at the shops?'

'Apart from the sneering teenagers in huge shorts, yes. And Phoebe's sulking because I won't buy her a wetsuit. I've suggested renting one, but that's no good, apparently.'

Phoebe's sitting in silence, reading a magazine. And occasionally sighing.

The local village is full of picture-postcard cottages with thatched roofs, and shops selling clotted-cream ice-cream, with extra clotted cream balanced on top, sort of like a heart attack on a cone. There's a fairly lively mix of happy campers and trendy surfing types in voluminous shorts with boards strapped to the top of their cars. The locals refer to the tourists as grockles or cockles or something equally derogatory, apparently; although they also seem perfectly happy to take their money off them.

'Do you fancy a cup of tea from the café?'

'Oh yes please. I was going to stop in the village, but Little Miss Hormones wasn't in the mood.'

'Phoebe, do you fancy an ice-cream?'

'Yes please, Annie.'

She gives me a dazzling smile. Mainly to annoy her mother, obviously. But still, it's nice to know that an ice-cream can still make the sun come out.

'Charlie, do you want an ice-cream? James?'

Silly question really.

But then things go slightly downhill. One minute all three of them are scampering up the beach to choose ice-creams, and then they mount a surprise pincer movement and I'm not only getting ice-cream and two polystyrene cups of tea, but somehow we're queuing up at the shop to rent neoprene wetsuits and bodyboards for all three of them as well. Charlie's thrilled. He's been desperate to have a go ever since we got here, but we've been trying to hold out for another day or two because renting all the kit for all three of them will cost us a fortune.

'You should get a wetsuit too, Mummy.'

I can't decide on the wetsuit front. On the one hand if I do get one I'll be able to lurk in the water without getting cold, and stop them requiring the services of air-sea rescue when they head out towards the rocks. But on the other hand I'll also run the risk of being mistaken for a beached whale and having people dripping cups of water on my back while they try to refloat me. So on balance, probably not.

Actually getting them into their suits turns out to be a fairly epic undertaking. Charlie gets his leg stuck and falls over and gets covered in damp sand, and James can't get his arms into his sleeves.

I'm completely red-faced and knackered by the time we get back to Kate.

'How on earth did they con you into this?'

We're lurking at the edge of the sea until we're satisfied that they're not going to get into trouble. But the waves are fairly big, so it's taking them all their energy to get out to even waist-deep.

'I don't know.'

'Well, they're loving it anyway. And at least Phoebe's stopped pouting.'

'True. She's too busy trying not to drown.'

'Oh it's not that bad. They're not going out too far, and it looks totally exhausting. You never know, they might all fall asleep really early tonight.'

By the time we're ready to head back up the path to the hotel all three of them are so exhausted they can barely speak. It's brilliant. If we'd known about this hidden bonus we'd have had them neoprened up on the first morning. Getting their suits off takes up their last glimmers of energy, and Charlie doesn't even whine when he trips over one of his sandals. This just gets better and better. I think we'll definitely be renting suits tomorrow as well.

We go for an early supper because they're all starving, even though we usually avoid the restaurant at peak children's mealtimes. The combination of bowls of lukewarm spaghetti hoops and lots of toddlers screaming blue murder isn't a very good one, but after a quick wash and brush-up, when I discover that my nose is now bright red and I've got a definite line where my sunglasses have been, which makes me look rather unhinged, we're sitting at our table and trying to persuade Charlie and James not to have a swordfight with their forks.

The couple at the next table are trying very hard to impress the rest of the room by talking in loud voices about which new car they should buy for their nanny. This makes me feel slightly outclassed, not least because I don't even provide Edna with a moped, but then we notice that their daughter has a face like a piglet, with pale, thin, white eyebrows and tiny little eyes. So that cheers us up. We start playing animal, vegetable or mineral, and then the chips arrive and we get a bit of peace.

Charlie's practically falling asleep in his ice-cream, and James is too, so we take them straight up for baths and bedtime and miraculously there's a complete absence of the usual counter-bedtime manoeuvres, and even Phoebe's asleep by nine.

We go out on to our balcony to celebrate, and Kate pours us both a gin and tonic from the minibar.

'It's still early, you know. We could go down to the bar, if you like.'

'What, and give the babysitter thing a go?'

'Oh yes, I'd forgotten about that.'

We asked reception about babysitters when we arrived, in the vague hope that we might be able to slope off for a child-free dinner at some point, but the hotel's version of babysitting turned out to be leaving the phone off the hook in the room, while the receptionist listens in for the sound of smashing furniture. And since we both know Charlie and James would simply replace the receiver and then set about trying to get scary movies on the hotel TV we've sort of agreed that we're stuck with them for the duration.

'Oh look, there's that couple who were on the beach. The ones who were arguing all the time. It looks like they're at it again.'

They're mid-bicker as they walk across the lawns and we keep catching snatches of their conversation. We've got the perfect vantage point up on the balcony: we can hear them, but they can't see us. Mum would love it here.

'I was only saying. There's no need to be nasty.'

'I wasn't, but you asked me what I thought. I only said I preferred the other one.'

'Yes, but which other one?'

'The blue one.'

'I haven't got a blue dress, Steven.'

'Yes you have. You wore it last night.'

'That was olive green, and it wasn't a dress, it was a skirt and top. You were there when I bought it, for god's sake.'

'Don't start swearing – I knew you shouldn't have had that second glass of wine.'

'For god's sake isn't swearing, Steven.'

'No, but it's not very nice, is it?'

'Oh just piss off.'

Kate starts giggling.

'This reminds me of Phil – we always ended up fighting on holiday.'

There's a sound of chairs scraping on the terrace, and the couple go back into the bar.

'God, you don't think they heard me, do you?'

'No. Too busy glaring at each other, probably.'

'I used to dread holidays with Phil, you know, I really did. And I don't think it was much fun for the kids either.'

'I bet they didn't notice.'

'Sometimes they did. Like the time I left Phil by the side of the road, when we were in the New Forest.'

'Did you? How brilliant.'

'Yes. But I went back for him. And then he sulked all the way home. Does Mack sulk?'

'Not so far, but he might take it up once he starts working with Barney. What about Gabriel?'

'No. He goes quiet, but nothing really Sulky.'

'And it's still going well?'

'Oh yes.'

'You don't sound too sure.'

I've noticed she's been a bit hesitant over the past couple of weeks whenever the subject of Gabriel has come up. They're definitely at the couple stage now, and he stays at her house a few nights a week, and then leaves at the crack of dawn so the kids don't get too rattled.

'I think he's too young for me.'

'Don't be daft, Kate.'

'No, I don't mean it like that. It's just he wants the whole thing, marriage and kids. And that's great, obviously, but I don't think I do.'

'Oh.'

'It's the baby thing really. I've been thinking about it, and I don't want another one. I'd only be doing it for him, to keep him, sort of thing. And that's not a good enough reason to have a baby, is it?'

She sounds really sad.

'No. Not really.'

'So I'm going to have to be a grown-up and stick to my guns. Tell him that I don't think it'll work, not in the long run. Be honest with him.'

'But are you sure, Kate, about the baby thing, sure he wants one? Have you talked about it?'

'No, but I know he does. He's really fond of Phoebe and James, despite them giving him a hard time sometimes. He's really patient with them. But when I think about another baby, well, I just feel exhausted. And it's not fair on Phoebe and James – they've had enough to cope with. But I really like him, you know. I feel different when I'm with him.'

'I know. I'm really sorry, Kate. It's such a shame.'

'Isn't it? I marry someone who doesn't really want kids – I had to persuade him, you know, he kept going on about the bloody mortgage – and then I fall for someone who's desperate for one, when I'm not. It's absolutely bloody typical. Has Mack said anything about having more kids?'

'No, not really. I think he's got his hands full coping with Daisy and Alfie.'

'That's the solution, you see, meet a man who's already got children.'

'Yes, but then you've got the wicked stepmother thing to sort out.'

'But you were fine with them, last year, weren't you?'

'Sort of. But it wasn't easy. And I don't know how Charlie's going to feel, if it gets more permanent. I'm trying to ignore it, actually. Take it one step at a time.'

'Very sensible.'

'Otherwise I feel completely overwhelmed by it.'

'Yes, but that's part of it, isn't it? Feeling overwhelmed. If it's worth it. And that's the thing – I'm just not sure it is, for me, with Gabriel, I mean, not if it means a baby. I only wish it was.'

'I know you do. Look, let's have another drink or something. Shall I go down to the bar and get some chocolate?'

'Tea, please, or I'll end up in floods. And I bought some biscuits, when we were out, clotted-cream shortbreads, about ten thousand calories each. They're by the kettle.'

'Shall I bring the packet?'

'You do ask silly questions sometimes.'

We spend the rest of the week stuck on a blanket while the kids play in the water and have surfing lessons. It's brilliant. We find a great woman who teaches classes to beginners, and they all lie on the beach balancing on their boards and practising standing up before charging into the water and getting buffeted about by the waves. They get so knackered we barely hear a peep out of them in the evenings.

Charlie decides he's going to be a top surfer when he grows up, and is busy brushing his teeth before bed and telling me he's going to Hawaii, for the waves.

'And I'm going to be a Vulcan too.'

'A what?'

I wonder if I'll have to get him a special Star Trek costume or something.

'A Vulcan. And not eat cheese. Vulcans don't eat cheese, and I hate cheese for my packed lunch at school. So that'll be all right.'

'I think you mean vegan, Charlie.'

Christ. I'll have to learn to do things with tofu and nut cutlets. I don't think so.

'So no bacon then? Or sausages?'

'Oh yes, I'll still eat them, just not cheese.'

How bloody typical. I've got the only meat-eating vegan in the South of England.

'Charlie, either you're a vegetarian, or you eat meat. And if you want to be a vegetarian that's fine. You can eat lots of macaroni cheese and tomatoes and broccoli, and get your vitamins that way. And when you're older you can become a vegan too if you want, when it's you doing the cooking. But not now.'

'It's not up to you, Mummy. I'm getting bigger now and I can make my own mind up.'

'Not about being a vegan, you can't.'

He does a bit of stamping, but he's too tired for a full-blown wobbler.

Time for a quick counter-manoeuvre, I think.

'Shall we get some more ice-cream tomorrow? You could have a two-scoop one, if you like.'

'Yes please, and we can decide about me being a vegan when we're at home. And I'll ask Nana what she thinks.'

'All right.'

If he's thinking she'll back him up on this one he might be in for a bit of a surprise. She's only just getting over Lizzie going vegetarian, and that was ten years ago.

Getting home from Devon takes ages because we have to stop at Stonehenge so the boys can have a pagan moment. I've always thought the stones looked rather tiny when I've driven past them, but when you're actually standing next to them they're pretty mind-boggling. It's all very organised with lots of ropes and coach parties, and a concrete underpass underneath the road, and I'm slightly worried that Charlie's going to be disappointed. Especially when we hear a couple from one of the coach parties discussing how on earth they managed to get the stones

298

through the underpass. But he's in bliss, especially when he spots a nutter in a white frock wandering about chanting quietly to himself.

Charlie and James decide he's a Druid priest and race over to introduce themselves before we get a chance to stop them, and spend what seems like hours talking about ley lines and sacred rituals, while we lurk close by in case he turns out to be a Druid child abductor. But actually he's really sweet, and tells them he's called Thorn, although I'd bet serious money his mother doesn't call him that. He gives them all sorts of top tips on how they should be celebrating the autumn equinox. Leaves and candles seem to be pretty much de rigueur, and when we finally persuade them that it's time to leave he rootles round inside his canvas haversack and presents each of them with a string with a sacred acorn on it. They're both thrilled, and rendered completely mute.

But Kate's always polite, even in the most trying circumstances.

'Thanks very much, um, Thorn. That's terribly kind of you.'

'It's nice to see the young ones so passionate about the old ways.'

Time to go, I think, before he tries to recruit us too.

'Well, goodbye then, and thank you again.'

'Travel well.'

Which turns out to be easier said than done when you've got to get past the bloody gift shop first. And English Heritage are not going to miss the opportunity of offloading a load of old tat, however pagan the site may be. Despite their new sacred acrons both Charlie and James are desperate for a nice bit of consumerism, and even Phoebe rallies at the prospect of a spot of shopping.

We get them back to the car after a fairly determined

tussle about whether we do, or as it turns out do not, urgently require a boxed set of stones at thirty-two quid, and finally emerge with posters, a book and some sweets. And two wooden daggers. For sacred ritual purposes only. Not poking people's bottoms in car parks.

The traffic's a nightmare, and the boys keep whining that they're starving, so we have to stop at a Little Chef and have the Obese English Breakfast Special, with extra sausage, and then we have to practically roll them back to the car. By the time we get home I'm completely exhausted. That's the trouble with holidays with children. You always need another one when you get home. Charlie races round reacquainting himself with all his toys, and then practically collapses and I have to carry him up to bed, which almost finishes me off completely.

I'm tucking him in and praying to the gods of sacred acorns that he'll go to sleep straight away, and not Chat.

'Mummy.'

Great.

'Yes, Charlie.'

'I want to start collecting leaves for our equinox.'

'Right.'

'And I want Nana to come. And Grandad. And we can have a bonfire.'

'Right.'

I'm looking forward to it already.

'And, Mummy, if I had a ferret he could come too.'

I'm adopting a new ferret policy: totally ignoring the issue.

'We'll have to go round to Uncle Monty's tomorrow and see how your pheasants are.'

'Yes. And I can show them my acorn.'

'They might try to eat it, Charlie.'

'No they won't, they're pagan pheasants. They know you don't eat sacred acorns.'

'Oh. Well, that's good.'

'Yes. And, Mummy. When I grow up I'm going to be like Thorn.'

'Are you, darling?'

So not a doctor or a lawyer then. Excellent. A person in a white frock who travels well. Oh well, as long as he's happy, I suppose.

'Yes. Or I might be a space pilot, and discover new worlds. I haven't decided.'

A pagan astronaut. Houston. We might have a problem.

'Well, there's no rush, Charlie. You might think of something else by the time you're grown-up.'

'Like what?'

'Oh I don't know. Maybe you might want to work helping people, be a doctor or a teacher or something.'

I'm thinking nice pension plan. No worries about being burnt to a crisp when you re-enter the earth's atmosphere, or someone forgetting to tighten the screws on the rockets.

'Don't be silly, Mummy.'

'Night, Charlie.'

I go back downstairs and phone Mum, and then Leila and Sally, and I'm just about to go up to bed when Mack calls.

'So how did it go?'

He had his big meeting with the Board today.

'Oh it was excellent. They went completely tonto.'

'What happened?'

'Well, their first plan was to get security to escort me from the building.'

'Christ, and did they?'

'No, not when I reminded them just how well that would

play with the clients, and my team. Half of them are threatening to bale out already.'

'So what happens now?'

'They're trying to find a way to get me to go quietly. And I'm starting to get noisy.'

'You sound like you're really enjoying yourself.'

'Oh I am, they're such a bunch of wankers. Anyway, enough about all that bollocks, how was your day? Journey home all right?'

'Fine. We stopped at Stonehenge and met a Druid called Thorn.'

'You pretty much live on another planet to the rest of us, don't you, babe?'

'He gave Charlie an acorn.'

'Did he, why?'

'They're sacred.'

'Oh a sacred acorn. Now you're talking.'

'Will you be back by next weekend, do you think?'

'Maybe. Why?'

'It's a surprise.'

'You haven't got me a sacred acorn too, have you, sweetheart?'

'I didn't say it was a nice surprise.'

'Not more headlice? I hate that fucking shampoo.'

'No. Just a family lunch. Mum wants to give you the third degree. And Monty's bound to find something he'll want to give you. You don't need a mangle, by any chance, do you?'

'Funny you should ask, I was just thinking this morning, what I really need is a good mangle.'

'Good. Well, that's sorted then.'

He laughs.

'Night, darling.'

The line goes dead. I really wish he'd stop doing that.

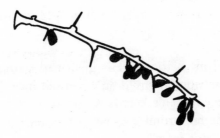

IX

That Old Black Magic

IT'S MONDAY MORNING AND I'm in the kitchen washing up the breakfast things after dropping Charlie off at school. The school holidays are finally over. Hurrah. They went back last week, and Miss Pike's got a new classroom assistant, a rather nervous-looking woman, an ex-lawyer, apparently, who thought it would be a good idea to spend a few terms in a classroom with our little pagans before deciding whether to go into teacher training. So bang goes another graduate trainee.

I'm trying to decide whether to wash the kitchen floor, which is so filthy your feet actually stick to it if you don't keep moving, or indulge in a spot of daytime telly without a small person complaining that he's Bored every five minutes, and telly's definitely winning, when Leila rings, sounding furious.

'You might have bloody told me.'

'Told you what?'

'That Mack's moving into directing with you and Barney.'

303

'Christ, that was quick – he only came back late on Friday. Who told you?'

'I never reveal my sources.'

'Right.'

'I don't.'

'OK.'

'It was Tom Bettinger. His girlfriend works there. But the real question is why didn't you tell me?'

'Because you can't keep a secret to save your life and Mack made me promise to keep it secret squirrel.'

'Yes, but not from me.'

'I think your name might have been specifically mentioned actually, sweetheart.'

'Bloody cheek. Well, it's top news anyway, darling. Did he get a huge pay-off?'

'I don't know, but he's had to sign something promising not to work for a rival agency for two years.'

Actually, I do know, and he got a staggering amount of money, but I'm trying to be discreet since I'm not sure how much Mack wants people to know.

'Well, that was clever of him, since he was never planning to move to another agency. Very clever. But I don't suppose they knew that, did they?'

'Let's just say he was pretty pleased with himself when he got back here on Friday.'

'I bet he was. Well, there'll be no stopping you now. Working together. Playing together. Clever you. When will you be moving up to town then?'

'Who said anything about moving up to town?'

'Just checking in case there were any other developments you'd forgotten to fill me in on.'

'No, nothing major. We've got a lunch at Monty's on Sunday, a three-line whip with Mum and Dad, but apart from that, nothing.'

'So your mum can give Mack the third degree?'

'Yes. She's working on her written questions now.'

'And how's mad Monty? Still a few sandwiches short of a picnic?'

'A whole loaf. He's going everywhere on that bloody lawnmower now. He even gets his pension on it. And he's got an enormous pair of rubber fishing waders that he wants to give to Mack.'

'Is Mack into fishing then?'

'No.'

She laughs.

'Well, at least he's not a flasher like my Uncle Peter.'

'Is he still doing that then?'

'Only at family parties.'

'Nice. I'm up in town on Friday if you're free for lunch.'

'Perfect. I've got some bastard client in, but I'll move him.'

After a delightful couple of hours lounging on the sofa watching telly, and learning how to make an elegant table decoration out of three limes and about two hundred quid's worth of white roses, I finally pull myself together and belt round the supermarket, and by the time I've finished stuffing things into the freezer it's time to pick Charlie up from school. Kate and I are taking them fishing in the stream on the way home, because the weather's gone boiling hot again and we can chat while they plodge about with their nets. Kate's still trying to sort things out with Gabriel, who's maintaining that he doesn't mind about not having children, but she thinks he's just being nice – which is why she likes him so much really. So it's all rather complicated.

We're lurking behind a bush having a quick fag without risking Comments from Boys.

'Where's Phoebe today?'

'Tea at Gemma's, so she'll come home and moan about how much nicer her house is than ours. She's driving me bonkers at the moment, she's always sulking about something. I've pretty much given up trying to keep track of what my latest crime is. It's like Chinese water torture, constantly dripping away.'

'Talking of dripping . . .'

We both look towards the stream. The boys have moved on from standing peering into the water and are now using their bamboo net poles for duelling purposes.

'Stop that, Charlie.'

'We're having fun. Honestly, Mummy. You spoil everything.'

'One of you will fall over in a minute.'

'No we won't.'

They carry on clashing poles. And then they both fall over. The stream's only about ten inches deep, but they're certainly making the most of it. Charlie's lost both of his wellies, and James has let go of his net.

'If you're not out by the time I count to ten, James, I'm making omelettes for tea.'

James starts splashing towards the bank, while Charlie claims his wellies are full of water and he can't move.

'Yes. Well, that's what happens when you lie down in rivers. Now hurry up, or I won't make any tea at all.'

He gets up, carrying his wellies, looking very bedraggled, with a large piece of green weed stuck to his back, and starts moaning about having trodden on something.

'It was probably just a stone, Charlie. Stop fussing and get out.'

'Yes, but it really hurts.'

He sits down on the grass and sticks his leg up in the air and we all peer at the sole of his foot. Christ. There's quite a lot of blood. He goes very pale.

'Let me wipe the mud off and I'll have a look.'

He starts shrieking while Kate finds clean tissues and we dab and peer.

Bloody hell. It's quite a big cut, and it all seems very red for such a small white foot.

'I think it might need stitches, you know, Annie.'

Charlie yells even louder.

'I don't want needles.'

Christ. I hope he won't need any injections. The thing he hated most when he was ill last year was all the injections into the drip in his hand, which kept blocking. Holding him while they changed the drip was one of the worst things I've ever had to do.

'Let's get you to the hospital and they can have a quick look, Charlie.'

He carries on yelling as we get him into the car, and then Kate offers to go home and collect some dry clothes while I drive him to hospital.

He's slightly calmer by the time we arrive, but I'm not. There's blood all over the back seat, and I can't work out where to park because the car park's full and the only other time I've been here we were in an ambulance. Only I'm trying not to think about that. I finally find a space and stagger in with him, but as soon as we get through the main doors he starts yelling again.

I'm trying to calm him down and book in with the receptionist when a nurse with a grey perm and a pale-grey uniform comes over.

'What's all this noise about then, young man?'

Oh great.

307

'You'll have to be quiet in here. There are other patients waiting too.'

I try smiling at her.

'You must keep him quiet, you know.'

She's glaring at me as well now. And Charlie's sobbing. Really sobbing. Oh fuck this.

'Actually, if you don't mind, you're only making things worse. He's not too keen on hospitals – he had a pretty horrible time last time we were here.'

'And was that for a little cut too?'

'No. Meningococcal septicaemia.'

She blinks and looks rather startled.

'Oh.'

'Yes. And getting annoyed with him isn't really going to help.'

The receptionist actually sniggers at this point and we both turn to look at her as another nurse in a navy-blue uniform comes over and picks up our form.

'Is there a problem?'

Oh great. Now I'm alienating someone else. If I carry on like this they'll be calling security.

'Let's have a look, shall we, poppet? Can you bring him over here, please?'

She walks into an area with cubicles curtained off and produces a sweet wrapped in cellophane from one of her pockets, and offers it to Charlie, who takes it and unwraps it very slowly. He's still clinging on to me, but he's definitely calming down, and she smiles and hands him another one. And the really great thing is you can't really go in for much in the way of shrieking with your cheeks bulging with sweets. How very clever.

She looks at his foot very gently, talking to him all the time.

'Well, that looks fine. Just a few stitches, and it'll be all fixed.'

'Will I have to have a needle?'

He's clinging on to my arm again.

She smiles and explains that they have stick-on stitches now or special glue for little cuts, but she'll need to find a doctor to check, and there might be a bit of a wait because they're quite busy today, and then Kate arrives with James, still dripping wet, and enough dry clothes for a small army of boys. We get them both changed and James is wide-eyed with sympathy at Charlie's tragic plight, which really cheers him up, and the doctor comes in and tries to look at Charlie's foot, which prompts another burst of hysterics until the nurse has a little word with him, whereupon he instantly transforms into Dr Geniality and says the stick-on stitches will be fine but there might be a slight wait because they've got two ambulances due in any minute.

'Shall I go and get some more tea then?'

Kate's being such a star.

'And maybe a KitKat, for people who are sitting nicely?'

James hurls himself down on to the floor and sits with his legs crossed like they do in assembly, and Charlie sits up straighter on his bed.

'Looks like two KitKats then.'

'OK, but I'll go, Kate, I need to find a loo as well.'

I manage to find the loos by following the signs, but on the way back I somehow take a wrong turn and start wandering down a corridor that seems vaguely right but isn't. And then I suddenly come to a complete stop outside a familiar-looking door. It's really strange. I've got no idea where I am, but I'm suddenly standing staring at the door and my heart's racing and my mouth goes all dry. And then I realise. It's the room. The actual room. Where they brought Charlie, on the trolley, last year. Oh Christ. The corridor's deserted, and I'm standing frozen to the spot like a total nutter.

And then I open the door, like I'm on automatic pilot or something, and I'm suddenly faced with the empty bed in the middle of the room, with a trolley and a drip-stand next to it. The mattress is covered in plastic and the grey paint on the metal frame is all chipped. And even though I know he's sitting on the bed in the curtained-off cubicle waiting for his KitKat I can see him lying here at the same time.

'Can I help you?'

A nurse comes into the room.

'I'm sorry, I got lost, and my son was in here last year, in this room, and – '

She puts her arm round me. Which nearly finishes me off completely.

'Deep breaths.'

Actually, that's quite a good idea. I think I've been sort of forgetting to breathe.

I walk backwards out of the room and close the door, which feels great.

God, I really wish I hadn't done that. I feel completely shattered as I walk down the corridor and through the doors. I remember them now. And then I'm back in amongst the curtained-off cubicles and Charlie's playing I-spy. I give him a hug, which annoys him.

'Where my KitKat, Mummy?'

'I got lost, sweetheart, sorry.'

Kate's giving me a rather concerned look.

'Are you all right?'

'Fine. I just went down the wrong corridor, that's all.'

'Shall I go and get that tea then?'

'Yes please.'

'And a large brandy?'

'Even better.'

The boys are eating their KitKats when a young nurse wheels a trolley in and does a bit of dabbing with cotton wool, which Charlie just about tolerates although the grip on my arm gets pretty intense, and then she sticks on little white strips over the cut and covers it with a plastic-coated dressing.

'There you are, all done. And you get a sticker, for being so brave.'

He's completely silent with a combination of relief and exhaustion. I think he's been convinced that they were suddenly going to produce a large needle. She gives me a note for the GP, and a leaflet about wounds, just in case, and says he should keep off his foot for the next few days, and no baths for at least a week, which goes down extremely well, and then she finds us a wheelchair and he's installed amidst huge amounts of fussing, and we're off back to the car. He's waving goodbye to everyone and has chirped up significantly.

I've got a parking ticket when we get back to the car, because I somehow missed the pay-and-display signs while I was busy Panicking and Staggering, but I don't really care. I just want to get home.

'Mummy, I was very brave, wasn't I?'

'Yes, darling.'

'I feel like I've lost a pound and found a shilling.'

Since he's never clapped eyes on a shilling I think this must be another one of Nana's handy little phrases.

'Well, never mind, we'll be home soon.'

'Yes, and I should get a prize, shouldn't I, for being so brave, shouldn't I?'

Oh here we go.

'Yes, maybe a little one, we'll see.'

'Mummy.'

'Yes?'

'You know the Lego castle? The big one.'

Excellent. More bloody Lego to tread on in the middle of the night.

'And, Mummy. Can I borrow your phone, because I want to call Nana.'

Even more excellent.

Mum's waiting when we get home, desperate to turn the house into a sterile zone, and Dad's mowing the lawn, for some reason. Charlie spends ages deciding what he'd like for tea, until he finally chooses toad in the hole, but done by Nana, which is a bit of a result all round really, since Mum gets to feel like a champion sausage-cooker and I get to grab a quick bath.

She brings me up a cup of tea, and says Dad's watching *Star Trek* with Charlie.

'Was he all right at the hospital then? He showed me his sticker. He's very proud of it, you know, bless him. Where you anywhere near where we were before then? In that room?'

'No, Mum, in a completely different part.'

I really don't think there's any point in both of us having flashback moments.

'Good. Well, at least he's all right, and that's the main thing.'

'Yes.'

'I'd better get back downstairs then. Supper in about half an hour?'

'Lovely.'

I call Mack while I'm drinking my tea. At least I'm in the bath if I spill anything.

'Good day in the office, dear?'

He's had his first proper meeting in the office with Barney today.

'Yes, Barney says Lawrence practically committed ritual suicide in reception when he told him, but you've got to hand it to him, he rallies well. Couldn't have been more helpful, busy sorting me out a desk and all that bollocks.'

'So I'll be back in the basement then.'

'That's the general plan, I think. And Barney says Lawrence will be my producer, on my first few jobs at least. What do you think?'

'Good idea.'

'Why doesn't Barney ever use him on jobs then?'

'Because he panics.'

'Oh, great.'

'No, he'll be fine, Mack, just what you need when you're starting out. He'll play things safe and make sure you don't get too many surprises.'

'I suppose so. He's got some cat-food script he wants me to look at. He says Barney's not up for it.'

'No, he hates cats.'

'Well, so do I. I had one next door to the apartment, used to jump over the balcony wall and crap on my terrace. It was called Cecil.'

'Well, don't use a cat called Cecil then. And don't choose a black cat either, because – '

'I know, Barney's already told me. They're quite tricky to light.'

'Quite tricky? We spent days locked in that bloody studio, with black cats and miles of black velvet. We couldn't even see the fucking things most of the time.'

'You don't fancy coming up for lunch tomorrow, do you?'

'Well, that's one of the reasons I'm calling you, actually. Charlie cut his foot in the stream today, after school. Five stitches, but only the stick-on ones.'

'Christ. Is he all right?'

'Yes, now we're out of the hospital, but he'll be off school for the rest of the week.'

'So Friday's off then?'

'Probably. Let's see how it goes.'

'They heal up really quickly at his age.'

'I know. But I'd rather be here with him, and you're coming down on Sunday still, aren't you, for lunch at Monty's?'

'Anything you want me to bring?'

'A large bottle of Valium?'

'No problem.'

Charlie spends the night in my bed, after playing his I Am Injured trump card at repeated intervals until I finally cave. And then he flings his arms about and rolls himself up in the duvet so I can't get to sleep. I'm just not cut out for this earth-mother thing, and I'm seriously considering prodding him until he wakes up and telling him to shove off back to his own bed, but then I manage to fall asleep, only to be woken up what seems like minutes later by someone poking their finger into my ear and announcing they'd like some toast and honey.

He spends the morning watching cartoons and occasionally requesting light snacks, and Kate rings and says she'll come round after school with Sally, and the kids can all have a picnic in the back garden, which is brilliant because it'll take Charlie's mind off his foot, and I'll get to talk to somebody who doesn't keep using their special whining voice.

I can't work out how to get Charlie up the lane to the shops so I can get some extra picnic supplies without having to get the car out, which I'm sort of avoiding because I still haven't sorted out the bloodstains, and then I have a flash of inspiration and decide to wheel him up the lane in the wheelbarrow. He's not too sure at first, but when I line it with a blanket and a couple of cushions he's rather impressed, and we're soon squeaking our way up the lane, with Charlie waving his Stonehenge dagger and generally having a fabulous time. He weighs a ton, and I'm really glad the shop's not far.

'Can I come in the shop too, Mummy?'

'There isn't room for the wheelbarrow, Charlie.'

'Can you carry me then?'

'No I can't. You're too big now. Just stay here and I won't be a minute. You look like a little prince, you know, lying on your cushions.'

This goes down rather well.

I race round the shop casting the occasional anxious glance through the shop window to make sure nobody's wheeled him off while I'm choosing crisps, although if they did I'm pretty certain they'd be wheeling him straight back pretty sharpish. Mrs Thompson on the till is very impressed with my ingenuity, and says her mother once did the same thing in the war when the wheel came off her old pram, and she had three of them under five, and she was going strawberry-picking for jam.

'Not that you could get the sugar, mind, but she used to save up our ration for weeks, but it was – good Lord, what's happened now?'

There's a combination of screaming and barking coming from outside, and I've got visions of Charlie being savaged by a pit bull as I grab the door. But it's more like the other way round. The wheelbarrow's tipped over and Charlie's lying on the floor yelling, and our Vicar's wife is trying to untangle herself from her dog lead while her ancient collie dog cowers behind the metal bin and barks hysterically. Christ.

'Oh dear, I'm so sorry, we were just saying hello and he

leant over to stroke Sadie and the whole thing tipped over.'

By the time I've got Charlie back in the wheelbarrow, we've attracted quite a little crowd of elderly ladies who are waiting for the Whitstable bus. They're all highly amused, and whilst it's nice to do your bit for cheering up the elderly, obviously, frankly, I just wish they'd leave us alone so I can calm Charlie down a bit.

One of them has gone into the shop to get him a lolly.

'Here you are, dear, poor little thing.'

Charlie's loving all the attention.

'I've got five stitches on my foot, you know. And there was loads of blood. Loads.'

'Have you, dear? And how did that happen then?'

They all lean a bit closer.

'I was fishing in the stream, and I fell over. And my wellies just came off. Not on purpose or anything.'

They all chuckle. Yes. Highly bloody amusing, I'm sure.

'Well, boys will be boys. My two led me a merry old dance, I can tell you. My Tom was a terror, we practically had our seat at the cottage hospital.'

The bus arrives, and they all shuffle off in a sort of flock of waterproof macs and tartan shopping bags, waving to Charlie as they get on the bus. The Vicar's wife has finally recovered, and I retrieve my shopping and we squeak off down the lane, while I try to remember if I actually said 'Christ' out loud when I first opened the shop door and saw him sprawled on the ground.

'That was nice, wasn't it, Mummy?'

'What was?'

'Seeing Sadie and all the nice ladies, and the Vicar lady. She comes into our school for hymn practice sometimes. But me and James don't go, because we're pagans. So we do drawing.'

I bet she's back at the vicarage right now telling the

Vicar all about the little pagan being dragged round the village in a wheelbarrow. They must think I'm a complete halfwit.

'Mummy.'

'Yes?'

'Did you get crisps?'

'Yes.'

'Oh good, because I'm absolutely starving.'

Kate and Sally arrive with extra picnic supplies, just as it begins to rain, so we get them all-settled in the living room with *The Lord of the Rings,* a large blanket spread over the carpet and plates of ham sandwiches, and a rather optimistic bowl of oranges and apples that Sally has peeled and cut into segments. I've got chocolate mini rolls and crisps for later, but we're keeping those in reserve. We make tea and sit at the kitchen table with the door open so we can race in and adjudicate in case of Disputes.

'So how's the wounded hero been then?'

'Driving me mad.'

I tell them about the wheelbarrow moment, which makes Kate choke on her tea so we have to bang her on the back.

'Did he sleep all right?'

'Oh yes, fine. Once he was in my bed.'

They both smile.

'They're a nightmare when they're ill, aren't they? William sort of regresses to being a baby, at the slightest sniffle. Wants his milk warmed up in a plastic cup, stuff like that. I hate it.'

'Charlie was like that last year, when we got home from the hospital. Wanted everything cut up for him, and he'd only eat with a spoon. It took me ages to get him to eat with a bloody fork again.'

'Yes, but that was different. That wasn't just a cold. Do you think he remembers much about it?'

'Mostly the injections, I think. He was out of it for most of the time. I don't think he's got any memories at all of being in intensive care at Guy's, thank god.'

'It's nearly a year now, isn't it?'

'Yes.'

'Well, I think you've done brilliantly, both of you.'

'Oh I don't know, Sal. He has, well, apart from the needles thing, and I think he'll get over that. But I'm still hopeless when he's ill, even a cold, or anything. It's like he's a baby again, and part of me is always on the look-out. You know, when you keep checking to see they're still breathing and then you gradually start to relax, and you build up a sort of barrier around them, where you trust that they'll be fine. And then suddenly you're sitting in intensive care listening to the beeping of machines and willing them to get through it, and it's gone, the confidence thing. You know there are dragons out there. It's like part of me is always bracing myself, and I know I've got to stop it. But I don't even know I'm doing it half the time. I'm so angry about it all, that it had to happen to him. Every so often, it's just sort of overwhelming. I'm still frightened I'm going to lose him. And it'll be all my fault. Because I haven't kept him safe.'

Crikey. I don't know where all that came from. Sally puts her arm round my shoulder.

'Sorry. Just ignore me. I didn't get much sleep last night.'

Sally smiles.

'You're processing. I read about it in *Good Housekeeping*. That's what happens when you've had a traumatic experience. Once you get over the initial phase, of coping with it all, you have to process it.'

'And then make your own chutney, right?'

She laughs.

'Yes.'

Kate smiles.

'More tea?'

She gets up to put the kettle on and Sally passes her our cups.

'Well, I think you've been amazing. I think I'd be a total basket case.'

'No you wouldn't, Sal. You'd just get on with it – you don't really have a choice.'

'Maybe.'

'Do you think I'll ever get over it? I mean really?'

'Do you want the truth?'

'Yes.'

'No.'

'Oh. Great.'

'I think you'll forget, most of the time. But it'll always be there.'

'Well, I don't have the worst dreams any more, the ones where he's on the trolley and they're turning all the machines off, and I'm driving home without him.'

Kate flinches as she pours the tea.

'You know, I can still see James lying at the bottom of the tree in the garden, you remember, when he fell out that time. And just for a few seconds, while he was lying still, before he started yelling, I thought he was dead. I could hear the birds singing and the sun was really bright, and he was just lying there. I'll never forget it.'

'Has Phoebe ever had any heart-stopping moments?'

'Not really. She went through a terrible phase when she was little, falling over things, down steps, that kind of thing, but nothing major. I'm just waiting for hers really. Going out with unsuitable boys, with tattoos and motorbikes. And then there's booze, of course, and drugs. She's just the type. Anything to annoy me.'

Sally smiles.

'There's so much to look forward to, isn't there?'

'Hobnob?'

'Please.'

They're both looking rather depressed, which is probably my fault.

'Well, before they all roar off on motorbikes snorting illegal substances shall we sort out what they're going to be doing in bloody *Mary Poppins*?'

Ginny's divided up all the classes and Sally and Kate and me are down for Charlie's class and we've got to choose which song we want to do.

'Good plan.'

'Actually, I've just had a rather brilliant idea.'

We both look at Sally.

'You know last year's nativity, when Charlie had that pheasant costume? Well, why don't we do the 'Feed the Birds' song? They can all be sparrows and blackbirds and chaffinches, and we can bulk-buy feathers and make them all beaks.'

Kate laughs.

'Good plan, but bags I don't have to be the one to tell James he's got to be a chaffinch.'

'Well, he can be a pheasant with Charlie. They can all be pheasants if they like. Or robins. Parrots. Whatever they like.'

Great. More sticking hundreds of feather on to pairs of thick tights.

Terrific.

* * *

Mack comes down on Sunday morning with a huge box of Harry Potter Lego for Charlie, which goes down extremely well. We drive round to Monty's, and Mack gets taken off on a tour of the farm while Charlie makes a start on Hogwart's.

I'm in the kitchen trying to get the crackling to crackle when Mack comes back in covered in mud. I pass him some kitchen paper and put the kettle on while he cleans his shoes.

'We'll have to get you some wellies.'

'No thank you, darling. Monty's already taken care of that. He's just given me a pair of enormous fishing boots.'

'Oh yes, sorry, I forgot about that. I meant to warn you.'

'They've even got rubber suspender things.'

'I know. Sorry.'

'Does he think I'm some sort of nutter?'

'Probably.'

'I might have to wear them at lunch if I can't get the mud off these.'

I hand him a coffee.

'How were the kids yesterday?'

'On top form. Alfie broke two glasses, and Daisy threw a total strop because I'd got the wrong kind of bread. But I took them to the British Museum and they loved it, just like you said they would.'

'Good. Oh god, here's Mum and Dad.'

Mum bustles in and starts fussing about the lunch, but quickly abandons this so she can concentrate fully on Mack. She's asking him where he went to school while Dad pours us all a sherry from the bottle Mack brought down with him, and Monty offers to show Dad his lawnmower, for the umpteenth time. Mack moves on to helping Charlie with his Lego while I set the table and Mum gets in the way, and then Mack pours her another sherry, and she starts getting quite giggly. He keeps winking at me when she's not looking.

By the time we're sitting down to lunch Mum has had a third sherry, and has whispered to me in the kitchen that she thinks Mack is lovely. Dad keeps raising his eyebrows, and before we know it she's on to her second glass of wine and telling Mack that Aunty Brenda can't make a Swiss roll.

'She just hasn't got the temperament for sponge. It's like the stuff you put under carpets. All flat and rubbery.'

'Underfelt. That's what she's talking about.'

Monty's being helpful.

Mack's trying very hard not to laugh.

'Charlie, don't eat with your fingers. I've told you before.'

'But, Mummy, my meat won't cut up. It's got me by the short and twirlies.'

Mack chokes on a sprout, and Monty goes rather pink. I think he might have been teaching Charlie a few new phrases when they're out in the fields on their walks.

Dad and Charlie help me clear the table while Mack makes coffee, and Monty shows Mum some photographs he's found in a drawer.

'Well, he seems all right, your Mack. Handy with the sherry anyway. You could do worse, I suppose.'

'Thanks, Dad.'

'Your mother seems quite keen anyway, but that might be the sherry talking.'

'True.'

'Just don't let him talk you into anything you don't want to be doing. He seems like he'd be quite good at that. Mind you, I think he's probably met his match with you.'

He smiles.

'Thanks, Dad.'

We sit reading the papers by the fire, and Charlie flings

Lego all over Monty's carpet. Mum has a light doze, and so does Monty, and then I make a cup of tea for everyone, and Mum and Dad go home because Mum wants to be back in time for *The Antiques Roadshow*, and Monty and Charlie go out to feed the pheasants.

I'm doing the washing up and Mack's drying. I don't think he's terribly experienced on the tea-towel front, but he's doing a very thorough job. In fact he's taking ages.

'Speed up a bit, Mack. There isn't any room for the plates until you do the bowls.'

'If a job's worth doing, it's worth doing properly, I think you'll find.'

'Yes. But not if I have to stand here balancing wet plates.'

He tuts.

'Your mum seemed very happy.'

'Yes. And pissed. Clever plan to keep filling up her glass.'

'It's a technique I've been perfecting over the years. You have to judge it just right, though, or they end up slapping you.'

'Oh do they?'

'Yes. Or they eat your pudding. Stuff like that. It can get quite tricky.'

'I only did that once, and it was chocolate soufflé and it's my favourite.'

'Well, I'll never order it again, that's for sure. Or I'll order two for you and something else for me, or I won't stand a chance. You'll have me right by the short and twirlies.'

I laugh.

'You better believe it.'

Mack goes back to town late on Sunday night because he's got an early meeting tomorrow morning, with Lawrence, about the cat-food job.

'Glamorous life this directing's turning out to be. Not.'

'I know. Just wait until you're on a deep-sea trawler in a howling gale.'

'Can't wait. I could stay here and leave really early, I suppose, but it would have to be really early.'

He gives me a rather searching look.

'You could.'

I'm half hoping he doesn't, because he hasn't actually stayed the night here, not since last year. And Charlie's been fine about him being back on the scene, so far. But I don't really want to push it. Not with the foot thing and everything.

'You don't sound very keen.'

'Of course I am. I'd love it if you stayed.'

'That's all right then. Actually, I should probably make a move though, much as I'd like to stay. Or I'll be wrecked tomorrow.'

'Fair enough. And I'm in the office tomorrow anyway, around lunchtime, so I'll see you then.'

I think I'm getting the hang of this. What he wants is for me to be keen for him to stay. And that way he'll be happy to drive back to town. Whereas if I'm reluctant he'll get slightly huffy about it.

'Great. And I'll help you move your desk back up from the basement.'

Charlie goes back to school on Monday, with a rather tragic limp that gets much more pronounced whenever he wants something. His foot's almost completely healed, and Miss Pike says she'll keep an eye on him, and then hands me a bag of feathers that one of the mums who keeps chickens has collected for us. Sally and Kate have already started on the wings, and we're trying to work out how to make thirty-two beaks without calling in professional help.

I drive up to town, and when I arrive Mack's already

in his second meeting of the day with Lawrence and the agency about the cat-food job.

Stef's just taken the coffee in.

'He's driving me crazy.'

I'm hoping she means Lawrence.

'Why?'

'Going on about sugar again.'

Lawrence thinks it's vital that we have brown chunks of sugar for client meetings, and not just the usual bowl of white. And warm milk, in a little jug.

'And I said to him, I said look, if I wanted to spend my time steaming milk I'd have got a job in Costa fucking Coffee, wouldn't I, and then I wouldn't have to put up with crap from you.'

'Did you really?'

'No, but I wish I had. But your Mack was brilliant. He said he didn't think anyone really gave a toss about stuff like that. And if they did, they were wankers, so it didn't matter. He's lovely, isn't he?'

'He has his moments.'

'I bet he does.'

She sniggers, which makes me laugh.

'What are you two cackling about? And what do I have to do to get a clean cup round here?'

Barney's not looking pleased.

'Sorry, but the white ones are in the meeting room with Lawrence, and I just put the rest in the dishwasher – the cleaners didn't turn up again.'

'Well, ring that bloody agency up and sack them. Christ. And then go and buy some more bloody cups. If that's not too much to ask?'

'No, I'll call them right now.'

Stef starts walking back to her desk.

'Thank you. And what are you looking so happy about?'

He's giving me a pretty ferocious look too.

'Oh, just how lovely it is being in the office, watching you demonstrate your fabulous personnel skills. Really inspiring. Anyway, I'm just off to Starbucks. Do you want anything?'

'No I bloody don't. I just want an ordinary cup of coffee, not a carton of froth. I hate all that skinny decaf soya bollocks.'

'I'll tell them that then, shall I? I'm sure they'll be devastated.'

He smiles.

'I hate lippy women.'

'Well, thanks for sharing that with us, Barney. So anyway, moving swiftly on, that's one non-frothy coffee then. Oh, and you couldn't lend me a fiver, could you? Only I haven't been to the cash point yet.'

He hands me a twenty-pound note.

'Get some of those muffin things too, for you and Stef, and Jenny.'

I give Stef a wink and get my bag as Barney goes back upstairs.

'I don't know how you do that.'

'What?'

'Get him over it, when he's throwing an epi.'

'Years of practice. And the occasional slap.'

'You've never actually hit him, have you? God, I wish I'd been there.'

'No. But I've come pretty close.'

'That's the thing about Barney, though, isn't it? He pushes it, but he always does something really sweet in the end, so you forgive him.'

'I know.'

'Silly old bugger.'

Quite.

I'm back at my desk and drinking my coffee when Mack comes out of his meeting. They've got the job and he's really excited about it, and Lawrence is busy booking studio days and sorting out a crew.

'Do you fancy lunch, darling?'

'Great.'

I can't decide if I mind him calling me darling at work. Maybe I should ask him to keep it more professional. But it's definitely better than babe, so perhaps I should quit while I'm ahead.

We go round the corner to his new favourite café, an Italian greasy spoon that does a great cooked breakfast, and he's greeted like a long-lost friend by the owner, Enzo, and then he goes into hyper-work mode and talks about budgets and schedules.

'Christ, it's complicated, isn't it?'

'It gets easier.'

'What if I'm crap?'

'You won't be.'

'But what if I am?'

'Then Barney will turf you out and we'll think of something else.'

He smiles.

'How did Charlie cope with going back to school? I'm guessing he wasn't exactly keen?'

'Still limping, and pretty miffed, but fine.'

My phone starts beeping. And then one of Mum's special hieroglyphic texts pops up on the screen.

'Oh bugger.'

'What?'

'Mum's sent me one of her mad texts that you can't actually read. She must have some sort of crisis on. I'd better call her.'

'Why didn't she just call you then?'

'Because I've just realised it's been on voicemail. Charlie was fiddling with it this morning and I never checked.'

His phone starts beeping too. Actually, it's playing the American national anthem.

'Why's it doing that?'

'Someone's calling me, that's how phones work, darling.'

'I meant why is it playing that tune?'

'Because it reminds me of how glad I am to be back in London.'

'Aren't you going to see who it is then?'

'They'll leave a message. And I'm having lunch with you. Who else could I possibly want to talk to?'

'Oh. Right. Good answer.'

He smirks, and picks up his phone.

'It was Stef, to say your mum's trying to track you down, because Monty's had an accident.'

I call Mum's number.

'Engaged. How am I meant to call her if she won't put the bloody phone down.'

My phone goes again.

'Mum?'

She's hysterical. Monty's somehow fallen off his lawn-mower in the barn, and hurt his leg, and had to crawl back to the house, where instead of calling an ambulance like a normal person he called me, only I wasn't there so he called Mum and asked her to give him a lift to the hospital. By the time she got to the house he was sitting in his chair wincing and trying to pretend there was nothing the matter.

'But he was ever such an odd grey colour, and honestly, thank heavens your father was there because I'd never have got him into the car by myself, and I nearly fainted, you know, it was all such a shock. Anyway, he's on the ward now, and they say it's just a fracture, although at his age

328

that's no joke, you know. And they've put him in plaster and they'll keep him in for observation, and I'm supposed to be going up to Lizzie tonight, they've got some work thing and she won't leave Ava with anyone else, so can you go in and see him later? He's on Jenner Ward, and take him some pyjamas, and then I'll go in tomorrow. He says he doesn't want me fussing, and you know what he's like, and I think he'd be better if you were there, and, Annie, are you still there?'

'Yes, Mum, and it's fine. I'll go tonight.'

'Good. And remember the pyjamas. I don't want him in those hospital ones. People will think nobody's bothered about him, and someone might have died in them – or anything – you just don't know.'

'Yes, Mum.'

'Marks do some nice blue ones, and you don't want to get him those ones in the packets because – '

'Mum, I've said I'll do it. I'll get the blue ones. But I've got to go now, I'll call you later, all right?'

Christ.

Mack's smiling.

'What's happened?'

'He's fractured his leg. Falling off that bloody lawnmower. And they're keeping him in. Christ, I might as well buy a nurse's uniform.'

'What a good idea.'

'It's not funny, Mack.'

'Sorry. Well, they're certainly keeping you busy, aren't they, the boys in your life. First Charlie and now Monty.'

'Yes, so watch it. Or you'll have something in plaster next.'

'Can't wait, if you'll be wearing a special uniform. Poor old sod. He'll hate being in hospital.'

'I know. I'll have to take him things to cheer him up.'

'I'll get him a bottle of something. What does he like, whisky?'

'I can't take an eighty-two-year-old a bottle of whisky in hospital. They'll throw me out.'

'I'll get him some miniatures then, and you can smuggle them in.'

I finally get to the hospital at around seven after a tricky moment in Marks when I tried to find someone to help me work out what size pyjamas to get and ended up with the head of bloody menswear giving me the run-down on the new autumn range. And I've got him some fruit and a couple of sandwiches too, and then I nipped into home on the way to check on Charlie, who's had a good day at school, and is now busy making a card for Monty while Edna fusses over him and practically spoon-feeds him jelly which she's made as a surprise for tea. She's very sympathetic about Monty and says bad luck is supposed to come in threes so could I please drive carefully and watch where I'm walking. Actually, I bloody hope I won't be the next member of the family with something in a bandage, because frankly I'm just too busy.

There are spaces in the car park this time, thank god, and I find Jenner Ward fairly easily, only it turns out they've moved him to the geriatric unit because they needed the bed, and it's right at the other end of the hospital, in what looks like an enormous old hut.

I see Monty as soon as I walk through the double doors into the ward. He's sitting in a chair by his bed, marooned inside vast pyjamas and looking very pale and fed up.

'Hello, Monty.'

'Annie.'

He smiles as I bend down to kiss him and grabs my hand and starts whispering.

'You've got to get me out of here. I can't stay here with this lot. They're all on their way out, absolutely round the twist. And that one over there keeps shouting all the time.'

The old man in the bed opposite appears to be having some sort of argument with an invisible visitor, poor thing. He's shouting at the chair next to his bed and waving his arms about.

'How's your leg?'

'It's fine. I've told them. I just want to get off home. And I'm not getting in this bed. Even if it takes all night. I'll sit here until they give me my pass.'

I sit down on the bed.

'I've brought you some sandwiches, and some fruit.'

'Very kind of you. But I'm not eating anything until they let me out of here.'

Oh great. So now he's on hunger strike as well.

'Monty, you've got to eat.'

'No I don't. Not until I'm home.'

'Have they told you how long they want to keep you in?'

'You can't get any sense out of them. They just keep saying we'll see.'

'Shall I go and ask someone?'

'Would you, love? And tell them, I'm not getting into this bloody bed, so they can think again. I just want to get home. There's Tess to feed, and the sheep to see to.'

'Dad's fed Tess, Monty, Mum told me, and the sheep will be fine in the field, won't they?'

'Yes, but there's Charlie's pheasants.'

'We'll do them after school tomorrow.'

'I just want to go home, Annie. Please.'

Oh god.

'I'll go and find someone then, shall I?'

'Yes.'

331

'Only you'll have to let go of my hand first.'

He sort of coughs and looks embarrassed.

'Sorry.'

I track down a doctor who's sitting in the office writing up notes, and he's fairly brisk and dismissive and says he's not sure how long Monty will be kept in, but probably at least a week.

'But he's refusing to get into bed.'

'Oh he'll soon get over that. A lot of them make a bit of a fuss when they first arrive, but they soon settle down. We can give him some tablets if he has trouble sleeping.'

'And he's not eating.'

'As I said, he'll soon settle, they all do. Now if you don't mind, I do have other patients. We'll call you if anything changes, but if I were you I'd just see if you can't persuade him to get into bed, and then pop by tomorrow.'

'But he wants to go home. I can't leave him like this.'

'I understand he lives on his own.'

'Yes.'

He gives me a nasty sort of smile.

'Well then. Unless you're willing to take him on, I'd leave him to us.'

And in a way he's right. It's very simple. Either I'm prepared to take Monty home with me, or I'm not. He can't go home by himself. And this is the best they can do. So I should bugger off and leave them to get on with it.

'Is there any medical reason why he should be here?'

'Well, technically no, but as I said – '

'Well, in that case I think I'd like to take him home, to my home, and look after him there. Or maybe back to the farm, I think he'd prefer that. He's worrying about the animals.'

He seems to soften slightly.

'It's a very simple fracture, nothing to worry about. He

just needs lots of rest. And his GP can get the district nurse to look in on him. If you're sure.'

'I'm sure.'

'Well, good for you. Why don't you go and tell him the news then, and I'll do the paperwork.'

Bugger.

Monty's delighted, but isn't keen on coming back home with me.

'You just drop me off home, love. I don't want you running round after me, and – '

'Monty.'

'Yes?'

'Shut up. Right now. And do as you're told. Or I'll leave you here and come back in tomorrow with a bunch of grapes.'

'I was just saying.'

'I know what you were just saying. But you're coming home with me and that's final. You can stay with us for tonight, and then tomorrow I'll take Charlie to school and then sort our things out and we'll come and stay on the farm with you for a few days. And you can look after Tess and tell me what needs doing with the sheep. And Mum will come round and wash things. And you'll be nice to her. Deal?'

'Yes.'

'And no ranting about bloody women fussing. And you've got to promise to lock the gun away while we're there, and no talking to Charlie about shooting things, not even with air rifles. Not even with rubber bands.'

He nods. But he's smiling now.

'Good. Now do you need a hand getting dressed?'

He gives me a very affronted look.

'No. I do not.'

Thank god for that.

'Right, well, you get ready then. I'll go and find the doctor – I think there's something you've got to sign. And then we'll find you a wheelchair.'

'I'm not getting in a flaming wheelchair – I'm not that bad.'

'Oh yes you are. The car's bloody miles away.'

'Annie?'

'Yes?'

'Your Aunty Florrie always said you were a good girl.'

Charlie's loving us staying on the farm with Monty. He's completely got over his limping routine now, and we check on the sheep after breakfast every day, which was rather nerve-wracking at first but basically if they're not lying on their backs waving their legs in the air they're fine. They rush up to us when we go into the field to fill up the water trough, and I'm starting to recognise different ones now. There's one with a black face who's always the first to come up and nudge you, just in case you've got any sheep nuts in your pockets, and a really nervous one who always moves to the other side of the field as soon as you open the gate. Tess trots round with us, which Charlie loves, and it's all very *Little House on the Prairie*.

Mum's been bringing round emergency casseroles, and having a great time washing and cleaning and getting into cupboards. We've sorted out the little back bedroom for Charlie, so he's not in the spare room with me now, which is a bonus. And Monty's much better, although he's spending a fair amount of his time asleep in front of the fire. But he can hobble round with a stick now, without going a pale-grey colour, so I've hidden the keys to the lawnmower just in case.

* * *

Mack's come down for the day on Saturday, with Daisy and Alfie, and I'm standing in the kitchen with one of Mum's pinnys on, making lunch, and feeling like I've slipped into a Stepford Wife twilight zone. I'll be making jam next and panicking about getting my whites really white. Charlie and Alfie are outside building a bonfire for the autumn equinox extravaganza tonight; Kate's bringing James round, and they've been going on about it for days. We're trying to downplay the pagan thing and make it into a more general bonfire tea, but they keep muttering about sacred oaths so it's not looking good.

'They're having a brilliant time out there. They're making a camp in the barn now. And Daisy's taken a real shine to Tess. She's always wanted a dog, but Laura wasn't keen. Any chance of a coffee?'

Mack's been out supervising the bonfire construction.

'Sure.'

'Good apron, sweetheart, very WI.'

He's raising his eyebrows and doing his flirty smile, and we're in the middle of a clandestine moment when Daisy comes back in. And she's not happy.

'Do you fancy helping me make some buns after lunch, Daisy, for the bonfire party?'

'No thank you. My mummy says we shouldn't eat cakes, they've got too much sugar. And sugar's very bad for you. We make banana bread instead.'

'Oh, right. Well, we can make banana bread, if you like.'

'Only my mummy knows how to make it.'

'Oh, right.'

Mack's frowning.

'Daisy. I'm sure Annie knows how to make banana bread too.'

She ignores him. Oh dear.

'Actually, I don't, not really, so maybe I'd better just do

the buns. Kate's bringing flapjacks, and we can have fruit for people who don't want cake. Do you like flapjacks, Daisy?'

'Sometimes.'

I'm guessing probably not today, but we'll see.

Charlie and Alfie race in, breathless with excitement.

'Mummy, come quick, we've made a camp, and it's brilliant, and I'm going to sleep in it tonight, and have candles. It'll be great.'

Excellent. Candles in a barn. With bales of hay. Maybe I'll just call the fire brigade now and book a slot for later.

'You can have a torch, Charlie. And we'll see.'

'And Alfie wants to stay too.'

Alfie's looking very determined.

'I can, can't I Daddy?'

'Not this time, Alf – we've got to get back home tonight.'

'That's not fair.'

'I want to sleep in the camp too.'

Daisy's looking very put out.

'Well, you can't. It's not for girls.'

Alfie grins. Finally a chance to get one over his clever big sister.

Everyone looks at Mack. Who says 'Christ' rather loudly and walks out into the garden, followed by all three of them lobbying him for camping rights.

Lunch is rather tense, since Mack has adopted the take-that-look-off-your-face approach during the camping negotiations, and is now busy ignoring some very sustained sulking. Monty's talking to Mack about the war, and why the RAF need taking down a peg or two. And by the time I bring in the apple crumble they're on to EU farming subsidies and why the French are all bastards and Monty's waving his fork in the air.

I've got strawberry ice-cream for people who don't want crumble, and I've just passed Daisy her bowlful when Alfie announces he doesn't like strawberries and he doesn't like crumble either and bursts into tears.

Mack's furious.

'For Christ's sake, Alfie, give it a rest.'

Alfie cries even louder.

'Mack.'

'Yes?'

He's glaring at me now too.

'I think he just needs a pudding he likes, that's all. Shall we go into the kitchen, Alfie, and see if we can find you something else?'

'Yes please.'

He's still doing the heaving-shoulders routine, but at least he's stopped crying. And Charlie's now eating his pudding as fast as he can in case something glorious emerges from the kitchen.

'There's yogurt, or apples. Which would you like, Alfie?'

'An apple cut up?'

'OK. Daisy, would you like an apple too?'

'Yes please.'

'Charlie?'

'What?'

'Do you want an apple?'

'Yes.'

'Yes what, Charlie?'

'Yes, cut up in a bowl?'

'Charlie.'

'Yes please.'

So that's three apples cut up then. Christ. Maybe I should just go on a catering course.

Mack comes into the kitchen while I'm making coffee.

'Sorry about Alfie.'

'He's only little, Mack.'

'He's a little sod.'

'Yes, but the trick is to make him your little sod.'

'He's still on about that bloody camp.'

'You can stay if you like, you know.'

'I'd love to, but I've got to get them back to Laura early tomorrow. She's got her parents for lunch. Will you be up in town this week?'

'Thursday. The duckpond job's a definite now, and Barney wants me in for the casting.'

'Shall I book somewhere for supper then?'

'That sounds nice, Mum's said she'll stay the night here. As long as I'm back in the morning to do the sheep.'

'What a thrilling life you lead, sweetheart.'

'I know. Talking of which, I was rather hoping you'd be offering to do the washing up. But since you haven't, I'm volunteering you.'

'Haven't you got him a dishwasher yet then?'

'What do you think?'

'Christ.'

The bonfire's a huge success. Kate brings some red candles, which are vital for equinoxing, apparently, and they march round in circles chanting, with Charlie and James wearing their sacred-acorns on strings and Alfie wearing oak leaves tucked into his woolly hat, and it all starts to get a bit *Lord of the Flies*. Phoebe and Daisy are very aloof at first, but then they can't resist, and James gets his *Bumper Book of Pagans* out of the car so they can remind themselves what they're meant to be chanting, and they circle the bonfire and thank the gods for a good harvest and wish for peace and happiness, and then they make a secret wish. Which all seems fairly harmless, and Kate and I are quite relieved because we've been bracing ourselves for Buffy-

338

type moments with garlic and pointy bits of wood. Monty's delighted and says it's just like the old harvest suppers he used to go to when he was young, and it's nearly ten by the time everyone's left and I'm tucking Charlie into bed.

'Mummy, our equinox was very good, wasn't it?'

'Yes, Charlie.'

'Only we need mistletoe for next time.'

'Right.'

'And green candles. The book said. Shall I tell you what my secret wish was?'

'If you want to.'

'I wished that we could live on the farm for ever, with Monty. And the pheasants. I told Uncle Monty too.'

'That was nice, Charlie.'

'Yes. And I could have a ferret if we lived on a farm. Couldn't I?'

'Night, Charlie.'

It's the day of the duckpond shoot, so we're in Wiltshire at five in the morning stumbling round in the dark and trying not to fall in the sodding pond after spending most of yesterday in the studio getting the pack shots done. It's freezing and once the dawn does appear we'll only have a few minutes to get the shots we want, or we'll have to come back tomorrow. So it's all getting rather tense. We've hired a flock of tame ducks to sit in the middle of the pond, but so far they're not having any of it and are sitting huddled under the trees sulking. The animal trainer's starting to panic, and so am I.

And then Barney has a brilliant idea.

'Tell him to tie some string to their legs and tie bricks on the other end, and then he can plant them in the middle of the pond where we need them.'

'I beg your pardon?'

'Just go and tell him.'

'Barney, I think I can safely say that's one of the daftest ideas you've ever had.'

'How else are you planning to get the fuckers to stay where we want them then?'

I go over and talk to the trainer. And surprisingly he thinks it might be worth a try, and starts measuring the depth of the pond with a stick. Dear god. I'm surrounded by nutters.

Half the crew hunt for bits of old brick and big stones, and after a great deal of quacking and flapping the ducks are grouped in the middle of the pond, and the trainer rows back in his inflatable boat to check they're in the right position.

Barney's delighted.

'Perfect.'

The trainer looks very relieved.

'They'll settle down in a minute or two.'

And they do. Just as the light starts to change. And we've just got the first shot when I notice that the ducks seem to be shrinking.

The cameraman notices too.

'Guv, aren't they getting a bit low in the water?'

'What?'

'The ducks.'

'What about the fucking ducks?'

Barney's been concentrating on making sure the actor's in the shot as he walks past the pond, playing a farmer on his way to his fields, to grow the perfect frozen peas: 'We get up early to make sure you don't have to.'

'I think they're sinking. That one in the middle is nearly up to its beak.'

'Jesus Christ.'

The trainer's noticed it too. 'Stop. Stop. They're sinking. You're drowning my ducks.' He's running towards his boat.

'Oh great. What's he doing now?' Barney turns to me, looking furious.

'He's rescuing his ducks, Barney. Before someone calls the RSPCA.'

'Just give me another minute.'

The duck man's in the boat now, and the ducks are getting even lower. The stones must be sinking into the mud or something. Christ. I wonder if you can do mouth to mouth on a duck. Because I've got a horrible feeling we're going to find out in a minute.

Barney's looking at the monitor.

'Fine. He can get them out now. We've got it.'

The ducks are all absolutely furious by the time they're back on dry land, and pecking anyone who comes near them. And I don't really blame them.

And the animal trainer's livid and marches over to Barney.

'These ducks are highly trained, you know.'

'Well, maybe you should train them to untie string then.'

I take him off for a coffee and try to calm him down, making hand-gestures behind my back at Barney as we go.

Once I've got him settled with a coffee I go back over to Barney.

'Thanks so much, Barney.'

'What have I done now?'

'You know. And don't pretend you don't. Are you off now then? Or are you hanging on here to see if you can really upset him?'

'It's your own fault, darling. I've told you. No more jobs with fucking animals.'

'No you haven't, Barney, you just said no cats.'

'Or dogs. Not after those fucking St Bernards.'

'All right, no cats or dogs. You never said anything about other animals.'

'Oh yes I did. It's just you never listen. What about that bloody camel who wouldn't lie down? When we had to turn all the studio lights off and stand outside in the car park until it relaxed. Christ, three fucking hours that took.'

'Right. So that's no dogs, cats, or camels. And now we can add ducks. But I don't know why you're telling me anyway. Tell Lawrence. He's the one that keeps getting the scripts in.'

'Oh I can't tell him, he just agrees with everything I say. Where's the fun in that?'

'Piss off, Barney.'

He grins.

'Bye, darling. I'll call you later. When you've calmed down a bit.'

God, I could slap him sometimes. I really could.

By the time we've packed up and I've apologised to the animal trainer for the fifteenth time it's nearly half-past ten. And I'm completely knackered. And then Monty calls. I've bought him a mobile since Charlie and I are moving back home at the weekend and I want to be able to call to check up on him without him having to be by the phone. He's completely fallen in love with it, and keeps calling me to tell me he's in the barn.

Only for some reason he's decided you have to speak in code.

'HELLO, THIS IS MONTY. REPORTING IN. EVERY-THING'S FINE. OVER AND OUT.'

'Hello, Monty. I'm just on my way back, is Mum there?'

And it turns out that yes, Mum is there, and she says

if I'm going past the butcher's on the way home could I get her some pork chops, but not the small ones.

And Monty wants a paper.

'ONLY, NONE OF YOUR LEFTY RUBBISH.'

'I'll see you later then, Monty.'

'UNDERSTOOD. OVER AND OUT.'

Dear god. I'm now officially living in the twilight zone.

I get back to the farm at around four, after stopping off at the butcher's to get Mum's pork chops and some sausages for supper, only to be met by Charlie hopping up and down with excitement because Mum's promised he can have pancakes for tea. And Monty's sitting with his leg propped up on a chair watching the racing, and yelling at the television. Mum says she's done the batter and it's in the fridge, so she'll be off now to do Dad's tea, and she tried to have a quick run-round with the Hoover only Monty's been fixing up one of his old lamps so he's taken the plug off.

After a bit of nifty manoeuvring I renegotiate the pancakes into toad in the hole, and then we feed the pheasants and take Tess for a walk while Monty shouts at *Newsroom Southeast*. I nearly fall asleep while I'm reading Charlie his bedtime story, until he pokes me rather sharply and says I've already read that page, and I'm just getting into bed when my mobile goes, and Barney's name flashes up on the screen. Oh great. Just what I need. It's his home number. If this is more about those bloody ducks I'm just going to switch my phone off.

'Annie?'

It's Sandy, Barney's wife.

'Hello, Sandy.'

God, I hope she's not trying to track Barney down. Maybe they've had an argument or something.

'I've called the boys, and they're on their way home, but I didn't know what to do about the office, and I thought maybe you'd call people for me.'

'Sorry?'

'I thought you'd probably be the best person to call.'

'What's the problem, Sandy?'

'We were crossing the road after the theatre and he was in one of his rants, you know how he gets, and there was a car, and he sort of pushed me out of the way, and then, well, I don't really know how it happened, but the car must have hit him, and he was on the road. Lying on the road.'

There's a silence.

'And then the ambulance came. And he looked like he was asleep, and the people were all standing watching us.'

Christ.

'They all just stood there watching.'

'Sandy. Is he all right? Is he in hospital?'

I hear her take a deep breath.

'No, Annie, he's not. He died. About three hours ago.'

X

In the Wee Small Hours of the Mourning

THE DAY OF THE funeral is rainy and freezing, which is just the kind of weather Barney would have ordered, only he'd probably have gone for thunder and lightning too. There are already a few people outside the church when we arrive.

'I don't know if I can do this, Mack, it makes it too real.'

'Yes you can. Look, there's Leila over there waiting for us, and Lawrence.'

Lawrence has been brilliant, and we've taken it in turns to sit with Sandy and try to help: making phone calls, arrangements, that kind of thing. Not that anything really helps. But he's been great, and he's the one who sorted the flowers, and the readings for the church service. Sandy doesn't really care. It's all too hard. But I know she will, at some point in the future. She'll want it all to have been done properly. With style. Like he would have wanted.

Leila's all in black, with a big black hat with a veil. She looks like Greta Garbo.

'I thought he'd probably want the maximum fuss. Yes?'

'Yes.'

She squeezes my hand.

'All right, darling?'

'Not really.'

'Me neither. Have you seen the flowers?'

'The ones in the church?'

'No, the other ones. Come and look. Every agency in the Western world's sent something.'

There's a mountain of mega-wreaths, each one more tasteful than the last, and lots of smaller bouquets and little arrangements from the crews we've worked with over the years. George and Kevin. Chris. Johnny, Cathy. Other directors. Oh god. I think I'd better stop reading the cards.

Lawrence comes over. He looks very pale, and I think he's been crying.

'Shall we go in? Sandy wants us sitting in the front. With her and the boys and the rest of the family.'

'OK.'

Oh Christ. I really don't think I can do this.

Inside the church there are lilies everywhere. Huge bunches of them, and candles. Not too many. But just enough. The whole church smells wonderful.

'The flowers are beautiful, Lawrence.'

Leila smiles at him.

'Do you really think so? I wasn't sure, and you know how much he minds about details like that.'

He suddenly looks very close to tears, and Leila puts her hand on his shoulder.

'Lawrence.'

'Yes?'

'Just bloody stop it, all right? Or you'll start me off. And if I get this bloody veil wet I'll kill you.'

He smiles.

More people are arriving, and there aren't enough seats. Everyone's squashing up and whispering hellos, and the organ starts playing and Sandy arrives, with the boys in dark suits looking very grown-up, and not, at the same time. She looks like she's sleepwalking. And then the coffin is carried in, by the men of the family, including Barney's two brothers, and Sandy's brother. I know they've all been really nervous about this moment. But they manage it beautifully.

And I almost make it through the service. The Vicar's chuntering on and it's almost all right, if you forget why we're here. But then Barney's oldest son Theo gets up. He's written a poem for his dad. And I'm finished before he even gets to the lectern.

It's pouring with rain when we get outside into the churchyard. I'm standing to one side with Mack and Leila sheltering under an enormous black umbrella that Lawrence has magically produced from somewhere. I'm trying not to watch what's actually happening at the graveside. I'll come back later, and say goodbye properly. And then Sandy shouts something and kneels down on the ground, in the mud, and starts making the kind of noise she's been wanting to make ever since it happened, only she's been trying to look after the boys. And everybody freezes. The Vicar tries to talk to her but she can't hear him. And in the end it's me and Lawrence who get her back up and walk with her towards the car, wiping the mud from her hands with tissues and telling her it'll be all right, when it obviously won't, with the boys trailing behind us looking desolate.

I've almost pulled myself together by the time we get back to the house, but then I see Barney's car, parked right outside, which sets me off again. It feels so wrong to be going into the house without him.

There's an uncomfortable mix of family – all in black or navy and looking stricken and awkward, the boys trying to circulate with drinks and be proper hosts – and loads of work people, milling about, talking and getting on with business, networking like it was just another drinks party. Sandy's upstairs with her sister-in-law Amy, and a man's sitting on the stairs talking on his mobile about budgets.

Leila's furious.

'Someone should throw these bastards out. What kind of sad fuck turns up at a funeral to network?'

Mack glares at the man on the stairs, who finally realises he's being watched and lowers his voice.

'I suppose they just reckon life goes on.'

'Not if they try talking to me it won't.'

Once the last people have left we say goodbye to Sandy and the boys, and go back to Mack's house for a drink. Lawrence offers to take Stef and Jenny home in a cab; today's been really hard on them both.

Stef's been drinking gin all day, and is now completely past the point of no return.

'He was a stroppy fucker, wasn't he, Annie?'

'Yes, Stef, come on, let's find your coat.'

'Yes, but at least he was alive. I mean before he died I mean. He was alive. He didn't put up with any crap, did he? Didn't settle for second best.'

'No, Stef, he didn't.'

Jenny comes over.

'Stef, the car's here, come on, you're pissed.'

'Sorry. Lawrence? Where's Lawrence?'

'I'm behind you, sweetpea, holding up your coat.'

'Oh right. You know, Lawrence, I used to think you were a bit of a tosser. But actually, you're all right, you know.'

Lawrence smiles.

'Thank you.'

Leila holds the umbrella while we get Stef into the cab, which is easier said than done because she suddenly gets weepy, and then we stand waving them off as the car drives down the street.

It's getting colder, and Mack puts his arm round me.

'Christ, what a day. Shall we order in Chinese or something? I'm starving.'

'Good idea.'

We go back inside and Mack orders the food and pours us all a glass of vodka while Leila takes her shoes off and stretches out on the sofa, still looking fabulous, mainly because she's still wearing her hat.

'The food should be here in about twenty minutes.'

'Great. So what's the plan now then?'

Leila's looking at me.

'I think I'll have another vodka.'

'No, darling, I meant about work.'

'Oh, right. Well, I'm not sure really.'

Mack sits down.

'We'll carry on, of course, and make sure Sandy gets her fair share. We'll have to get the lawyers to sort out the paperwork but basically we'll just carry on, keep the office going, maybe change the name. We'll have to talk about that, but Lawrence has already said he wants to stay.'

'Has he?'

'Yes, today, at the house.'

'Oh. Right.'

'And I've told Stef and Jenny they've still got jobs if they want them. And I'll get more work in, I hope, and we'll see how it goes. And I think we should get another director in, people are already calling me, maybe someone who's worked in the music business. What do you think?'

He looks at me.

'What about?'

'Getting someone else in.'

'Oh I don't know, Mack, I suppose so.'

Leila holds up her glass for a refill.

'Well, what about Ben Lippsey? He's looking for a move, I think. He did that gas job for us, and he does music stuff too. He's really good. And he's just sharing a desk at Lemon, I think. I bet he'd be up for a move.'

'I've already talked to him. I'm meeting him next week for a drink.'

Leila smiles, and they talk about work and I know they're right, and it's good that Mack's been thinking about it. But I just can't do it right now. I'm not sleeping: I keep having dreams where Barney gives me long lists of things to do and I always forget something crucial, or I leave him stranded somewhere, only I can't remember where. And I'm just not sure I want to carry on with work, not without Barney. Which is a bit of a problem because apart from anything else I need the money. But I'm hoping I'll get over it in the next few weeks, now we've had the funeral, because at the moment it feels like I'd be happy if I never set foot in the office again.

The food arrives and I bring some plates in from the kitchen. It all looks delicious, but I'm not really hungry.

'Let's drink a toast.'

Leila raises her glass.

'To Barney.'

We clink glasses.

'What would he say, if he was here now, do you think?'

Leila looks at me.

'He'd be absolutely furious. But he'd like your hat.'

She smiles.

'And then he'd say it was all bollocks. Total bollocks.'

'That sounds like another toast to me.'

We raise our glasses.

'Bollocks.'

It's a week since the funeral and I still haven't been into the office, but at least I've stopped waking up in the middle of the night. I've talked to Sandy on the phone, and she seems to be coping. Well, surviving anyway. I think the boys are helping. And Mack shot his first film yesterday: Lawrence rang me late last night to say he'd done a brilliant job and the client's thrilled. I offered to turn up at the studio for moral support but Mack said he was fine, which was a bit of a relief, to be honest. He's getting deluged with offers from young directors wanting to join the firm, and he seems to have assumed that I'll be up for producing for them, and maybe I should. I'll be running out of money soon, so I'll have to get something sorted.

But I'm sort of avoiding the issue by panicking about Mary Poppins instead; I've been making beaks ready for some of the kids to try on and I'm meeting Kate and Sally at school this afternoon for our first rehearsal with the whole class.

They're both in the school hall when I arrive.

'Do these look all right?'

Kate's covered two wing-shaped pieces of material with feathers, so we can see what they look like.

'We can do them in different colours to make them a bit more varied.'

'They look great. How long did it take you?'

'Bloody hours.'

Sally looks worried.

'We're never going to get this done in time.'

'Well, I've done a few beaks, only one of them got a bit bent when Charlie tried it on and tripped over.'

I hold up a rather tragic-looking tin-foil beak.

'And I thought we could do papier-mâché ones too, and paint them, get the kids to help, maybe, at the weekend?'

'Good idea, but bags it's not round at my house. James is terrible with paint.'

Sally laughs.

'Well, come round to us, if you like, Roger's always saying he wants to be more creative.'

The next half-hour is a complete nightmare. Charlie and James sulk because they don't get to wear the beaks – we're trying not to show favouritism. And the children who do get beaks all promptly start pecking each other. Cecily's wearing the prototype wings, and flaps so hard her elastic snaps. And the noise is terrible; most of them seem to vaguely know the song, but they're not exactly what you'd call natural musicians, and Jack Knight seems to be singing an entirely different tune to everybody else. The recorder group have been practising so they can accompany Mrs Pemberton on the piano, but they keep finishing at completely different times, and there's lots of shrill squeaking, which makes you want to put your hands over your ears. In fact the whole thing makes you long for a good pair of earplugs, which isn't exactly what we'd been hoping for.

Miss Pike's lurking at the back of the hall while we struggle to keep them all standing in a semicircle on the stage, but then Harry Chapman pushes Tom Trent, who falls on to the PE trolley, and she can't stand it any longer.

'Fingers on lips everybody. Now.'

One of the boys with a beak puts his hand up.

'And people wearing beaks can just stand nicely.'

He puts his hand down.

'It's nearly home time, but before we line up I've got something very important to say. And I want you all to listen. And that includes you, Sophie. And Alice. Because this is very important. Grace Pettifer, why are you hopping? Stand properly, please. This is very important. Now we all want our concert to be really special this year. Don't we?'

There's a muted chorus of 'Yes, Miss Pike'.

'And we're very lucky to have our three mummies helping us. Sam Barrett, leave your beak alone. It is not a hat. So we need to be very sensible and show them just how good our class can be. Not how silly. Or how noisy.'

They all shuffle and look at their feet.

'And anyone who can't be sensible can come and sit with me when we have our concert. And they won't have a lovely costume at all. Is that clear?'

There's another round of 'Yes, Miss Pike'.

'And, Barry Morgan.'

'Yes?'

'I've been watching you and you've been especially silly today.'

Christ. What was Barry doing? I never even noticed him.

'Now everybody, very quietly, line up, ready for home time.'

She turns and smiles at us.

'They're all just rather excited. I'm sure it's going to be lovely.'

'Bloody hell. This is going to be a disaster.'

Kate's looking really worried.

'Do you think we could develop a mysterious illness, something highly infectious, so we're in quarantine?'

'We could try.'

We arrange to meet up at Sally's after school tomorrow

to work on the costumes, and our emergency escape plan, just in case.

'Mummy, can we go and see Monty after tea?'

'Oh I don't know, Charlie, maybe tomorrow.'

'But I need to see my pheasants. And it's not fair to leave Monty to do it all. You said.'

'I suppose.'

'Good. And, Mummy. In the concert. Me and James don't want to be pheasants now. We want to be eagles. So we can claw Harry if he pushes us. He's always pushing people.'

Excellent.

Monty's very pleased to see us, and says he's been hoping we'd call round because he wants a word.

'Have you eaten yet, Monty?'

'Yes, I had that ham you brought round. Good bit of ham, that was. But a cup of tea would be nice. And I got some of those biscuits Charlie likes from the shop.'

He follows me into the kitchen.

'Now then, I've been thinking, have been for a while now, long before you were so good about my blasted leg and everything, so I don't want you thinking that it's because of that. Because it's not. It's just . . . well, I want to keep it in the family.'

Oh god. Not another rusty old mangle.

'Monty, it's very kind of you, but – '

'I know what you're going to say. But I'm not getting any younger and it's got be dealt with. So I've decided I want you and Charlie to have the farm when I'm gone. I went to see old Bill Mansfield, to find out about doing a proper will and everything, only he says we'd be better off sorting it out now or the bastards will have it off you for taxes. And you wouldn't have to farm the land, you know, when it comes to it. Jim Markson would rent the fields off you, and he wouldn't cheat you. He's always on at me to rent him more land. Or you could carry on with the sheep, if you wanted. But it's only an idea. You can say no, if you like. And no hard feelings. I want to make that clear.'

'Monty, I don't know what to say. I never thought – '

'You wouldn't have to be here, there'd be no need for that. Only I know you've been worrying about your work and what you're going to do now, without Benny.'

'He was called Barney, Monty, and I shouldn't have said anything to you about it really, I was just upset, it was the day after the funeral, but I'm fine now, honestly. I've still got a job, so there's no problem, you know. That's not why you're saying this now, is it?'

'No, it's like I said. I want you and Charlie to have it, keep it in the family. Be a nice start for Charlie, when the time comes. And you'll know you've always got something to fall back on. And the barn would make a nice little house, you know, if you wanted to make a start on it. You could rent it out or something, or go in for that B & B lark. So what do you think?'

He's gone quite flushed.

'Monty, you don't think I've been coming round here after your money, do you, because honestly – '

'Of course not. Heaven's sake. If I thought that's what you'd been after I'd never had let you in the door.'

'Well, if you're sure, then I think it's lovely, Monty. Really lovely. And thank you, ever so much, and thank you from Charlie too.'

I give him a hug.

'Steady on, girl, or you'll have me over.'

I kiss him on his cheek, which he seems to like.

'It'll be a lot of work, you know.'

'I know, but it'll be worth it.'

He smiles.

'I've always thought so. Well, I'll get old Bill over and we can talk about it again with him, once you've had a chance to think. Now are you making that tea, or what?'

Bloody hell. I can't quite believe it. But the more I think about it the better it gets. I could sell up and use the money from the house to do up the barn, although I might need a loan as well, but I'm sure I could do it. And maybe I could do a course on sheep, and go organic and do farmers' markets. Mack could come down every weekend, and be based here during the week too depending on how busy he was. And we could make proper bedrooms for Daisy and Alfie so they felt part of it at weekends. And there'd be lambs in the spring, and Charlie could have a dog. It could be perfect.

I ring Mack as soon as we get home, but he's got his voicemail on so I call Mum and Dad, and Mum confesses that Monty's already mentioned it to them, to see what they thought.

'I can't believe you kept it a secret, Mum.'

'Well, it was Monty's secret, and you know what he's like. He got quite rude about it, actually.'

'You don't think Lizzie would mind, do you, Mum? That's the only thing I'm not sure about.'

'Well, I've had a little word with her, your father said she'd be fine, only I wasn't sure, but he was right, as usual; she's pleased for you, and she said she'll do you some drawings for the barn. Started going on about walls of glass – you know how she gets.'

'Oh well, that's great.'

'And you'll have to sell your house, you know, before you can afford to do any work, and it'll be a lot of work keeping tabs on that silly old fool. And Lizzie wouldn't want to be doing any of that, so it's fine, love.'

'The barn could be really beautiful.'

'And Charlie will love it.'

'I know, but I'm not saying anything to him about it yet, not until it's all definite, all right, Mum?'

'He could have a dog.'

'Yes, but it's the ferret that's the real worry.'

'Nasty dirty things.'

'I'm not planning on getting one, Mum, but let's just keep it quiet for a bit longer, until we're sure it's really happening.'

'Monty thinks Charlie wants to be a farmer, you know, he was telling us, when we were over, the way he's so mad keen on animals. He said he was a country boy and anyone could see that.'

'Well, he might be, you never know. But either way it's very kind of Monty.'

I spend the rest of the evening on the phone. I call Lizzie to check that she really doesn't mind, and she doesn't, and Mack thinks it sounds great, only he's still on a bit of a high about work and he wants to talk through the new scripts that have come in. Leila's really keen too, although I'm not sure she's entirely grasped the kind of budget I'll have because she's already on at me to put in an infinity pool and turn it into an upmarket spa hotel where she and Tor can come for weekends.

We're round at Sally's after school the next day, sewing on feathers like our lives depend on it, and I'm telling them both about the farm idea. Sally says one of the teachers at her school lives with a farmer who's gone organic and she'll ask them round for a drink, if I like, and Kate thinks there are grants you can get.

'So when will you sell your house then?'

'I don't know really, we're only just talking about it.'

Sally gets up to put the kettle on.

'Well, Roger will help, if you like. I know he will.'

'Thanks, Sal. I was thinking I might talk to him. Make sure it really is the right thing to do, from Monty's point of view.'

'Of course it is. He gets to have you near by, and the farm stays in the family. It's perfect. And I'm so pleased, because we thought you might be moving, off up to London, with Mack.'

'Well, that's the only problem really. I'm not sure he's as keen as I am, about the farm idea, I mean. I think he wants to be in town more, not less.'

Kate passes Sally the cups.

'It's so difficult, isn't it, trying to balance everything. Gabriel's really good about things, he really is, but it's not easy, is it? You're very lucky, you know, Sal.'

'Oh I don't know about that. You two make me feel so bloody boring, like my life's set in stone or something. I was reading a magazine about it at the dentist. Spice up your life, before it's too late, but it was all rubbish about dressing up and making special suppers. If I opened the door stark naked to Roger one night he'd probably call the police.'

Kate laughs.

'Yes, but you love him anyway.'

'I know, but that doesn't stop it being boring.'

'Yes, but you've got the deep peace of the double bed and all that.'

Sally smiles.

'Yes, but that doesn't stop you fancying a bit of hurly-burly now and again.'

We all snigger.

'I thought I might buy us a water bed, as a surprise, for Christmas. What do you think?'

Kate laughs.

'Doesn't Roger get seasick? I thought you said he was really sick when you went to France that time?'

'Yes, but he could take tablets.'

'What, every night?'

Poor Roger. He'll have to bulk-buy Kalms.

'Why don't you go away for a weekend instead? I'll have the kids, Charlie would love it, and you two can go off somewhere.'

We run through our top venues for a weekend away, and Sally starts getting really excited about the idea.

'I'd love a weekend in Venice. I've always wanted to go there.'

'Great. Well, that's you sorted then. Go and book it tomorrow and start saving up.'

'Blast.'

'What?'

Kate holds up a half-completed wing.

'I've just sewn this on the wrong way round.'

'It doesn't matter, does it?'

'It does when I've already stuck feathers on the other side.'

Sally laughs.

'Biscuit time anybody?'

Mack calls late on Friday night, just when I'm putting the finishing touches to the lasagne for tomorrow's lunch. He's coming down for the weekend and lasagne is one of Daisy's favourites. Sometimes.

'Is there any chance you could come up here this

weekend, only there's stuff I need to do in town. I've got no clean suits left, and I need some new shirts and things.'

'Not really, I'm up to my neck in beaks.'

'What?'

'Beaks, for *Mary Poppins*.'

'Mary Poppins doesn't have a beak, darling.'

'For "Feed the Birds", I told you, Charlie's class are all being birds, in the concert, and anyway I've said I'll do lunch at Monty's on Sunday.'

'Oh.'

'And I want us to have a proper look at the barn.'

'I've seen it, Annie.'

'I know, but I'll make us supper, and keep Charlie up late on Friday so he goes to sleep early. And I've been thinking, and it could be great, you know, the farm idea. I could have a go at being organic with the sheep and maybe do bed and breakfast – the stables would make great little cottages. What do you think?'

'I think you don't know the first thing about sheep.'

'No I know, but I can do a course, and Monty will be around, and that way we could have the best of both worlds.'

'You could, you mean. I'd spend half my life in the fucking car.'

'No you wouldn't, Mack. It's only a couple of hours. And you don't need to be in the office every day, you know that. You could do loads of it from down here – Lawrence would be fine with that. Barney was always disappearing off in between jobs.'

'Yes, but I want to take on more people, not just be a one-man band like Barney.'

'Oh, right.'

'I'm only just starting to think about it, but I think we should hire a big hitter from one of the agencies, to bring us in more work.'

'That all sounds great, Mack.'

'But?'

'There's no but, it sounds great.'

'So you're up for it then?'

'Me? I've just said, Mack, what I want to do, about the farm.'

'Yes, but that could be a background thing, couldn't it? Get the place sorted out, for weekends and stuff, holidays with the kids, that kind of thing.'

'I think it would need more time than that, Mack.'

'Well, we could pay someone to do it for us then, because to be honest I think I'll need to be up here most of the time. We can buy a bigger house, if you like, and find a good school for Charlie. But that's what I want. And the rest is just detail, isn't it?'

'Not really, Mack. I don't want to live in town, you know that. We've had this conversation.'

'You're still upset about Barney.'

'Yes, I am, and I don't know if I want to work for anyone else, on shoots, I mean. It just wouldn't be the same. But that's only part of it. I want more time for the things I really want to be doing, not less: spending more time with Charlie, and being around to keep an eye on Monty, that kind of thing. I'm really excited about it, Mack, just like you are about your ideas for the office.'

'How can you get excited about sheep?'

'Mack, you know it's not about the sheep.'

'Well, what is it about then? Dedicating your life to a kid and a barking old sod who probably won't even know his own name in a few years' time?'

Oh god. He's getting really angry now. I don't think I'm handling this very well at all.

'It's not about dedicating my life to anyone, Mack. It's about what makes me happy. It's all so fragile, Mack, and

361

you never know how long it'll last, the time you've got with the people you love. And taking care of Monty is the right thing to do, that's all; he just needs a hand.'

'But who'll give you a hand, when you're old? Charlie will have buggered off and have a life of his own. Or are you going to tie him to a chair?'

'Most of us end up on our own. One way or another. Some of us are just less scared of it than others.'

'I'm not scared of being on my own. Christ.'

'I didn't say you were.'

'No. But you're telling me I'm going to lose you to a load of fucking sheep.'

'Mack, you're not listening, you're not losing anybody. This isn't about Monty, or the sheep. But I don't have to be part of Mack MacDonald Enterprises to be with you, do I? I don't have to eat, sleep and breathe the business for us to be together. I'd be miserable, and anyway, it's not just about you or me, is it? It's got to be about the kids too.'

'Oh here we go.'

'What does that mean?'

'Now you're going to tell me what a crap parent I am for going off to New York.'

'No I wasn't.'

'But that's what you think, isn't it? Christ, you can be annoying.'

'Thanks.'

'So come on then, Miss Perfect Parent. How is living in the middle of fucking nowhere better for the kids?'

Actually, he's really starting to piss me off now.

'Don't be obtuse, Mack. It's better for Charlie because all his friends are here, his school, his family, Edna, everybody. Little things like that. And as for Daisy and Alfie, they need a routine, a base with you, and yes, you can do that in London, of course you can. But we could do it on the farm too. And there'd be lambs in the spring, and we could keep chickens. They'd love it. We could even get Daisy a dog.'

I'm sounding desperate now, and I know it.

'I love my kids and they know that, and that's all that matters.'

'Yes, of course it is. But it's about the boring stuff too. Homework, and school shoes, that kind of thing. Not just swooping in with half of Hamleys in the boot. Because however big you grow the business, the money won't matter, you know. What matters is that you know what Alfie's favourite pudding was when he was little.'

'Well, fuck you.'

There's a silence.

'Actually, on second thoughts, I don't think I'll bother.'

The line goes dead.

Shit.

I ring Leila.

'I thought this might happen.'

'Did you? Well, you might have bloody told me. I'm so angry with him. I never said I wanted to live in London, or work full-time running his new bloody empire. He just assumed. I've been telling him for weeks now, but he never fucking listens. It's all about what he wants. And anything else is just not an option.'

'I just can't see him in wellies.'

'I never asked him to wear wellies, Leila.'

'No, I know, darling, but he's an all-or-nothing kind of man, isn't he? He wants you to be totally devoted to him.'

'Well, he'd better grow up then. I'll be devoted to him when he's devoted to me. Otherwise it's just bollocks; and he'd be better off hiring a good PA. Because that's what a lot of this is about, I'm sure it is. He wants me near by so there's always something for supper in the fridge, and his suits are dry-cleaned. Jesus, he'll be asking me to do fucking dinner parties next.'

'God forbid, darling. So are you going to ring him back then, try to talk him down?'

'No, I'm bloody not. He's being ridiculous. And it was him that put the phone down, so he can be the one to ring back and grovel.'

'That's my girl.'

It's been nearly four days and he still hasn't called. I've gone past the glancing-occasionally-at-the-phone stage, past the checking-my-mobile-has-a-signal-every-thirty-seconds stage, and now I'm at the Sod You stage. Thankfully Charlie doesn't seem to have noticed, and being surrounded by bloody beaks and feathers is actually helping to take my mind off it all, along with constant supportive moments from Leila and Kate and Sally. But still. Christ. I'm giving it one more week and then I'm going to ring him and tell him to fuck right off. With knobs on. Probably.

Leila rings at teatime on Tuesday.

'I saw him at lunch today, with a load of people from Mackenzie's, but I managed to collar him on his way out.'

'Leila, you didn't say anything, did you?'

'Of course I did, someone's got to tell him. He went all grim-looking and said it was all too complicated for him.'

'Oh well, at least I know he hasn't broken both his arms and been desperate to call.'

'You haven't heard the best bit yet.'

Oh god. I've got a feeling Leila's had one of her moments.

'You didn't throw anything at him, did you?'

'Of course not. I never throw things.'

'What about that time you threw a kiwi fruit at James Jarvis from the sixth floor and gave him a black eye?'

'That was different, he was practically begging for it. No, I just told him, very calmly, that I thought he was being a wanker and it was only complicated if you were a complete moron. And if he didn't pull himself together soon I'd be forced to send the boys round. And he made some joke about checking for horses' heads in his bed.'

'Right. Well, that sounds all right.'

'And then I biked him round a little present this afternoon.'

Oh Christ. Leila's rather fond of sending unusual gifts to people who annoy her. She once biked a pig's head to an ex-boyfriend, and she goes in for bunches of dead flowers, and buckets of manure too; you name it, and she's probably sent it to someone balanced on the back of a bike.

'What sort of little present, Leila?'

'Two dead fish, in a box. Cod, actually, cost me a bloody fortune, but still. I think he'll get the message. Sleeps with the fishes is Mafia for get a fucking grip, isn't it?'

'Yes, I think so.'

'Good. So are you liking it then? The idea of him opening the box and seeing the fish? Because I am.'

'Yes, I'm liking it very much.'

'Excellent. I thought you would. And don't forget. Call me, if you start to crack, any time. Day or night. Because it's vital you don't call him now. Promise?'

'I promise.'

* * *

365

It's the night of the *Mary Poppins* concert and I'm trying to get Charlie to stand still so I can sew the last few feathers on to his wings. He's in brown corduroy trousers and a brown T-shirt, and keeps pinging the elastic on his beak.

'This doesn't look like an eagle, you know, Mummy. I need claws. I told you.'

'You're a pheasant, Charlie. Look, see.'

I've sewn a couple of pheasant feathers on to each wing, donated by Monty. God knows where he got them from, but Charlie's pheasants were looking pretty nervous last time we fed them.

'Is Nana going to meet us at school?'

'Yes, with Grandad. And Monty.'

'Good. And is Mack coming?'

'No, darling, he's busy.'

And he still hasn't called, the bastard. It's been two weeks now, and I've practically had to sit on my hands to stop myself from calling him.

'Nana will love seeing me in the show, won't she?'

'Yes, darling, I'm sure she will.'

Or, if the last rehearsal was anything to go by, possibly not.

We arrive at school to find the place in an uproar. Ginny's trying to separate Travis and another boy from Reception, who are having a battle with their papier-mâché giant teaspoons. But at least they're singing 'A Spoonful of Sugar' while they bat each other, so that's quite encouraging. Assorted chimney sweeps are wandering about, and I think some of them must have gone the method-acting route and used real soot, because there are black footprints everywhere. Charlie's very impressed.

'I wish I could have been a sweeper.'

Two boys from Year Six go past, looking like gangsters in borrowed jackets with padded shoulders. They're doing the Bankers' song: 'Tuppence, prudently, frugally, invested in the bank'. Except for Justin, who's being the Tuppence in a bronze foil outfit that he's designed himself, bless him. It's really fabulous. Phoebe's being a Banker too, but she's insisted on the Britney approach and is wearing a very short black skirt with a pink shiny crop-top. Kate says she's given up, and it was either that or leave her at home.

We spend a hideous half-hour in the classroom putting the finishing touches to costumes while Sally valiantly reads stories and tries to keep them all sitting on the mat. They're all completely hyper and there are feathers everywhere. And just when they start to calm down, slightly, Mrs Taylor comes in and shrieks 'Five minutes, everybody' and blows her whistle. Bloody hell.

We line up and hop and peck our way down the corridor, and lurk outside the doors to the hall listening to the finishing stages of 'Supercalifragilistic' from Year Three, who are all dressed as Pearly Kings and Queens. Whoever sewed on all those sequins deserves a medal. Sally thinks it was Dawn Linton – she's got a special sequin attachment on her sewing machine, apparently, but even so it must have taken her weeks.

And then we're on. We've given up on the recorder thing because it was just too stressful, but Mrs Pemberton does a valiant job on the piano. They're all rather quiet at first, standing completely still and looking pale and terrified. But by the time they get to 'Listen, listen, she's calling to you' they perk up and start belting out the chorus, and flapping the occasional wing. Barry's beak keeps slipping down so he's rather muffled, which isn't entirely a bad thing, and quite a few people are waving at their special members of the audience, which is rather sweet. Jack Knight actually takes a step forward so his mum can get a proper look at his wing-span.

And then they're finished, slightly ahead of Mrs

Pemberton, but not as much as in the rehearsals, thank god, and the applause is thunderous. Monty stands up and whistles, very loudly; I suppose it must be all that practice with the sheep. And Charlie does a little twirl for him, nearly knocking James off the stage, and then there's a slight lull while we get them down the steps and past the chimney sweeps – who are already lined up in the corridor and raring to go – trying to stop them getting tangled up in all the brushes in the process. Ginny's almost hysterical, and Mrs Jenkins has got black marks all over her face, but they lead their sweeps in with fixed smiles on their faces and we get our lot back to the classroom.

Miss Pike comes in and says how proud she is, of all of them, and could everybody just be extra sensible for a little while longer and line up very quietly again, and could the people with kites please find them now, and then we're back out in the corridor again ready for the 'Let's Go Fly a Kite' Big Finish.

The Year Six Bankers have stayed on stage and are now pressed up against the wall by an assortment of chimney sweeps, Pearly Kings and Queens and birds, and the occasional giant teaspoon, with children sitting in front of the stage and down the sides of the audience, and then the excitement gets too much for Mrs Pemberton, who starts playing before we've got all of them in place, but it doesn't seem to matter. They all wave their kites, and Travis falls off the stage, and then gets back up and does it again until Mrs Taylor retrieves him. Cecily snaps her elastic, again, and gives me a stricken look but then tucks it under her arm and carries on singing.

The audience clap hysterically, and Mrs Taylor makes her way to the front after handing custody of Travis over to Miss Pike, and produces small posies of flowers from behind the piano for all the helpers, and a bouquet for Mrs

Pemberton, who gets another round of applause, and is inspired to stand up and make a little speech all of her own, which is a surprise to Mrs Taylor, I think, but she handles it very well. I suppose all those years on playground duty means not very much actually throws her any more. Mrs Pemberton says she's had a lovely time, and will never be able to think of *Mary Poppins* in quite the same way again, which I'm sure is true, and how nice it is to see the children taking music so seriously, and I don't think she's being sarcastic, and Mrs Taylor asks everyone to give Ginny Richmond a round of applause for all her hard work in organising this evening, and everyone does, even Mrs Harrison-Black, who's looking thunderous in the front row.

And then Mrs Taylor asks everyone to remain seated, and put their trays in the upright position, which is rather witty, although some parents do look rather anxiously at the seat in front of them so perhaps on balance she's rather wasting her time.

We march the kids out as quickly as we can and Miss Pike somehow manages to magic herself back to the classroom so she's standing waiting for us by the door clutching a tin of Quality Street and congratulating everybody all over again. There's an enormous amount of flapping and pecking, but we're past the point of caring. Charlie's delighted and is now wearing his beak as an eye-patch.

We hop back towards the car, being congratulated by lots of parents, and Sally looks particularly exhausted. William's giant teaspoon took ages to dry, and she was up late painting it last night.

'Well, thank god that's over with. Now we've just got Christmas to get through and it'll be nearly time for Venice.'

Roger starts whistling 'Just One Cornetto'.

'Please stop doing that, Roger, or I promise you I'll be

pushing you out of the first gondola we get into. Night, Annie. Where's Wills got to?'

They go off bickering, with Roger still whistling, and Kate says she'll call me tomorrow, and don't I think it's just typical that Phil couldn't even be bothered to turn up, which I do, and wasn't it nice of Gabriel to come, which it was. He's busy refereeing between Charlie and James as to who can do the most bird-like flapping, and telling them all about a parrot he has to see at the surgery, who regularly bites chunks out of his hand. Which of course they both think it absolutely delightful, and I can foresee parrots moving to the top of the Most Wanted Pets list fairly soon.

'Mummy?'

Here we go.

'Don't you think we were good in our concert?'

'Really good, Charlie.'

'Yes. So do I get a prize then?'

'No.'

He flaps his wings in his annoyance.

'That's not fair. You should get a prize if you try hard. You said.'

'Yes, but your prize was having the audience clap for you.'

Even I can see that this is pretty weak, but it's the best I can come up with.

'Mary Poppins was practically perfect in every way you know, Mummy.'

'Yes, I know.'

Oh good. Maybe he's fallen for the bit about doing it for the love of performing. How very gratifying.

'Yes. But you're not. You're totally horrible in every way.'

He stamps off towards the car.

* * *

370

We're round at Monty's for Sunday lunch with Leila, who's come down for the afternoon unexpectedly because Tor's gone off on a Yoga Day and she's bored. She's inside the house with Monty looking at bits of old tat, while I'm outside trying to move the sheep from one field to another, which isn't exactly going to plan. I think I'm going to have to work on my technique. I've got most of them through the gate, but a few are still in the far corner of the field and I'm doing the bucket-rattling thing but so far they're just ignoring me. Bastards. I don't know why Monty couldn't have done it himself but he says his leg's sore today, although that hasn't stopped him taking Leila for a tour round.

Charlie's in the barn, building another bloody camp, which means he'll want his tea out there, and I'm seriously considering borrowing Monty's shotgun to see if that might persuade the sheep to quicken up their pace before it gets dark, when Leila appears carrying a white box.

'This just came for you.'

'What?'

She holds the box up a bit higher and smiles.

'By messenger.'

'Leila, what are you talking about?'

'Just open the box, for Christ's sake.'

I open it, and there's a small toy sheep in it, nestling in pink tissue paper.

'Oh Leila, thank you, how sweet.'

'It's not from me, you idiot. Read the label.'

There's a label tied round the sheep's neck.

Dear Annie. You win. Would like to rejoin flock. Dinner? Will bring own wellies. Mack.

And then I see him, opening the gate to the field, looking rather nervous, and carrying a very pristine-looking pair of new green wellies.

Leila smiles.

'I know. It was all his idea. Honestly. Well, nearly all of it. Anyway, give me the box and I'll go back into the house and make sure Monty doesn't need resuscitating or anything. He's been so excited about our plan I thought he might keel over earlier on.'

'Does Monty know about this too then?'

'Yes. Why do you think he asked you to move the sheep? We needed to get you out of the way, so you didn't see the car. Now don't forget, make him beg, darling, and I'll see you in a minute.'

'Hello, Annie.'

'Hello.'

He hesitates.

'Did you like your present?'

'Yes, thank you.'

'She's a very determined woman, your friend Leila, isn't she?'

'She can be, yes.'

'Did she tell you about the fish?'

'She did.'

'I was in a meeting when they arrived, with half of DWP. Stef brought the box in, because it was marked "Urgent". So I opened it, in front of everyone. It was quite a moment, I can tell you.'

I'm trying really hard not to laugh.

'Yes. They all thought it was highly amusing too.'

There's a silence. And he goes rather red.

'So I was wondering, if I put these bloody boots on, and help you with whatever it is you're doing with these flaming sheep, can we assume that I won't be getting any more surprise parcels at work?'

'I don't know, Mack. Possibly. We'll just have to see how it goes, won't we?'

A NOTE ON THE AUTHOR

Gil McNeil is the author of the bestselling novels *The Only Boy for Me* and *Stand by Your Man* and has edited three collections of stories, *Magic*, *Summer Magic* and *A Journey to the Sea* with Sarah Brown. Gil is currently working on a new novel, *Divas Don't Knit*, and helps run the charity PiggyBankKids, which supports projects that create opportunities for children and young people.
She lives in Kent with her son.

Stand By Your Man Gil McNeil
£6.99 0 7475 6139 7

'A funny and touching novel … I wish I'd written it' Arabella Weir

Alice Mayhew, part-time architect and full-time mother to Alfie, is to gardening what Alan Titchmarsh is to deep-sea fishing. So finding she's been volunteered to design a new garden for the village comes as a bit of a shock. Molly O'Brien is finding it hard enough coping with Lily (aged four and likes washing up) and Dan (aged thirty-two and doesn't) before she discovers she's pregnant. And then there's Lola Barker, who causes havoc wherever she goes, and brings a whole new meaning to the word high-maintenance. Toddlers, jelly, bad behaviour, romance and gardening tips all loom large in Gil McNeil's hilarious and heartbreaking new novel. *Stand By Your Man* turns prejudices and assumptions upside down with humour and passion, telling it like it really is. Sometimes it's hard to be a woman …

'Thinking of moving to the country with your kids? Read this book instead' Phil Hogan

'The frantic pace of her juggled lifestyle, insane conversations with her Peter Pan obsessed toddler and the relief of swigging gin with her equally stressed friends is captured with biting humour and sharp, fast-paced dialogue' *She*

'This blast of fun and frivolity in the Shires is like a breath of fresh air' *Sunday Mirror*

To order from Bookpost PO Box 29 Douglas Isle of Man IM99 1BQ www.bookpost.co.uk
email: bookshop@enterprise.net fax: 01624 837033 tel: 01624 836000

bloomsburypbks

www.bloomsbury.com/gilmcneil